THE VARIANCE

THE TEST OF TIME

1

A.C. MARHOLIN

First edition. Published 2024.

Editing by: Tabitha Chandler @tabs.edits

E-book Cover by: Ivy @BeautifulBookCoversbyIvy

Physical Cover by: Selkkie Designs @selkkiedesigns

Map, Chapter Art, and Formatting by: Devin McCain @studio5twentyfive

ISBN (Paperback): 979-8-9917655-0-3

ISBN (Hardcover): 979-8-9917655-1-0

LCCN: 2024921632

To my Dat
I never could have done it without you. The many hours of reading and re-reading for me, offering suggestions and pointing out plot holes, to driving me around for hours so I could write and edit without distraction. Not to mention taking care of the house, the kids, the cars… You are the book boyfriend every woman dreams of.
With all my love,
Your Dere

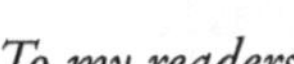

To my readers
This is dedicated to everyone who ever thought they weren't good enough. Who were told they weren't good enough. Who felt they weren't good enough.
You are good. You are enough.

FREDULIN GULF
ICE LANDING
DORNASH FOREST
FREDULIN GULF PASS
NORLET LAKE
WILTRIE RIVER
WILTRIE MARSH
CANTUË PLAINS
CALAMITY CAMP
ROTHESARD
ASHADIER
AMARANTH FOREST
TIVERVISTA
SHALIAL PASS
WINFAIR
AMIKET CITY
AMIKET BAY
THURHURST
BRUDERDON
BLOOMSISLE EDGE
KAHLI DESERT
DANJERI GORGE
GLASRIAL PASS
FORGONIE
ODEFT
DELJA
ZARVAN REALM

ZARVAN GUIDE

Months:

1. Ervi (er-vee): Goddess of Light to represent the new light dawning on the new year.

2. Shilium (shih-lee-um): God of Waters to represent the melting of the winter snows and ice.

3. Kassia (kas-EE-uh): Goddess of Chance to represent the chances people take after winter.

4. Ryo (ry-oh): God of Wisdom to represent the judgment and goodness of the Celestials.

5. Naheia (nuh-hee-uh): Goddess of Life to represent the new life of late spring and summer.

6. Tiulla (tee-yoo-luh): Goddess of the Hunt to represent the provision of the Celestials.

7. Udara (Ew-dar-uh): Goddess of Stars to represent the celestial bodies that decorate the skies.

8. Atar (ay-tar): God of War to represent the great wars and losses of the past.

9. Onas (OH-nuhs): God of Creativity to represent the creativity of the peoples.

10. Fymir (fye-mer): God of Fire to represent the fiery colors of nature in the fall.

11. Dhoemis (day-mis): God of the Dark to represent the coming long night.

12. Mesnata (mez-nah-tuh): Goddess of Midnight to represent the longest of long nights.

~

Celestials:

1. Madnja (mad-en-jah) – Celestial of Fire, female
2. Omros (om-rohs): Celestial of the Stars, male
3. Bretia (br-eh-tee-uh): Celestial of Storms, female
4. Sierin (see-eer-in): Celestial of Beauty, female
5. Udtis (yoo-d-tis): Celestial of Water, male
6. Cyllena (sy-len-uh): Celestial of Air, female
7. Iterin (eye-ter-in): Celestial of Death, female
8. Dealdin (dee-ahl-din): Celestial of Medicine, male
9. Arasil (air-uh-sil): Celestial of Home, male

Pronunciation Guide:

- Aerith – air-ith
- Amaranth – am-uh-ranth
- Amiket – am-i-ket
- Ashadier – ash-Uh-deer
- Bruderdon – broo-der-dun
- Cardis – car-dis
- Chance – cha-ntz
- Delja – del-Juh
- Eaglyn – Ee-glin
- Eloise – el-oh-Eez
- Gamet – ga-met
- Gilda – gil-Duh
- Giselone – jis-eh-lohn
- Gorduin – gor-Doo-in
- Halberg – hall-burg
- Hilda – hil-duh
- Illume – ih-loom
- Isynt – eye-sint
- Julieth – joo-lee-eth
- Kahli – kah-lee
- Leck – lek
- Mitac – my-tak
- Nyana – nee-ah-nuh
- Rothesard – roth-eh-sard
- Saada – shah-duh
- Selvia – sel-vee-uh
- Staksu – stak-soo
- Winfair – win-fair
- Zarvan – zar-van

PROLOGUE

Timekeeper

Time is multi-faceted. Fleeting. It has no beginning. It has no end. Everyone always thinks of time as linear, that you can never move backward. I have a different view. Time goes in circles. It decides when to start a turning of the age and when to end it. For me, it begins with a blank page and ends with halls of pages, leather-bound and filled with detailed stories and rich illustrations. They sit silently like the void, inoffensively, no matter the horrors they contain.

Unlike myself, they have no opinion, no thoughts, no mind. The end of this age draws near, which means the Variance will appear soon. I wonder who it will be this time.

As the revolutions grow long, the previous Variance and the destruction they wrought has been forgotten by those below. Typical. The clan leaders, or the Illume Council, as the people of this age refer to them, stop passing the legends down from generation to generation.

I have seen it in the annals of all the ages I have ever read and recorded, which has been many. The Variance always comes as a surprise to the Realm. Despite the warnings the Celestials pass down at the start of every age to stay vigilant and prepared, the foolish humans stop heeding the advice after a few centuries. They slowly sow doubt amongst the fertile minds, and those with less conviction begin to believe the old texts are a farce, something fanciful, a tale for entertainment but not to be thought serious. Only a few devout remain and maintain a diligent watch for the time.

I am one of them, but not among them. I have been watching and waiting for the next Variance to come. The One to make nation rise against nation, people against people; a revolution to end the revolutions. What I am waiting for though, is the one Variance who can reset time itself. Who can end its cruel rule over the Realm in its entirety.

Hidden carefully in my chamber is the oldest tome, the first tome. Its leather is cracked and worn with age; the parchment fragile. Within is a prophecy, protected from time and the Celestials, promising that there will be one who can do it.

It's frustratingly light on details. What prophecy isn't? What details remain are spotty at best from faded ink, but it does say there is One.

My hair grays, my skin wrinkles, my back hunches, but still, I watch, I wait, I hope. Every age, I wait. Even with all the revolutions afforded to me, far more than the mortals, I am still racing to beat time.

My workspace, a huge library lined with polished oak shelving and white marble streaked with black, as though someone took quill ink and spilled it everywhere, and is home to all the written history of time. Other than that one.

I run my hands over the others lightly now, each one bringing bursts of memories to my mind's eye as I pass over them. The faint smell of dust, old leather, and old parchment floods my nostrils. I sigh. Some of these stories are delightful, most of them grim.

My hand pauses, and I freeze, a gasp escaping my lips as I come to a particularly painful point in history. This is Faizu's age. I recognize the desolation.

The Realm is laid bare before him. I can smell the burning flesh. Blood bathes the ground, like a canvas painted with rust. Vultures circle overhead in the cloudless sky, their raspy hissing sounds calling for more. They will need an entire kettle of vultures to handle the corpses spread out before the iridescent-skinned man. His hair shifts color with the shifting of the winds. Beautiful man yet so wicked.

A grisly smile, his teeth far too white for the blood and dirt he is covered in, splits his face. He laughs, a deep, hearty guffaw of derision. Those who have finally managed to capture him, an entire league of magic-wielders of every color, have brought the body of the iridescent man to his knees, but not his spirit. Never his spirit.

Even to the last moment, when the Black Warrior before him reads his charges, he only smiles. His pride evident, indomitable. Even as the blade comes out, he does not struggle. He stares his captor in the eyes.

"I will be back," Faizu declares. His equally iridescent eyes flashing in the sunlight. The blade swings through the air, severing his head from his neck, and his blood sprays, covering the Warrior standing in front of him. Faizu's body collapses, his eyes finally going black like his soul has recently become.

"Doubt it," the Black Warrior states flatly before turning and walking away.

I manage to pull my hand away from the painful tale; I don't need the rest to play out in front of me. I wipe the tears falling off my cheeks. So many lives lost in that age, so many good people.

I had thought when he was revealed, that Faizu was the One I had been waiting for. Unlike previous Variances, who came in destructive at the outset, he moved quietly amongst the nations. He was politically wise, having been raised amongst the most cunning of nobles. He seemed concerned with the overall well-being of the people, trying to offer them a better life by working with rulers to increase food production, decrease the cost of goods, increase trade…but then. Then.

I close my eyes at the harrowing memories as if closing my eyes will make them go away any more than taking my hand off his book did. Faizu, like all the rest, proved to be as power-hungry as every other Variance. Under the guise of "best for the Realm," he slowly took more and more control. Before even I, with my birds-eye view, realized it, he had amassed an incredible amount of power. The kings and queens bowed to him, cowed to him, and if they didn't, they were forcibly disposed of.

By this time, the rulers had given him control of the markets and trade. A mistake it turned out; if any of the rulers didn't accept his demands and stipulations, their people starved. In the end, enough rulers banded together their magic-wielders and eliminated him. Too late. To destroy a Variance was to destroy the Realm. It was effective; it did reset the age, but once again, it was through force and time ticked on…

I move away from the annals of destruction, hoping distance will relieve me of the ache in my chest.

Despite my aging body, I amble easily among the light-colored marble halls until I reach the last row of shelves. I pull one of the few remaining sheets of blank parchment and sit at my dark walnut table in front of the large, arched window; double my height and equal in width. Outside, white, fluffy clouds gather, disperse, and swirl around my quarters. Below those clouds is the Realm, the ones to whom I am beholden to pen their stories, their life songs.

Using a bony but dexterous hand, I pick up my red-tailed hawk-feather quill, my conductor's wand in this orchestra of life, which is heading swiftly for its crescendo. Unlike a conductor, however, I am unable to stop or slow this one-man band any more than the mortals are. The clouds part when they sense I am seated and ready. I peer through, scrawling what I see in neat handwriting on the fresh parchment with rich black ink. I anticipate little rest between now and the end of the age for myself or for the transient lives currently blissfully unaware of what is coming…and soon. Time is not on their side, nor mine. I pray this one is the One. The One to fulfill that promise I have kept hidden and tucked away for eons.

PART I

The Gift

WISHING FOR WISHES...

Eloise

Revolution 1762, Tiulla 19 (R62T19)
2 Days Before the Quest
Ashadier, Amaranth, Isynt Vale

I WIPE the sweat from my brow with a beige cotton cloth, which was once white. It's the end of spring, but we seem to be having a heat wave to rival mid-summer already. I sit on the bench outside our small pine board cabin to take off my boots. I pause and look up at the village spread around me. Our land is set back slightly from everyone else's, closer to the pine forest that surrounds Ashadier, but not so far that we don't have neighbors. Not that it would matter much. There are only about four hundred Ashadierans, which means we pretty much know everything about everyone.

I wave to Miss Halsey as she walks by the house, her shock of Orange skin and hair giving her away even if I didn't have excellent eyesight. She waves back and keeps going on her way, dragging a trunk on wheels behind her, kicking up dust the whole way.

"Still have my dress?" I call out to her.

"You know it," she shouts back, not pausing. "I'm not selling it to anyone but you!"

Miss Halsey, an inventor by magic and seamstress by trade, has an elegant purple silk dress in the window of her shop. Every other day, I find my feet leading me to her shop in town. The dress form is my height, and when the sun is right, I can picture myself wearing the dress in the window's reflection, and I daydream. *What kind of person would I be in that dress? What would I be doing?*

Miss Halsey decided it was "my dress" when she caught me staring at it one afternoon in her shop window. At fifty silvers, it's not likely anyone here could buy it anyway. Especially not me.

Inevitably, the light shifts to show the person I truly am. Tall and sturdy, tan linen shirt with brown wool pants. Scuffed black knee-high boots instead of purple bejeweled flats. My long, brown, wavy hair sticking out every which way. Green eyes, more tired than I imagine someone in the palace would have, light brown skin which could be tan or dirt depending on the day. I always sigh with the reminder of reality before turning and treading home.

Maybe I will stop by tomorrow and look at "my dress."

Around me, cabins in similar states of disrepair as ours are buzzing with activity. To our right, Mr. Craser is butchering a deer he must have nabbed in the Amaranth Forest while his wife hangs laundry on the line. I can hear her giving him a lecture not to get blood on the fresh linens. He surely will, and she will likely be hanging the same linens again tomorrow. To the left of us, Miss Harrow is sweeping the dust off her porch, her black hair pulled into a bun on top of her head. It waves back and forth with her movements. She gives me a smile when she notices me looking her way and resumes her sweeping.

Before I left the garden moments ago, I had seen Cardis, my fourteen-year-old brother, chasing our cousins, Hilda, Gilda, and Leck, in the meadow behind our cabin. I can still hear their squealing now and their peals of laughter when he catches them and tickles them mercilessly.

I smile. This is Saturday in Ashadier. This is familiarity. It's not a ballroom, it's not a feast in a court, it's not perfect, but it's home. Sure, our house is too small for the eight of us living in it, the roof leaks in the rain, and the porch has a cracked board, but I don't want to be anywhere else.

My boots come off with a strong tug. The breeze feels good on my legs, which had grown damp with sweat under the black leather. Unfortunately, the breeze also brings the smell emanating from the boots. I hastily store the offending items under the carved bench, my handiwork, thank you very much, and get up. I take one last look at the happy town around me and step inside the cabin.

It's quiet when I enter. Maybe Saada isn't home after all. I know Gamet, Saada's husband, is likely in town. He's one of the few in Ashadier with magic and it earned him an automatic spot on the town board when he moved here. He could have refused, but he didn't and stated he'd be happy to serve the people.

"It's not a job," he always says, "It's a duty." He doesn't get paid for it, so I'm not sure it could be called a job anyway. I don't point this out to him, though. I know it makes Saada proud which makes him happy, too. He would do anything for her.

Every week, Saada straightens his bowtie before the town board's Saturday meeting and helps him flatten his hair. Then he will tease her about her "fussing" and walk out with her still putting a handkerchief in his pocket. He will be there the majority of the day. He doesn't share town board business with us, but I know they talk about troublemakers in town and punishments. I only know this because Gamet has helped Julieth over the years. My stomach turns sour at the thought, and I push it aside.

The door opens into the living room. A rickety wooden rocking chair and a threadbare brown couch are placed around an oval wood table on which are a few candles and one lantern, which we rarely can afford oil for. A small rectangular yellow rug rests on the floor in front of the hearth. The mantle above it contains a few small painted portraits of our family. My mom and dad, both gone now, stare down, smiling at me. I smile back as I always do. The middle one from several years ago is comprised of Julieth, my now eighteen-year-old sister, myself in the middle, and Cardis next to me. The other one contains our merged family of eight. Leck was only an infant at the time. Now, he's a rambunctious six-year-old. I notice the smiles in that one, but I know the artist took some liberties. At the time, Julieth wasn't smiling at anything, and I was likely scowling at her.

"Hello?" I call out from the entryway when no one greets me. "Anyone home?"

I hear shuffling feet, and my shorter but older aunt, Saada, appears from the small kitchen around the corner to my right, wiping her hands on her blue apron covering her pale-yellow dress. By the white patches of flour that appear on the fabric, she is baking. Another Saturday routine. Saada may have left Unchanged from the Quest when she entered ten years ago, but she can work her own magic in the kitchen. I use my nose to see if I can guess what she's making. I inhale the aroma of fresh rosemary and smile.

"Rosemary olive bread?" I ask, holding my breath.

Saada smiles in return. "Your favorite."

It's one of the few things I can remember of my mother, and warmth radiates through my chest as happy memories come to mind. My mother, with her long chestnut-brown hair, pulled back behind her head in a tight bun, kneading the dough carefully, her silver-blue eyes shrewdly assessing the quality of the dough in her nimble fingers. If it wasn't good enough, she would turn it into something else. Nothing went to waste, but she wouldn't turn it into my favorite bread if it weren't perfect.

She used to hum while she worked. It was always a slow song that was completely at odds with the fervor with which she would pound the dough after proofing it. Puffs of flour would fly around the kitchen like the puffs from dandelions we used to make wishes.

"Baking," she would whisper to me conspiratorially, "is meant to be messy." Then she would poke my nose, leaving a bit of flour behind, and I would giggle. Together we would shape the loaves or rolls and put them in the oven over the fire. I smile, gripping tightly to those moments and return my focus to Saada.

"What's the occasion?" I query as I close the cabin door behind me and hang my bag on one of the iron hooks to the left of the door.

"I figured we would have some with dinner and save some for Monday. Have you thought about what you're going to take in with you?" Saada walks back toward the kitchen.

I stop in my tracks. I had forgotten. For every day being similar to the one before it, Monday, Tiulla 21st, is the summer solstice and is anything but a normal day. Every year on the dawning of summer solstice, every seventeen-year-old in Zarvan Realm, or person who will be seventeen before winter solstice of that same year, prepares to enter the Quest.

Both a test and a rite of passage, the Quest tests each and every one of us for one of the eight different magics: Red, Orange, Yellow, Green, Blue, White, Black, or Brown.

We've been taught about the magics in school. Even though other cities and lands commonly mock us for not having magic-wielders, we still have to learn about them. It's a slap in the face to hear about all the things the magics can do and know the odds are heavily slated against us to be gifted with any of it.

Before the Quest, no one knows if they have magic within them; however, we can guess what the odds are based on family history. One whose parents have magic is far more likely to express magic. My family has no magic. Zilch. Nada. Zero. Therefore, my chances are also zilch. I'm not too upset, though. While having magic could make some things easier, magic-wielding requires two years of training in Amiket City to learn control over that magic, so they don't accidentally hurt someone. I'm not keen to leave home for that long. They need me too much.

My mind drifts to the garden in the back, the goat I helped obtain, the soap and knives I make and sell. My eyes drift to the coin jar on the mantle. Woefully low on coin despite my best efforts. I push away thoughts of our beleaguered finances and focus on the Quest.

As a child, I learned from the traveling salespeople that each region within Isynt Vale uses a different place for their tests. Until then, it hadn't occurred to me that not every town has a forest. They told me villages in Kahli use the desert and the towns in Delja use the ocean. As someone who cannot swim, this is a terrifying prospect.

In Amaranth, though, it is the forest. For this one period, the large pine forest is imbued with magic by the nine Celestials. No one shares details about the Quest, only that they were put through tests. I still don't know what "tests" they are. I used to think I would have to sit at a desk and answer questions.

"What kind of test is it?" I had asked, my curiosity inexhaustible at seven. Everything in my world revolved around asking questions and getting answers. "Do they move desks into the forest for it? Why not do the test here?"

My teacher's eyes narrowed in annoyance. "It's not that kind of test."

"But then what do we do?"

"You go into the forest," she replied.

"Oh!" I exclaim. My chest puffed out, my confidence soaring. "I've been in the forest lots of times. Why don't we do the test now?"

Some of my classmates murmured in agreement. Many of us went into the forest in the summer to cool off in the creeks or to play in the veritable wonderland of ice and snow in the winter. We weren't afraid of the forest.

"You can't go in until you're seventeen," she said, rubbing her temples. "And just because you know what the forest looks like now doesn't mean you know what it will look like then. No one knows what it will look like during the Quest. It's different every time."

Looking back now, I realize she had been exasperated and haunted. I never got a chance to figure out why. Once we learned that school couldn't prepare us for what was to come, at least half the class lost interest in what she had to say.

I shake my head at Saada. "I'm not going to take much in, like everyone else."

Most Ashadier citizens keep it simple for Quest supplies. Something for water, something to be able to hunt for food, something to keep warm. We don't have many people in the village who have needed to stay long in the forest. Often, we are out after a handful of hours. The longest any of us has ever stayed, in recollected history, was two days, and he came out with black hair, but Unchanged skin and eyes: a Warrior, not an overly powerful one, but a Warrior, nonetheless.

If he had been more powerful, he would have been a dark color in hair, skin, and eyes. That would have labeled him a Prime and made him valuable. Tales told at night to scare children around the bonfires are that other Vales have spies who have tried to kidnap our Primes.

Even though the Black magic-wielder didn't have a lot of magic, he was still taken to Amiket City to train. He never returned, and rumors still abound regarding what happened to him.

Saada's green eyes, similar to my own, seem to have a troubled look, but it comes and goes so fast that I can't be certain. I guess that maybe it's a look of disappointment.

"Saada," I sigh exasperated, "no one in our family for all the revolutions in this age has ever entered the forest and not been told to leave within the hour, right?"

I pause and wait for her acknowledgment. She doesn't; instead, "Maybe you'll be different, Eloise. You don't know."

"We do know. It's not likely. What's the point in packing all my stuff up only to unpack it again? I'm not interested in practicing my organizational abilities, you know."

"They could use some work," she mutters, and I know she's affectionately referring to the mess in the room I share with the other girls in the house. I've never been fond of cleaning or making my bed. I always wondered what the point is when I'm going to make it all a mess again later. Why not leave it undone?

"Don't worry, Saada, I'm not going anywhere. You're stuck with me no matter what." She brightens a little, but her facial expression still perplexes me.

"Fine, but you will take some of this bread with you." She winks. "Just in case." She turns on her heel back to the kitchen, flicking her golden blonde hair over her shoulder.

"For fun," I hear her call to me, and I wander closer to the kitchen, where she is pounding down some proofed dough. "What would you choose if you could pick one?"

"Pick one, what?" My heart lightens. I lean against the kitchen wall. Do I get to pick if she makes rolls or buns or a loaf? My mind races, thinking about what I might want. Rolls will be easier to take with me on the go, as I often do, but the inner parts of the loaf, so soft...so warm. The melting butter. My mouth waters.

"Zarvan to Eloise!" Saada has stopped working on the dough and has snapped her floury fingers in my face. I sneeze when the flour makes its way up my nose.

"What? Rolls!" I call out on a whim. Yes, rolls will be good. Easier to pack into the forest on Monday. If I get a little campfire going, I can warm it over the fire. If I need to even stay that long.

"Rolls?" She lets out a laugh, her cheeks dimpling deeply. "I asked what you would pick for magic!"

"Oh…um…I don't know. What would you pick, Aunt?" Saada and I have never talked about this. Not that it's ever been discouraged, per se; it just hasn't been brought up before.

Saada resumes her kneading and thinks for a moment. "Red, I think." I cock my head at her. I always think of Reds as angry, given their domain is over fire. Saada isn't an angry person. She's probably the very opposite. She never yells at us, has never raised her hand nor her voice to us. Even when some of us, like Julieth, have long since earned it.

"Red? Really?" I ask her.

"Yes, I think so. Think about it. The ability to bake and control the fire's temperature at every moment? Everything I baked would come out perfectly!" She spreads her arms widely with a flourish.

I chuckle. "Everything you bake *does* come out perfectly!"

She shrugs. "I said what I said. You don't get to rain on my parade. Now, your turn." She pokes her finger into my chest, leaving more flour behind on my linen shirt.

What would I choose… What would benefit us the most? "Well, I think Brown would be best for us. I could make sure our land is fertile and grow the best vegetables. Or I could go Green and help Cardis find animals to hunt for us, and we could sell the hides."

Saada gives me a knowing smile, her hands stilled in the dough. "Those would be beneficial for us, true. Putting aside wanting to help feed us or make money for *us*, what would your *heart* want?"

I hastily wash and dry my hands and cover them in flour. I begin to help Saada shape the dough into rolls. I contemplate the magic available. What would I want control over?

Blue would let me control water, but Gamet is Blue already. I'm not sure how much help that will be. And I don't like being in water much anyway. So that's out. I don't mind fire, but unlike Saada, I don't bake, so I don't have a need to control it. Yellow controls the weather, and while we get cold and hot, it's neither here nor there for extremes, so I'm okay without that one.

I don't feel the need to fight, and I've never been one for wounds, so that takes out Black and White. That only leaves Orange, and while I admire people who invent things, that's not where my mind goes. If we're wishing for wishes, though…

"There is one I would want," I finally declare after a long period of silence. Saada rolls the dough in her palms and adds it to the pan, waiting for me to continue. "It doesn't exist, but I would want the magic to stop you and everyone else from dying before you're thirty."

Saada pauses the rolling again, and I look up from my own dough to her teary green eyes. I give her a cocky grin, and she returns a sad smile. I grunt when she envelops me in a tight hug, covering us both in more flour.

WANT TO TALK ABOUT IT?

Eloise

I step out of the bathroom after a quick bath in our beat-up copper tub. I run my fingers through my wet hair as I pass through three kids fighting at the door for who gets to use the bathroom first. I sidestep past them and head back to the kitchen. The warm rolls on the counter draw me like a moth to a flame. I inhale their yeasty smell greedily, and my stomach grumbles loudly.

"Hungry?" Saada asks unnecessarily.

I nod eagerly. "Starving." I look hopefully in the oven. Empty. "Dinner?" I ask, straightening.

"Julieth," Saada remarks simply without looking up from the potatoes she is chopping.

My heart falls. "Oh."

Saada gives me a look, but I say nothing more and walk to the living room to sit in the rocking chair. Julieth. The one who disappeared for much of my childhood after our parents died. The one who caused us so much grief. The one who abandoned us as soon as her Quest was over. The one I cannot find it in myself to forgive. Saada and Gamet insist she's doing better, but I don't trust it. She's living with her girlfriend, Elaxi, who is part of a bad crowd, and I'm convinced that crowd is the one who encouraged Julieth to dodge her responsibility.

Julieth comes to visit from time to time, sometimes bringing food from the bakery where she works. That must be the plan for tonight. I hope she doesn't bring Elaxi. I can't promise to be civil if she comes with.

Saada emerges from the kitchen and sits across from me on the couch. It makes some menacing and threatening sounds, but it doesn't collapse.

"Are you okay?" Saada asks, resting her elbows on her knees and leaning forward. "Want to talk about it?"

"No," I answer shortly. I don't want to talk about my good-for-nothing sister. No, I don't want to hear how I should give her some grace for her mistakes. No, I don't want to expend any more energy on a sister who can't expend any energy on me.

Saada sighs and leans back. "Look, I know things with your sister have been strained." I snort, and Saada pretends not to hear it. "But she's still your sister and had a hard time with everything."

"You think I haven't?" I scoff angrily. "You think Julieth is the only one who had a hard time after they died? Why does she get a pass?" I didn't cry then, and I don't cry now. "I didn't disappear for days at a time; I wasn't the one who was failing school or slept for days on end. I kept going, but *she* deserves to get a pass?" My anger rages in me like a storm. I feel my face flush, my breaths coming short and fast.

I pulled myself together. *I* kept going even when the images of my parents being lowered into the ground haunted me in my dreams. I kept going even when it hurt so bad that I would go to the bathroom and throw up until only dry heaves wracked my body. Did anyone tell me it was okay to fall apart? No. Never. Just, "you're so strong" and "you're doing great" and "we're so proud of you."

"I'm not saying she gets a complete pass, Els, only that it might help if you both work together on this. You three will always need one another."

I shake my head. "I have everything I need here." I wave around the cabin, gesturing to the family I care about. "I don't need my unstable sister, okay?" I get up stiffly from the rocking chair and stalk off to my room. I slam the door behind me and the window rattles threateningly in its frame. I fall into my bed with a loud thump.

Life isn't fair. My parents died. Both of them. Within six months of each other. It sounds like a tragedy, and it would be, and it would garner more sympathy if the Realm weren't filled with similar stories. I roll over on my bed and hug a small patchwork quilt to my chest. It's one my mother sewed for me when I was a baby. It's seen all my tears and heartbreak. It doesn't judge me for still being hurt by the loss.

I know, intellectually, that joining the Celestials is supposed to be a celebration, a cause for joy, but it's hard to find joy in seeing someone who was once so alive, vital, be lowered into the ground. Their minds intact, their bodies intact, but still, just…gone. Like that. I have seen so many "celebrations" over my seventeen years. Parties thrown for those passed on to the Celestials. Trite sayings about how the Celestials want us back with them as soon as possible. How we must be such good people to be taken to them so soon. Gag me.

I know I'm in the minority, but I can't help but think that they're full of shit. Both the Celestials and those who believe in their great goodness. The Celestials always seem to mess with us mere mortals. If they wanted to, they could stop people from dying altogether, but do they? No. Instead, they take us younger and younger. Everyone puts on a brave face, eats, drinks, and dances around the bonfire at the celebration of life and then moves on like nothing happened. But it's not lost on me. The haunted look many people carry after the celebration has died down, and the drinks have stopped flowing. For all the talk of the goodness, those who lost their loved ones are aching. At least, in that, I know I'm not alone.

I AM STARING into an ornate gilded mirror, admiring my reflection. *How did I get here?* The dress fits perfectly, the purple silk hugging my curves. A split in the front reveals a black layer beneath. It falls near to the ground but not long enough to cover the purple silk shoes I have somehow obtained. My hair is pulled up elegantly, with a few curled strands falling around my face. *Who did my hair?* Around my neck, a silver chain from which hangs a phoenix with a keen gemstone eye. *Where did that come from?*

As I reach up to touch the cold metal, I am suddenly dancing in a grand ballroom with dark marble floors and huge windows through which moonlight streams. The rays dance along the floor, creating an illusion that the floor is liquid. A hint of lavender and sage wafts by on the air.

When did it get to be night? A large golden chandelier hangs from the ceiling with only half the candles lit. The flickering light only allows me to catch glimpses of my dancing partner's face, but his green eyes are an unmistakable emerald.

The music fades and I'm next sitting at a feast in a court somewhere. *Where is this?* The rich redwood table is shiny enough to mirror us and our food. I look at the reflection, and my breath catches in surprise and fear. I gasp and snap my eyes away from the reflection, but it's no illusion.

All of the guests appear to be rotting where they sit, their skin peeling away from their skeletal remains. The smell of rotting flesh assaults me, akin to the smell of the rats I found in the rafters one year. I want to go back to the ballroom.

The guests smile at me, at least I think they do, but without skin, it is quite impossible to tell. As I stare, flakes of skin drop off of them and crumble into ash before me. The pieces float away on an undetectable breeze.

The feast before me sours and turns fetid on the shiny plates and silver trays, intensifying the rotting smell. I hold my hand in front of my mouth, gagging when maggots crawl out of the roast on my plate. I push it away.

Still, the guests continue to eat their food. I am speechless, and my eyes track the bolus of food of their own accord, following it as it passes their mouths and down until it falls out between their ribs and onto their bony thighs. The maggots crawl on their laps and the marble floor around their seats. Some escape the food while the skeletal remains chew, and they crawl out of the eye sockets and nasal passages. The sacks of bones don't seem to notice.

In spite of what must be a disgusting meal, they continue to eat robotically, staring at me with dead eyes. One eye falls out of the guest's skull directly to my right. I get up slowly from my golden chair, afraid to upset the dead at the table. As if my movement might alert them that something is wrong. Who knows what will happen if I disturb the dead? I excuse myself with a stammering apology. They pay no mind. Chew, chew, chew…swallow…plop. I have to get out of here.

I push my chair back under the table, pause, then turn and run from the room back toward the ballroom. I look over my shoulder, once, and notice no one moves to follow me. Relief surges through me. I race for the door which seems so much further than it was before. *Before…before when?* My dress flows out behind me. *What a strange thing to notice.* I rip open the door when I finally reach it, nearly doubled over. More guests, more rotting skeletons. I start to back up, feeling for the door I went through. The door is not there. I spin and notice there are no doors at all. I spin back. My green-eyed dancing partner is back and conspicuously not a corpse. He holds his hand out to me.

"Come," he urges, his voice deep and sure. *How can he be so calm?* "I will keep you safe."

I debate whether he can be trusted. *How is he unaffected by this disease, if it is indeed a disease? How am I unaffected? More so, how is he not bothered by the abominations around us?* As I reach my hand out to take his, deciding to trust him, a knocking sound causes me to turn. My hand drops to my side.

I still see no doors, but the ghoulish skeletons turn to dust at once. The knocking sounds again. I turn to face my dancing partner. His calm smile turns to a frown. "I'll be back," he tells me before he, too, disappears.

~

"Eloise?"

I blink my eyes open slowly from a nap I never meant to take. I feel faintly unsettled, but I can't put my finger on why. I try to recall the dream I had been having, but like water through a sieve, it slips away.

"Eloise?" I recognize Cardis' soft voice. He is treading carefully. Probably sent by Saada. As my favorite family member, if anyone can get me to calm down, it's probably Cardis.

"Julieth and Elaxi are here," he states, his voice lightly muffled by the door. I grunt in acknowledgment.

"Great," I mutter. I could stay here and refuse to go out there, but if I want to eat more than crumbs, I need to play nice.

"See you soon." I hear his footsteps retreating from the door.

I climb out of bed. At the door, I pause to take a deep breath. *You can do this. Be civil for dinner.*

In the living room, the kids are seated around the oval table, plates of food in front of them. I see my rolls on their plates alongside a roast and potatoes. Roast. How did Julieth get a roast? I suddenly have a flashback to when she was fourteen, and she went through a phase of stealing whatever she could hide.

Maybe she's graduated to stealing roasts now, too.

I see Gamet, Cardis, Julieth, and Elaxi at the larger round table near the kitchen. They're chatting lightly. At the sight of Julieth and Elaxi, my lips purse in irrational anger. Elaxi laughs, that high-pitched fake tinkle she does that grates on my nerves, and she flicks her long, perfectly straight blonde hair over her shoulder. She smiles at Julieth who moons back. Gross. Why doesn't Julieth see how fake this girl is?

"Sister!" Julieth exclaims, getting up from her seat. My mouth drops. *Sister? She's taking on more and more of Elaxi's less desirable traits.* Julieth grabs my shoulders, and I flinch. Not because it hurts but because I have no clue what is happening here. She gives me air kisses on either side of my cheeks while I stand stiffly.

She grabs my hand and pulls me along to the table. I stumble after her, my shock still not past. "Elaxi told me that's how they greet people in Amiket," Julieth babbles excitedly, sitting down and pulling me down to the seat on the other side of her. "That's where we are going, you know! Once we get the money and well…"

She holds out her right hand, and there on her middle finger is a simple metal band. Probably steel, if I had to guess. Definitely not silver. "We're getting married!"

Julieth is bouncing in her seat, clapping with delight, and Saada rushes in to look at the ring and congratulate Julieth and Elaxi. Cardis mutters a similar expression of happiness, if more forced. Gamet smiles, not saying anything.

Leave it to me and my big mouth, though; I can't accept this. "You…Her…What…I'm sorry, what the Abyss?"

"Well, I know it's surprising!" Julieth doesn't seem to notice that I am anything but surprised. "Well, we were waiting until we had the money, you know, to travel, but Elaxi asked why we should wait. We couldn't find a reason, so…she proposed!"

I look over to Elaxi. She's smirking at Julieth. Not smiling. Smirking. Like she's won a game. When her gaze meets mine, with those obsidian eyes of hers, I glare at her to let her know her act has not fooled me. To her credit, her smirk doesn't slip. Instead, it transforms into a wide, genuine grin. Furious, I stand from the table.

"Eloise?" Julieth asks, her chin trembling.

"I'm sorry, I'm going back to my room." I glance at Julieth's ring. "I'm—" I take a deep breath. "Congrats, I guess."

"You don't have to be jealous," Elaxi sneers.

"Jealous?" I blurt. "You think I'm jealous?"

"Eloise—" Saada interrupts, sensing I'm about to lose all control.

"Well, what other reason could you possibly have for not wanting to stay and celebrate with us? We brought a roast and all." Elaxi gestures to the plated meal Saada abandoned to come and congratulate the supposedly happy couple.

I lean forward, my palms on the table, and I get in Elaxi's face. "Rest assured," I whisper, my voice deathly quiet. "I could not be less jealous of Julieth. To be tethered to you?" I bark a laugh. "I would never even consider it." I turn my gaze to Julieth who sits with her mouth agape, eyes wide, brows furrowed. "Good luck."

"Sorry, Saada, I'm not hungry." I turn and leave the cabin. I can't stay there for another minute. I swear, if she said one more thing, I would punch her in the face.

...BEAUTY AND SPLENDOR...

Aerith

R62T19
  Amiket Palace
  Amiket City, Amiket, Isynt Vale

I SWEEP MY LONG, straight purple hair from my face. Today has already been unusual in many ways. Firstly, that I am being called to Dream.

My first ever Dreaming session has started with the rising of the sun, pulling me out of my bed chamber and my warm silk sheets, demanding I get to my place immediately. I barely remembered to put on my brassiere in my hustle to get out of the room. I'm pretty sure I left one of the straps twisted, though, and I try to fix it on the run. It would be so much easier to be a man. These damned things get obnoxious.

I can Dream anywhere, or so I've been taught, but it is supposed to be much stronger and more detailed when I'm on the carpet surrounded by the dreamcatchers, which is the only reason I left my room at all, requiring I wear appropriate clothing. I wasn't about to miss a dream because I was feeling lazy.

There are five Dreamers in the palace in Amiket City.

Not all of the nine magics have a designated Dreamer. The Celestials didn't see having one necessary for Red, Orange, Green, or White to have one. However, they created Purple magic for the sole purpose of foretelling. There is no Purple magic outside of the Dreamers, and since Dreamers only exist within the palace, most outside of the city don't even know it exists. It's only myself and, one day, my apprentice, Mancio, when he comes of age to complete his Quest. We know he will come out Purple, but he will finally gain access to his power. Dreamers are the only people in all of the Realm to know they have magic before the Quest. Until then, he and the other apprentices go to school and practice the motions of Dreaming alongside their mentors.

One of the purposes of Dreamers is to identify other Dreamers. When one is born, the Dreamer who saw them notifies the Council, who immediately sends emissaries to test them. If they do indeed seem to have the gift, they are brought from their village to train as apprentices.

I don't remember my test; I was an infant, after all. Naseem, the Yellow Dreamer and my good friend remembers her test as she was a bit older before she was identified. She said the emissaries, a delegation of every color magic except Purple, came to see her. Each of them looked at her then talked amongst themselves before taking her with them.

Even though it didn't sound traumatic to me, she had tears streaming down her face when she told me about it. She doesn't talk about it if she can help it, and I'm sure she only told me because I asked when she'd had a bit too much wine. I still don't know if she remembers telling me, and I have never brought it up again.

Once we are trained, we provide a valuable service, as the Illume likes to remind us. Besides locating others like us, each of the Dreamers helps predict looming disaster so it can hopefully be mitigated. Naseem predicts dangerous storms, Batair, the Black Dreamer, predicts the moves of the other Vales against us, and Wynn, the Blue Dreamer predicts changes in the water. It's not a bad deal on the whole. Some of us work harder than others. My work is lightest, and some of the other Dreamers look down on me for having so little use as if I'm not also frustrated by that.

I never have dreams outside of sleep, and those don't count. Anything I have seen to date lacks detail and refinement. This isn't because I lack skill, as my mentor used to reassure me when she was alive; it's because Purple Dreamers only get to see big changes in the Realm. She herself died without ever having a dream worthy of sharing with the Council. At the rate I'm going, I'm about to be the same.

This morning, though, everything changed. My amethyst orb, the talisman hanging around my neck, had turned hot and nearly burned me before it managed to rouse me from deep sleep. It's never done that before. I had leaped out of bed in shock before falling on my face in a tangle of uncoordinated limbs and tangled purple silk sheets.

I quickly pulled the orb away from my skin, settling it on the outside of my purple silk gown. Deeply unnerved, I scrambled off the carpet and changed into my Dreamer clothes: a purple silk skirt and purple silk collared shirt. My shoes are purple flats. We all wear the same items, like a uniform, but each Dreamer has their own color. I have always wondered if I like purple or if it's because it's the only color I've ever had.

I didn't bother to braid my long hair as I normally would; I just rush out the door. Completely out of sorts, picking up Mancio from his room slips my mind. I remember right as I get to the room, but by then, the heat from my necklace is starting to scorch my clothing. I had never heard of the amulets getting this hot before; is something wrong with it? The only way I think I might be able to stop it is to try to access the dream the Celestials were granting me.

I open one of the large fifteen-foot golden double doors to the large octagonal room in the tallest tower of the West Wing. It's empty, which isn't surprising, given how early it is. I step onto the carpet, my feet sinking into the velvety fibers. I leave my purple silk flats at the entryway; shoes are not allowed past the first two feet of the door. The room is surrounded by enormous spotless windows, and the sun's first rays are beginning to peek through them as it comes over the mountains surrounding Amiket City. The shine off the gems in the dreamcatchers creates a kaleidoscope of color on the white walls and vaulted ceilings.

Normally, I pause inside the doors and take a deep breath, enjoying the privilege of being in the room. Privilege is not always how I saw it, however. I wanted to leave five years ago when I was new to being the sole Purple Dreamer and feeling useless with nothing to share. I may have also been goaded by Naseem who frequently manages to sneak out of the palace. I'm still not sure how she gets away with it.

While the Council tried to reassure me I was doing a good job and was still very important, I felt claustrophobic and wanted out. Naseem didn't contradict me. She told me I would like it outside of the palace. She was wholly incorrect. That was the worst experience of my twenty-two years to date.

I didn't realize how privileged we are in the palace. I knew we had privilege. Anyone who has ever read a book about fairytales knows that you're spoiled in a palace, but I had no idea how hard life is outside of it.

The Illume agreed to let me go with a Warrior handler trained in protection. I was prepared to face the real world, at least I thought I was. Turns out I was woefully ill-equipped to survive outside of the palace. A major miscalculation on my part. Thankfully, the Warrior was there to help keep me safe.

I discovered outside of the palace a world of scratchy sheets, shared bedrooms, and bathrooms that are outside rather than attached to your room and don't even flush. Most were openings to holes deep in the ground, and the smell made me retch. The food didn't help this. If that's what it could be called. Each meal I ate or attempted to eat looked exactly the same, although I was assured it was different. I couldn't differentiate one bowl of brown mush from the next. They tasted the same, which was like nothing. My stomach disagreed, thinking it definitely was something to be expelled. And forcefully. I spent the first night hovering over the hole in the outhouse, leaning against the wall and praying to the Celestials to make it stop. I cried from exhaustion and the sharp cramping in my stomach.

I never did experience the lumpy straw mattress and tattered blanket that were in my room in the "inn" if that's what it could be called. It had at least looked like the proprietor had tried to keep it clean. I'll never know for sure.

I wanted to go back to the palace after the first night, but the smug look on my handler's face kept me from doing so. I figured I had chosen the wrong spot to stay, and we tried another "inn" the next night with comparable results. My handler didn't seem bothered, but he had probably come from similar circumstances. Everywhere I went, people stared at me and asked questions.

"What's the palace like?"

"Huge, drafty, but very clean and comfortable." I fidgeted telling them this, seeing the obvious lack around me.

"What does a Purple Dreamer see?" I hated this question.

"Changes in the world."

"What's coming for us?" About half the people who asked this had hope shining in their eyes, the other half fear.

"I haven't dreamt of anything big." Or anything at all, but I kept that part to myself.

For every question they asked me, I asked them questions in return.

"What is day-to-day life like?"

Most would laugh harshly. I learned they work hard with little protection from the environment around them.

Then I asked, "How do you earn money? "

This answer varied, but everyone, even children, had jobs that were hard labor. The mines, fishing boats, construction, cleaning, serving. A rare few worked for the palace; they looked slightly better off than the general populace.

"How is your food at home?" I wanted to know if they had better food. Selfishly, I thought maybe they would invite me over for a meal that wasn't mush.

The gist of their answers led me to believe it was scarce. The gaunt faces staring back at me confirmed that, and guilt twisted my stomach further. I wondered why the palace didn't help more people in their own city, it's clear they need it.

I quickly learned most of the population had extraordinarily little money, no better housing or bedding than the inns, many of them sleeping on the floors or outside. After another night in the outhouse, completely exhausted and dirty, I told my smug handler to take me home.

The first thing I did when I got back was to take a long bath and use the entire bar of jasmine soap to feel remotely clean. I didn't tell anyone about the tears I cried at having seen the needy people I was ignorant of around me. Not even Naseem. Slowly, the pain of what I had seen faded, but the need to leave never crossed my mind again.

∼

On this particular day, I don't take the time to admire the beauty and splendor before me or how spoiled I am. I simply find "my" spot on the carpet, the far-left corner of the large room. I fold my purple legs beneath me, hold the talisman orb on the silver chain around my neck, and begin to do my breathing exercises.

The talisman serves a few different purposes. The first is that it will heat up when the Celestials call us to have a vision, which is what woke me this morning. The second is to be a communication device for the Illume. When they call us to meet, it will turn cold as ice. It also tells the Illume members where we are and our general health status so they can make sure we are safe. That's the part I haven't figured out how Naseem sidesteps to leave the palace. Not that I'm interested anymore.

The last purpose of the amulets is as a personal focus point for each of us. To start our Dreaming sessions, we have to breathe deeply and deposit our thoughts, fears, and hopes into the talisman to allow us to see things without influencing them ourselves, which is a real and potentially fatal problem, especially for the other Dreamers who have the responsibility of being a siren call for disaster. Our talisman is designed based on what the Quest thinks we need and is either made of the gemstone of our color or includes a gemstone of our color.

Our Quest isn't like most other quests. On that day, we enter a mirror of the dream room and sit like we do every other day. While we do, we change color, and we also get our final official talisman. Evidently, the Quest thought I needed peace; that's what I was told my talisman represents. Some of us may have our first vision. I did not. Nor have I had any since.

Mancio has an iron owl amulet as a placeholder, his favorite animal. It may or may not respond to the Celestials, but it still serves all the other purposes. When he is seventeen, he will remove the necklace before entering his Quest to obtain his final version. We are told from the time we get our talisman that it cannot be removed. Doing so can result in our death as it is closely tied to our core being. I wonder who was the first to discover that little side effect.

I push this thought out of my mind and into the amethyst totem, along with all of the other thoughts and feelings in my head. After my mind empties, I drop the talisman, and the dream begins. I sit there still as a statue not moving once. In this dream state, I am unaware of time or discomfort. I watch the vision unfold with my mouth hanging open and my heart racing.

I AM YOUR EVERYTHING.

Eloise

I am unable to sleep. Tossing and turning in my small bed. Across the room, I hear Hilda and Gilda snoring softly. In the living room, I can hear Saada and Gamet; the walls in our cabin aren't very thick.

Saada must have sat next to him as I hear the springs on the ratty, brown loveseat creak. "Everything okay? That was a big sigh." Gamet asks, concern lacing his voice.

"Just tired. It was a busy day," Saada responds. She doesn't sound like she's being entirely truthful. I'm sure some of her sigh has to do with how dinner went…or didn't.

"Tell me what's really going on," Gamet asks in a more probing way. I can practically picture them sitting on the couch. He probably has an arm around her, absently rubbing her shoulder. The two of them are made for each other. They almost never argue, and they're always touching each other. They emulate the kind of relationship that I always wonder if I will find one day. When I was younger, it was almost disgusting how sweet they were together. As I've matured, I've realized that this is the way love should be.

"We are both getting older," I hear Saada respond softly. "Our time could be up any day. You have, at most, a couple of years left, and I have maybe three." She states it matter-of-factly, without sorrow. Like someone who has come to terms with her future. "Eloise and Julieth can't see a way to get along and even if they did, I'm not sure they should be the ones to look after the kids."

An arrow of pain penetrates my chest. How can she not trust me? I've told her I will, and on many occasions, I have watched the kids, even disciplining them when necessary. I can see why she doesn't want Julieth doing it, given her lack of desire and her unreliability, but I have been nothing but responsible.

"Julieth has no desire to take on the family, and I'm not sure she should. With her…issue." I don't have time to ponder what issue Saada is referring to before she moves on. "Although, she is getting married, perhaps it will help. Maybe she's growing up. But if she does want to leave Ashadier, she's not going to do it with five kids."

I don't know why Saada insists on seeing me or even Cardis as kids Julieth has to look after. In two days, I'll be an adult, and Cardis will be only a few years behind me.

"…and Eloise is so young and, after the solstice, may not even be here anymore," Saada continues, unaware of my listening ears and internal debate with her. "What happens if we die, and no one takes the kids?"

A pause, and I hold my breath to hear the response. I can bet Gamet is pondering what to say next. "They're good kids; they'll take care of each other. Even Julieth would help, I'm sure. And maybe it would help her."

Oh, Gamet, ever the optimist. Julieth always said she didn't want to lead the family because she wasn't good enough or whatever, but I secretly thought it was because she wanted to leave Ashadier. Now, with this "issue" Saada brought up, I wonder if there's something more that I have missed. My chest tightens, thinking I may have allowed my disdain for her choice to stop me from connecting with her. I shake my head. No. She hasn't earned the right to be close to me.

"But, if Julieth can't or won't accept the helm, all of them will be put into the orphanage in the village," Saada adds, her voice breaking on the last few words. I grind my teeth, my hands fisting at my sides. I will never let that happen, and I thought I had made that clear to Saada.

I can understand she doesn't want her kids to be in the orphanage.

The orphanage is a sad, under-funded, Amiket City-run business. The people who work there have little interest in the children nor their care. "Only enough to keep them alive" seems to be their motto. I can usually identify one of their charges on sight; they're always dirty and hungry. Ashadierans don't have a lot of money, but we pride ourselves on at least washing regularly and managing to feed ourselves. I always give those kids a bronze or one of the fruits of my garden when I can.

Amaranth isn't a prized land, despite its ability to provide wood, since it rarely turns out anyone with important or unique skills. Thus, we call for no extra care or concern. If we were one of the other lands that turn out precious metals or citizens with great magic…well, then it would be a different story.

Fortunately, Gamet's family didn't have any other children we needed to look out for. Not that they would have ever wanted us to take them. My understanding of Gamet's family is tenuous at best as he prefers not to discuss them, his face twisting in disgust when they come up. Gamet was a noble from Amiket City who decided to marry a non-noble in Saada, and his family disowned him as a result. Family was everything, that's what we had always been taught, but it seemed his family was one we could do without.

"Tell me, Wife, are you worried about the Quest?" Gamet asks softly; I hear his papers shuffling. "About the curse?"

The what now? I tune my ears in more finely. I went from passively listening to now aggressively listening.

"No, not so much. Well, maybe a little. It's all tied together." Saada sounds confused.

I feel bad for eavesdropping on my aunt's fears, but she would never disclose them and if there is any way I can put her at ease, I would do it. Sometimes, the most stubborn people are the closest to falling apart.

"If Eloise goes into the forest and comes out with powers, she goes to the city. Which is great, right?" Saada sounds falsely cheery. Like she's trying to convince herself while also being distraught. I huff. I want to tell her that, no, it's not great. Especially if one of them dies while I'm gone. Then, the kids would be at the mercy of Julieth and Elaxi or the orphanage until I could come back.

"She gets to have a better life, a more secure life. But what about the kids? Is it so terrible of me to hope that she doesn't have magic so she can take care of the kids when we die?" A pause, then, "Of course, it is. Who wouldn't want to wish that at least one of her kids got to have a future beyond the bare minimum?"

"Is that what you think we have?" Gamet asks honestly. He doesn't sound offended, but I am. "The bare minimum?"

"I didn't mean…" Saada starts, but Gamet interrupts her.

"I don't think we have the bare minimum. We have a house, we have kids who love us, we have each other. What do I always tell you?"

I don't need to hear it to know what it is that is going to come out of her mouth next.

"I am your everything," Saada says so softly I almost miss it. Every time one of them leaves the cabin, that's what they say. "You are my everything, don't forget!" Once again, it would be so cliche if I didn't know they absolutely meant it.

"That's right. Which means as long as I have you, and you me, we have more than the bare minimum. And one day, the kids will find their everything, too. Maybe they'll find it with magic, maybe they'll find it in a partner, maybe they'll find it in the simplicity of life. But they'll find their everything."

I hear crying, and I assume it's Saada because Gamet's next words come out clear. "Oh honey, everything will work out. Everything always does."

"What if it doesn't?" Saada asks tearfully.

"What if it does?" I roll my eyes at the two of them going back and forth.

"I guess we will find out in a couple of days," Saada finally resigns the argument and changes topics. "Anything good in the paper?"

I hear the papers shuffle again. "Depends on what you define as good. Most of this month is talking about the Quest coming up and speculating what might come out of it. Pieces on the noble families and their prediction of how fantastic their kids are and what magic will be revealed in their offspring."

Since we are so far outside of larger society, we get a monthly newspaper with a rundown of the past month and speculation on the coming months. I don't usually have much interest in it. By the time we get it, a lot of it is outdated anyway.

"Noble, sure," Saada scoffs. The couch creaks, and Saada's voice shifts away from the living room. "To me, noble means they would do the right thing and help the less fortunate. When was the last time you saw a noble person do something noble?"

This is an argument I have heard many times before, and I return to half-listening. "Yes, well, noble means only that they get to play with the other nobles, marry the other nobles, and breed more nobles. Lot of good it does them. They still die before thirty like the rest of us poor people."

Saada huffs in derision, her voice closer to the hallway leading to the bedrooms. "Thank goodness for that. They do enough damage in thirty years to last one hundred thirty years. Come, let's go to bed. Tomorrow will be busy with the market and getting Eloise ready for the festival."

I quickly close my eyes as Saada and Gamet come down the hall. They quietly open the door and check in on us, same as they have done every night for the last several years. The door closes with a soft click, and I hear their footsteps recede to Cardis and Leck's room.

I am not sure why Saada believes I could come out with magic. Nothing indicates any magic in our family. Which leads me to the curse Gamet mentioned. I wish they had said more about that. I also wish they had said more about whatever Julieth's issue is. Not that I'm being nosey, I want to know so I can help her. Honest.

My heart aches for both Gamet and Saada. I don't entirely blame Julieth for not wanting to have kids. Given the state of things. However, I can blame her for not being willing to help with the kids already here. I quietly rise from my bed and make my way out of the cabin. I don't bother with my shoes or a cape; I don't plan to be outside long, and there's some lingering heat in the soil.

I go out back, through the garden, stepping softly and using the moon to guide the familiar path. Behind the garden, through the whitewashed fence, is a meadow. Odd in its placement is a large weeping willow. It oversees the graves at the base of its trunk, standing like a guardian over my parents. Wooden plaques demarcate their graves. I run my hands over the engraved, polished wood. Familiar to my touch.

Familiar to my pain. I allow a few tears to fall as I kneel between the graves.

"Mama, Papa, I miss you so much." A slight breeze picks up, a soft whooshing sound through the spindly branches of the willow, bringing with it the smell of grass and pine. My hair tickles my neck. It's like they're here with me when this happens. I can almost feel them hugging me, holding me. Papa's reassuring hand on my shoulder, giving it a squeeze for bravery. Mama's hug enveloping me in comfort. If I keep my eyes closed, I can pretend they're still there. "I'm going to make you proud. I promise," I whisper.

"Couldn't sleep?" I jump as Cardis approaches in the dark. His feet are also bare. We both have snuck out of the cabin often enough to know how to avoid the creaks in the wood floor and to forego shoes, ensuring we won't be heard. Usually, we sneak out to do exactly what we are doing now; spending time with our parents. We seek advice, comfort, and celebrate, but it's always when we can't sleep.

"No," I say, "I take it you couldn't either."

He shakes his head and kneels beside me. "No. I'm worried." I look over at my brother, his glasses obscuring his blue eyes.

"What are you worried about?" I pull a few small weeds that have sprouted around the graves while I wait for his response. The dirt feels good on my hands. I think I know what it is, but I give him the space to reveal it himself.

"Your Quest." He croaks like he did last year before his voice dropped into a manly timbre. "I have a sense of foreboding. I can't put a finger on it, but it scares me, Eloise."

I smile at Cardis' ten-bronze words. "All that reading is making you smarter by the day, little brother." He scowls at me and my use of "little." He has always hated being the youngest of us three. I wrap my arm around him and pull him into me. He doesn't stiffen, accepting my hug willingly. Something he doesn't do in public. "I'll be right back, same as Julieth. You don't have to worry about me, Cardis."

"If I shouldn't be worried, then why are you worried?"

"Who said I'm worried?" I retort, outright lying to him and myself.

"If you're not worried, then why aren't you asleep right now?" Cardis quips.

"I'm not tired," I refute nonchalantly, but a large yawn stretches my mouth at that moment, revealing my deception. "Okay, I *wasn't* tired. Now I think I could sleep." I won't burden Cardis with my concerns or fears. I get up from the ground and put my arm around him as we walk back to the cabin in silence.

...OR A BRICK WALL.

Eloise

Sunday, R62T20
  1 Day Before the Quest

I BLINK MY EYES OPEN; I have a foot in my back and realize it's one of the girls who must have left her twin and joined me sometime in the night. Through the small window in the room, I can see the sun starting to shine through the trees. My stomach gives a little lurch. Today is the festival, tomorrow the Quest. But first, the market.

Last night, the Gophers will have arrived by wagon from Amiket City. The train cannot travel directly here, so they must travel in a less luxurious way from the train hub in Rothesard to get to us. I can almost bet the Gophers assigned to our area are being punished for something. No one from Amiket City chooses to come to this part of Amaranth of their free will. It's not got any nice inns, no fancy roads, and we don't have any of the amenities I've heard exist in the cities. The Gophers will come, turn their noses up at our village, and carry out their requirements. Then they will leave, likely with no additional passengers, and we will breathe easy again for another year.

Beyond overseeing the Quest each year, the Gophers are the eyes and ears of the Illume Council. While they don't visit us often, they can come if someone requests their help resolving a conflict, or they may show up to do a surprise inspection of the town.

The disdain between the village and the Gophers is mutual around here. They don't want to be around us; we don't want to be around them. It's not only their general attitude that gets to us; it's also the fact that they can take us away with no reasoning whatsoever. The Illume removed the law that required that they or anyone else acting on behalf of the Council have a reasonable cause to arrest someone. Their claim that they would get a trial in Amiket and, therefore, reasonable cause wasn't necessary is weak at best. True, the Gophers don't have the right to kill us without reason, but it's a small consolation when anyone they have taken to the city has never returned. They just…disappear. I find it hard to believe they get a fair trial and that *every* person brought to that trial is guilty of a severe punishable offense so as to prevent them from coming home.

I carefully and quietly climb over the end of the bed, trying not to disturb the sleeping gremlins. I grab some clothes off the floor that look to be clean—probably discarded in the hunt for other clothes—and head to the bathroom. This early, no one seems to be awake yet, and the bathroom is clear. I wash my face with cold water, comb out my unruly hair before tying it out of my face with a hair tie, and change into my clothes. I pile the dirties in the corner of the bathroom to retrieve later… if I remember. Not likely. After all, my clothes from yesterday's garden work are still in the corner, too. I reason that I can't possibly put them in the basket and risk waking the kids. That's what I will tell Cardis when he inevitably asks why my laundry is breeding in the bathroom.

I tiptoe toward the door, grab my leather satchel hanging beside it, and sneak outside. I sit on the small wooden bench again, feeling that sense of deja vu in reverse as I pull on my boots. My feet protest strongly.

"I promise to see the cobbler soon, see if he can make them bigger somehow," I plead with my aching feet. I stand and hiss with pain. The blister on my right foot has made itself known again. I grit my teeth, trot down the rickety steps to the little path leading off our property, and out the open metal gate attached to the stone half-wall which wraps around our abode.

Today is Sunday, market day, and with the Quest tomorrow, there might be some people interested in buying my wares. To help with family finances, I sell various items at the market. It started with vegetables from the garden and soap I made from the milk we got from our goat. When I got a little older, I started carving wood and selling decorative figurines and flutes. Most recently, I've been able to add knives with carved wood handles. These are more likely to sell today than any other day. While the Quest is touted not to be dangerous, kids still need a way to hunt. Someone might want a knife. Or maybe someone will want to congratulate their new almost-adult with one of the decorative items I have.

I know that tonight is going to be a late night, and I should be getting as much sleep as I can to prepare for it and the early day tomorrow, but I can't pass up the chance to add a little coin to the family jar.

It's too early for the market to be open, but vendors are already setting up little tables of wares and getting sorted. The earlier you get there, the better placement you get on the Clearing. It was once called the Green but since it has no green anymore, it was re-named. It is now a large circle of dust and old flagstone, which once made a winding path across the Clearing.

Ideally, especially in winter months, I get a place near the flagstone paths. The rest of the circular area turns into a mud pit, which means fewer people are likely to visit. I'm not a vendor with many essentials, so I try to rise before dark on Sundays in the winter and spring to snag a coveted spot. I'm less concerned with that today, though, as the heat wave has dried out the dirt sufficiently for shoppers.

There are no clouds, the sun is starting to shine brightly, and the smell of wildflowers is on the breeze. It's nice now, but it does portend a sweltering day later. No matter. While the market will last until the afternoon, I plan to only stay until mid-morning. I have a festival to get ready for. I plan to look at least somewhat presentable tonight. There's no one to impress, but there aren't many reasons to celebrate around here that don't revolve around death. It'll be nice to go to a dance that doesn't involve the hideous black dress in my closet.

I see one more open spot that looks promising. Near the start of the flagstone, where people have more money to spend. I rush down the grassy sloped path towards it, hoping to beat anyone else who might have eyes on it. Focused solely on that, I don't notice the man who is directly in my path, and I suddenly ram into him…or a brick wall. I'm not sure. My shoulder says it's a brick wall. The man grunts but doesn't even step back.

He steadies me by grabbing my upper arms, and I yelp in surprise and pain. I look up to apologize but the brick wall's gaze is lost to the present momentarily. I notice what he is wearing. A tan cloak, crisp white shirt that is a stark contrast to his deeply Black skin, and tan pants with neat creases. His shoes are perfectly shined, and his black hair, hanging down in locks, is pulled back neatly. Shit. He is definitely a Gopher. *Shit.*

The man shakes his head and blinks. The man stands several inches taller than me but also several inches wider…in muscle. Suddenly unnerved and afraid, I mutter a quick apology, keeping my eyes down and hoping he won't arrest me on the spot.

"Are you alright?" he asks in a deep rumble, looking me over. I fiddle with the edge of my shirt, realizing how wrinkled my clothes are and how dirty my boots are compared to his. I shouldn't feel embarrassed, it's nothing less than the Gopher would expect of me. Still, I want to cover myself.

"Yes, sir. Sorry, sir." My voice is shaky, and I hate myself for betraying my fear. His large hands drop from my arms, and he steps back away from me a little.

"Where are you going in such a hurry?" he asks. Surprisingly, he sounds more curious than accusatory as I would expect.

"To the market," I reply, keeping my gaze downward, "to set up. There is a good spot open, and I want to get it before someone else does. I'm sorry, I wasn't looking where I was going." It comes out of me in a rush, breathlessly. I look around him and groan. The spot I want is gone.

"If you're sure you're not hurt…"

"I'm not, thank you. Sorry, sir." I'm fidgeting in place, and I try to force myself to stillness. I chance a look up at him and he has a contemplative smile on his face, a dimple on the right, but not the left, and black eyes, deep and expressive.

I hold my breath, waiting for him to let me go. He holds out his hand. "Mitac," he introduces himself. "And you are?"

"Late for the market." I ignore his outstretched hand. Now that it seems like he's not going to arrest me, I am feeling a little bolder, and I dart away from him. "Sorry, sir, gotta run!" I call over my shoulder. He doesn't give chase; he merely looks at me with that little smile of his and waves me on. I breathe a sigh of relief. That could have been so much worse.

WHAT STRIKES YOUR FANCY, SIR?

Mitac

I watch the girl scurry from me to what must be the market she was speaking of.

Danger, the unfortunately familiar voice in my head returned when I touched the girl to steady her when she ran into me. I haven't heard it in years, not since my brother, Meinolf, left for Amiket City. I don't know where it comes from or why, but I know each time I've heard it, it's not been a good outcome.

I shake my head, trying to dispel the disquiet.

I see ramshackle tables set up around the dusty circle. Some look barely sturdy enough to hold themselves up, let alone the goods they're being tasked with holding. Fruits, vegetables, clothes, shoes, household items...there's something here for everyone. Villagers greet each other warmly; some shake hands or hug and help each other set up. This is certainly not unlike what it would have been like in the smaller towns of Delja, but Amiket citizens would never dream of helping each other. The city would just as soon stab you in the back while giving you a hug as help you.

It's my first time in Ashadier and Amaranth, too, as a matter of fact, as I had only taken a position with the Illume Council earlier this year and didn't have much time to travel before this assignment. As a newbie,

I was given what everyone considers the worst assignment for the Quest. Nearly every Gopher is assigned somewhere, and the posts in Amaranth, Ashadier specifically, are supposed to be the worst.

"No one magic ever comes from Amaranth," one of my new friends had ribbed while we were changing after a training session. "You'll probably be on your way home within a couple of hours of the start of the Quest."

"At least you won't have to stay long, Mitac!" another of my friends called from near his locker. "I went to Amaranth my first year." He scowled. "Foul, dirty, smelly, rotten place. No decent food, no decent people. A bunch of poor folks."

I bit my tongue and fought hard not to say something. Like how I had been a "poor folk" all my life until I came out from the sea all Black. How I had spent time sleeping on the street with hungry belly and dirty clothes. Contrary to widely held belief, the sea does not clean things well. It leaves them smelling funny and crunchy from the salt. My parents died when I was twelve, and I managed to avoid the orphanage in Delja proper by being sneaky. If anyone at school asked who I was living with, I managed to avoid the question, change the topic, or run off and find a new village to live in.

Sometimes, I found work on plantations, lying about my age, or working for those who either took pity on me or didn't care that much. But work meant I didn't have to steal from other folks; the rest of the time, I went without. It was a long five years with nothing to show for it other than street smarts, how to be sneaky, and how to sense trouble. When the Quest came around two years ago, I hoped upon hope I would Change so I could find a better life. While going to Amiket City wasn't my dream—I'd much rather have stayed in Delja, but with some money to my name would have been nice—going to Amiket meant I could train in something and, hopefully, snag a long-term job.

I got lucky. Coming out as Black as I did made me a highly coveted Prime. I was both dangerous—strong powers with no control—and endangered. Prime magic-wielders are the strongest of their kind, and I traveled under the guard of a few other Prime Black Warriors to the city center. There, I was given two years of room, board, and education. I learned that my particular brand of Warrior skill lay in Negotiation. It was hardly a surprise, given how I had spent five years either avoiding trouble or talking myself out of it. For the last two years, I had studied with other Negotiators, learning tactics for how to get the most out of someone else while giving as little of yourself or your land as possible.

When I finished with the Academy, the Council offered me a position. I could be a Gopher for them, paired with a Prime Green who was an ace in Tracking, and attend the Quest days. Together, our job was to watch those who came out, identify anyone with magic, and immediately abscond with them to the city.

Sometimes, kids went in and didn't come out, though. If anyone was unaccounted for, it was our job to go in and find them. My Tracker locates them, and I either rescue them from trouble, carry out the body, or convince them the city is a wonderful place to be. Something I'm still trying to convince myself of.

Some of the kids did not want to leave their families. A fact I could understand. If my brother hadn't left for the city, I would have had someone old enough to hold a steady job and help look after me. At the time, I imagined his fears were much the same, but the laws were clear. All people who came out of the Quest Changed had no choice but to return to the city. What really bothered me was that he had never returned after his training.

I spent the early part of my time training at the Academy, looking for my brother and trying to find out what happened to him. No one ever told me. He had come out of the ocean Black, too, but no one could tell me what happened after that. I did find in the Academy records that he finished his training, but I found no further records of him, and all my searches had turned up empty. Eventually, I gave up my search, deciding that the voice in my head had struck again, and he was dead.

I'm not particularly excited about separating families, so I hope what my fellow Gophers were jibbing me about is true and that no one with any real magic came from here. For one, I would get to leave sooner. For two, I wouldn't have to face tearful goodbyes.

Rabbit girl greets a few people on her way to the village center and sits on the ground. She pulls a small square quilt from her bag and lays it flat on the dirt. She takes several different items from her bag and puts them out for display on the quilt. Someone nearby brings her a low stool to sit on, and while I can't hear her, I can see the gratitude on her face. I wipe my brow and look up at the sky. It's going to be a hot one.

"Are you ready for this?" my Tracker asks as she sidles alongside me. She has short, jaw-length dark green hair that matches her dark green skin, though most of her skin is covered by her heavy brown cotton pants and long-sleeved tan cotton shirt. Despite her heavy boots, she made nearly no sound coming up to me.

"Ready for what?" I ask, still distracted.

"The Quest? Your first big mission?" She gives me a playful nudge with her shoulder. I shrug. Maybe I should be nervous, but she and I have worked on a handful of smaller missions before.

"Sure. Though, as I understand it, not much happens around here." I look over at Chance, not her real name. She won't reveal her true name to anyone, insisting she detests it. I don't push. Frankly, it doesn't matter what she wants to go by. She makes a good partner. While the assignments we have done together so far have been trivial things like finding lost kids in the city or helping track down thieves, she does her job, and we work well together. I don't want to share about my past. She doesn't want to share about hers.

"Is that why you're not carrying your weapons?" She eyes my back.

"I left the sword and the leiomano in the room. I didn't think it would be a good way to get the village's cooperation." When I graduated as a Negotiation Warrior, I was able to choose my weapons. I picked the sword because of my familiarity with it from training in the Academy. The leiomano is a traditional weapon of Delja. I carry it as a reminder of where I come from. Plus, the long, wooden sword-shaped weapon with shark teeth embedded on its edges is downright vicious looking. It can do some serious damage if I choose to use it. I hope I never have to.

Some of the Blacks I trained with were bloodthirsty and couldn't wait to become part of the enforcement squad or the army, but that's not me. It was a difficult two years of being relentlessly bullied for my gentle nature. And not only by the other students. I grind my teeth at the memories and shove them back into the box in my brain where I keep them locked up. Most of the time.

"True." She looks around. "Another small village with nothing to offer. Although, maybe we should see what they are selling. Sometimes, these little village folks have cool stuff we can't get in Amiket." Chance is no older than I am, but she traveled far more than I ever did. She never did reveal why, and I never pried. Whenever her past comes up, the subject quickly changes. Not all that indifferent to when mine comes up. Often, I wonder if she weren't so guarded, and I weren't so guarded…I shake my head. No point hoping for something that won't be.

Chance hoists her cloth bag to her shoulder and heads for the round patch of dirt. I follow behind. I have some money that could be spent here. Unfortunately, most vendors don't want to look at us as we approach. I understand. Gophers are persona non grata in most areas I've heard. I've never seen it so blatant before, but I think people in Amiket are more accustomed to seeing us.

Still, we are often only accepted and liked by the upper class in Amiket. That could also be because many Gophers look the other way at the misdeeds of those same upper class. I'm not among them, but the villagers here don't know that. They have no way of knowing that I mean them no harm and desperately want this to be the most boring Quest in the history of Quests.

I try to be casual, smiling at the vendors. I look around at the various products before me. I pick up a few and put them back when the sellers hold their breath for too long. I have my eye half on the girl who ran into me earlier but try not to make it obvious. I am eager to see what she has most of all. Someone bold enough to run from a Gopher and then set up shop in eyesight is someone I want to know more about.

I wander to the next booth over; a portly man in a white apron is selling some baked goods. He doesn't look away from me when I walk over, and the smells from his table have been assaulting me since I entered the market.

"Good morning, sir," he greets, smiling at me genially. "Looking for something to eat?"

I'm not particularly hungry, having eaten a little bit of bread and cheese in the inn before coming here, but I can smell something that is making my stomach grumble. Loudly. The man laughs.

"Sounds like your stomach is answering for you! Mr. Braswell, town baker." He holds out his hand for me, and I shake it with surprise.

"What do you have that smells so good?" I take a deep breath, pulling in the rich smell. I'm no culinary expert, but I am an expert at eating. If it weren't for my rigorous self-imposed training schedule, I would probably have quite the pot belly.

"I have sweet and savory. Some blackberry hand pies made this morning, along with rhubarb. If you want something savory, you might like the mushroom, chive, and goat cheese pie or the sausage and egg hand pie. What strikes your fancy, sir?" He stands, hands on his hips, clearly proud of his wares.

I ponder it. Everything sounds amazing. The golden crusts are begging me to buy all of them. I glance at Chance and wonder if she would like one, but if we are being honest, I have no idea what her preference would be. I hedge my bets. "I'll take a mushroom and a blackberry."

"Good choice!" We exchange some coins, and he hands over the pies. The mushroom and cheese is still warm. I hope Chance wants the sweet pie because I *really* want the savory one.

"Over here, Mitac!" Chance calls as though I'm not already heading her way.

She is standing in front of rabbit girl. I walk over and hand Chance the sweet pie, not offering her the choice. I think she would appreciate that, especially since I already took a big bite out of the mushroom pie. It is as delicious as I thought it might be. I almost close my eyes in pleasure as I take another bite.

"Aren't these amazing?" Chance asks, accepting the hand pie from me. She holds up a dark wood flute that has been carefully carved with various wood animals and vines. It is beautiful, and I tell Chance as much. She buys it and puts it in her bag before walking off. I bend down to take a closer look at the items the girl has laid out. Another flute is there, with flowers and trees on it, made of lighter-colored wood. Beside the flute, she has several bars of soap. I pick one up, and under her watchful green eyes, I smell it.

"Lavender?" I ask, turning it over in my hand. Even the soap has a carved decoration on the top. It looks like a bird of some kind.

She nods. "There's also a pine one. I'm sure that's surprising." I almost ask why before I remember a massive pine forest surrounds us.

I chuckle. "Indeed. Shocking," I deadpan. She doesn't smile. "What's even more shocking is that you know what soap is." I want to stuff my foot in my mouth. *Why did I say that?* But I needn't have worried.

She blinks and quips right back. "Yes, well, we only bring it out for special occasions. Seems like it's the same for you."

"I figured I would dirty down before coming to the backwoods. So I would fit in better." Still no smile. I'm glad I didn't try to pursue a career as a court jester.

"You failed." She pauses. "You smell worse than the pigs in the pen."

I choose not to answer the latest statement and look at the soap again. "A bird? Why does a bird need soap?"

"It's not merely a bird," she snaps, taking the soap and putting it back on the blanket. "It's a phoenix."

"Okay, why does a phoenix need soap?"

"They don't." She doesn't explain further, forcing me to ask.

"So why a phoenix?"

She shrugs. "I thought it was an interesting animal. One day, it can burst into flame and be reborn."

Interesting. "Is that something you'd like to do, Rabbit?"

She raises an eyebrow at me. Her green eyes bore into mine. "Not particularly. Burning up sounds painful. I could do without that."

"What about being reborn?" I ask.

She cocks her head. "Well…it's a nice idea, isn't it? With everyone dying so young, wouldn't it be nice to think we could come back and try again?"

I nod. "Perhaps. Depends on how much you enjoy life, I suppose." I'm not sure I would like to live this life again. A different one, perhaps. "Do you think you'd be destined to relive the same thing over? Or would it be completely different?"

"I have no clue," she states, a hint of annoyance in her rising voice. "The phoenix is a myth; how would I know if it relives the same life it already did before?"

I hold up my hand. "Sorry, I didn't mean to get into a philosophical discussion this early in the morning."

"Maybe we save philosophy for a more appropriate time…like when I'm thirty-one."

I laugh. "Deal."

She still doesn't smile, but I smile at her anyway. I pick up one of the knives she has on her blanket. It has an antler handle, and it, too, has birds carved into it. But this is delicately carved with ravens on tree limbs. I am surprised to find that it balances and fits in my large palm quite well.

"Did you make this yourself?" I ask incredulously.

"Yes," she responds defensively, her large green eyes narrowing, arms crossed. "I had some help from the blacksmith in town in shaping and sharpening the blade, but I made and carved the handle."

"It is very good." I try and fail to keep the surprise out of my voice as I make a few motions with the knife. "I did not expect to see anything quite so nice here."

"Here as in Amaranth or here as in from me personally?" Her tone holds a bit of disdain in it. Clearly the rumors about Amaranth are not known only to those in the city with more money than brain.

"From you, personally. You look young to be doing something so skilled."

"I'm seventeen, thank you, but I have been working with wood since I could hold a whittling knife and not unintentionally stab myself or someone else with it."

"Unintentionally, huh?" I smile.

"Yes, unintentionally. I have never intentionally used one to hurt anyone, either in case you were wondering. Are you going to buy that?" She jerks her head toward the knife I'm holding. "You're scaring off the other customers." I look around and notice other villagers giving me a wide berth.

I hold the knife more firmly in my hand. It is a well-put-together knife. Maybe even better than some of the ones I have gotten from Amiket City that are now on my person, hidden away. Leaving the big weapons in my room doesn't mean I'm completely defenseless. I make a few more slashing moves in the air and run my thumb lightly across the blade, noting how sharp the honed blade is. "How much?" I ask.

"Ten silvers," she counters firmly.

I whistle. "Eight silvers." This is the part I love about my magic. I don't buy anything at face value, even when it's worth it. Most of the time I don't even notice I'm doing it.

She smirks. "I'm sorry, did you take this to be a negotiation? Because it's not. Ten silvers, or it stays with me. I know what it's worth."

In all honesty, it is probably worth at least fifteen silvers but I'm not going to tell her that. "Fine, ten silvers but you give me your name."

Her smile slips. She hasn't expected that. In my world, information is as important as money. "Ten silvers. Eloise is the name." I relax. I didn't even have to put my magic out there to make that one work.

"Pleasure to meet you properly this time, Eloise." I pull the change from my pocket and hand it over. I palm the knife and quickly hide it away. "You're seventeen," I say it half as a thought to myself and half as a question to her. "Did you do the Quest last year, or is this your year?"

She sighs. "This year is my year." Clearly, she's not excited.

"I'll keep an eye out for you," I say. She stares me in the eyes and, other than when she ran into me, doesn't appear afraid. Nearly everywhere I go, people clear a path for me. Bowing, scraping, like I'm royalty. It's aggravating.

"You have to anyway, don't you? Being the Gopher and all? But don't trouble yourself," she retorts. "I'll be out within an hour."

"Is that so?" I challenge. Such confidence.

"Yep. Never been anything different for our family. Hardly been anything different in the entirety of Amaranth, especially Ashadier. I don't even know why you people keep coming."

"'You people'?" I quirk an eyebrow at her.

"Yes, you people," she waves in my general direction. "Council flunkies. It's a waste of time and money for all of you. Should leave us alone."

"Well, I do what I'm told."

She grunts. "Because the all-knowing Illume Council is perfect, right?"

I shake my head. "No, not necessarily. But thus far, I haven't crossed any moral boundaries."

"Moral boundaries? You have those? I thought they trained those out of you in the city?"

"No, Rabbit, though they certainly tried." I push down the revulsion of the training I received in the city.

"Why do you keep calling me Rabbit?" she asks, her eyes narrowing.

"You reminded me of one. The way you scurried away…" I scissor two of my fingers quickly to simulate running legs, "…Rabbit."

"Okay…" Boy, I'm dying out here. She looks around, smiling at a few people. I should move on so she can sell her items.

"Care to put a wager on it?" I ask not ready to end our back and forth yet.

"A wager on what?" she asks with curiosity.

"Whether you turn into a rabbit tomorrow," I jest. She still refuses to smile. If looks were venomous, I would be dying a slow painful death at this moment. "Whether you Change tomorrow, of course."

She kicks her feet out in front of her, crossing her ankles, and asks smugly, "Do you like losing?"

I shrug. "No skin off my nose."

"Of course not, it's only money, right?"

I nod, not missing her contempt. "Exactly. Let's see…if you come out in the first six hours Unchanged, I will give you a gold coin."

"Six whole hours, huh? And if I don't come out in the first six hours Unchanged?"

"Then you come with me to the city without a fuss."

She rolls her eyes. "I would already have to. That's the all-knowing, all-mighty, never-wrong laws."

"You missed the key words there, Eloise. I said, 'without a fuss'."

"Who's to say I would put up a fuss?" Her shoulders stiffen, and her spine straightens.

"A hunch." I hold out my hand for hers.

"Deal." She clasps my hand firmly, and we shake. "Get ready to lose your coin."

I pull it out for her to see, and her eyes grow wide. I suspect she has never seen one before. That stupid bit of gold is worth two hundred silvers. More than most people make in a few months. Especially in places like these.

...A REAL DREAM!

Aerith

As soon as the Celestials release me from my vision, I dash out of the tower and head to find Naseem. I nod to a few maids and servants cleaning rooms and floors. I try not to make it look like I'm in a hurry, but I speed up when the hallways are clear. At one point, I almost take out a messenger who rounds a corner at the same time as me. I apologize profusely, then keep going.

The palace is a bit of a maze; when Naseem first got here, she frequently got lost. All the rest of us had grown up in the palace and learned the layout as we got older. Since Naseem wasn't immediately identified at birth, she learned the hard way. That's one of the reasons we became good friends. I had come out of a class and found her in an alcove between the legs of a suit of armor. She was curled into a ball, crying. The other kids had kept going, a few going so far as to laugh at her, but I knew what it was like to be the outsider and the one mocked.

"Hey," I said, walking over and sitting beside her in the tiny alcove.

"Hey," she replied, wiping her nose on the sleeve of her shirt, looking up at me with her then brown eyes.

"Want some help?" I asked when she didn't offer anything more. Her blonde hair was a mess of tangles. I reached out to help untangle it, and she flinched. I dropped my hands.

She looked at me hesitantly, then nodded. "Okay."

"Where are you supposed to be next?" I got up from the floor and held out my hand to her. She took it and climbed out from under the statue.

She pulled a piece of parchment out from the pocket in her bright yellow skirt and glanced at it. "English. I think? What day is it?"

"It's Tuesday," I looked over her shoulder at her schedule.

"Yes, looks like you have English. You're in luck, so do I." I clasped her hand, and together we walked to English class. I didn't have English lessons at that time, and I got weird looks from our teacher, who had seen me earlier that day. I held my finger up to my lips and explained the situation later.

A compassionate woman, our English teacher saw to it that my classes were switched to Naseem's for that year. The school council refused to do it again, but they allowed it this time since Naseem was struggling so hard. As far as I know, she never found out. She needed a friend, and, honestly, so did I. Ever since that day, at the tender age of seven, we have eaten every meal side by side and spent much of our free time together.

You couldn't get two girls who were more different from each other. Like magnets, we were drawn to each other anyway. She is as messy, chaotic, and wild as the storms she predicts. I, however, am neat and proper. Obedient. Naseem disparages the Council regularly, much to my angst, and I remain convinced once her apprentice can take over for her, she will find herself locked in the dungeons. She always shrugs off my concerns.

"The Council isn't everything, you know," she tells me when I tell her to hush or at least keep her voice down. "There's more to the world than this."

I roll my eyes. "I know. I've heard this before."

"Well, I've heard your lecture, too, Aerith. You don't remember what life before the palace was like. You feel beholden to them. I do not."

That's all she would divulge on the subject. When Naseem first showed up, I had asked my mentor why she hadn't come sooner. She told me Naseem lived in Halberg and because the ice bridge hadn't frozen over, they couldn't go get her.

Nonetheless, as different as we are, I would still do anything for her, and she would do anything for me. I also trust her judgment, most of the time anyway. I know I can tell her everything I have seen so far, and not only will she not judge me for not bringing in Mancio, but she will also give me solid advice. I've never had a reason to bother the Council with anything before, and I think this may be one of the times I should call them. I'm terrified of calling a meeting and making them angry for something they perceive to be needless. Naseem has had to call them before, so she will know if this is worthy.

I approach her doors, white double doors that mirror my own, and knock, excitement barely contained. When she opens the door, she gives me her usual smile and hug before ushering me in. I wonder if she can tell I'm bursting with news.

"I'm so glad you're here!" I tell her as I enter her room. Then my face falls. She has clothing everywhere. On her bed, the floor, I even find a piece of undergarment hanging from a painting. "I'm sorry, do you need some time to clean up?"

She laughs heartily. "Oh, Aerith, you think you would know me better than that by now! No! I was looking for a ring I had bought in town and well…I finally found it." She holds the gold ring with a diamond in the middle up in triumph for me to see.

"But why is everything," I gesture around us, "everywhere?"

"I started to panic when I couldn't find it, so I started pulling everything out of my dresser drawers. I was so sure I had put it in there."

Having a feeling I knew where this was going, I asked, "And where did you find it?"

"In the last place I looked!" she exclaims. Same old joke, same old Naseem. I smirk at her. "In the bathroom. Silly me. I must have removed it when I took a bath and forgot to put it away."

As I thought. Another difference between us, Naseem is quite forgetful while I have a steel trap for a memory.

"Oh!" I said, suddenly remembering why I was in such a hurry to get to Naseem.

She starts to put on her yellow coverlet chuckling at me and misinterpreting my sudden outburst. "That hungry, eh?"

I shake my head. "No, not that! I'm so excited I can't possibly think of eating anything!" Her face falls at the idea of missing lunch, but she looks at me curiously. "I had a dream! And not a night dream, a real dream!"

Her mouth forms a small "O" in surprise. She immediately sits down on her unmade bed, the yellow silks in disarray, and motions me to do the same. We turn to face each other. "Tell. Me. Everything," she demands.

"Well, I was sleeping comfortably this morning. All warm and cozy. The bed was exactly right. Whoever put the hot water bladder in my bed did it perfectly." I giggle. I can tell Naseem's getting annoyed by my long-drawn-out story by the way she fidgets on her bed. I'm messing with her, and she knows it, but who knows when I will ever have something so juicy to share again?

"Get on with it!"

"Fine, fine. Ruin all my fun. Where was I?" I pause dramatically while she huffs. "Oh right, I was in my bed. Warm, cozy, all that. I felt my talisman go hot, scorching even! So, I got up even though it was dark outside." She waves her hand, telling me to move it along. "Anyway, I get to our wing, sit down, and Dream! And that's all!"

"Aerith! I swear to the Celestials that I will tickle you mercilessly if you don't tell me what you saw. Right. Now!" Her now golden yellow eyes narrow at me, her hands come up in claws, prepared to attack.

I hate to be tickled, and Naseem knows all my ticklish spots, so I relent. "Okay, so the first dream I saw—"

"You had more than one?" She interrupts me. "In one morning?"

"Do you want to hear this or not?" I raise my eyebrows at her. Now, I'm the one getting impatient.

"It's highly irregular to see more than one dream at a time," Naseem explains.

I ponder this but press on. "Okay, let's circle back to that. Anyway… the first dream didn't make a lot of sense. I saw a couple of boys and a couple of girls. They were traveling together, somewhere. I couldn't tell where they were coming from or where they were going. In front of them, Zarvan was in chaos and ruin. As they passed, the land grew peaceful and began to grow new life."

Naseem considers this. "So, it's not like…real events?"

Oh no…what if I wasn't seeing the future? What if I was imagining things?

"I don't know, I mean. What are your dreams like? My mentor never had any to share with me."

"They're pretty literal," Naseem clarifies. "They show me where, approximately when, and show me exactly what. What good would they be if I can't direct warnings where they are needed?"

"Oh…well, maybe mine are more symbolic?" I'm grasping at straws. I had heard the other Dreamers share their visions with the Council and they had sounded literal, but I thought they were skilled at interpreting them.

Naseem nods. "It's possible." But her pursed lips and tilted head tell me she is no longer sure.

"Is that a thing?" I ask hesitantly, desperately wanting her to confirm it.

"Maybe. What else do you have?"

"The next dream showed one of the girls. Again, I don't know where she is, but she was old." I pause. Naseem looks less surprised than when I told her I had a dream. "Old, Naseem! She had wrinkles and grey hair!"

"Old," Naseem repeats, rolling the word around in her mouth. As unfamiliar to her as it is to me.

"Yes, old. Way past thirty. I saw similar things with the other three. They're old, too."

"Wow…I wonder…" Naseem rises off the bed and paces her floor. "Anything else?"

"Nothing that makes any sense. What do you wonder?"

She shakes her head. "Nothing. A fleeting thought. Have you told Mancio about this?"

"No…I didn't wake him on my way to the wing. I was too excited."

"Good," she says absently. "Good."

"Huh?" I scratch my head. Why shouldn't I tell Mancio?

"I mean, it's good that you're finally getting the call of the Celestials."

She doesn't sound truthful, but I decide to let that go. For now. I have bigger questions to ask. "What do you think? Is it Council worthy? Should I tell them?"

"Those are two different questions, Aerith. Is it worthy? Definitely." My heart leaps at the thought of being able to share something. I reach up to my talisman hanging off my neck, prepared to call them for the first time before Naseem's hand gently closes over mine. She looks me directly in the eyes, her golden eyes meeting my purple ones with great intensity. "*Should* you tell them? No."

"But why not? If it's something worthy of them knowing, I must tell them!" They are supposed to know about anything significant as soon as possible. Naseem's desire to keep it from the Council confuses me. She's always kind of done her own thing, been a woman with her own mind, but she's never told me outright to disobey the rules. She's encouraged me to do things we aren't supposed to, but this is much more than that.

"No, you don't." I look at her quizzically. What can she possibly be talking about? "Aerith, you're my best friend here, and I love you dearly, but you lack knowledge."

I bristle. "I've had the same education as you. In fact, more than you because I started at four, and you didn't get here until you were almost six!"

"I mean you lack practical knowledge. You're naive, Aerith. For you, the Illume is everything. They know everything; they act in the best interest of everyone. Right? But I hate to tell you this, they don't. They are human, flawed, same as everyone else, and…I'm not saying you shouldn't ever tell them, but I would wait until at least our next meeting before you do. Think about it. See if you can gather some more information for them to make better, well-informed decisions. Everything you saw is something, but it's also nothing. It doesn't tell us anything about who, when, where, or even what."

Naseem expresses all of this softly, with kindness, but I am still upset over her "naive" comment. She moves her hand to my arm, and I look into her pleading eyes. "Please, think about it." I make a non-committal sound, and she drops her hand. "I would probably wait to tell Mancio, too. He can be a bit chatty, and the Council might find out about everything too soon."

"Yeah…I guess. I'll wait for now to tell anyone else."

She smiles, her face relaxing. "Lunch?" she asks.

I nod. "Lunch." And like that, we let go of the tension and return to our normal. Even as we walk, though, I think about my dreams and Naseem's advice. She's never led me dangerously wrong, but this time she might be. The question is, is she doing it on purpose to get me in trouble? I can't fathom it.

I BARELY RECOGNIZE MYSELF.

Eloise

I watch Mitac walk away with his Green Tracker in tow. I'm excited. Tomorrow, I will have a gold coin to add to the family treasury. Saada's eyes are going to bug out of her head! I could keep it myself, but I owe so much more to Saada and Gamet for taking us in than I can ever pay back. I turn my attention back to the customers milling around the Clearing, greeting anyone who comes by and answering questions from the occasional customer who is unfamiliar with my wares. Most everyone here already knows who I am, but I don't recognize these people, so they must be from surrounding areas. A few people buy their Quester a knife, and my regulars come by to restock their stores of soap, and it sells out quickly.

Towards midday, Cardis joins me and sits on the ground next to me. I should have left already, and I think he is surprised to see me still at the market, but I can't resist the opportunity to sell a little bit more.

"I can stay and finish here if you'd like," he offers, chewing on an apple he must have bought since our tiny orchard hasn't yet produced any good apples. "I'll only charge a bronze for each sale I make." He smiles cheekily.

I shove him gently. "I'm so sure." Cardis has watched the goods for me several times in the past and knows as much about selling as I do, but today, I am in no hurry to leave. My stomach churns; thinking about tonight and tomorrow and being here takes my mind off everything.

"I'm going to miss you," Cardis leans on me in a quiet lull between customers. He eats the apple core, and I flinch when he does. I don't know how he can do that. I'm all for no waste, but that's one step too far for me. He puts the seeds in his pocket for his seed stores.

"What do you mean, Card? I told you I'm not going anywhere."

"You might. The Quest is unpredictable. I've heard kids talking at school about people with no magic in their families coming out Prime. Then they're ripped away to the city. What will we do without you? What will *I* do without you?"

I wrap my arm around his shoulder and pull him close against my side but unlike last night, he stiffens and pulls away. I forgot that teenage boys don't like public affection. I release him. "I don't think you have anything to worry about, but if that happens, I'll refuse to go. I'll run away if I have to. I'll live in the forest until the Gopher and Tracker have forgotten about me. Then I'll come back, right as rain!"

He looks away, unmollified by my promises. Never mind that I have never once broken a promise to him. He brushes his brown hair out of his face.

"When are you going to let me cut your hair again?" I ask, ruffling his brown locks.

He laughs. "When you promise you won't cut my ear instead!"

"It was one time!" I may have gotten a little close to his ear when I went to cut his hair the first time. I didn't actually cut his ear; well, I stopped before I sliced it off anyway. He's had Saada cut it every time since.

"It was also the only time." He straightens his hair again. He touches the tip of his left ear. There is no scar other than the one he carries internally. "For good reason."

"It's getting too long." I reach over and muss it up, pushing it back in front of his eyes. He leans away from me and fixes it back in place a third time.

"My hair or my ears?" he smiles.

"Haha. Very funny," I snark back at him.

"I'll let you cut it if you come back after the Quest. It'll give you a reason to come home." And like that, the mood turns sour again.

"Oh, Cardis, I don't need a reason to come home. You and the family are all the reason I need." I turn and hug him tightly. This time, he returns the hug before remembering he's fourteen and shouldn't be showing me physical affection in public. He pushes me off, then looks around, probably to see if any of his friends noticed the hug. I shove him gently. "If you don't stop that, the next time your friends are around, I'm going to lick my thumb and wipe dirt off your face!" He looks at me horrified, and I laugh. He joins me, but he's still clearly worried I will do it.

Soon, I see Saada, Gamet, and the kids coming our way. Saada hands a couple of bronze coins to the girls, and they run off, brown pigtails flapping wildly as they go. I know right where they're going—the pastry cart. It's a little Sunday treat they sometimes get if they haven't tortured their little brother during the week. Later, they'll be even wilder and more unruly with sugar in their system.

I wave to Saada and Gamet and they come over briefly. Saada has a woven basket on her arm with some vegetables and other goods from the market we haven't been able to grow in the garden.

"Anything special you want for tomorrow?" she asks me, looking around the market and the displayed goods as though she might have missed something.

"No, Saada. I told you. One hour. I'll be out." *I better be out. I want that gold coin.* It takes everything in me not to gush excitedly about it to Saada. But don't count your chickens before they hatch and all that.

She shrugs, that strange look on her face again. "What about for the festival tonight?"

I shake my head. "Nothing I can think of."

She nods. "How are sales?"

I gesture to my few remaining wares. A couple of knives and the flute with the flowers. All the soap already gone. "Not bad, sold most of it already."

Saada smiles. "Make sure you keep some of that money for you. No sneaking it into the family jar."

I nod obediently, knowing full well that other than spending a little with the cobbler, all my money will end up in the family jar. Saada will then find creative ways to give it back to me. Putting it in my bag, my coat pocket, my shoes… One time, she even sewed it into my brassiere. All I did was carefully extract it and return it to the jar. The problem was that I wasn't as good at sewing as Saada, so my brassiere now has some uneven stitching and puckering on one side.

Eventually, Saada loses track of how much money I put into the jar, and the game stops until the next week. I don't want anything special, and it's a good way to show Saada and remind her that I can take care of the kids. Saada has shown me what it takes. She denies any luxuries for herself, favoring to give them to us instead. I will have to do it without Gamet's income, which will make it harder, but not impossible. Nothing is impossible.

Saada, Gamet, and Leck wander off with a wave, and Cardis heads off when he sees a friend of his. I see Saada stop to pick up the girls from Mr. Braswell's cart. It looks like they were expertly guilting Mr. Braswell into letting them have two pies for the price of one. Saada scolds the girls and takes one pie to split between them. I giggle. Those two are trouble with a capital T.

After the market concludes, I get the last goat meat pot pie from Mr. Braswell to take home with me as a surprise for the family, or at least a surprise for Saada so she doesn't have to cook tonight. The rosemary from the gravy is sneaking out of the vents in the crust. I move it closer to my nose and inhale deeply. Tantalizing. The sun is starting to come down from its high point in the sky. It's still hot, but it is starting to cool some. I realize then that I only have a little bit of time left to get ready for the festival. The shoe cobbler will have to wait for another day. Maybe tomorrow after the Quest. My feet can make it one more day. Never mind that I've been telling myself that for weeks.

I hang my bag beside the cabin door and sneak my coins quietly into the family jar on the mantle of the stone fireplace. They make a light clinking sound when they hit the pitiful number of coins already there.

Luckily, the bathroom is unoccupied, so I quickly wash my face and hands. I change my clothes into something relatively clean, pick up my dirty clothes from this morning and last night in the bathroom, and take them back to my room. I feel proud of myself for remembering them.

Will Cardis praise me for this massive effort? No, of course not. He says I should do it automatically. I roll my eyes.

In my room, I start pulling on my least threadbare socks. Not that anyone will see them, but I do it as a favor to my feet and the blister. I inspect it now; it's open and raw. I grab a cotton roll from my big pack in my room. I roll a bit out and use one of my knives to slice it off. A knock sounds at the door. Too heavy for Cardis.

"Come on in," I call as I finish wrapping the blister. The cotton sticks to itself, and I hastily pull on my sock, figuring the knock is Saada. I don't want her to see what my shoes are doing to my feet.

I'm right. She enters, holding a brown wrapped package in her hand. "I got you something for tonight."

I frown at her putting my newly wrapped and socked foot on the floor. "I told you I didn't want anything."

"I know what you said, but you only get one festival before your Quest, and you should have something special for it. Besides, I am sure you put the money back I told you to keep, so don't worry about the cost." She hands me the package.

I narrow my eyes at her and tilt my head. I frown. "You and I both know you're going to do everything you can to give me that money back."

"Yeah, buuut…you still haven't found all of the last ones I hid." She gives me a wink and I know she's being evil now. It's going to drive me crazy that I haven't found all of last week's money. I thought for sure I had.

The package has no bow, no tag, nondescript. It's soft and squishy, and I suspect I know what's inside. I know Saada has caught me looking at it. I could have bought it myself, but I didn't have a place to wear it, nor was it worth the cost. It was twenty silvers, and that amount could not be recouped easily for something so frivolous. I didn't look in the tailor's window today, so I have no idea if "my dress" is missing, but I would almost bet the gold coin I was about to win that it now is.

I pull apart the brown packaging and carefully remove the dark purple silk dress. Tears fill my eyes. Celestials, it's even more stunning in my hands than in the window. Maybe because it's mine. My first thought is to fold it up and promptly return it. The family jar had so many bronze coins and so few silvers in it; twenty more in there would look so much better than this dress. I put it back in my lap, debating what to do with this. Meanwhile, Saada is standing in front of me, beaming with pride.

This isn't for me, I realize. This is for her also. Saada's giving me a gift is the same as her receiving it. Because she was able to get it. For me. She truly doesn't want it for herself; she wants me to have it. Wants me to own it because she knows how much it means to me, and that means… well, that's everything. I know I'll keep it forever. If I need to, I will wear the damn thing every day to make her happy and know she didn't waste her money on this gift. With as soft as the silk is, I don't think I would mind wearing it every single day. I would only feel bad if I ruined it.

I hold up my arms, so it won't touch the ground as it unfurls, shimmering in the dimming light. It has a corset back with silver silk ties and cap sleeves made from a thin, sheer material. The dress has elegant silver embroidery on the bodice. The bottom of the dress flares slightly on its way down to the ground, the purple splits at the waist, and underneath, I see the peek-a-boo black silk skirt. I hold my breath, as though breathing will make it disappear.

"Saada…this is…"

She holds up a hand. "If you say it's too much, I will literally slap you."

"But Saada…"

"No, not a word. You are worth it. You contribute so much to this family and never ask for anything. Miss Halsey is waiting for you at her shop to do any final adjustments."

"Saada…"

"No complaints, missy. Get going! It's getting late!"

"I was going to say, I don't know what shoes I'm going to wear." True, I had considered arguing about taking it, but she doesn't need to know that.

Saada holds up a finger and disappears from the room. She comes back a moment later holding a pair of black leather flats up triumphantly. They are a pair I have never seen her wear before.

"I got these from your mother for my festival. Hopefully, they'll work for you too. If not, boots it is!"

We both giggle a little. I hug her tightly in gratitude for what she has done, and I feel the tears escaping down my cheeks.

"There's a meat pie in the oven," I tell her as though my little gift could come anywhere near touching what she has done for me in this moment. "It's for the family. I will meet you at the festival. Flats or boots."

She shoos me out of the cabin, dress carefully refolded in its packaging for transport. I hustle to the tailor, boots on, flats in hand so they don't get dirty on the way.

Fortunately, Miss Halsey doesn't have to make many adjustments. She fusses for a while, repeatedly brushing her bright Orange hair out of her face. She places pins here and there, thankfully not poking me in the process, then gets me out of the dress so she can quickly stitch the places she's marked with a little machine she's invented herself. Miss Halsey's Orange magic has made her the inventor of all things fashion.

While she does this, I slip on one of the black flats. Something rubs my toe, and I'm disappointed, thinking they won't fit after all. I take off the shoe, prepared to put on my boots when a necklace falls out of the toe. I finger the delicate silver chain with a silver phoenix in profile on the end and a small gemstone in the eye. I have never seen this necklace before; I would remember it. Still, it seems oddly familiar somehow. Like a memory, but I can't place it. I turn the phoenix this way and that, noticing the gem changes color slightly depending on which way the light hits it.

"Oh, my girl, that will be perfect!" Miss Halsey startles me. I hadn't even noticed she had returned with the purple dress. "With the sweetheart neckline, you'll need something on your neck!"

"I'm not sure whose this is, actually. It was in one of the shoes Saada gave me."

"Well, then it's yours, my dear!"

I shake my head. "No, I'm sure it was a mistake. I'll take it back to Saada."

Miss Halsey's face falls but she helps me into the dress. Somehow, she then manages to talk me into trying on the necklace. She's not wrong; the long chain hangs center chest, right above the cut of the dress. Miss Halsey ties up the corset back with a neat silk bow. In her full-length mirror, I barely recognize myself. She hands me a few hair pins and a purple hair tie she fashioned from the trimmings off the bottom of the dress. I deftly sweep my hair into a single braid down the middle of my back. I fold it up onto itself and tie it with the tie. Using the bobby pins, I secure the stray hairs away from my face. I slide on the black flats again, this time fitting perfectly.

Miss Halsey stands behind me, giving me an approving look over my shoulder into the mirror.

"I will take your stuff back to your cabin. You get on to the festival. You're already late." She ushers me out of the store as I thank her. Too late, I realize I never took the necklace back off.

HAZARDS OF THE TRADE.

Mitac

I stand at the back of the large cream-colored tent that has been erected over the place where the market was, watching the festivities. It probably hasn't been used much since the last Quest; it has a musty smell, but the foods covering the large, rectangular, wooden tables in the tent are doing a good job of trying to overpower it. Cakes, pastries, roast, bread, cheese, fruit…all of it looks delicious and makes me hungry. In the center of the tent, a dancing area has been cleared on the uneven flagstone, colorful rugs spread out over it, and small tables and chairs have been placed around the outer ring of the tent. At the front, a small band is playing lively music with various stringed instruments. Torches light the area around the tent, erected on long poles, casting a golden, flickering glow on everything. A few people are already dancing, but most are milling around, talking to each other while nibbling on small bites of food.

Chance is crouched in the corner of the tent with her own plate of food in her hands. Most people here are being offered food for free tonight, but not the Gophers and Trackers; we aren't one of them. I don't mind much and don't blame them. The amount of hospitality they show each other tells me that they are a people who take care of each other quite well. I also know that people like this will close ranks quickly if an outside threat is identified. Right now, I'm an outside threat based on the looks I'm still getting. I vow not to make them a full-blown enemy.

I wouldn't even be here tonight if it wasn't required. The city mandates we attend all pre-Quest activities the villages, towns, or cities put on so we can help maintain the peace and see who it is we will be ushering into and out of the Quest.

I watch as more people come and go from the tent, more people coming than going. Most of them are clearly kids preparing for the Quest tomorrow. They have a nervous edge that others do not have, the same nervous edge I felt myself the night before my Quest. They laugh a little too hard with their friends, bite the inside of their cheek when no one is watching, pace when left alone too long. The Quest decides their prospective future, and unlike kids in other areas, these ones hope they come out with *no* magic.

The flaps to the tent open, and I see someone in a dress enter. This in itself isn't entirely unusual, but not as common as the majority around me are dressed in casual, everyday clothing. I can't make out the face thanks to the remaining sun directly backlighting them. When the flaps close, I gasp. It's Eloise. The rabbit with the knives. She looks stunning in a purple silk dress, and her hair pulled up. She walks in with a confident but unassuming grace. If she is nervous about tomorrow, she is hiding it very well. With no conscious thought, I find myself walking over to her.

"Welcome," I greet her with a smile.

She jumps slightly at my voice coming from behind her. "Make some noise next time!"

"Hazard of the trade," I joke. "All of my training directly contradicts that exact statement."

She rolls her eyes. Unimpressed, evidently. Glad we can continue to point out how unfunny I am.

"Can I escort you in?" I ask, offering her my arm. I emulate what I have seen from nobles at other more formal dances I have had the complete displeasure of having to attend.

"In case you haven't noticed," she retorts, waving around us and ignoring my arm, "I am already inside."

I shrug, dropping my arm back to my side. I'm actually relieved. I'm afraid the voice will return if I touch her again. "I suppose that's true." I feel the same strange pull I had felt earlier at the market. A weird need to protect her.

Danger, the voice whispers again. I check myself. I'm not touching her this time. I stiffen. I can't tell if the voice is talking to me or telling me to warn her. I have only heard this voice a couple of times in my lifetime. The first time I was ten, and my dad was getting ready to leave for work. The voice had said, *Danger* when I hugged him goodbye. I had written it off as nothing at the time. He went out to fell trees that had picked up a rot. He ended up being the one felled that day. He underestimated how much the interior of the tree had rotted away, and it fell toward him instead of away. The second time was when my brother was leaving for the city; it told me *Danger* then, too. Given that I never saw him again, I assumed it had been right.

It's jolting to hear it again now. Both of the other times, the person I was around ended up dead. Not good. I don't know how to tell her or if I should. Would she even believe me? Probably not.

She stares at me oddly in the silence that follows my statement. She absently fidgets with a silver necklace on her neck. I wonder where she got something so nice.

"I think I will go talk to my friends."

"Alright then." I offer her a smile and walk away back to the edge of the tent as she wanders off to find her people. Truthfully, I'm grateful she didn't take the dance. I need some time to think about the voice. I try talking to it like I did the other two times.

Who is in danger? I ask. *Is it Eloise?*

Danger, it repeats.

Yes, I get that. What kind of danger? Give me something more. Something to make her believe me if you actually want me to warn her.

Danger.

Excellent. Helpful. I know I must look deranged with my face contorting while I try to converse with a voice in my head. And maybe I am. Still, it can't hurt to try to warn her, right? Does it matter if she thinks I'm deranged?

Eloise moves among everyone easily, giving the impression of being happy to see them, but her smile doesn't quite reach her eyes. I pull my gaze away from her and watch the other kids. These are the kids whom tomorrow I will need to make sure I account for but also notice magical changes and bring them back with me if they occur. Once more, I pray to the Celestials I don't need to.

According to Amiket City, I should have fifty-eight kids entering this portion of Amaranth Forest tomorrow. Forty-two are coming directly from Ashadier, the other sixteen from surrounding villages. Of course, with villages this far out, the counts could be off. Technically, every birth is supposed to be recorded and reported to the city. It is well-known, though, that many in areas like here would prefer not to be recognized by the city which means there are likely plenty of people who remain unaccounted for.

If the city doesn't know about them, they don't have to do the Quest. However, if not everyone shows up for their Quest that *is* on my list, we have to find them and bring them to heel. They won't get to do the Quest; they'll end up before the Council. Celestials, I hope they all show up tomorrow morning.

The sounds of joviality in the tent are increasing. As the sun continues its journey below the horizon, more people enter the tent. I can see the kids talking to each other, greeting old friends, and making new ones.

The dancing picks up as people finish eating their food and everyone gets more comfortable. I set my plate into a bin for dirty dishes and thank the shopkeepers for their delicious food. I pay for a mug of punch and down half of it in one go. The heat in the tent is starting to get to me, and I've begun to sweat. I take the mug with me and mill among the people. Conversations pause as I get near, so I don't stop at any of the groups. I merely nod and smile at them, cataloging and watching for potential trouble. I don't predict any, but my training never lets me fully relax.

I end up on the other side of the tent where Eloise is laughing with her friends. She seems to have relaxed some. She doesn't notice me at first, so I enjoy watching her. When she does notice me, she doesn't stop talking like everyone else does. She gets louder.

"Have you noticed the Gopher they sent for us this year?" she asks her friends while giving me a side-eye.

The others haven't noticed me standing nearby and I smirk at her. Such a bold girl, to risk my wrath and retribution. Surely, she knows I could arrest her on the spot. I won't, but it is interesting that she would risk it.

"Sure looks like they dragged the bottom of the barrel to find one to send to us," one of her male friends says as he drinks his punch. He looks around but fails to look behind himself to see me standing there.

I sense a bit of jealousy in his tone. The kid isn't bad looking, but he's scrawny, and I'm betting he wishes he had the muscles I did. I was once scrappy, too. It wasn't until I hit puberty that my muscles started to build. This kid is beyond that stage, so he'll probably always be a beanpole.

"Of course, they always do," another girl agrees. "No one wants to come to us."

I clear my throat softly. "Actually," I butt in, "I wasn't upset to be coming here."

I enjoy watching her friends panic and turn to face me, but Eloise only raises an eyebrow as she turns fully to face me. Her friends are falling all over themselves to apologize, and I hold up my hand to stop them. "Don't worry about it," I tell them. I should scold them; heck, I should arrest them and teach them a real lesson. It's what any other Gopher would do, but I don't see the point. It will only give them more cause to hate us. Ruling by fear only makes people more sly, not obedient or loyal.

"Is that so?" Eloise challenges me. "Please enlighten us as to why you *chose* to be here."

"I didn't get to choose," I clarify, coming a little closer. She doesn't back down, merely tilting her chin to continue to look me directly in the eye. "But I was glad to be chosen for this assignment. I don't want to have to separate families if I don't have to. While others may not want to come here because there's no glory in it, this reduces the likelihood I have to bring any of you back with me, which is good. The carriage to get here from the train is small and I don't imagine it would smell good with one of your lot in it."

Eloise's face scrunches with disdain. "I'll have you know I showered the other day. I make soap, remember?"

"Making it doesn't mean you use it. But I'm sure you wanted to look good for us Gophers, eh?" I return sarcastically.

She scoffs. "Hardly. You were lucky that it's bathing month." I'm sure she's joking, but I know this is the reality for some of these kids. It was for me. A proper bath was a luxury I could ill afford.

"Indeed," I mutter. "Lucky me." The voice in my head is getting louder and distracting me. Eloise's friends have found somewhere else to be suddenly, and I'm grateful.

"Care for a dance?" I ask, pressing my luck and her good humor. She looks surprised, and I'm surprised to be asking it, but part of me wants to see if the voice says anything more if I touch her again. I also enjoy catching her off guard.

"I'm not sure you want to dance with me," she sneers. "I probably smell too bad. Should stick to your Tracker." She motions with her head to where Chance is crouched, seemingly bored. I know she is keeping as close an eye on everything as I am. She has the benefit of looking less obvious in doing so.

"I could, but you're all dressed up, and you haven't even danced yet. Would be a waste of a beautiful dress, even if it is on you." I goad, but I am hoping she says yes. *Come on, say yes.* I waft some magic her way, and a jolt runs through me when it hits a wall. That's weird…

The pull to her vibrates in my chest. The voice is repeating itself in my head. With my father and brother, it had been a single warning. Does its insistence come because the danger is greater? And what danger is greater than death? Or…is it warning *me*?

Eloise narrows her eyes. "Fine. One dance, Gopher," she snarls.

I hold out my arm to her, and this time, she takes it. Immediately, the room around us disappears. I'm standing in a forest. I'm fighting someone and I spot Eloise, for a moment. She's on the ground, holding someone covered in blood. The vision disappears as quickly as it appears. My heart hammers against my ribs. That's never happened before.

Eloise tilts her head at me, knitting her eyebrows together. I remember what I was supposed to be doing.

I lead her to the crowded floor.

The voice is screaming now. I want to hold my head and block out the noise, but I manage to keep my composure. No one notices as we join the fray. She's a surprisingly good dancer. I'm not as quick or light on my feet but I do manage to avoid stepping on her toes as we move around the floor.

This is a dance I recognize from home, and I let my feet do the work for me. My brain is on leave while I think about what I saw. What was that? I've not had visions before; that's a Dreamer's job. Not a job for a lowly Negotiator.

Who was Eloise holding? It had looked like… I shake my head. No, it can't have been.

Danger, the voice repeats.

It would be more helpful if it would give me a repeat of the vision or whatever I had seen, so I could confirm some things. We continue moving around the floor, Eloise, myself, and the voice. The protective urge I feel toward her is at ease when I have Eloise in my arms, even if the voice is not.

"Be careful tomorrow," I whisper in Eloise's ear, the urge to warn her becoming unbearable. The voice finally quiets some. I hope the warning is for me, not for her, but the moment the warning crosses my lips, it rings true. Like a piece of something sliding into place. I wonder if this is what Truth Finders feel when someone speaks the truth around them. I didn't test well for that particular sect of Black magic, but I wasn't completely without the skill. It just takes an exorbitant amount of energy for me to do it since it's not my innate magic.

"What?" she asks. She pulls back from my arms to look at my face, stopping our dance. A few other couples bump into us before seeing we've stopped.

"Be careful," I repeat. "In the Quest," I say more sternly, more clearly. I feel my magic extending toward her and trying to push the words into her head. I'm jolted when the threads hit that wall again. That's never happened other than with my trainers, who were trying to block me. My threads try to find an opening, there's usually one, especially in someone who hasn't learned their magic. With her, I can find none. She continues to stare at me, confused by my warning or my lack of movement since, I'm not sure which. "Just…be careful." My magic tries to reach out one more time. The block stops the threads, and they retreat back to me once more.

She shrugs and urges me to continue our dance. "I never had any intent not to be." I don't move for a moment. It'll have to be good enough. Celestials, let her take me seriously.

NOW HERE IT IS AGAIN...

Saada

I watch as Eloise dances in the arms of the Gopher. It makes me uneasy. Gophers have never been known to be nice or kind. How she ended up with him, I do not know. I had waited to finish dinner at home before I came with Gamet and Cardis, leaving the twins in charge of Leck. Once we got into the tent, Cardis darted off to hang out with his friends, and I see him dancing and jumping to the music. I smile until I glance over to Gamet and see a similar look of disquiet on his face while he watches Eloise. He has much more experience with the Gophers and the city than all of us. If he's worried, then I have good reason to be, too.

Eloise looks so beautiful and relaxed. I could almost mistake her for having fun. I decide to give her one dance and then I am going to interrupt. For her own good. For all our own good. No Gopher in the history of Gophers has ever had good intentions with anyone outside of the city, and their intentions are questionable even within the city. Maybe especially within the city.

The song comes to a resounding finish, and the dancers on the floor applaud loudly. I rise from my seat and make a beeline to Eloise and the Gopher. I gently tap on her shoulder. "Eloise, it's time to go."

She looks confused, but one look at my face, and she seems to understand my meaning. She curtsies in an antiquated, overdramatic way to her dancing partner. He offers a bemused smile.

"Gopher, this is my aunt," Eloise introduces us. The one time I wish she would forget the manners we had tried so hard to drill into her head. I purse my lips and look over the Black man before me. "Saada, this is the Gopher we are so privileged to have assigned to us this year." I don't offer my hand to the Gopher and wince at Eloise's heavy sarcasm. I will her to stay quiet going forward.

"Pleasure." I spare him one more glance then reinforce my earlier intentions. "Come on, Eloise, it's going to be a big day tomorrow. You'll want your rest."

I notice with a start that Eloise is wearing a necklace that I have not given her to wear. I won't ask her about it in front of the Gopher, though. He's liable to think she stole it if he finds out I didn't give it to her, and we don't need to be memorable to a Gopher.

The Gopher backs away slightly from us. "You don't have to go. I'll be heading out shortly," he says, correctly interpreting my haste to get Eloise out of the tent. He glances at Eloise, looking at her with what could almost pass as respect. If I didn't know better. "I got what I came for."

"To leer at my niece?" I spit out before I can stop myself. I bite my tongue. *Stupid, stupid, Saada.* My mom always said my quick wit and sharp tongue would get me into trouble one day.

"No, ma'am, to see who the Questers are for tomorrow, so I know who I am looking for as they come out." The Gopher bows as dramatically as Eloise's curtsy and takes her hand to kiss it. "Have a good night, Rabbit; I look forward to seeing you tomorrow. And remember what I said."

"Yeah, see you tomorrow," Eloise calls at his retreating back. "So you can pay me!"

I can't tell if he's heard her, but it looks like his shoulders might have risen with a slight chuckle. He disappears from the tent, and a Green Tracker I hadn't seen in the corner rises smoothly and exits with him.

"What's that all about?" I ask Eloise as I bore a hole into the back of the retreating Gopher.

"I presume that wherever he goes, she goes," she replies glibly.

I roll my eyes, shifting my gaze back to her once I see the tent flap close behind them. Relief flows into me knowing they're gone. At least for now. "Don't be obtuse. You know what I mean."

She sighs. "Let's just say, tomorrow we will be one gold coin richer."

The prickle of unrest is back. "No, no, let's say more."

"It's nothing, Saada; a little bet the Gopher and I have." I start to lead Eloise back to the table I was sitting at. She sounds bored. She needs to be afraid. Fear around those from Amiket is necessary. Protective.

"It's not wise to associate with the Gophers," I call back over my shoulder. "They are closely tied to the city and the city's motives. We don't know what his real purpose is here."

"I'm sure it's the same as every Gopher ever has been, Saada; monitor the Quest and get out of here as fast as possible afterward."

"Yeah, taking the kids with them."

"Only the magic ones."

I stop in my tracks, and Eloise nearly runs into me. "So that makes it better, Eloise? As long as it's not you, it's fine?" I clench my jaw, desperately trying to control my anger. Sometimes this girl...

Eloise stops a couple of steps ahead of me and turns to face me. "I didn't mean that. Only that you don't have to worry about me. Of course, I don't want them to take anyone from their family, but..." she sighs, "do you ever wonder if there could be a better life if one of us worked for the city or had more magic?"

"Yes," I answer honestly. "I think about it all the time."

The memories of before, of my own Quest, threaten to rise and overtake me. My vision reduces to a tunnel as my breathing grows shallow. Dark images flash in front of me. Blood, arrows, and the pounding of my feet and heart... I shove the memories back down where they belong. Where they're safe and can hurt no one. I pray that Eloise's Quest doesn't go the same way mine did. She fingers the necklace on her neck again. I take a deep breath, praying she didn't notice my near panic attack. Luckily, she seems oblivious.

"By the way, where did you get that?" I ask her, pointing to the silver phoenix.

"Oh yes! It was in the shoes you let me borrow. Miss Halsey practically forced me to put it on." Eloise chuckles. She reaches up to take it off. "Here, I meant to ask you about it and give it back to you."

I put my hands on hers, pausing her efforts. "Don't. Keep it. It looks good on you." It's true; it does look good on her, but that's not the reason I tell her to keep it. Not really.

She looks at me quizzically. "Are you sure?" I nod. "Thanks! I'll give it to you after tonight, okay?"

"Not necessary," I wave her off. "It's yours now."

"Where did it come from?" She drops her chin and examines the phoenix, moving it in the light. Examining it much the same way I had.

"It's been passed down through the family for quite some time. I forgot I had it, honestly." A lie. I hadn't forgotten about it. I didn't want anyone to once again face the choice I had. I thought I had gotten rid of it, but it had come around and chose her anyway. I held no illusion that it did so to spite me. It didn't work like that, but it felt personal anyway. Leigha, my sister, had once worn it. Then it fell off and was lost until before my Quest, when I found it and put it on.

I tried to remove it so I wouldn't lose it in Amaranth Forest during my Quest. Every time I tried to remove it, I would suddenly get busy or remember something else I was supposed to be doing. I grew suspicious of it the more it happened but was relieved when it fell off during my own Quest. I knew, when it showed up on Julieth a few days before her Quest, that it was no ordinary necklace. I had attempted to retrieve it from her, but once again, we both would find ourselves waylaid and distracted from doing so. She also wore it the day of her Quest, and again, it fell off when she came home. I threw it in the fire, and it was no more. Or so I thought. Now, here it is again, around Eloise's neck, a reminder of the past, a promise of trouble in the future. It didn't even look like the fire had touched it, even though I had watched the damned thing melt.

"Well, thanks for letting me have it," Eloise says brightly, unaware of my dark thoughts. "I'll probably take it off for the Quest, though. You'll keep it safe for me while I'm gone, right?"

"Sure," I nearly choke on my false cheer. I am not prepared to have this conversation with her. Hopefully, tomorrow, the damn thing will come off her neck and leave again. I wonder what it will look like on Cardis' neck. I laugh and Eloise looks at me oddly.

"You okay, Saada?" she asks me.

I nod. "Yes, a funny thought. Tomorrow, you'll be an adult. Officially."

"Okay…why is that funny?"

I struggle to come up with an answer that makes sense. "Because I still see you as the little girl who came to the cabin, scared and sad. In spite of that, you refused to let me see you cry. Do you remember that?" She nods, clearly not understanding why I would laugh. "Julieth was crying, Cardis was crying, and there you were. Straight-backed, arms wrapped around the both of them. Giving them comfort like you hadn't also lost your parents. You aren't the oldest, but in that moment, you acted like they were your responsibility."

Eloise shrugs. She's clearly uncomfortable with this line of conversation. She never has been good with emotions. "Someone had to stay level-headed. If they couldn't do it, then I would."

"But none of you had to," I point out, both relieved she's forgotten why we started this conversation and grateful to have a reason to probe at her emotions a little. "Gamet and I were there for you. To be the strength you needed. I am sad that you couldn't see it at the time. I hope you know you can still lean on us."

"Not forever. Soon, you'll die. Then I will be on my own to comfort Cardis *and* your three." I flinch. She doesn't mince words, that's for sure.

"One day, that wall to lean on will be gone. It's okay to fall apart while you have someone to help you put the pieces back together; otherwise, you'll crumble from the inside out, and no one will be here to show you how to put yourself back together."

She looks away. Like she always has done. I pat her hand on the table and get up. I give her a hug and wave Gamet over from where he is dancing, trying to keep up with Cardis and his friends. I smile. Sometimes, he's a kid at heart. It's so easy to forget we are technically still young adults. We had so much growing up to do so quickly. The sorrow I feel over all the kids in the tent facing much the same dilemma is overwhelming. I push it away. Maybe I'm not so different from Eloise after all.

"We will head home for tonight. Don't stay out too late. I will be up with you in the morning."

Eloise simply nods. "You do look beautiful," I tell her, tilting her chin to look at me. She sniffles. "I am so happy to give you that dress. You deserve it."

Eloise nods again. I suspect that if she tries to talk right now, her voice will fail her. Gamet comes over, and we walk out together, reminding Cardis to be home in the next half hour.

PART II

The Quest

...A DESOLATE REALM.

Aerith

Monday, R62T21
The Day of the Quest

THIS MORNING, I remember my apprentice. Problem is, I only stood there outside his door with my orb warming more and more around my neck. I debated if I should bring Mancio in with me for several minutes. I am supposed to. That's the reason he's here, after all, but I remember Naseem's words and decide not to bring him in. If questioned, I cannot explain why, not with any reason that would be acceptable. So far, no one has caught me in the room Dreaming by myself. I know I have been lucky. I also know that when check-in occurs in a week, I will have to answer for my crimes. Technically, I could claim I didn't know my visions were significant, but that lie would fall apart as quickly as it came to my lips. The Council would know. I have long suspected the Black Council representative to be a Truth Finder.

In the front, a woman with iridescent hair and skin, her eyes flashing various colors. Before her, a desolate realm. Dried earth, scorched from who knows what, mankind suffering and dying. Buildings are crumbling or fallen over. I can feel the pain of the people, I can hear their cries for help, I can smell the death.

From the woman's fingers, magic flows. In front of her, some people cower, others strike out with magic and weapons. Fruitless. She fights back with all the magics at her disposal, it seems. She flashes color after color. Those who fall rapidly decay, then turn to ash before being blown away. She then turns her attention to someone else. The petite Purple woman on her right holds the scales of justice and whispers in the iridescent girl's ear before her attention shifts.

That's how she's deciding, I realize. The Purple girl of justice is telling her. I'm excited to see another Purple; maybe we will finally do something of import!

The Silver man on her left flank has a small cat sitting on his shoulder. He walks with a Blue woman and a Brown man. I don't have time to think of how odd a Silver magic-wielder is nor to contemplate the cat he has perched on his shoulder; there's too much to see. *The Silver stops to heal those caught in the crossfire while the Blue conjures springs of water beneath the ground for the thirsty populace. The Brown brings forth plants from the fertile ground, creating instant gardens for starving masses. Directly behind the iridescent girl is a man who looks ordinary, but he, too, conjures magic, flashing the color of the magic he uses before returning to an Unchanged look.*

The Green behind them calls animals forth, willing sacrifices for the people in need of meat. A raven sits on his shoulder. Even further behind is an Orange man who is helping to rebuild buildings, putting houses right, and creating things I have never seen nor have any name for.

Even further back are Red, Black, and Yellow, each doing their duty to right the destruction in front of them in their own way. When they weary, the Silver lays hands on them, providing them with energy so they can continue.

Behind this large group of destructive yet redemptive magic-wielders are multitudes of Changed and Unchanged. They're following her, and the following is growing by the second. They are jubilant, alive again; they dance and sing. They hug and cry. Before my eyes, they age, getting older and older.

The iridescent woman has around her neck a large time piece and if anything shows her tiring, it's when she checks this ticking clock dragging her down. Nothing the Silver man does changes the speed of the clock nor makes it less burdensome for her. She looks up, seeming to look directly at me. "That's enough," she says.

I am pulled instantly out of my dream.

I get up from my position on the carpet and stretch. Another dream, butterflies take flight. That was definitely much clearer, and I feel like I will need to tell the Illume, and soon. I start to head to the doors to return to my room when they begin to open of their own accord. I have a moment of panic and indecision, then decide to act casually.

I make an about-face and head back for my place on the carpet, pretending I had walked in moments before. I turn to look to see who has entered and smile as my apprentice, Mancio, enters the room. He looks at me and gives a little wave. He is wearing his Dreamer garments, a light lavender silk shirt with opal buttons down the front and lavender silk pants with wide legs; he discards his white sandals at the door as I have taught him to do. He brushes his deep brown hair from his face, strides over to where I am, and takes a seat in his spot. One day, his spot will belong to his apprentice and my spot will be his.

"My my, good morning, Mancio; how did you rest?" I greet him calmly, my heart slowly returning to its normal rhythm after the scare of nearly being discovered a moment ago.

"Well, thank you for asking, ma'am," he responds politely. "I am surprised to find you here so early. The sun has only risen a couple of hours ago."

I smile at him. "We don't have a specific clock. Only the call of the Celestials on our time," I flash him my talisman. "What brings you here, though?"

"I felt the call of the Celestials, too!" He smiles at me and sits a little straighter. He holds up his talisman as well, and I touch it. It feels hot, like mine did this morning. He seems proud of his achievement, and he should be. Until now, I have had to come and get him for sessions. Of course, I've not had the call of the Celestials. All of our Dreaming has been a fruitless endeavor until now. A way to practice the necessary steps but without any outcome.

"That is wonderful, indeed," I reassure him. Inside, I am torn. Normally, it would be a celebration to have an apprentice feel the call of the Celestials, especially so young, but this is not normal. He might walk in on me if he can feel the call the same as me. I do not want to share the things I am seeing yet. The warning Naseem gave me still runs through my head. If she's right, which is potentially a big if, all of us could be in trouble. Me included. I can tell some of the things I have seen the Illume are not going to like, but the more I see, the more it seems like it's not only necessary; it's for the greater good. *Surely the members will see that. Given enough detail?* I repeat it to myself several times a day, and it sounds less and less convincing each time.

I regather my thoughts and adjust my position on the carpet. I smile at my young apprentice. "Well then, Mancio, let's talk about today's lesson, shall we?"

Mancio can't see yet. He has no access to his powers, same as everyone else. Our ability to dream makes us special, but not so special the Celestials allow us access to our magic early. In lieu of having the apprentices sit around waiting until they're seventeen, we teach them other skills they will need to be successful in their craft. All young Dreamers attend school to learn to read and write from the ages of four until they're eight, then they spend most of their time with their mentors learning about the art of Dreaming and a few hours a day continuing studies in history, language—sometimes our visions are not in languages of our own. There's also social studies and disaster control.

Additionally, depending on their magic, the apprentices are assigned specialty classes to help them. Blue and Yellow study weather patterns, Black study war strategy, and Brown study geography and land movements. Us Purples will join in various aspects of all those classes as we never know what we will see and what may end up being useful for us one day. Right now, I wish I had paid a little more attention in my classes. I don't even know how to handle what appears to be a Realm-wide war, or at least a Vale-wide one.

With my apprentice in front of me, we talk about how to quiet the mind and use the talisman placeholder he has around his neck to keep his thoughts in. Then, I will try to Dream while he sits with me, watching and learning. This teaches him to keep his mind calm for extended periods of time, to hold his stance steady. It's a challenge, especially at the start, because kids have little patience where much is needed to truly see. When it is over, I share with him what I have seen. At least, I am supposed to, to help sensitize him to the feelings the visions may cause, as well as help him learn how to handle those emotions.

We start with situating ourselves comfortably on the gold carpet. While it is usually very pleasant, I have already sat for a couple of hours this morning, so I am feeling sore. I would be surprised if the Celestials share more today, but it's been a strange couple of days and Mancio's amulet did heat up. I surreptitiously feel mine, but I can't tell if it's warm or if it's been sitting against my skin for too long. If there's a call there, it's faint.

I correct Mancio's form, as usual. He tends to hunch his back, which will cause him pain in the future, causing distraction. He sits up straighter. We cross our legs, sitting as flat on our butts as we can, keeping as much contact with the carpet as possible. The carpet isn't magic, any more than the dreamcatchers that dot the room, but the sensation tends to be soothing and keeps us grounded. We begin our breathing exercises. Deep breath in followed by a slow, even breath out. There is a slow metronome on a small table nearby that helps Mancio keep time for his breathing. As he gets better with this exercise, we won't need the metronome. I look forward to that day, the metronome is quite distracting to me.

"Close your eyes," I tell Mancio. I don't need to open mine to tell that his are.

"How do you always know?" he asks, irritated.

"I just do. I'm like a mom, I have eyes on the inside and the outside of my eyelids."

"How would you know what a mom has?" Mancio tends to be mean when he's corrected on his poor behavior. He has always struggled against my authority over him. From the day our apprentices come, we become their overseers. This can be a little challenging for everyone involved since we might be quite young when they arrive. I was eleven when Mancio arrived. I was enamored with the idea of this tiny baby, only a few months old, being in my care. I quickly stopped enjoying it when he cried frequently at night. I tried to wheel his bed into the hallway, and I received a severe talking to by my mentor. She reminded me that I had been similar, and it was my job to make sure Mancio's needs were met, short of nursing him, which was the job of the wet nurse. It was a rough first year.

I thought it would get easier…it didn't. As he got older, he got more rebellious and more mobile. I started missing the days when I could put him down, and he would stay there. I lost him a lot in the first five years. I would have to search for him and, a few times, I would have to go to one of the Illume and beg them to locate him by his placeholder talisman. I received severe punishment each time that happened, so it was truly my last resort.

"It's something I heard, let's say." I don't have the energy to scold him for his behavior in this moment. I want to get this over with so I can go talk to Naseem. I will probably pay for not rebuking him now on the back end, but I hear Mancio's breathing steady with the metronome, and I can tell his eyes are closed. Success for now.

"Now, feel the carpet beneath you, put your hand flat beside you, run your hand across it. Feel the soft fibers on your palm. Hold your amulet in your other hand." I hear rustling, which tells me he's doing so. "Focus on that feeling. All other feelings, gather and focus on your owl. Put all your emotions in there. Happiness, sadness, confusion, anger, tiredness, everything goes into the amulet. Feel the smoothness in your fingertips and the weight of it in your hand."

Mancio's breathing stays steady. I focus myself, letting my feelings go to the smooth round stone in my own hand. "Push aside your needs, your wants, your desires into the owl," I guide softly. "You can have them back after your lesson. Once you have moved everything into the owl, drop your other hand so it too can connect with the carpet."

I finish moving everything in my mind to the stone and drop my hand as well, the orb dropping to my neck. I hear Mancio's hand drop, too.

"Now, focus inward and wait for the dream to come to you. You can't rush it; you can't force it. It will either come, or it won't."

I know he can't see anything yet, but these continued reminders to him will one day be a mantra he will use on his own apprentice or to remind himself of what he's supposed to do; the way they do for me. I silence myself, feel the carpet with both hands, and wait. I go through the motions, expecting nothing, but I push that same thought into the stone with the rest and wait.

If I could feel surprise, I would. I begin to Dream again.

...BUT YOU HAVE A CHOICE...

Eloise

I wake to someone shaking my shoulder and calling my name. I groan and try to roll over. There's a twin there, evidently, by both the lump and the lump's dissatisfied grumbling. I open my eyes. It's still mostly dark outside, and it's Saada who is interrupting my slumber. I rub the grit out of my eyes, my vision slowly clearing.

I didn't leave the festival until late last night. After Mitac left, I spent the night laughing and dancing with my friends. We partied like it was the last time we would see each other. Which is silly, especially since we would probably all be present this evening in our own homes.

"Why," I ask, "are you waking me up so early, Saada? The sun hasn't even thought about waking up. I don't need to be out there until before dawn."

Saada doesn't smile. Her brow is furrowed in the dim light of the candle she holds. I sit up abruptly, suddenly wide awake. A rock drops in my gut. "What's the matter? Is it the kids? Cardis? Julieth?" I see gremlin two on the other bed, sleeping soundly. Gremlin one behind me rolls over. I breathe a sigh of relief; that's half of us accounted for.

Saada shakes her head and motions for me to follow her out of the room. I disentangle myself from the twin in the bed and follow Saada to the couch in the living room. We sit down and turn to face each other.

A chill runs over me, my cotton pajamas not quite warm enough for the coolness of the room in the dark. I rub my arms lightly while Saada lights a couple more candles on the coffee table and takes a deep breath. "I need to talk to you about the Quest."

"Okay, what is it? What has you so worried?" I recall the mention of a curse when she was talking with Gamet the other night. Is it related to the Quest?

"You might get in there, and…things aren't the same as when you go in the rest of the time." Saada twists her fingers in her lap, her gaze not meeting mine. The dark rings under her eyes and her disheveled hair tell me she didn't sleep last night. I don't remember her being awake when I came home a few hours ago.

"What do you mean?" I ask carefully. "We've been told that the forest changes, one of my teachers told me that a long time ago, Saada. She told me that I wouldn't recognize it. Is that what you're talking about?"

"Yes and no, we aren't supposed to tell you before you get in there, but you'll be tested in different ways. Ways that are meant to call forth your magic."

"Old news, Saada. We all figured this out from the things others have said. They never said what the tests are, only that they are tests. Are you going to tell me what the tests are?" I smile, rubbing my hands together in anticipation. Anything that helps me prepare will help calm my churning stomach.

"No, I can't tell you what the tests will be." My smile drops. What's the point of this conversation then?

"Okay…but if I don't have any magic, I'll be right back out, right? There's nothing for the forest to test me for. Like you, Mom, Julieth. Everyone."

Saada shakes her head. "You very likely have magic. We come from a lengthy line of magic folks, but you have a choice, in there, to use your magic or to hide it."

This is news to me. My mouth falls open, my eyes widening. I'm certain I heard her wrong. That's impossible. "What on Zarvan's Realm are you talking about? We all come out quickly. None of us has ever Changed."

Saada only nods. "Yes, but it's because we shielded ourselves from our magic."

I feel cold and clammy, and my vision is narrowing. Saada is speaking, but she sounds incredibly far away, and I am no longer processing anything. I break out in a cold sweat.

"If this is true, why haven't you said anything before?" I blurt out, interrupting whatever Saada was babbling about. My mind is reeling. Magic, us? Our family? We are the most bland and boring folks ever. Actually, the fact that Saada married someone with even the smallest bit of magic was shocking. I rock slightly on the couch, wrapping my arms around myself. This changes…everything. Everything I thought I knew, everything I ever expected, my whole world has fallen out from beneath me like someone has pulled a trap door.

"I couldn't tell you sooner," Saada defends, possibly repeating herself. She rubs her hands on her thighs. "I wasn't allowed to."

"Weren't…allowed to? What does that mean? What? Who…who told you this?"

"Your mother told me; now I am telling you." I can't understand why she is so calm. Her face is straight. Like…oh…it's a joke! It must be a joke. I suddenly smile and let out a laugh. Saada looks nonplussed. I must have figured out the joke too fast for her to have fun.

"This is some trick! Is everyone getting the same lecture I am?" I get up from the couch to look out the window, eager to see if candles are alight in nearby houses. Everything is dark in the pre-dawn light; a few stars still twinkle in the sky. I keep staring, hoping that I'm right, *needing* to be right. I *need* this to be a joke, like I need air to breathe. If it's not… I can't even fathom it. I shake my head.

"This is no joke, Eloise!" she hisses. "Julieth thought it was a joke, too. It wasn't easy for her to accept either, but it's the truth."

"Julieth knows, too?" Now I'm *really* mad. "My good-for-nothing sister, who essentially abandoned the family, got to know the family secret before me? What. The. Abyss?"

Saada looks taken aback. Maybe from my anger, maybe from the name calling. "Language," she warns.

I bark out a laugh. "You would think of all times it's okay to cuss, the moment you're told that you have a massive family secret would be one of them!" I'm no longer trying to keep my voice down. "So, I repeat, what the *ABYSS?*" I emphasize the word, practically spitting it at Saada. To her credit, she slowly closes her eyes and opens them again.

"We are not supposed to tell you until right before you enter the Quest."

"I don't understand, Saada. I don't get it. Make it make sense. If we have magic, why don't we accept it? You yourself have said you think we could have a better life if we had magic." Saada looks at me in bewilderment, and I realize a hair too late that I've revealed my own eavesdropping.

"I have never told you that, Eloise." She runs her hands through her hair. "I have made very, very sure to never say anything of the sort around you kids."

I shrug. "I may have overheard a couple conversations between you and Gamet," I confess and immediately jump to defend myself. "But I wasn't trying to! The walls are thin and…I know you won't tell me what's upsetting you. I figured I could at least use what I heard to help you."

"It is not your job, Eloise, to try to take care of me or the family. Not yet, anyway." Her nostrils flare, and I feel guilty.

"How else was I supposed to know we were struggling for money? Or that you were worried about whether we would have enough food in winter when the garden stopped producing? I used that information for good!" I protest. "I expanded what I was selling to more useful items, less decorative. And in the fall, I planted winter crops, so we had vegetables to harvest nearly year-round. We had tight months, but none of us had to wear our smaller clothes last winter!"

"It was not your concern." She lifts her chin. I feel suddenly guilty. I don't want to make Saada feel bad or that she's not doing enough. "We figure it out. We always do."

"Are you saying you don't appreciate my help?"

"That's not what I'm saying, and you know it. It's not what we wanted for you, though. It's why we didn't talk about it in front of you kids."

"Well, my help came in handy anyway, didn't it?"

Saada shakes her head slowly. "You don't get it, do you? I have never used the money you earn from the Market. Not once." Saada gets up from the couch and walks over to a small broom closet. One I never go into. She reaches in and backs out with a sizeable jar in her arms. It's full of coins. Bronze and silver alike. "This is all the money you kept putting into the jar. When you thought I 'forgot' how much you had put in, that's when I would pull it out and put it in this jar. I figured you could use it one day." I don't know how I feel about this development. On one hand, I am grateful there's a rainy-day fund. On the other hand, I feel suddenly useless. Here, I thought I was helping the family, and it turns out they didn't need it.

"I don't know what to say," I respond honestly. Saada puts the jar back. "I thought I was doing the right thing."

"You were," she says. "But you could have been having more fun, and I am gutted that you felt an obligation to provide for this family long before you ever needed to. I'm sorry, Eloise, that you didn't feel secure enough in our care." A singular tear rolls down her cheek.

Oh geez, now I feel very guilty. This was not at all what I was picturing for the morning. "I'm sorry I didn't trust you. I...thank you. For saving the money."

Saada nods and clears her throat. "Back to what I was saying..."

"Right...what were we talking about?" I murmur. I don't even know. I can only sit on the couch and stare at the jar of coins. All my hard work. There's the evidence, in the jar. If I had to place bets, I would place a hefty one that not a single coin is missing from the money I had brought home. I don't know what to do with this information.

"You asked why we don't accept our magic." I turn to look at Saada again.

"Yes, that. I don't understand. If you truly believe that we would do better with magic, why not take it when it's offered?"

A dream of a better life for me and the family crosses my mind again. Then I remember what leaving to train would mean. It's clear that they don't need me to survive monetarily, but they still use my vegetables. *Someone else could learn to garden.* The thought comes unbidden. Could I leave? I could...I wonder if the city would let me come home if Gamet or Saada die while I'm training. I open my mouth to ask if Saada knows when she starts speaking again, apparently having gathered her thoughts.

"This is where it gets complicated."

"Only just now?"

She gives me a wry smile. "Yes, well, this is where it gets more complicated. As has been passed down from person to person for as far back as possibly time itself, failing to shield ourselves from our magic will end in the destruction of the Realm."

I stare at Saada. Searching for a lie. "Destruction of—"

"—the Realm, yes."

"Who—where—are you sure?"

"I do not know where it started, only that I was instructed to tell you as you prepare to enter the forest. So here we are. Your mother, I, Julieth, your grandparents…we all hid our magic. Shielded it, buried it, however you want to look at it. We cannot access it, but it keeps the Realm safe."

I swallow, my throat tight. I haven't had a panic attack in a long time, but I feel like I'm about to have one now. "We are people from Ashadier, the duds. We are nothing. Powerless, weak, barely surviving."

Saada half-smiles at me. "Seems ludicrous, doesn't it?"

"Do we have any evidence that we have magic? What if it's a lie?"

She shrugs. "Well, if it's a lie, no harm, no foul if we take steps to shield it, right? But if we take the chance, and it's not a lie? The ramifications are beyond our control."

I'm perplexed. Baffled. Honestly, a little hurt. A lot hurt. How could Saada keep this a secret for seventeen years and never warn me sooner? How could my own mother hide it from me? I was old enough before she died to be told about legends of this import about our family!

"Why now? Why not years ago? Why does it have to be at the Celestial-blasted earliest hours of the morning?" I know this isn't what I'm truly upset about. It's not the getting up early. It's not the disrupted sleep. What bothers me is that everyone lied to me.

"We don't mess with magic, Eloise. When someone or something magic passes down a warning to share and when to share it, you do it, lest you face unpleasant and unknown consequences."

I turn from the couch angrily. "No, I don't accept that. You lied to me for seventeen years."

Saada looks down. "I didn't lie, I didn't tell you."

I snort. "Same thing. So, I have to bury my maybe magic, or else I'll destroy the Realm one day?"

"Yes, Eloise. It's your choice, of course. I can't force you to shield yourself, I can only tell you what the possible meaning is for you and everyone else if you do."

I remain silent. What kind of choice is that to have to make? How is this fair? Other people get to have magic, magical lives, good jobs, and good houses, and it's there in front of me. Within reach, and I only get to have it if I'm willing to sacrifice the very Realm I want to live in. Yeah, that makes sense. What's the point of having all the magic in the Realm if there's no Realm left? I run my hands through my hair in exasperation, wincing when I hit the multitude of tangles I haven't combed out yet.

Saada presses on as though sensing my interior resolve to avoid this curse. "You don't have to bring forth your magic, Eloise. You can keep it behind a wall within yourself. Shield it. Then you can return from the forest Unchanged. It's the same choice we have all had, and we have all taken."

"So how do I do this? This shielding thing?" I'm still annoyed with her, and my questions come out aggressively. I wouldn't even ask her; I'm so angry with her, but I need to know how to do this.

"When faced with something that seems too difficult to manage without magic, you run. You don't fight; you don't try anything miraculous. You run."

"So...I run from my magic is what you're telling me. That's it?" I'm picturing myself running through the forest with a glittering rainbow chasing me, and I chuckle. "Sure, I think I can manage that. As long as it doesn't make me run too fast, that is."

Saada frowns. "It sounds easy until you're faced with those situations. Three times you must run, then you will have shielded your magic sufficiently to be safe. The forest will tell you that you're free to leave."

"I guess I'll wear my good boots, then."

Saada nods. "Yes, your good boots. Take your knife or multiple knives. And pack your bag. You must not let on that you plan to do anything other than go into the forest like everyone else with no prior knowledge of what might happen."

I turn on my heel, not acknowledging Saada any further. I glare at the jar of coins still sitting on the floor. Evidence of more lies. Is anything I know real?

I grab my bag from beside the door and shove some clothes in it, barely paying attention to what I'm doing. I strap two knives to either side of my waist and a canteen to the back of my belt. I pull on a light cape, in case of rain, and put on my good socks and good boots, the ones that are too tight. But they're good in the sense that their soles are still intact. By the time I finished, I have calmed down some. I can kind of understand why Saada wouldn't risk the family or me by telling me early, but it doesn't mean I'm happy about it.

I try to imagine what I will do with my own offspring. Will I tell them early? Would I risk something awful happening to them because I did so? As I look at Gilda and Hilda sleeping soundly in our room, I know I would do the same as Saada. I could never risk them, and they're not even my own kids. At least now I know I can and will win the gold coin. All I need to do is run away three times and I'll be done for the day. I hope the challenges come fast. I don't want to stay long.

I hoist my backpack to my shoulder, lean over to press a light kiss on each girl's forehead, and head out to the kitchen. There, Saada looks more put together. She gives me a brown package with bread and jerky. I tie it closed with twine and tie it to my belt.

She gives me a hug, which I return reluctantly. This fracture in our relationship saddens me, but I do not have the words yet to forgive her. I'll do it after the Quest. I nod in her direction and head out the door. Cardis, Julieth, and the kids all wished me well last night before the festival, so I feel no need to wake them for the pre-Quest wait.

BE CAREFUL.

Eloise

There's a slight chill in the pre-dawn air, making me grateful for my little cape. I know that later I will be carrying it as it will get hot, even in the forest shade, but right now, it feels good to have. I notice a few other kids my age heading toward the table set up near the forest. A lantern sits on it, and a few small torches on poles surround the area, lighting it. I see Mitac sitting, impeccably dressed in his uniform. He looks positively fresh and clean. Damn him. In front of him are several pages of parchment and a quill and ink. A small line has formed in front of him.

Most of the kids look sleepy, probably not unlike my own look; some look bored and a rare few look nervous. I wonder if any of them have a legend or curse on their family passed down to them from who knows when or where. I get in line behind a girl I don't know and wait patiently for my turn. Mitac asks for each person's name in turn, has them sign their name, then directs them to his Tracker friend to wait in yet another line. The pile of bags near the village Healer's house grows steadily as each child is processed and taken to the forest edge to wait. Most of the bags look light.

Per everything we have been taught, we are supposed to pack everything we would want with us in the city. Should we come out with magic, we will be immediately pulled out and held in isolation away from things we could accidentally damage and people we could accidentally hurt. When people are first able to wield magic, it's unpredictable, uncontrolled, and it may be used entirely unintentionally.

We will have a few minutes to wish our families goodbye, but we have no time to go home to pack. Knowing that Amaranth doesn't turn out magic, almost nobody packs the bag the way they are supposed to. It's simply performative at this point. Another step we are required to take.

Occasionally, a kid will pack properly. They're the hopefuls. The ones who hope they get to leave the village. They usually come from the orphanage. I couldn't blame them for wanting to hold out hope. That place is awful, as are the people who run it. With no family to keep them here, those kids have a real reason to want to leave.

I finger the necklace at my neck, realizing I forgot to take it off in my anger. Guess it will have to wait until after the Quest.

"Good morning, Rabbit." Mitac greets me with a smile. I don't return it.

I mumble what must resemble a friendly good morning because his smile neither slips nor is he deterred from wanting to talk to me. "Are you ready for today?"

I shrug. "Have your gold coin ready?"

He reaches into his pocket and pulls it out for me to see again. He flips it lazily and snatches it out of the air. "Ready when you are."

I smile. That gold coin is mine. I have the secret, and he has no idea. It feels like cheating, and I almost feel bad. Almost. He is a Gopher, after all. He will easily get another gold coin. Probably from some nobleman who pays him off to look the other way while he trounces over the less fortunate. I snort in disgust.

He puts the gold coin away and begins riffling through the papers.

"Ah, here we are." He pulls out a piece of paper and hands me the quill. "If you'll read and sign."

I glance at the paper. It simply states that I am who I say I am and that signing for anyone else would be punishable by death. I laugh. "Who would want to sign for someone else?"

"It happens. In some other cities, it's an honor to have magic, you know. They're eager to get a second chance at the Quest, or they want to get in before they're seventeen."

I shake my head. Idiots. I sign my name with a flourish. He takes my paper and looks at it for an inordinate amount of time in the flickering torch light. "All looks to be in order. Head over to Chance, and she will take you to where you will wait for dawn. Good luck today, Eloise." More softly as I walk away, I hear, "Be careful." I don't acknowledge his parting words and join my second line for the day.

The deep Green woman approaches me with no smile, no false niceties. Here is someone I can relate to.

"How is it working for the Gopher?" I ask.

The Tracker looks at me sharply. "I don't work *for* him," she snaps. "We work together. He's better with people, so I let him do that while I stay in the background."

I nod. "What's your job like when you're not here?"

She shrugs. "We do various jobs in the city. It's not bad. I like finding lost kids and helping them get home and bringing people to justice."

Silence falls. I find it uncomfortable, so I keep the conversation moving.

"What do you think of being out here?"

Another shrug. "It's nice, actually. I've never been here, but I've been to a lot of other villages, even in Amaranth. What you all have here—it's clean. The air is clear, the souls are clean."

"Our souls are clean?"

She nods. "Yes. What I do is smell the traces of people. The city is full of dark souls, dirty and it makes it difficult for me to enjoy any time there. Here—" she gestures around, "—you must be good people. It's so very clean."

I am unsure what to say to that, but I'm saved from response.

"Stay here," the woman says. "When the Quest announces it's time to enter, that's when you go in." The Tracker's voice has returned to all business. "Good luck."

She turns on her heel and marches back toward the next waiting kid.

Good luck, indeed. Run. I just need to run.

...FREE TO DIE...

Timekeeper

"No, no, no!" I scream, throwing down my quill in frustration. It leaves a dark mark on the parchment in front of me before bouncing to the floor and leaving another drip of black ink on the white marble. She's been told! We need the Variance. We need her to end the age! Every generation, every single time, they all refuse to accept their magic. They refuse to go.

I pace my quarters. The clouds outside reflect my mood. Dark, thunderous, and stormy. Curse the Celestials for ever telling this family the secret to avoid their magic. What can I do? Time's wasting is all I can think. The Variance has not appeared in so long because the Celestials, or rather one Celestial, thought it would be funny to see what would happen if the lineage that creates the Variance knew a way out.

"Well, HA-HA!" I yell at the gilded ceiling. "Well done! Humanity is going to die out because you decided to play a joke!"

Thunder answers my ranting. The Celestials hear me, and I should care, but I don't. I must do something. I think about my options. There aren't many of them. As the Timekeeper, I'm restricted in what I'm allowed to do. I'm not allowed to meddle; I'm not allowed to go backward. I'm not allowed to go forward. I'm not allowed to do anything! Oh, how I wish I could do *something*. Never before have my constraints felt so…constraining. I stay up here, alone, day after day, with nothing and no one but time. It's incredibly lonely. Time is not kind to me.

I have been the Timekeeper for so long even I have forgotten how long it's been. I was granted the choice to be immortal if I would merely watch the goings on of the silly humans and write what happens. In exchange, no pain, no fear, no hunger, no death would ever know me. To a young, dumb, and chronically sick twenty-two-year-old, this sounded like a grand plan. Death would come eventually…or it could not as long as I was there, they said. I only had to sign. I signed the dotted line, so to speak, and became the new Timekeeper. The ages started anew, and I recorded them.

At first, it was great, but no one told me that the reason I would never feel hunger is that I could never eat or that I would never feel pain because I could never feel anything at all. I still age, it turns out, but incredibly slowly. I won't die here because they'll find a new Timekeeper by then and send me back to the mortal realm, where I will eventually die anyway. Always read the fine print… Lovely lot, those Celestials. The immortal beings also conveniently failed to mention that I would be "ALONE!" I yell into the void.

Thunder resounds again, sounding akin to a chuckle, which only serves to needle me further. I am not afraid of them; they can't technically do anything to me until they have a new gullible sot to take my place. I have made it my mission to thwart every attempt they make to replace me. Not because I want to keep doing this but because I have other plans that don't involve them getting the pick they want.

I remember the last one who showed up to be wooed by the Celestials.

The young man walks around the marble halls, his hazel eyes bright and wide. He looks even younger than I was. From my hiding place in the stacks, I hear the usual spiel.

"This will all be yours," Udtis says, gesturing around the place. He causes the waters to rise in the fountain.

"You don't have to worry about where you will sleep anymore," Bretia states, clearing the clouds around the windows to display her beautiful stars. I should spend more time looking at those.

"Or what to eat," Sierin prompts, whispering in the young man's ear from behind him. She grows a flowering cherry tree at the top of the fountain. Its branches spread out, the floral smell is delightful.

I shake my head. Even the speech and knowing what's coming doesn't make me immune from the power.

The man spins on the spot. "It's all mine?"

"Yes," Iterin whispers. Silver-tongued devil, that one. "You only have to spend parts of your day recording what's going on below."

"We will teach you exactly what you need to do," Onas encourages, pulling some parchment and beautiful quills out of thin air. "You will play an important part of history. Be remembered forever in the writings you leave behind."

The man's eyes flash. Desire glowing strongly. He's almost ready to sign. But he's not the right one. I can sense it.

"Stop!" I yell and reveal myself.

The Celestials groan and reveal their ugly, angry selves.

They have started the same con several times. They sweet talk the person; promise them the same promises they gave me with their silver tongues. They bring them up and show them where they will get to stay, which is quite stunning objectively. Huge room with a big soft bed—they'll never use it; sleep isn't a thing—a large tub with running water, they even lay out platters of food. It's funny. A beautiful song and dance that I always manage to ruin.

Right before the new prospect signs, I find a way to "accidentally" tell them the downsides. I've left letters for the prospects, played charades for them, used a flashing sign once. That was fun. I paid dearly for that. Darkness, but no stars or moon, surrounded my quarters for nearly two years for that one. It worked, though. The prospects always refuse to sign. As much as I would love to be free, even free to die, I will not allow them to do this to others. Not yet. I am waiting for the right person who can manage it, maybe even undo it.

I think about my limited options for how to help the Variance wield her magic, and one keeps coming to the surface. I know I am going to get into so much trouble if I am found out, but it's a necessity at this point. I pick up my quill and wipe away the ink before sitting down and plotting my next moves.

...THE QUEST OF 1762

Aerith

The dream I have this time is far different than the previous dreams I have had. This must be what the dreams are like for the other Dreamers. It feels real like I'm there watching actual events, not symbolizations of events.

I watch as one of the young girls I've seen before, her brown hair tied at the nape of her neck, follows a Green Tracker to the Amaranth Forest. She is dropped off at the edge of the forest and told to stay there. The girl pats her waist, checking the security of the knives she reveals there. She reaches around her back and feels the brown package and canteen tied there. Seemingly satisfied, she sits on the ground, no doubt waiting for the announcement to enter. It's nearly dawn there. How odd to be dreaming about a Quest on a Quest day.

Not much happens for a little while. She simply sits and waits. She appears bored, and I feel bored as well. She pulls a knife off her belt and pulls a fallen tree limb closer to her. I watch as she starts shaving off long strips of wood. I think she is trying to make a spear until her stroke changes, and she starts gouging and carving into the wood. I see she's working on something decorative. A bird, maybe. I lose interest and try to shift my vision to see what else is going on, even though I know better. I cannot look around in my dreams. I can only see what time chooses to show me when it chooses to show me. That's what we are always taught.

Time must be feeling kind because the vision shifts exactly as I wanted it to. I am facing the Gopher assigned to the region. He has finished processing the last of the kids, and his Tracker is taking them to their place at the edge of the forest. The Gopher stands from his small wooden chair and stretches. He follows the torch lit path to the bags and pulls a gold coin out of his pocket. He looks over the bags, searching for one specific one, and gets nearer to it when he finds it. He looks around before he slips the gold coin in the pouch. He smiles and walks off to his Tracker, who has reappeared.

The two converse. I cannot hear what they are saying, so it must not be important to what I am meant to see here now. The sun is starting to peek over the top of the mountain. A supernatural announcement booms from out of the forest. "Enter now, all who qualify for the Quest of 1762."

I realize with a start that this is happening now. It's as though I am looking through a portal to events happening in the moment. While it is nearly dawn there, it is more than a couple of hours past dawn here. This young woman, who I have now seen several times before, is getting ready to start her Quest.

My surprise causes my view to falter.

This is unheard of. Dreamers dream of the future. Usually, a week, maybe two. The Purple Dreamers are slightly different in that we can see things further into the future, but I have never heard of them seeing something in the here and now. Nor have I ever heard of them seeing anything in the past. I don't know what to make of this information. My mentor never said she saw things in the past or the present; she described amorphous blobs. Much like I have seen all my life. I wonder if other Purple Dreamers who actually saw things had similar experiences. It would make sense for a Purple Dreamer to have visions of the far future since we are supposed to see change. But…why now? What is the purpose of this girl? Why am I seeing her current events and not what she will be doing?

I force the surprise out of my mind and return to passive observation.

I watch as she puts down her decorative whittling. I can tell she's debating taking it with her or leaving it behind, but in the end, she must decide against it. She stands up and lazily brushes off the needles from her pants. She looks around, finds a rock, and puts the stick on top. Perhaps she intends to retrieve it after her Quest. I can't see what kind of work she's done on it, but it appears to be an intricate pattern. The girl double-checks her supplies again and steps into the forest.

My view dims and goes to black. I calm my mind and emotions, attempting to bring it back, figuring my investment in this girl has caused another faltering. It does not return. I have seen all I am going to see for now. Time's up.

I take a deep breath and allow my feelings and emotions to return to me from the stone on my neck. I open my eyes. Mancio also opens his eyes, the slight changing of my position alerting him to the end of the vision. He looks at me expectantly. I smile. This is something I can share with him. Nothing major happened, a vision of a girl going on her Quest. I do not want to draw attention to her specifically, so I quickly think of some ways to alter the vision, to still teach him as I am supposed to but shift focus from her. However, I cannot stray too far from the truth, or the Council may sniff out my lies in our next meeting.

I tell him what I have seen in hushed tones, or at least what I am willing to tell him. A young boy, entering Amaranth Forest, for his Quest. The boy seems excited and anxious. I tell Mancio nothing of the Gopher's actions and avoid mentioning the girl at all. I also avoid telling him that the Quest is happening today. Close to the truth but not too close.

Mancio looks at me with awe. "How are you not super excited?" he asks.

If only he had seen me after my first actual vision. "I am," I reply quickly, "but remember that we are supposed to maintain control over our emotions. This is what that looks like."

"Oh." A pause, then, "What's it like?" Mancio asks too loud for the space. I remind him to keep his voice down. We have been joined by several other pairs of Dreamers. Our talking could distract them.

"What's what like?" I reply.

"What's the Quest like?"

"I don't know," I answer honestly. "Like you, I was brought here as an infant. I have never been on the Quest, at least not their Quest, and I have told you about our Quest." He touches his owl. I know he is eager to get his true talisman, same as I was.

"Oh," he repeats, his face falling. "I thought maybe you had Dreamed of other people in the Quest."

"Mancio, you know I've not had a real dream until today. Remember that many times, we Purple Dreamers will not have any dreams, or they will have no real definition to them. As I have told you before, the Illume almost wants us *not* to see anything significant. Whatever it is we report, it could cause major upset."

"So…if you do dream something, and you tell them, what will they do?" His head is cocked to one side, an inquisitive look on his face. Here, in this moment, he looks every bit the twelve-year-old child that he is.

"I don't know, Mancio. I suppose they will make whatever preparations they need to make."

"Will they come after you?" For someone so young, Mancio has good questions and great insight. He puts voice to my own concerns.

"I don't think they will. I am not the one causing those things. I will merely be relaying it to them." I spout it off with certainty, but the conviction within myself is weak; I'm still a little shaken by Naseem's statements about the goodness of the Council and I'm starting to doubt them a little more myself. I can't imagine they will take the end of the Realm in stride and pave the way for this girl to do what she needs to do, even if it's for the best. I myself struggle with whether I should tell them to get them to stop her. I hope, however this goes down, I'm not on the wrong side of it. As each day passes, I am picking a side. Even if I'm not ready to declare it.

CELESTIALS, WHICH WAY DO I GO?

Eloise

As I am sitting when the announcement comes, I enter the forest a couple of minutes behind everyone else, at least those I can see on either side of me. I hear crashing and bumbling about and shake my head. Clearly, we don't have Trackers in this group.

I walk forward slowly, taking a deep breath of the pine and sap smell emanating from the forest ahead of me. I remind myself I need to run. *So why am I suddenly afraid?* Probably has nothing to do with the potential to destroy the entire Realm if I don't do this right. My shoulders drop, but I stiffen them. I can do this. Everyone before me managed to do this. Even Julieth and I won't be bested by the likes of her.

I step into the forest, and everything suddenly goes silent. Curious. I turn around to step out to see if sound comes back and gasp. There is only forest behind me. No exit.

Okay… It is magic today. Saada did warn me. Who knows what else it can do? It doesn't do much to settle my nerves.

I start forward slowly, keeping my eyes peeled. The complete silence is extremely unnerving. I don't hear even the birds or the rustle of rabbits and squirrels that normally live here. I purposefully brush up against a bush and am grateful to hear the leaves rustle. So, I haven't suddenly lost my hearing. I'm relieved, although it was an incredibly low likelihood. Low but not zero.

Like your magic you had a zero percent chance of getting, right, Eloise? I tell my inner thoughts to shut up and go away.

In this place that once was familiar for berries and small game hunting, I am frightened of the eeriness. Nothing looks right. The trees loom over me ominously where before they were a comforting sight, a place of play, rest, and comfort. The bushes snag on my cape. Normally, the paths are wide enough to walk down in pairs, but now they're so small I have to turn sideways in many places. The rocks I'm used to dodging or picking my way over have all moved out of position. Fallen trees crisscross the path, forcing me to climb over them. This is not the forest I know. My teacher from so long ago was right.

I remove one of the knives from its sheath on my belt and hold it in my palm, feeling safer having it at the ready. We have been told that the Quest is safe. Nothing here will harm us, but it doesn't mean that we can't harm ourselves. Other people have also told me not to believe a word of the Council's propaganda. I trust the people who tell me not to trust a whole heck of a lot more than those who tell me to trust. Especially right now. A branch cracks and I jump and turn toward it. I realize I'm the one who broke the branch and try to laugh at myself. It comes out a hoarse rasp instead.

I wipe the sweat off my brow. It's not hot by any means, but I'm covered in a light layer of moisture. I move forward slowly, uncertain what might happen next. I try to keep my breathing steady, reminding myself that I need to save my adrenaline for running when it's time, but it doesn't have any effect. I'm wound tighter than a spring on the carriages.

I get to a small opening and pause. There are a few trails in front of me. None of them give me any information on which way to go. I jump up and down on the balls of my feet a few times, trying to release some of the anxiety. It helps a little.

Celestials, which way do I go?

They look identical. I stare at them for several moments. This shouldn't be this hard. I decide to walk down the one on the right.

Maybe it's one path for each time I need to run? Does everyone get tested three times? I wish someone had given us more information.

I walk along the small game trail in the shadow of pine trees and sunlit ferns without incident for a while. I turn another bend in the path and jolt to a stop. There, in a widening on the path, is a girl curled into a ball whimpering in pain. One of her legs is twisted grotesquely at the wrong angle with a large open gash. I rush forward, not even pausing to think.

I crouch at her side, getting a closer look at her wound. "What happened?" I ask her as I look over the rest of her. I don't see any other obvious wounds. Her cream-colored shirt and black pants are covered in dirt. Her black hair has fallen around her face, pine needles collecting in it from the ground around her head. She doesn't answer my question; she only moans.

The gash is bleeding at a good clip. I don't know a lot about healing, never having felt an aptitude for it nor a desire to learn it. That's Kinta's job, our village Healer. She had given a few small classes on basic wound care, and now I'm kicking myself for not going. Might have been useful.

"I'm Eloise," I tell the girl, brushing hair away from her face. She's extremely pale, and her head feels damp. "What's your name?"

She doesn't answer, but she's still wincing and moaning. At least she's still conscious. I turn my attention back to her leg, whatever it was that caused the gash went deep. I don't know much, but I know stopping the bleeding is probably a good start. That means I should put something in it to staunch it. I'm proud of my fledgling logical thought. At least my brain hasn't completely fled.

I look around, and I see several possibilities of what to put into the wound. Maybe some leaves and moss would work best. Yeah, I like that. It's not the cleanest, but it has to help somehow, right?

Clean…that triggers another thought.

I should clean the wound first. Yes, clean. See the breadth of what I'm dealing with.

I look at the pants; they're encroaching on the wound. I need to clear more space around it.

"Hey…uh," I stop, realizing I don't know what to call her. "I'm going to cut your pants some more to see what your wound looks like. Then I'm going to rinse it and try to stop the bleeding."

No response. I look up at her. Her eyes are closed, but she's still breathing. If she did pass out, it's probably for the best. I use my knife to cut away at her pants and free some space around the bleeding wound. My knife is sharp but not sharp enough, and I inadvertently pull on her broken leg as the pants give way to my knife. She starts whimpering again. Back to the land of the conscious, I guess.

I grab my canteen and realize with dismay that it's still empty. How could I have forgotten to fill it? I was sure I had filled it before I left the cabin.

"Hold on," I tell her. "I'm going to get some water to rinse your leg. Unless you have some?" I look at her hopefully. She only shakes her head slightly, tears forming in her grey eyes.

"There's a creek nearby; I'll fill the canteen and come back." I hope the creek is nearby. With everything being so different, the creek could be gone altogether.

I rise, and she does not try to stop me. I move quickly and carefully through the forest. I head in the direction of where I think the creek should be. A dip down off the side of the path, and yes, there it is.

Oh no…it's dry.

I let out a howl of frustration. This creek runs all the time, even in the dead of summer when it's excruciatingly hot and nearly everything else is dry. I dig frantically with my fingers, hoping the water is right under the surface. I accomplish nothing other than a few broken nails and dirt wedged far under my remaining nails.

I sit back on my heels and ponder what to do. I know, I *know* there is water here. I pick up a small branch nearby and poke and dig at the dirt in the bed. I dig down, using the stick as a makeshift shovel. Hoping, praying. No water, not even some damp dirt. Damn this magical forest!

I slam my hand on the creek bed, completely annoyed. I've been gone for several minutes, and I worry for the girl I left behind. I can't be gone too long; her unconscious episode earlier has me worried. Plus, I know she has to be scared. I refuse to acknowledge that I may also be scared.

I hang my head in defeat and start searching my memory for where else I have seen water in the forest, hopefully somewhere not far from here. As I search my memory banks, I hear a trickling sound, and my head snaps up. There, from one of the holes I have dug, water is coming out as if I have hit a spring. I don't stop to analyze it, chalk it up to good luck, and start gathering the clean water that bubbles forth into my canteen. It's clear and clean and, at this moment, one of the best things I have ever seen.

When my canteen flows over, I cap it and head back quickly to where I left the girl.

She hasn't moved, still in the fetal position. She looks limp, and my heart stops. I approach her and put a hand on her shoulder.

"I found some water." She doesn't rouse. "This is going to hurt," I tell her unconscious form as I kneel beside her, "but it needs to be done."

I try to straighten her leg, so I won't get her other leg wet when I go to rinse it, but she wakes and screams, so I stop. At least she's awake again. I don't know what I'm doing, but I hope I'm not making it worse. I pour some water on the gash, trying to direct the liquid to the dirtiest and deepest areas to wash them out. It's an imperfect job, especially with her writhing in pain and my limited supplies.

"What's your name?" I ask, trying to take her mind off my ministrations and keep her awake.

"Selvia," she replies faintly, too faintly. She moans again.

"Are you from an outlying village?" *C'mon, keep talking*, I beg her internally.

She shakes her head in response. I'm surprised. I don't know everyone in Ashadier, but I would remember if I had seen this girl, I'm sure. Her black hair is not common in town. I wonder how our paths had not crossed before.

"I live in the village here, too."

"I live—in the…in the orphanage," she stutters out. That explains why I haven't seen her. Poor girl.

I keep pouring the water, directing it to the wound, trying to waste as little as possible. It slowly clears, the older blood dripping down to the forest floor. The smell of iron is pervasive. Fresh blood begins to mix with the water in the wound. The dirt has cleared. It is deep, as I suspected, but I'm not seeing muscle or bone. I sit back on my heels and look at my handiwork.

Selvia is quiet again. I look over at her. Eyes closed, still pale, but still breathing.

"Okay, Selvia." I nearly shout and I let out my breath when her eyes flutter back open. "Your leg looks badly broken. I'm going to see if I can find something to wrap it and brace it. And something to fill this hole in your leg. Maybe we can get you up and out of here." I look around, remembering how the exit disappeared earlier, and amend my statement. "Or maybe we will have to wait for the Gopher to come get you with his Tracker."

Selvia nods, tears snaking down her cheeks, leaving tracks in the dirt on her face. She looks so much younger than seventeen. Looking at her, she could be one of my little cousins rather than one of my peers. She must be one of the youngest in here. Probably barely of age.

I gather the cleanest clumps of bright green moss I can find. I shake out any pine needles and bugs that have taken residence within them. Then, I gather some large leaves from some of the plants nearby. With luck, if I tie them down, I'll be able to get the leaves to hold the moss in place. What a mess.

I look around the clearing for something to brace her leg with. I see nothing obvious. Too easy, of course. I expand my perimeter a bit and find some large branches. Thankful that I have two knives, I begin whittling the branches into smaller, usable braces for her leg. This knife won't be the same once I'm done with it. Not until I can get it honed and sharpened again. Hopefully, anything else I need to do today will only take one knife.

I find some blackberry vines and work to cut off the menacing thorns, cutting my hands in several places. I ignore the stinging and keep working until the vines are clear. I cut them into four equal parts and weave them into the best rope I can fashion in a hurry.

When I return to Selvia, she has managed to sit upright against a tree. Some color has returned to her face. I am pleased to see her rallying.

"Can you tell me what happened?" I ask her again when I kneel next to her once again. I gently start pushing moss into the wound. It looks like the wound is smaller than I remember, and the bleeding has stopped. I'm glad for that. Funny what anxiety will make you see.

"I was running," Selvia answers, closing her eyes against the pain. "I thought I heard something chasing me. Something big." She shudders and opens her eyes again. "While I ran, a big branch caught me along the leg, and I fell down a ravine. I tumbled head over heels until I got to the bottom. I could still hear the big thing chasing me, so I managed to crawl out and keep crawling until I didn't hear it anymore. Then I collapsed here, until you found me." She pauses and looks at me with watery eyes. "Thank you. For helping me, you know. Not everyone would."

I smile at her. "What else do I have to do? The forest hasn't told me to leave yet."

"It told me to leave." She hangs her head. "Almost as soon as I entered. I didn't want to leave yet, so I kept going. This," she waves at her leg, "is my fault. The forest sent the thing after me, I know it, and this is the result."

I want to tell her she's being stupid, but I think she may not be wrong. I have never heard what happens when someone stays in the Quest after being told to leave. Perhaps that is when the Quest gets truly dangerous. I wind the vines around her calf, holding the leaves and moss in place. This, at least, is going as I had planned.

When that is complete, I turn to the bigger of the two challenges.

I brace her leg with the branches and the fashioned rope. Each brace placement, tie, and knot I create causes Selvia to wince and moan. "I'm so sorry, Selvia, I'm trying to be as gentle as possible."

She nods. "I know. Thank you again." She bites down on her lip to stay quiet as I finish my work. I sit back. I nod in satisfaction; it looks decent. I am still perplexed as to what to do with her.

Next logical step. "Uh, did you have stuff when you came in?"

"I did, but I lost it when I was running." She stares down at her empty hands.

"Should we go looking for it?" I ask, looking around to see if I can spot anything obvious. I don't even see the ravine she said she crawled out of.

She shakes her head. "Not necessary, I don't know where I was when

I lost it, and I'd rather get out of here. I think I've tempted the forest enough for today."

"Well, Selvia," I stand and brush off my pants. I reach out for her hand. "I'm not sure how we are going to get out of here. The exit disappeared when I came in."

"That's okay. It's right over there. Can't you see it?" She's pointing west of where we are. All I see is more forest and I tell her as much. I help her up onto her good leg. I wonder how much blood she has lost to make her so delusional as to see things that aren't there. I decide to humor her since it will at least get her moving somehow. She wobbles uncertainly on her feet.

"You okay?" I ask, wrapping an arm around her waist to stabilize her.

"Yeah, a little dizzy."

I look over where she was lying. The blood from her leg is slowly seeping into the dirt, but there's a lot there. No wonder she's lightheaded.

"Ready." She leads us forward.

Together, we perform an awkward and very slow three-legged race toward what she insists is the way out. When we have been hobbling along for several minutes, and the foliage has not changed, I feel like I need to address her hallucination of the exit.

"Selvia, I don't think—" Suddenly, my face hits something solid, and I fall backward, bringing Selvia down with me. She cries out in surprise and pain.

"What was that?" she asks, alarmed.

"I don't know," I rub the new sore spot on my head. I look around and see nothing I could have hit. I get up and help Selvia up, too. "I think we hit a barrier."

"Not we," she giggles. "You. I was still moving forward when you hit it." She pauses momentarily. "I think I'm allowed to leave, but you're not. Maybe that's why you can't see the opening in the trees."

As ridiculous as it sounds, it wouldn't surprise me on this day. "Oh. Well, can you get out okay?"

"I think so, my leg feels a lot better now. Thank you."

"I hope it heals alright, Selvia."

"I hope so, too. Next time, I will wait until I'm supposed to be here to come. Good luck, Eloise."

I want to address how foolish she's been, but I am fairly certain she knows that already. That explains why she looks so young. I wonder how she got past Mitac and his Tracker. Sneaky girl. She might be a Green when she comes in the next time when she's actually supposed to be here. For her sake, I hope she does have magic. Anything to get out of the orphanage.

Selvia turns and, lightly touching the toe of her bad leg to the ground, she hops away, tree to tree for support, and disappears from view. I shake my head, trying to clear my vision to see her, but she doesn't reappear. She simply vanishes. I walk forward gingerly with my hands stretched in front of me and feel a solid barrier right where Selvia walked through. I marvel at this crazy magic and turn around.

I hastily return to the clearing we were in previously and gather my discarded canteen. I make my way back to the creek bed to refill it and drink deeply. That took a lot of work and was completely unexpected. At least it took my mind off of everything for a little while.

I have been here for at least two hours by my estimation, and I still haven't been challenged yet. I can practically hear the clock ticking on my six-hour time limit. That gold coin is sliding out of my reach.

I decide it's time to pick up my pace. I have to get this over with. If I don't, my heart may give out before I even make it to the first challenge.

FOOLISH GIRL!

Mitac

This part of the job is boring. No one talks about the waiting. All you ever hear about is who found the Primes and how many came back this year for training. The waiting, however, is interminable.

On her covered porch, the Healer, her brilliant white hair pulled back and spooky white eyes half-closed, is on stand-by if we need her. She, too, is waiting, rocking rhythmically back and forth, making me drowsy. *Creak, creak, creak...* My head drops off my hand, jolting me awake. I need to move. I get up and stretch, trying to bring myself to wakefulness. The fitful sleep last night isn't helping.

The inn was comfortable enough, but I was dreaming of Eloise. It started innocuous enough. I would be walking through the forest, calling out for her, desperate to find her and protect her. When I found her, though, she called me hateful names then fled from me. I would wake, my hand outstretched in the air, trying to grab hold of her.

I tossed and turned, trying to shake it off. When I finally did, I only managed to sleep long enough for the nightmare to repeat itself.

I roll my shoulders and jog a few steps toward the forest and back. It's still early, and while a few kids have already come out, I still have a lot on my parchment who have not.

Chance is wandering the edge of our part of the forest. Other

Gophers and Trackers are tasked with other villages and towns in Amaranth, which also use the forest. Ashadier is the smallest and the furthest west. Bruderdon, Rothesard, and Winfair are larger and more easily reached by train and carriage. My back still aches from the bumpy ride into Ashadier a couple of nights ago. The roads here are not as well-traveled or well-maintained. The carriage had bounced uncomfortably over rocks and small branches.

Chance paces, I pace. She waits, I wait. And we watch. Everyone is supposed to come back through us so we can check them over, but inevitably, there are those who will be so relieved they head straight for home. Or others who don't want to come to the city. These are the stories I have been told by everyone anyway.

After another hour, Chance comes around supporting a young girl with a strange limp. Her right leg is bandaged, and she's got some sticks attached to her legs. *What in Celestials is this?*

"Healer!" I call out to the woman in the rocker. She isn't paying attention, but jolts promptly out of her reverie and hustles right over with me.

"My girl, what happened?" The Healer drops to a knee to look at the leg paying no attention to the dirt getting onto her white outfit.

"I was being chased," the girl replies in a small voice. She appears ashamed, and I can't tell if her shaking is from pain or fear. I look at her closely. I don't recognize this girl from the festival last night nor sign in this morning. There weren't so many kids I could have forgotten one.

"Chased? By what? Do you—" The Healer looks around. "Do you mean to tell me you went into the forest?!" Why is the Healer so upset by this? The Quest requires it. My eyes narrow behind the Healer's back.

The girl hangs her head. Her hair a black curtain in front of her face. "I wanted to try."

"Foolish, girl! You're only thirteen; what were you thinking?!" Suddenly, it comes together. I didn't recognize the girl because she *didn't* come to see me this morning. She snuck in somehow. I scrutinize the girl more closely.

The Healer leads her away, supporting her right side while the girl leans on her. I follow. "No, don't put your foot down, hop instead." The girl obediently keeps her leg up in the air and hops. "How did you manage to bind your leg this way?"

She begins undoing the creative wrapping on the girl's leg. The girl winces, her grey eyes releasing several tears as the packing in her wound is removed.

"I didn't," she tells the Healer as she is lowered into one of the chairs on the porch. "A girl, Eloise. She did it for me and cleaned it up. It looks and feels much better than it did."

At the name, Saada comes running over. "Eloise?" she asks. "You said Eloise helped you?" The girl's eyes go wide at the intensity of Saada's questioning. "Well, did you?"

She nods almost imperceptibly. "Y-yes."

"How is she? Is she okay? Is she coming out behind you?" Saada looks back at the forest, her hawkish gaze trying to peer through the trees.

"N-no. She couldn't leave with me. She was fine, though." Saada's face falls and she walks away dejectedly.

"Don't worry," I tell the girl, "She's anxious for her niece. It doesn't have anything to do with what you said."

The girl nods and focuses back on the Healer's work. She hisses through her teeth when the bulk of the packing comes away. The Healer tuts. "This is quite deep, and this," she stares at the moss and leaves in her hand, "is not good packing. Not at all."

"It looks better than it did," the girl insists. "And it hurt less. At least, until you started doing that."

"Yes, well, I am not the best with wounds. I am better with medicines and such. I will do what I can. This is going to take a while to heal."

The Healer disappears into the cabin and returns with clean bandaging. I wander back to my table, confident the girl is in competent hands. I smile to myself. Eloise is still inside. I don't think she's going to win the coin, so I am glad I put it in her bag already.

Last night after I left the festival, I wandered Ashadier, checking out the sights. I saw Eloise's family leave the tent and head to a run-down cabin on the edge of the forest. I wasn't stalking, I told myself, only curious. I followed them silently, trying to remain inconspicuous. A bit of a challenge given my size, but I had done well in my stealth studies at the Academy.

The cabin was mostly kept together, maybe more by the sheer stubbornness of its occupants than anything. The tin roof had patches in several places, and I could almost bet it leaks when the rains come. The stone half-wall was quickly becoming a quarter-wall in many places due to the crumbling architecture. Given that it's likely decorative, I am not surprised it hasn't been prioritized for repair. Folks around here don't seem to have enough to worry about looks. Function is what matters.

The majority of the houses looked to be in similar condition. By all accounts, Eloise's was probably one of the best ones around. Since her aunt's husband has a faint tint of blue to his hair and skin, I can safely guess that he holds a position that pays better than most for the average Ashadieran.

Around the back was a large garden with netting over top. I guessed it was to keep the birds out of the fledgling plants, but I didn't know. Gardening wasn't a hobby I had the choice of luxuriating in. No permanent housing means no garden. Now I have a small apartment in Amiket, but it has no outdoor space.

Inside the cabin, which I was definitely not peering into in a stalker way, candles had been lit, and I could see Saada moving around inside ushering little kids towards what I presumed were bedrooms. Gamet was seated on a wooden chair, talking animatedly with an older boy with brown hair similar to Eloise's. If I had to hazard a guess, I would put him and Eloise as siblings.

Having gotten a decent look at the dwelling, I moved on. I didn't want to get caught, and all the husband or the presumptive brother would have to do is turn toward the window, and I would likely be seen. I'm a dark Black, but I am not invisible. There are other Warriors better suited to that skill.

A screech brings me out of my thoughts. I whip my head around to see a big, beefy woman with short, spiky blonde hair, giving the girl with the injured leg a stern talking-to. Maybe talking is the wrong word. She is yelling loud enough for Amiket, six hundred and seventy-five miles away, to hear from here. I approach carefully. The Healer is working on the girl's leg while she sobs. It's hard to differentiate if the crying is from the continued efforts of the Healer or the abhorrent treatment by this woman.

"How dare you! You moronic little brat!" The large woman's jowls shake with anger in her round, red face as she points a beefy finger in the girl's face.

"Excuse me, ma'am," I interrupt softly when she takes a breath, clearly ready to continue her screeching.

She whirls to face me. "And what do you want, Gopher?" she spits in my direction. I wipe some of the spittle off my face, making a show of it.

No love lost here. "I wonder if we can maybe reconsider yelling at the girl?" I gesture towards the pitiful thing who has curled in on herself.

"Why do you care? She is a damned idiot. Entering the forest at only thirteen years old. And you!" She turns her ire toward me. "Where were you and your Green dog at when she went in?"

I narrow my eyes at her. I don't appreciate her calling Chance a dog, but I am glad she has stopped yelling at the girl. I can take all the abuse given to me, no problem, but this woman should be grateful Chance didn't hear what she said. Years of being a street rat will teach you to let insults roll off you. If you don't, you end up in worse situations. Chance, however, holds no such compunction and would have only been too glad to give as good as she took.

"I assure you; we will be investigating that exact thing when the Quest is complete. We will question her."

The girl's head snaps up, and her fearful eyes meet mine. When the large woman isn't looking at me, I wink and smile at the girl to let her know not to be afraid, then school my face back to neutral before the angry woman rounds on me again.

The fight in the woman seems to turn to self-righteous satisfaction. "Well then, an inquisition by a Gopher will do her some good! That will be excellent punishment. You'll make her go without food, too, right?"

I nod enthusiastically. "Oh, of course, we are quite harsh with our prisoners. Your daughter will certainly learn her lesson."

"Daughter, hah! This brat is not one of mine. Oh, ho! She wishes!" The girl's face shows she wishes for anything but that. "No, this thing is from the village orphanage. No parents, no family. Abandoned to our care, which we do dutifully, willingly, and with great sacrifice, and she still has the nerve to complain and be unhappy." I nearly laugh at the woman playing like she's a victim here.

Things start to click into place at the woman's statement and anger roils in my belly. I want nothing more than to arrest this woman in front of me, but I know she will only be replaced by someone the same as her if I do. She wouldn't even get a mild reprimand. Likely, she would get a promotion to a better orphanage for dealing so harshly with her charges. Bile rises in my throat at the thought of this little girl being in her care. An idea comes to me.

"Well, how about this? Since she's in the orphanage, I'll take her back to the city for questioning. She won't even need to return to you." I don't know what I am saying, or what I will do with her, but this girl can't stay here.

The girl looks startled but hopeful. The woman is looking away, and I give the girl a warning glance to put her head down. If she shows hope, this foul woman will keep her out of spite. It certainly wouldn't be out of some misguided sense of duty.

"Yeah, but I would need something," she turns her round brown eyes to me and scratches her chin, where she has several hairs growing impressively long. "We get paid by the child, you know, and while it's one less mouth to feed, she does some work around the orphanage. Albeit terribly." She glares at the child again. "I would need to hire someone to do the work she does."

I can see through to her true intentions, a benefit of my magic. She wants a payday. "Oh yes, ma'am," I say. "I wouldn't want to take capable hands from you. Shall we say fifteen silvers, and I'll take her away for good?" I keep my voice smooth and convincing. Allowing my magic to do some of the work for me.

The rotund woman thinks about this. I suspect most of the money given to the orphanage goes to this woman's large waistline. "Hm…" she taps her chin, the hair on the mole bouncing when she taps it. "I'm not sure it'll be enough. Let's make it twenty."

I frown, acting put out. One negotiation technique: pretend the options provided are less than ideal for yourself, then concede. I don't have to use much of my magic to get over on this woman. She calls the girl foolish, but here she is the fool. I would pay anything to rescue this girl who reminds me so much of myself. "I think I can make that work. Wait here."

I go back to the table and my leather coin pouch. I pull out twenty silvers and hold them out to her in an open palm, like offering a horse a slice of apple. I almost laugh imagining her as a large Clydesdale only far less majestic. The woman snatches the coins, turns on her heels, and clomps away, not unlike a horse. Get that woman a farrier! I snort. A little cruel, but I won't take it back. I take another three silvers and give them to the Healer for her work on the girl's leg. Thankfully, that's over. The girl and the Healer both look up at me.

"Thank you," they say in unison.

I chuckle. "It's nothing. What's your name?" I ask, looking at the girl I've essentially paid to release from the orphanage.

"Selvia," she replies.

"All done." The Healer stands wearily. "She's going to have to take it easy on that leg for a little while, but whatever Eloise did, she did a respectable job. In a few weeks or so it'll be as good as new." She looks at me curiously. "You're an odd Gopher."

I expect her to say more, to ask questions. What I have done is way outside of protocol. It's nothing I have ever seen or heard of being done. I don't think it's illegal, but I am sure that I'm in a grey area that the city won't appreciate. As odd of a Gopher as I am, I want to ask her how a Healer with enough power to be Prime ended up here but take her lead. The Healer reconsiders and wanders off to sit down, closing her eyes in seeming relief.

"Well, Selvia," I clap my hands. She looks up at me. She looked appeased before and now seems afraid since she's been reminded I'm a Gopher. "Looks like you're coming to the city with me."

"Okay," she answers quietly. "Then what happens?"

I shrug. "I don't know. I've never done this before. At the very least, we can get you to the city orphanage. It's better than this one. Or at least I've been told it's the best. How's that sound?" The girl's face twists, but she attempts a smile. "A carriage ride and a train ride await you. And some food. But we won't tell her." I jerk my head in the direction of where the Clydesdale stalked off to.

She perks up. "I get to ride the train?" She truly is a smaller version of myself. As scared as I was to go to training, I couldn't wait to see the Vale. I had been one of the few bouncing on the balls of my feet when we collected our train tickets. Others were stoic or resigned. The few who were excited sat together, guessing what the city and our training would be like. We were very wrong. I shake off the memories and turn my attention back to Selvia's fervor.

I laugh. "Yes, it's several days to get back to the city. Even by train."

"We will cross the mountains?"

I nod. "And the rivers, and the plains, and the desert." I'm starting to sound like a travel brochure. I chuckle.

I see her eyes shining with elation now. "I've never been outside of Ashadier. The orphanage wasn't big on trips." Her face clouds over, probably remembering something unpleasant from her time with that horrible woman.

"For now, though, we must wait for the Quest to finish. You were the first out…probably because you weren't supposed to be in there."

She blushes deeply. "I know. I just…I wanted to try."

"Well, you did. How did you achieve that, by the way?"

Selvia shrugs, her eyes alight with a little pride. "I snuck around the houses, and when the announcement came in, I jumped into the forest when she happened not to be looking."

"You must have been utterly silent."

She nods. "I am good at sneaking up on people."

"I'm impressed. But don't go doing something that stupid ever again."

Her shoulders droop, the pride leaving her eyes immediately. "Yes, sir."

"You could have gotten seriously hurt." I look at her leg. "Well, even more seriously hurt. That's the last I'll say of it."

"It was worse," she replies, "Eloise helped me a lot."

"Did she turn White?" *If she has Healing powers, she should have turned White. But then, why didn't she come out?*

Selvia looks confused. "What?"

"Did Eloise turn White when she helped you?"

"No," Selvia cocks her head, looking a little confused. "She looked the same as when I first met her, except for a sore spot on her head." Selvia giggles.

At my confused look she relays how the two of them got Selvia out of the forest. Maybe Eloise doesn't have Healing magic, but it had sounded like it from the description of events. Of course, Selvia could be embellishing how bad her wound was, in the way kids will do to seem braver. I am a little disappointed. I wanted Eloise to come on the train ride with us.

I give Selvia my water canteen and set off to find Chance so she can yell at me away from Selvia. I am sure she will not be excited about my tagalong for the trip home.

...WHY DID YOU DO IT?

Mitac

"You did WHAT?" Chance yells.

I glance back over my shoulder to Selvia. Thankfully, she's not paying attention. Or she's pretending not to.

"Chance, please, she doesn't belong in an orphanage."

"So, she has parents or family?" Chance looks at the girl, too.

"Well, no," I admit.

"Then an orphanage is exactly where she belongs. That's what those places are for!"

"I'm well aware of what an orphanage is, Chance," I grind out. "Those places are awful. Did you hear that woman yelling at her? Belittling her? You tell me, is that where you would want your family?"

I'm taking a risk, appealing to Chance's human side. She's never shown much empathy before. Chance is straight forward, lacking emotion, tightly wound, and controlled. That she's even displaying her rage at my actions is a strong indication of an absolute hurricane raging inside of her. I know one way to convince her, but I refuse to use magic on my partner.

Chance, predictably, glares at me. "I don't have family."

I forgot. Maybe I should use my magic anyway. I shake my head. That's a line I will not cross.

"This is your deal," Chance holds up her hands. "If this goes wrong, and it will, I am not taking the fall with you."

I hold up my hands. "I have no intention of making you do anything for her." I turn to leave, then shoot over my shoulder, "I do need you to watch her if we stay overnight, though."

I jog off, not giving her time to refuse. I hear her angry grumbling behind me.

As I approach Selvia, I give her a warm smile. There might be a lot of uncertainties, and I might get into serious trouble, but I will never be sorry for removing this girl from that situation. I wonder how many more like her are in the orphanage. I can't afford to rescue all of them, and I have no long-term plan for one kid, let alone many of them, but I add it to my long list of things I would like to change. In case I ever get the chance.

"I'm sorry if you heard any of that," I tell Selvia. "Chance wasn't expecting to bring someone back with us who wouldn't be heading to training."

Selvia shrugs. Tears well up in her eyes. Gosh, I forgot how often kids can cry and break your heart. "I can go back to the orphanage. You don't have to take me with you." Selvia sits hunched in her chair. I imagine this is bringing forward all kinds of abandonment issues.

I quickly correct her, waving off her suggestion. "No. I paid for you and intend to bring you with us." Her face shadows as though reminded she's been purchased like a slave. Isynt doesn't have any slaves, but the other Vales, Eaglyn has them. Or is it Staksu? I can't remember which. Maybe both.

"Erm…mister. I'm sorry, but I don't remember your name." Selvia blushes furiously.

"I don't think I gave it to you, Selvia. My sincerest apologies. I am Mitac." I hold out my hand to her, and she shakes it briefly.

"Thank you, Mr. Mitac, for stopping the mistress' yelling. I have been subjected to them many times, and they can go on forever." She twists her hands in her lap, clearly uncomfortable with revealing this information. Likely she would get in trouble for doing so.

"It's no trouble," I reassure her off-handedly. In truth, it's probably going to be a lot of trouble. A lot of work.

"I don't mean to sound ungrateful…but why did you do it?"

Memories bloom in my mind. From my time on the streets. I was not treated kindly, not that I expected to be. I would take it sitting down, letting them hurl insults, but when it happened to someone else? Anger would roar to life, and I have more than one set of bloody knuckles from then. Along with more than one warrant for my arrest. The Council keeps those covered up for me. Another reason I need to stay in their good graces. I could end up in jail if they decide to act on those warrants.

"I don't like to see kids mistreated. What she was doing was inappropriate. You didn't deserve it, regardless of what she thought." I look over to the orphanage. "No one deserves to be there with her."

Selvia shakes her head. "She's like that mostly with only me. She's not particularly kind to the others, but she seems to dislike me even more."

"Well, I'm not sure whether that's good news or not. Either way, there's nothing I can do about the rest of them for now. We will leave together, and maybe one day I can do something to help them."

She sits quietly for a moment. "How did you end up there, anyway?" I ask, curious to know where the rest of her family went.

I almost immediately regret asking. She glances away, biting her cheek. Before I can let her off the hook, she answers.

"My—my dad…he wasn't a good person. To me or my mom. One night, my dad was being extra cruel. He…he had me in a corner." I tense. I can picture the scene in my head and wish I couldn't.

"He was yelling at me. Saying terrible things about me. My mom came up behind him and hit him with the cast iron pan. He fell to the floor immediately, but she didn't stop. She…she killed him." Tears fall freely from her eyes into her lap. My heart cracks a little more.

I hand her a black kerchief, and she wipes her eyes and nose. "It happened during Quest time. The Gophers who were here found out and took her in. I tried to explain why she did it, but they dragged her off anyway. That's the last time I saw her."

She tries to hand the kerchief back, but I ignore it and kneel in front of her. I look into her grey eyes, moving my head to maintain eye contact even when she tries to look away. "I am so sorry, Selvia. That should never have happened. None of it. It's deplorable." I pause. "I knew a couple of people with similar backgrounds, with bad people for parents. I remember them being uncomfortable with being hugged. So, I'm asking you for your permission. Can I give you a hug?"

Selvia's eyes widen and she draws back. I think she's about to tell me no, when she nods wordlessly and I gather her into a big hug, and she sobs harder. All I want to give her in this moment is the safe place her father should have been for her.

I wait until her tears stop before I let her go. My knees ache, but it's background noise.

"I'm sorry for your shirt," she apologizes, finally pulling back.

"It needed a good washing," I jest. She giggles then claps her hand over her mouth.

"You can laugh," I tell her. "At least *someone* thinks I'm funny."

"When will we leave?" she hesitantly asks, her smile returning.

I look up at the sky, doing some math. "Well, the Quest has been underway for a few hours now. Your friends should be coming out soon. When everyone has been accounted for, we will get to leave, after you tell them goodbye, of course. Maybe a day at most."

"I don't have friends. No one in there cares about me." She fidgets with her hands.

I wonder how she can think that. "That doesn't seem true. Eloise took care of you."

She nods. "That's true, but she's not a friend. She's nice and all, but she doesn't know me."

I'm not sure how to respond to that. I clear my throat. "Well, be that as it may, I still think we will get to leave for the train tomorrow and be on our way to the city next week."

"Where will we sleep?"

"If we are here tonight, you'll stay in the room with Chance. I don't think you want to room with an old man. As for after, we will travel by wagon back to Rothesard, which will take us about six days or so. We have tents to let us get out of the wagon for the night, but you may want to sleep inside of it. I'm not sure how you feel about camping?"

"It's no problem for me," she answers my half-asked question. "I once spent three days in the forest alone, and it was winter." She lifts her chin, puffing out her chest.

"Well then, tents it is. I'm sure Chance will let you share hers."

Or she will once I pay her to do so. Selvia looks less certain.

"Don't worry, Chance looks grumpy, but she's actually fairly nice. She may be bitter about you sneaking past her, but she'll get over it." At least, I hope she will. I look over at the forest right in time to catch a boy walking out. "Oh look, here comes someone now. I'll be right back."

Time to get back to my actual duties. I recognize this boy, now man, I guess, from last night. He had been dancing with Eloise's brother for a little while.

"Hold up," I tell him. He was headed straight for his bag. Startled, he jolts to a stop. "I need to check you over. How was your Quest?"

I'm not supposed to make conversation with the Questers; strictly inspect them and direct them to where they need to go. That feels so clinical and uncomfortable, so I make small talk.

"It—it was fine, I guess. It said I could go, the voice. So…can I go?" He looks at me expectantly. I look over his skin and hair. Then I look him closely in the eyes, the part that makes everyone flinch and look away.

"You're clear," I tell him. He visibly deflates and runs off to his bag.

CLIMBING OR RUNNING...

Eloise

I continue my journey further into the forest at a brisk walk. At one point, I come back to the opening with the same three paths. How is that possible? I was pretty sure I wasn't walking in circles. How many three-path options are in this place, though? One way to be sure. I could walk back down the right-hand path and see if I end up where Selvia was.

On the one hand, I could satisfy my curiosity. On the other, I could be wasting my time. Looking around the shadows, I have plenty of curiosity but not plenty of time. I decide on the middle path.

This path is much less clear than the first one was. I climb over fallen limbs, some fresh from the last storm in the spring, others nearly rotten through, being taken over by the moss and mushrooms of the forest. There's something in that about the circle of life. If I stop to think about it, I'm sure I could find something poetic about what I am going through now and what the forest does to its fallen, but I don't pause to think. Besides, Julieth is the one to wax poetic, not me. I barely even register what I am seeing. I focus only on the path in front of me and keep my eyes and ears open for something, anything out of place.

Now that Selvia is out of the forest, it has gone silent once again. Every snap of a branch under my booted feet sounds a thousand times louder than usual. I am not particularly quiet whenever I do visit the forest, but it doesn't normally sound this loud. I flinch when a particularly large branch breaks underneath me as I jump onto and off it. It was more rotten than I realized; one of my feet catches in the hole, and I fall on my face.

Angry, I get up, brush myself off briskly, and move forward more slowly. Time is passing, and I still haven't done anything. How am I supposed to get that gold coin if the forest won't do something for me? If I end up out of here late, I wonder if Mitac will give me a time allowance for helping Selvia out. That wasn't Quest time, after all.

"Anytime now!" I yell, turning my face up to the dense canopy. I'm confident no one can hear me since I couldn't hear Selvia until I could see her. Nothing responds to my angry yell, not that I expected something to. "Gah, what a waste of time! Let me leave, already! I'm not going to take the magic!"

More silence. Meh, it was worth a try. I wonder if anyone else thought to try it.

I keep walking, looking this way and that. I see some movement off to my right and halt my progress to watch. It doesn't look human. I pull both knives off my belt and hold them steady in my hands. Typically, there's nothing too big in this forest. The worst peril you'll find is getting lost in the cold or stumbling too close to an elk. I am neither cold nor lost, at least as far as I know, and the moving thing is not tall enough to be an elk.

The thing to my right keeps moving forward, occasionally stopping to smell the air as if hunting something. Most likely me. There's no discernible breeze where I am, so I cannot tell if I am upwind or downwind from the animal. It looks big enough that I think I would prefer not to have an encounter with this creature. Climbing or running seems to be my best choice. Running will create too much noise, and I fear I will bring the creature directly to me. I look around, and a lot of broad trees great for hiding behind greet me, but not even one looks good for climbing. I'm not a strong climber, but it's also doubtful that whatever is hunting will be frightened of my two little knives. I'm hopefully a better climber than this hulking figure.

I back away very carefully from the path, keeping a close eye on the animal and trying to watch where my feet are stepping.

I worry my heart is pounding loud enough to be heard by the animal on the hunt, even if my occasional missteps aren't. I've managed to get off the path and further into the depths of the forest as I search for a suitable tree. I look behind me again, I don't see the animal, but I'm not dumb enough to be relieved…yet. I turn back to watch where I'm going, and run directly into a smaller tree in front of me. This is not a good day for me and obstacles.

I examine the tree, paying particularly close attention to how far I will have to go to get to some sturdy branches. I hear some crashing in the forest behind me and decide the time for inspection has passed. It will have to do. I quickly stash my knives and start trying to climb the tree.

It's slow-going, with many starts and stops and several embarrassing falls back to the ground. My boots may have a decent sole, but they're not made for climbing trees.

Finally, I make it to the first sturdy limb, but the animal turns off the path and takes the same path I did to get to the tree. If I keep climbing, I am sure I will draw its notice. If I stop, I leave myself open to anything that can reach up to about six feet. I hedge my bets and stop here, judging the limb strong enough to hold me. The hulking figure walks into a sun ray, and I see with alarm that it is a sizable brown bear. It has massive paws with long, sharp claws. My heart is hammering harder in my chest.

The bear smells the air again with its black nose, scrunching its muzzle, which pulls its lips up, revealing large teeth. My heart nearly falters in fright. It's as though I can feel the teeth sinking into my flesh now.

I try to think if I have ever heard any facts about how to avoid bears, but nothing comes to mind. I curse myself for not listening to Cardis' droning about some book or another he read. Somewhere in there, I bet he had read something about bears and told us all about it. And I listened not one bit. A mistake, I realize, but who knew a place with no bears would suddenly spawn a freaking bear?!

The brown beast sniffs around where I was on the path, and I stay as still as possible. I don't know much, but I do know bears can climb. I also know that this bear will be taller than six feet when on its hind legs, not good. I contemplate my options. If I climb further, I may not climb fast enough to get out of the reach of this thing's gnarly claws or, worse, slide to the ground altogether. If I jump and run, I will only make it chase me. I would love to think it's not interested in me, but it's already retracing the steps I took minutes ago. I don't think it has spotted me yet, but my smell will lead it to me. If not the scent of me walking through the brush, then the smell of the copious amount of sweat I'm suffering from. I can't take on a bear alone, I'm going to die out here. I know it. I decide my best option is to go down fighting.

I crouch on the branch, leaning on the trunk to keep me steady, and quietly release my knives from my belt. My palms are sweaty, and I almost drop one to the ground. I take a couple of steadying breaths, doing my best to calm myself. I need all the adrenaline I can get for what's coming, and it won't do me any good to panic now. The bear is taking a direct path through the forest where I walked. As it approaches my tree, I stand on my limb. I send a prayer up to the Celestials to make sure my body can be found, and take a deep breath…

A LONG TIME AGO...

Aerith

It's report time. Anxiety twists my gut. I run through every possible excuse I could use to get out of it or delay it. I'm still not sure what I'm going to do.

I could make an excuse, tell them that the call of the Celestials is on me to dream right this moment, but then I would definitely be asked for a more thorough report the moment I finished. I contemplate what I am going to do. The only sound I hear is the panic in my thoughts and the swishing of my purple skirts. Mancio is walking softly beside me as we head to the meeting chamber.

All of us Dreamers come with our apprentices if we have them. I hate that I lied to him earlier, but I was hoping I would have a little more time before report was called. Usually, we meet once every two weeks to fill in what we have seen since our last meeting. It has only been a week since our last report, which must mean the leaders have reason to believe that one of us has something of interest. Is it possible that it's only because of the Quest? Or is something going on in one of the other Vales? I hope this is the case. Anything to take the focus off me.

The cream-colored marble halls, which normally seem so long, feel so short today as dread and indecision settle into my gut. I hear slightly raised voices, and my name, in the last hallway before the doors to the room. I hold out my arm to stop Mancio when I recognize one of them to be the Orange Illume. I signal to him to be quiet so we can hear.

"What if it *is* time?" I hear him ask someone.

"Then we will do what we must." It's the voice of the Black member. He's the unofficial leader of the Council. Usually, whichever way he decides to go, the rest of them do as well. He's also the one Council member to fly off the handle and make rash decisions. Usually, those decisions aren't towards me, so I haven't been bothered by it...until now.

"Would it not be wise to try to guide this person?" the Orange asks, almost pleading. "To help them rather than stop them?"

The Black laughs darkly. "No, it would not. You've read the history books. When has this ever gone well?"

"No one has tried to guide them, though. If we can..."

"No! They cannot be guided. They never have been, and I will not have the Illume, and this land, taken out by them!" Someone's fist hits one of the walls in the hallway, and I jump. I suspect it's the Black. "We are not prepared, we are not ready, not yet!"

"But how are we going to reset—"

The Black interrupts. "It's not for us to worry about. We must take care of this person. At once. The same way the earlier Illume Councils should have. They all died, you know. Do you want to die?"

Reset? Reset what?

"Well, no." The Orange sounds defeated, resigned.

"Come, this is no place to discuss such sensitive topics." Feet start shuffling away from us.

The Black's voice slowly fades as he continues, "We identify them and take them out before they take us out. Come on, we need to get to the meeting and find out what the Purple has been up to. She should have—"

I can guess what I should have done. What I *should* have done was notify the Council. What I *should* have done was not listen to Naseem. However, it turns out that what I did was exactly what I needed to do.

I stay where I am, Mancio waiting next to me with wide eyes. "What was that about?" he whispers. "What do they think you've been up to?"

I shake my head. "I don't know," I lie.

They're talking about one of the kids I've been having visions of. I can nearly guarantee it. My indecision resolves itself as I realize... Naseem was right. The Illume can't be reasoned with. Not right now. And it sounds like the Black knows what's going on already. How can I reason with someone who has more information than I do?

⁓

Two dark Black Warrior guard the white double doors for the Illume's meeting room. Their eyes glance over us, reading through us; their black eyes so dark they seem like holes into their souls. They are probably the darkest of their kind. The Illume members must be kept safe, so it only makes sense they keep the strongest Warriors themselves. They confirm who we are with visual and voice recognition and swing the doors open to permit us entry.

The round room is about thirty feet in circumference. In the center, a large rectangular redwood table stands, polished so perfectly that you can see your reflection. Behind the table are ten high-backed chairs with red velvet cushions and gold inlay on the redwood frame. Each spot is currently empty, but this is not unusual. The Council always enters after the rest of us have arrived. Sometimes, we wait a few moments. Other times, we wait for more than an hour.

This has always bothered Naseem, who is a little too impatient to be sitting around waiting to give report.

The tall walls that make up the room are full of large round windows of varying sizes. Almost like bubbles in a bubble bath, only the walls are tan, not blue. The carpet here is also tan, giving the illusion that the walls have bled paint onto the floor or that the floor has started crawling the walls. The other four file in shortly after I arrive. They must have been in their quarters. Mancio and I had been on our way to the kitchens to get a snack when we were summoned. Both of our talismans turned ice cold, and we turned around and headed back the way we had come. We didn't even have to say anything to each other. We both knew what to do.

I smile at each of my fellow seers in turn. They give smiles back, even if some of them are forced. Naseem's smile is genuine, though.

We gravitate toward each other; our apprentices begin chatting with each other. Given the amount of time Naseem and I spend talking, our apprentices have made friends with each other as well. Thankfully, this leaves Naseem and me free to chat.

"Is this about you?" she asks me.

"I would bet that it is," I reply quietly.

She shakes her head, her curly yellow hair falling out of its bun. I smile. Naseem's hair has always been a point of contention with the Illume. She is supposed to be prim and proper. We all are. She never took that lesson well.

I reach over and help pin it back in place like so many times before. I cast a furtive glance at both sets of doors. The ones we came in and the ones the Council will come in. The guard at the entry door is standing at rest, so I assume I have a few minutes to fill Naseem in.

I take a deep breath. "I heard the Orange and Black members talking before I got here. They were talking about 'taking care of' someone and in a permanent way." Her yellow eyes flash in surprise. "I think it's probably about one of the kids I've been dreaming about."

"How many more visions have you had since we talked?" she asks earnestly, her words rushed.

"A couple. This morning, I saw someone entering the forest for the Quest. Today."

Naseem gasps, and a couple of the others glance our way. She gives a little chuckle as though I told a funny story, effectively throwing them off. They return to their own conversations. "You saw the past?"

"No, I saw it as it was happening. In real time."

She contemplates this. "A dream, in real time. What's the purpose of that?"

"The same question I've been asking myself," I mutter. "I thought maybe you would have an idea."

"No clue, Aerith. It's always been future stuff for the rest of us. I don't know how you Purple Dreamers work. The more you tell me, the clearer it is that we know nothing of your craft."

"They also said previous Councils should have done what they planned to do and dispose of this person or people. The fact that they didn't ultimately led to their death, and they aren't going to make the same mistake." Naseem continues to stare at me in silence. "The Orange also said something about resetting something. I don't know what that means."

Naseem takes a deep breath and, in a hushed, reverent voice, "It is time."

"Time for what?" Naseem shakes her head, clearly reluctant to share anything more.

"Naseem, please," I beg, "Please tell me what is going on. This girl, probably the others, they're going to be in danger if I don't do something, right? Or maybe if I do. What are we looking at here?"

She looks around, her yellow eyes wild. "I can't tell you everything, mostly because I don't know everything. A long time ago…"

The guard at the Council entry door shifts position to a stiffer stance. They are on their way in.

"Later," she hisses as we scurry back to our positions. Naseem casts me a worried glance, and I give her a sad smile. I hope, beyond all hope, that I can fool the men and women streaming into the room now.

...THIS QUEST IS UNPRECEDENTED.

Aerith

The Illume enter the room in a single-file line. They're dressed in their finest. While we wear silks, the Council wears blood-red velvet cloaks, the silks underneath matching their respective magic, or lack thereof. The Unchanged representative wears a cream color, dark enough not to be mistaken for White, not dark enough to be mistaken for Brown. The idea is that everyone is represented equally, and therefore, no one magic has more control than any other.

Technically, everyone in the Realm also has a say in who represents them. Every two years, the whole Illume is put up for re-election, and occasionally, there are those who challenge for positions and those who die between elections. The problem that even I have noticed is that the voting only takes place in Amiket City. Anyone who wants to vote from an outlying area must come here to do so. For most, this is not a feasible task, which means those outside of the city do not end up choosing their representative. Those running for position focus all their efforts on keeping the citizens of Amiket City happy, especially the rich ones. As a result, everyone in this group taking their seats in front of us is a noble. Not one layperson has ever held this position of power.

Each representative takes their seat according to their magic: Red, Orange, Yellow, Green, Blue, Brown, Black, White, and Unchanged.

There is no Purple, of course, since so few of us exist, and as the only magic we have is dreaming anyway, there's not much we need representation for. Although, considering what I am about to do, it would be nice if someone up there was automatically on my side. At least in theory.

"You are probably wondering why we have called a special session," the Red states. I nod alongside the other Dreamers. I am relieved to see that the others look confused. Maybe the details of my secret are safe.

"We have reason to believe that this Quest is unprecedented, so we want to check in with all of you to see if there's anything we should know," he clarifies for everyone.

This is what I was worried about, and I break out in a sweat. I was already pretty sure what our discussion would be about today, but the last of my hope officially fizzles like a match put underwater. Deep, deep, underwater.

If they know I have been dreaming of something and didn't share, why call a whole meeting? For my humiliation? To drag it out? To make an example of me?

As is normal, the Council goes in order of color. Red and Orange have no Dreamers, so Naseem is the first to speak. When the Yellow woman calls her, she steps forward with her apprentice, as is customary, and they kneel. When acknowledged by the Council, Naseem and her apprentice stand with their hands folded behind them.

"Nothing to report," she says flatly, bored. "I see nothing ominous in the weather."

The Illume look at each other and nod, clearly pleased with this result. The Yellow Council member waves her back. Naseem and her apprentice duck their heads and return to their place. Naseem resumes looking bored, but I catch her gaze drifting toward me when others are not paying attention.

What was she about to tell me when the Council interrupted us? She has answers and it's frustrating knowing I cannot get them from her. I make it my mission to seek her out as soon as is safe after this meeting.

Wynn is called forward with his apprentice by the Blue man at the table, skipping over the Green woman with no seer to call. Wynn and his apprentice also kneel and stand, hands clasped behind their backs.

"I have nothing to share." His stance is wide, confident, his voice a natural booming sound, like waves crashing on the rocks. "I see no changes with the water at this time."

The Illume again nod and dismiss them. They return to their places.

The Black and Orange look bored, and I catch them staring directly at me more than once, but I keep my eyes averted. I try to pretend to be interested in the other reports, as I have been so many times before. And also try not to let on that I know why this session was convened.

Poriforio, called forward by the Brown, is next to report on land changes. He, too, has nothing, followed by Batair. My hopes rise. If anyone would have anything to take the heat and attention off me, Batair would be the one to do it. Usually, the Council eats up what he has to say and barely pays attention to my reports. Of course, my reports have always been devoid of anything worthwhile.

"I have seen some disturbances coming from outside threats." The Council erupts in a quiet buzz behind the table. "As well as inside threats." The murmuring grows louder. I hope that the men and women up there will forget about me altogether. Especially if only two of them are aware of anything. I am sweating profusely, but I hope my discomfort isn't noticeable from a distance. Unfortunately, silk isn't great at hiding nervous sweats.

"What kind of threats, Batair?" the Black asks his charge.

Batair shakes his head. "Too soon to tell, the dreams are weak and ill-formed. I hope to have more for you next week at our regular meeting."

He emphasizes the word "regular" which makes me flinch. Clearly, he's trying to make it understood to everyone in the room that they would have more answers if they didn't call meetings outside the normal ones. Batair is the only one who could pull off that kind of thinly veiled reprimand without getting thrown into solitary. The Black member stares at him momentarily before dismissing him and his apprentice back to his normal place.

"Perhaps we should adjourn?" the Unchanged woman asks. "To discuss these possible threats?" The Black looks over at her and she quails under his glare.

"Call your Dreamer forward, Imrian," he orders, skipping over the White who also has no Dreamer.

She waves us forward. Mancio walks beside me, myself on shaking knees, and we complete the ritual of respect to those at the table. My mind is spinning for what to share. If I say nothing, then Mancio is liable to contradict me, which would certainly get me in trouble. If I report what I have seen, then Mancio will be confused, and the girl I have seen will likely be in trouble. If I try to lie and they catch me, I am not sure what the consequence will be, but I am positive it will be unpleasant. I feel dizzy when I stand again.

I decide my best option is to tell them the same story I gave to Mancio and hope it's enough to prevent raising eyebrows.

I am thankful I can hide my shaking hands behind my back. "I have seen something, but it's not yet clear what it might mean." I lean into Batair's defense. I'm proud of myself for coming up with a plan so quickly. I give the impression that if I have more time, I will be able to present something more complete. It's not totally untrue, I have seen an incredibly detailed dream, but it is also incomplete. I don't intend to share any of it with them though if I can help it.

Most of the Illume look shocked, and I hear gasps from behind me. Never before have I had anything to share, and they look rightfully uneasy. All except Orange and Black. So, I was right. They are the only ones who knew I would have anything to share. Imrian, the Unchanged Council member and theoretically "my" representative, waves me on. "Tell us what you have seen so far."

I gulp. Now it's time to lie.

"I saw a boy," I clear my throat, trying to clear the wavering in my voice, "he must be sixteen or seventeen, obviously, as he was entering the Quest. He looked quite nervous, maybe a little excited." I stop. They wait expectantly for more.

"What else?" The Black Council member asks, clearly expecting something far more than what I have provided.

"What did he look like?" Orange asks while Red asks, "Which place was he entering?"

I search my brain for which question is safe to answer. It appears my first lie caught them so off-guard they didn't sense it was a lie, but I must tread carefully, or I will surely give myself away. I decide to start with the where.

"It was the Amaranth Forest," I try to calm my heart, present confidence. That is truthful, so I hope I stay under the Black Warrior's radar. He's staring at me with those black eyes. I feel an unpleasant prickling along my skin. Magic? Or my imagination?

They gasp. "Amaranth?! When was the last time we had someone from the forest who was significant?"

"Could it truly be time?"

"There have been other concerning signs."

The Illume are talking amongst and all over themselves, thankfully, and not directly to me. I am not paying attention to who is speaking. All I can feel is the strange sensation on my skin and the pounding of my heart. At the sound of "other signs," I snap out of it. I wonder if that's what Black and Orange were discussing in the hallway. I wait to be dismissed, hoping they will forget they had asked other questions and want to retreat to solitude to discuss.

"If it is, we need to do something right away—"

Black cuts off the Yellow and calls the meeting back to order. "What else can you tell us, Aerith?" he reiterates. His voice is stern, and I think this is the first time anyone behind the table in front of me has ever used my name.

I shake my head. "Nothing. I told you I didn't have a complete dream to share yet."

Kind of true, kind of not. I can share more, but I don't want to. So, technically, I don't have anything else to share. My palms are clammy, and it feels like I am standing directly under the sun for how hot it feels in the room. Everyone else appears perfectly comfortable so I know it's only me.

The Illume discuss and murmur to each other. They keep their voices low, so I cannot hear what they are saying. Finally, they break up their little sidebar. The Unchanged waves me off. I nearly collapse right then and there, but I manage to calmly back away from the Council to my spot and try to keep my face stoic, Mancio by my side.

"We will meet as normal next week," the Green dismisses us, and relief rushes through me. "We hope you will have more for us then." She looks pointedly at Batair and me. "Until then, we will get in touch with our Gophers in Amaranth and check in on our borders."

Relief quickly gives way to fear again. If there are no males who come from the forest Changed, I am in so much trouble. My lie will be very clearly revealed. I desperately wish I could get hold of the Gophers there to get them to extend my lie. However, it will take a few days for the message to reach Rothesard and another week to get to Ashadier, the furthest forest village from the train stop. Then another ten days to get a response… Of course, if they are already on their way back on the train…I have, at most, three days before the jig is probably up. Having not visited Amaranth, I am not sure which village exactly the girl is from. If I'm lucky, it's Ashadier. My head is starting to hurt. No matter what kind of mental gymnastics I do, I need a game plan and quickly.

OVERACTIVE IMAGINATION?

Mitac

So far, fifty of the fifty-eight kids who went into the forest this morning have come out. All Unchanged, to my relief. It is now nearing noon, and I still have not seen Eloise. I am feeling better about having hidden the gold coin in her pack. It doesn't look like she's going to win it from our bet, and I would rather she have it. I could see the stress on her aunt's and uncle's faces when they were buying goods at the market. They were pinching their bronzes to make them last, and my chest ached. I know exactly how that feels.

The Healer, whose name I had learned is Kinta, set Selvia up with a lounging-type chair that kept her leg up, and she is snoozing in the shade. She'd had quite the morning. I unwrap a pastry I bought from the pie shop in town and eat mindlessly. It is delicious, like the previous day's pastry, but the disquiet I have about Eloise's fate causes it to turn to dust in my mouth. A swallow of water from my canteen doesn't help much.

I have no reason to be worried about her. People had stayed in the Quest for much longer than she had been in there already, but something is nagging in the back of my mind, and I don't like it. That warning I gave her yesterday to be careful, the voice in my head reminding me she's in danger; I don't like any of it. That voice has a horrible track record of being right.

I am tempted to send Chance in to see if she can find her, but I would be breaking at least half a dozen Quest rules if I did so, the biggest one being not to interfere with the Quest itself. I wrap up the other half of the pastry.

A kid comes bolting out of the forest looking terrified. "Bear!" he yells loudly. He stops a hundred feet outside of the forest, doubled over and panting. "I barely escaped!"

My anxiety ratchets up. I look at the forest. A bear? The forest and all of the testing areas are supposed to assess the kids enough to reveal their magic but not put them in imminent danger. A bear would be imminently dangerous.

I approach the boy at the same time Kinta does. He's shivering violently. Kinta deftly pulls a small vial from the pouch on her hip and hands it to the boy. He uncorks it and downs the blue liquid in a quick gulp. A sense of peace seems to overtake him. I glance at Kinta and wonder if I can get some of those for myself.

She catches the direction of my gaze. "Potion of Calm," she explains. "I make a large amount on Quest day. Kids get scared, and this helps."

"Do you often have scares like this?" I ask but then clarify, "With bears or large predators?"

She shakes her head. "No. Usually, kids get scared because of the Quest itself, not after the Quest unless they think they're Changed."

I nod. "What do you make of this?"

She shrugs. "I don't know. Overactive imagination?"

"I'm not imagining it!" the boy exclaims loudly, his shivering reduced to mild tremors. I had forgotten he was nearby. "Do you imagine this?" He shows us his pants, which appear to have a big tear in them from multiple sharp objects.

"Okay, not imagination. How did you get away?" I ask, feeling like his story has actual merit.

"I was near the exit when it showed up. I was already running full out to leave and it chased me. It swiped at me, but then it quickly turned and left like it was after something else. I bolted out before it decided it wanted to play some more."

"Are you injured?" the Healer asks, suddenly all business. She looks him over closely as do I. She is looking for injuries, while I am looking for skin, hair, or eye changes. Neither of us see what we are looking for.

"You can go," I tell the boy, "when Kinta says you're clear."

I walk off away from the two of them to find Chance. She is crouched, bored, by the edge of the forest. The excitement of the boy bursting out interested her only minimally.

"Did you catch that?" I ask her.

She nods, not even bothering to get up. "A bear."

"Yes, a bear. What do you make of it?"

She shrugs. "No idea. I've never heard of Quests causing serious harm. Usually, if the kids get hurt, it's because they didn't pay attention and fell or hurt themselves in some way. The weapons they take in are for hunting, not for defense."

I think back to my own Quest. "I needed mine for defense." Chance jerks her head to look at me.

"Really?" she asks.

I nod. "A boy came out of nowhere and tried to attack me. I fought back until I managed to disable him. Then he disappeared, and I turned Black." That's the short version of it. It sounds so much cleaner than what had actually happened.

My Quest had shaken me, truthfully. In Delja, our Quest took place in the ocean. At dawn, we all rushed from our places on the beach to take our chances. We swam out at great distances from one another, which turned out to be completely unnecessary. With even minor swells, it was easy to lose sight of the others.

Some of the kids dived down, but I preferred to stay on the surface. I bobbed, feeling quite stupid for a while. Suddenly, another boy came out of nowhere. No one I recognized, but given my travels to different areas, I didn't take the time to get to know the people in all the places I stayed. I had started to ask him what he thought we should be doing when he tried attacking me. His knife appeared, almost like magic, and he started slashing at me. I swam away as fast as I could, but he would not stop coming at me.

I talked to him, tried to reason with him. I thought he was another kid on his Quest. Maybe confused. I was exhausted from swimming, so I pulled my knife, flashing it at him in warning. He paused momentarily before he came at me again. I got lucky and was able to grasp his wrist. He dropped the knife, but another appeared in its place. A dagger with a serrated edge. In the end, I lost my innocence that day. His blood stained the water and my mind's eye. To this day, I still dream of his lifeless body.

It didn't matter that precisely like he appeared, he disappeared. It didn't matter that he was probably an illusion. That day, I discovered a dark piece of myself. A shadow that I worked very hard never to let out again.

Once he disappeared, I turned Black as a moonless midnight sky, and a voice boomed that my Quest was over. I never left the ocean so fast in all my life. To this day, I still don't like combat or killing. I don't like being in or on the ocean, either. It causes debilitating flashbacks.

"Well, maybe we have a Green in there whose specialty is taming wild animals?" Chance offers. "Or a Warrior?"

"Could be, but why would it attack someone else? None of this makes any sense."

"Dunno."

Chance's curt answers are frustrating. Normally, I appreciate her lack of chatter, but at this moment, I would have preferred someone to spitball ideas with me. She's perfectly okay with everything, but then again, she doesn't have this voice in her head screaming about danger like I do. That would make a difference, I'm sure, but I won't share it with her. I don't need my partner thinking I've gone round the bend.

"Maybe something has gone seriously wrong with this Quest." I shift my weight, foot to foot, antsy to contact someone in the city to report this and see if there have been other instances. The idea that maybe we have a Green in the forest is one thing, but the Quest is individualized to the participant. Why would the bear attack someone whom it wasn't targeting? I don't think it should even appear until it's needed.

I look over at Kinta and the boy. She must have released him because he is nowhere to be seen, and she is sitting in the shade again. I look at Selvia, who is still sleeping. She must have slept through the whole thing. Suddenly, I wonder if the Healer gave her something for sleep. I would take one of those, too, along with a bottle for calm.

I return to my table and put a checkmark next to his name on the list, hoping Eloise's is the next name I can mark off.

BEST LAID PLANS...

Eloise

I watch the bear as it stalks closer to my spot. It is stalking my scent, I know now. Heck, even I can smell the fear coming off of me. The knives are tight in my hands, ready for my feeble plan. When the bear gets directly below my tree, it pauses, smelling around it, recognizing the scent but noticing it dissipates.

My hope that it will give up disappears as it looks upward and spots me on my little limb. It stands up on its back legs, and my heart stops. So does my brain. All thoughts of my grand plan flee in fright. I'm lucky my bladder doesn't give out.

It's colossal, so much bigger up close. It growls, its black eyes menacing, its breath overwhelmingly terrible. I nearly fall backward off the limb but maintain my composure by merely a hair.

The bear pulls its massive paw, and I scarcely manage to lift my legs quickly off the limb and scurry around the backside of the tree. This is what I was expecting, but it's no less frightening because I had an idea it was coming. The claws demolish my safe landing place, turning it into chunks and splinters. It leaves me unharmed, but one of my knives slips from my hand and falls uselessly to the ground. I'm panting and desperately trying to hold onto the tree. My boots keep slipping, and I'm slowly sliding down.

I curse myself for not stowing the knives. Fortunately, the second one stays trapped between my palm and the bark, but it doesn't allow me a whole lot of purchase with the tree. Maybe I should have jammed the knives into the tree, like handholds. So far, the plan is going...not well.

"Curse the Celestials!" I yell as my legs slip from the tree. The bear has repositioned underneath me, preparing to rise and swipe at me again. Not giving it a chance, I push back from the tree a little, and drop onto its back, my one knife positioned point down to stab it in the neck. Unfortunately, its skin and fur are thicker than I expect, and my knife barely scratches the beast. *Best laid plans.* I would have expected it to be a bit thinner coming out of winter hibernation, but it looks like this bear has been busy fattening back up.

The animal immediately rises on its hind legs in surprise, roaring loudly. I latch my arms around its neck, trying to keep hold of my knife in the process, but the bear shakes me off like a fly it can't be bothered with.

If only I could fly... I do fly, but not gracefully. I hit a large fallen tree trunk with a painful thump. I'm seeing stars, but I have managed to keep hold of my one remaining knife. I quickly scramble over the fallen tree and hide behind it, hoping the bear will give up. It's not to be my luck today, however. It takes only a few seconds for the beast to locate me again, and it turns its ferocious snarl my way.

I hold my knife in front of me, preparing for death, my hand shaking. The bear approaches slowly as though sensing I am stuck. I could probably make a run for it if my brain were working properly, but all I can think about is my family and how they will make it without me. Even if I did have my wits about me, I am sure this thing can run faster than I can, and it has already proven it can climb better than me.

The bear stalks closer until I can see the individual hairs in its fur. Its black eyes aren't black at all but a deep dark brown with a few gold flakes. The bear's eyelashes are long and fine, and if it weren't for being eaten by it, I would pet this bear and be friends with it.

I shake my head. Is this what happens at the end of your life? You start noticing things that don't matter? I thought your life was supposed to flash before your eyes.

An inexplicable impulse makes me duck, right on time, too. The bear swipes at me as I do. My knife was still pointed toward it, and I manage to stab the bear's paw. The knife does its job; it sticks well but then is flung off into the forest. There goes my last hope of defense and attack.

As afraid as I am, I try to keep my eyes on the animal. I am not going down like a coward. I look it dead in the eye, attempting to scare it off, but I am sure if it could laugh, it would. I swear it's smiling at me.

I stare it down. "Well, get on with it if you're going to eat me."

It cocks its head at my voice and freezes, its mouth open and ready to bite the arm I have lifted in front of me.

"Just, please, leave enough of my body for my family to identify me," I murmur quietly. I'm not sure if it's a prayer to the Celestials or a plea to the bear.

The bear must have heard me, and it looks confused. Then, it suddenly sits on its haunches and licks the wound on its foot. I stare, more confused than the bear at the sudden change of tactic. What is this? Some kind of bear game to play with its food? Give the meal a sense of safety before eating it?

I'm shaking, but I lower my arm. The bear seems entirely engrossed in its paw. I test out trying to stand up and groan in pain; my back is beyond pissed by being thrown into a tree. The bear looks over at me, and I freeze partly upright. It blinks a few times at me, but it makes no move to get nearer to me nor to attack me. I stand the rest of the way upright and watch it.

I don't know if the bear forgot about me or if it lost interest in food that fights back. How long is the attention span of a bear? I will have to ask Cardis when I get out of here. Either way, it limps off back the way it came and disappears around the bend I had walked down earlier. I watch it stalk off, and after ensuring it isn't returning, I lean against the tree and sigh in relief.

My legs nearly give out again when I see the chunks of the fallen pine tree it had taken out. That could have been my head. I thank the Celestials whom I was cursing earlier and head back to where I last saw my knife. So much for us only needing our weapons for hunting. How about for not dying? If I ever meet anyone from the Council, I will be sure to tell them they misinformed all of us about how "safe" the Quest is. And possibly also kick them between the legs. For good measure.

I find the knife I dropped fairly quickly but it takes me about twenty minutes of searching to find the one the bear flung into the bushes. I refuse to leave without it, given my most recent encounter. I clean both off on my pants and put them back on my belt before sitting on a nearby tree stump to let my adrenaline come back to normal.

As it fades, I shiver, and my teeth chatter. I pull my cape tight around me. I feel absolutely exhausted now, but I don't have time to stop. There's a gold coin in the balance. I look up again; the sun is no longer visible above me. It must have dropped to the other side which, I realize with dismay, means I have been in here more than six hours.

I howl in frustration. "Dang it! I lost the bet!" I stare at the canopy above me and yell, "Can I be done now?"

The forest either doesn't hear me or has no interest in letting me go yet. I take a deep breath and get up off the stump with a groan. Onward, then, I guess.

I pick my way back to the path and continue forward. I wonder if it's wise to continue on the path when, so far, I haven't had anything but bad luck on it. It's still the easiest way forward, though, and I want to get this over with. As I walk, I stop in my tracks.

"Oh no," I moan as realization hits me. "Oh no, oh no."

ONE FOR ONE?

Saada

I have been sitting outside in the weather for the last ten hours, waiting to see Eloise come out. I have seen person after person come out Unchanged and return happily to their families. I have watched the Gopher's exchange with the Amiket orphanage crone. As much as it begrudges me, he gained a little bit of respect from me for stopping her and finding a way to save sweet Selvia from her clutches.

I had seen Selvia around the village a couple of times, running errands, but she never stopped to socialize. I realize now that it wasn't necessarily her choice. I vow to make it a point to help at the orphanage in my spare time and keep a closer eye on those poor kids. One day, my own could be there. I rub my chest where a sharp pain blooms at the thought.

"Dear Celestials, please don't let that be so."

I chew on my fingernails with worry. On my Quest, I was able to leave within a couple of hours. My tests arose quickly. Bile rises in my throat as the memories threaten to overtake me again. I push them away and swallow hard.

I'm not sure what to make of the fact that Eloise still hasn't appeared. When the boy came running out yelling about a bear, I grew even more anxious. That was hours ago, and still more people have come out, but no Eloise.

The Gopher is pacing. He, too, looks nervous, although it's hard to tell what he is nervous about. By all accounts, his job here is easy.

To take my mind off Eloise's absence, I get up from my spot on a tree stump in the Clearing and walk over to him. Cardis watches me before turning his attention back to the book he and Selvia are reading on Kinta's porch.

"Hey," I greet the Gopher, and he turns to face me. I can tell he is surprised to see me here. I am a little surprised to see myself here, but I cannot sit around any longer. "Thanks for helping Selvia." I gesture to the girl.

He shrugs. "It's nothing. It's the least I can do."

I shake my head. "No, it's really not. This town and I should have been doing more all along."

"Don't blame yourself. People like that woman," he hooks his thumb over his shoulder in the direction of the orphanage, "know exactly what to do to keep control of their underlings and control their image." A shadow crosses the Gopher's face.

"Oh. Well, thank you anyway." I wonder how he knows about this kind of person. I've never met anyone like that in Ashadier. I glance around nervously at the forest, and he turns to look. Another girl has come out.

"Excuse me for a second." He turns and walks to the girl and checks her over. He directs her to the few remaining bags, and she trots over to pick hers up and runs off to her waiting family. Tears collect in my eyes. *Where are you, Eloise?*

The Gopher comes back to me, his walk confident, but I can tell he's getting tired. "How many are still inside?" I ask, trying not to betray my anxiety.

He picks up his list from the table behind him. "Looks like we have three left."

"You're sure Eloise hasn't come out?" I fidget on my feet.

He gives me a knowing smile and sets his list back down. "I am sure. Chance would not have missed her."

"She missed Selvia going in, though; what's to say she didn't miss Eloise coming out?"

He stiffens at my implication but doesn't get angry. "What makes you think Eloise would have done anything other than go directly home?"

"Yes, you're right." I swallow back tears. "I'm sorry."

"I can't imagine how hard this must be. I would tell you to go home and relax, but I know that's not something you're going to do. Maybe you should send Cardis home?"

I smile. "You would be correct and Cardis isn't going to go home any more than I will."

He sits down and unfolds a small stool from under the table. "Have a seat, Saada. Tell me about your family while we wait."

I hesitate. I don't want to tell this man my story. The less the Gopher or anyone from the city knows about me and our family, the better.

"How about you tell me about yours?" I counter.

He thinks about it then nods. "You've got a deal. One for one?"

I nod and sit on the wooden stool, determined to keep my answers brief with as few details as I can get away with.

"I grew up in Delja," he starts when I show no indication of doing so. Delja, huh. I would not have placed him there. I always pictured him as maybe a Kahli kid. Something about him doesn't seem laid-back enough for Delja. At least, what I've heard about people from Delja. Laid back, friendly folks.

"It was only me, my parents, and my brother," he continues. "My parents died when I was nine. My brother went into the ocean four years later on the cusp of his seventeenth birthday, one of the youngest, and came out Black. He went to the city." Hurt flashes behind his eyes. I am about to ask what it's about when he sits back and smiles. "Your turn."

I take a deep breath and try to stick to basic information. "I grew up here," I wave around, "Never left. Never felt the need to. When my sister died, I took in her three kids, Eloise being one of them. None of us has ever Changed."

Not a lot to hunt us down with if he ever wanted to. Of course, he's been here for more than a day, so he's probably figured out everything he needs to know about us. If Amiket did ever have interest in us, I'm sure we would have to abandon Ashadier entirely. Normally, I wouldn't hesitate to tell someone about my family. I am proud of them.

My loving, optimistic husband, Gamet, works as much as he can to find clean water for the village and earn a living for us. Julieth is working hard and saving money to go see the Realm. Despite the troubles she has had, she has been free of drink for several months. As far as we know, at least. As much as it scares me, she's determined, and I love that about her. And now she's getting married. I may not like her choice of partner, but I'll support her to my dying day.

Eloise is practical, level-headed—most of the time—caring, and ultra-protective. Cardis is so smart none of us can quite keep up with him. He's itching to get out of Ashadier, too. As much as he doesn't see it as possible, I secretly think Julieth is waiting for him so she can take him with her.

Hilda and Gilda, my twin terrors who are full of life and spunk. And Leck, my soft-hearted baby. They're everything to me. Losing Leigha was so difficult, but having her kids helps. I get to see some of her in them every day, and I am so grateful to the Celestials for at least that.

Thinking about my family makes me more curious about his living family. "Where is your brother now? Do you work together?" I ask gently.

His smile slips before he has a chance to recover. "No, we don't. I don't know where he is."

"I'm sorry. Were you two close?" I feel sympathy for him. What would it be like to have family that you can't find?

"When we were younger, yes, we were close."

"What happened?" I had started asking more questions than answering to deflect from myself. Now, I'm asking because I'm genuinely interested.

He rubs the back of his neck. "When our parents died, he leaned hard on the parent role, and I resented him for trying to take their place."

I nod. "That's something I can understand. For a little while after Eloise, Julieth, and Cardis joined us, they had a tough time adjusting to our new family dynamics. I wasn't trying to take their parents' place, but I had to find a way to keep some kind of structure."

Those were wild days at first. Julieth was moody and emotional; she had multiple outbursts a day. When we discovered her new drinking habit, we came down hard on her. It made things so much worse. As much as we tried to control her, to keep her away from the friends leading her down a dark road, she kept finding a way. At one point, even running to them and staying with them. We tried to keep it from Eloise and Cardis. We explained she was having an extended stay with one of her friends. Luckily, they were young enough and caught up in enough of their own grief to buy the story.

When we saw her next, she was sobbing on our doorstep. Too afraid to knock. Too afraid we would turn her away. That was when we realized she needed a softer hand. We spent the next several years walking the fine line between discipline and grace. We weren't very good at it. As soon as her girlfriend found a place for the two of them, she left us. I worried for her. Whether she was doing okay. Elaxi was as much a part of the group that led her down the road of her addiction as anyone else. When she came over to bring dinner and announce her engagement, she looked bright-eyed and happy. It's all I can ask for.

Cardis had buried himself in his books, of which he only had two at the time, but he would read one, put it down, then start the other. Then start over again. Those two books, which had been old at the time, were falling apart before we could get him some more. He said he wanted to learn, so he focused on non-fiction books. Where I had wanted to read books to remove me from this world when I was younger, Cardis delved deeper into the reality of the world around him.

Eloise worried me the most at the time. She acted like nothing had happened at all. The only time she had any reaction was if we started to talk about her parents. Then, she would roundly shut down or leave the room. It took more than a year for us to get her to open up at all. When she had, it was still tightly controlled; she never let go completely. I was sure she still hadn't processed her loss. Her outbursts of anger rarely have to do with the matter at hand.

"I know," Mitac replies, pulling me from the past, "he was trying to do his best. He was twelve; he didn't know how to be a dad any more than I did. But I was a young, dumb kid who thought he should be allowed the freedom to make his own decisions and do whatever he wanted. He had his own ideas of what needed to be done. Things like working, finding food for us, a roof over our head…" The Gopher's voice cracks, and he swallows hard. I can tell this is painful for him. "He managed to keep our house for us. Until he went to the city."

I have a sudden urge to hug him, but I push it down. I remind myself that he's a Gopher and can't be trusted.

"When he came out of the ocean…I hated him. I spit at him when he left." He can't hide the regret from that decision, unshed tears shine brightly in his eyes.

"I'm sure he knows you love him," I say softly. "Family always knows."

"I should have told him, though. I shouldn't have let him leave without telling him to his face. I hope he knew I loved him."

The tense change doesn't get past me. "Knew?"

"Knows. Sometimes, it's easier to think of him as dead rather than that he never came back for me or looked for me."

I am about to hug him, after all, to try to soothe those aches when another girl jogs out of the forest. The Gopher gets up to check her out. I can sense he's steeling himself, putting on a façade before he gets to her. His shoulders straighten, and his back stiffens. I can't hear their conversation, but she must be Unchanged as he directs her to the few remaining bags off to the side and she takes off to her waiting family.

I begin biting my nails again. Terrible habit, and if my sister were here, she would scold me for doing so. Since she isn't here and it's her child I'm waiting for, I think she will find a way to forgive me this once.

I look back at Cardis. He's looking at the girl who left the forest, his face falling the same way mine probably had. Two more kids left. "Where are you, Eloise?" I ask softly. "Please come home soon."

...THE WORST GOPHER ANYONE HAS EVER SEEN.

Mitac

My chat with Saada was supposed to help keep her mind off her anxiety. While it may have helped with that, it brought back a lot of my past I preferred not to think about. I usher the girl off to her bag and her family before returning to where Saada sits waiting for me.

"So, tell me, Saada," I settle back into my seat. "What do you do for fun?"

She drops her fingers from her face; she looks surprised by the question. Or maybe she's surprised by the sudden change in conversational tone.

"Well, Gopher," she makes it a point to use my title instead of my name, "I don't have a lot of free time. Keeping six kids alive and the house going takes most of it."

"But surely you must do something for fun. For yourself or in the village?" It's been a long time since I've indulged in my hobbies, but I used to do a lot of manual work. Not only to live but for fun. My favorite jobs were the ones that got me working with my hands. Working on houses, fetching coconuts out of trees, repairing broken carriages…they were perfect jobs for me. Kept me busy and sometimes fed.

She chuckles. "Gopher, I'm going to forgive you your lapse of judgment, seeing as you never had a family to try to keep up."

I give her a thin-lipped smile. "No, but even when I was on my own, trying to keep away from people who wanted to put me in the orphanage, avoiding street thugs, trying to keep myself clean and fed and still go to school from time to time, I still found some form of fun." I bite it out with a little more vehemence than I mean to. Her face shows she's been wounded, but I am past caring. Sometimes, I get tired of people assuming I had an easy life. "And the name is Mitac, by the way, not Gopher."

She flinches. I stand again from my chair, not bothering to excuse myself, and walk away to find Chance. It's starting to get darker out, and I want to come up with a game plan for the night with two kids still in the forest.

"Chance," I call out to the motionless Green woman blending into the tree line. She stands up nimbly and comes over to me. "What's the plan for tonight?"

She looks thoughtful. "I hadn't given it much thought. I figured we would be long done by now. Should we go in after 'em?"

I shake my head. "Rules say we have to wait at least thirty-six hours before we go looking for dead or injured." I mentally recite the rules I had drilled into my head when I accepted this job:

Don't interfere with the Quest.

You must wait thirty-six hours before going to look for anyone.

If you enter and find they're on their Quest, you must leave them, no matter their state, to finish.

If you find someone injured after they have finished their Quest, you may bring them out.

And the biggest one I'd already come close to breaking:

Don't get familiar with the questers or their acquaintances.

Oops.

"No one in Amaranth ever takes that long," Chance reminds me, interrupting my run-through of the rules. She looks around as though expecting to see the remaining kids coming out.

"I know, but those are the rules. I won't compromise the Quest." I don't care about compromising it, more so that I don't want to run afoul of the Illume Council. In my short time in the capital, I have gotten quite used to having regular meals, a bed to sleep in, and a roof over my head. If I don't toe the line, even the ones that push the boundaries, I could be without a job. I'm not sure what I would do if I had to start over.

"Fine, I guess I can stay out here tonight," Chance sighs. "You take yourself and the tagalong back to the Inn for the night. Come back to relieve me at dawn."

Shit, Selvia. I had nearly forgotten about her. I will need to feed her soon. I tell Chance I will leave in a couple of hours and return around dawn. I turn and head back to check on Selvia. Saada has left my table, and I'm ashamed of how relieved I am by that fact. I'm not ready to go digging into my past some more. Something about her makes me want to open up. Not a good thing for someone like me.

Selvia and Cardis are talking to the Healer animatedly. As I approach, I hear them discussing the healing properties of some plant or another. Healing was never in my wheelhouse. It's nice to see Selvia so excited, though. She has been so subdued the whole day, clearly uncertain of her place. Now, however, she's debating with Cardis and Kinta with the best of them.

I smile when they look over at me. "Looks like you all are having fun."

"Yeah! Cardis has a delightful book!" Selvia turns the book to show me.

"I'm glad Cardis had something more interesting for you than sitting here waiting for me." She nods in agreement. "I've noticed it's getting late, though. Are you hungry?"

She nods again, more enthusiastically. "Okay, I'm going to see about getting us some food. Do you want to come with or stay?"

She looks longingly at the book, currently in Cardis' hands. "You can choose to stay," I reiterate. "I won't be offended."

"I'd like to stay." She makes a choice, but it's hesitant; her eyes are wide, and she's physically as far from me as possible. It's like she's never been allowed to choose for herself before. That might be the case, I remind myself. I head off to the baker and find him as he's getting ready to head my way with some more hand pies.

"I was worried you were going to forget to eat," he laughs. The apron he has wrapped around him today has multiple mysterious stains on it. Some of them red, like blood, but I assume this is from berries of some kind. At least, I hope it is.

I smile at him. "Thank you, sir. I need three pies tonight. I have an extra person to feed."

He opens the basket on his arm to show me a trio already nestled inside. "I heard what you did for Miss Selvia, and we are sure grateful. This one," he points to the one on top, "is for Selvia. When she thinks I'm not looking, she likes to come and take blackberries off the bush. This one is blackberry, goat cheese, and lamb. She'll love it."

I glance back at Selvia and then look at him in surprise. "She steals from you?"

He laughs heartily. "Don't arrest the poor girl! Is it stealing if I know it's happening and let her do it?"

I scratch my chin. "I guess not…" I wouldn't arrest Selvia anyway.

"She was likely being starved in that place, poor kid."

I nod. I'm touched by his thoughtfulness and reach into my leather pouch to pull out some bronzes. He takes his spare hand and lays it over mine. "Nonsense, you don't get to pay."

"Please, sir, I want to. Your pies are the best I've had in an exceptionally long while, probably since my mother's. It's only right that I pay you for them."

"I won't hear of it. You've been kind to this village since you've gotten here. The best Gopher I've ever seen."

Which, by the city's accounts, would make me the worst Gopher anyone has ever seen.

I duck my head and put back my coins. "Thank you very much." I retrieve the pies from the basket. Still warm. "I'll be back early to trade places with my Tracker. What time will you be around?"

"Normally, I don't have anything to sell until an hour after dawn," Mr. Braswell answers, "but I'll have something ready for you early. Any requests, or would you prefer to be surprised?"

I contemplate the question for a moment. "Surprise me." I smile. "I have a feeling nothing you give me will be less than spectacular."

"You got it. I'll have three pies ready for you before dawn so your

Tracker can leave and get some rest." He's about to walk off when I stop him.

"Make it two," I order, "Selvia will be at the inn for breakfast."

"Got it, two surprise pies before dawn." He gives me a wide grin. What a kind soul.

"If you do this, I insist on paying for it."

"And I will insist on not letting you." He gives me another toothy grin before leaving with his basket and heading back towards what must be home.

I shake my head and return to Selvia and Cardis. Stubborn people, these Ashadierans. It's a wonder more Negotiators don't come from here. They seem to be mighty adept at it.

Back at Kinta's porch, I give Selvia a pie, and she smiles brightly as her stomach grumbles loudly. "Looks like I wasn't a minute too early," I chuckle. She giggles and takes a big bite. "Sorry, Cardis, I should have gotten you one!" I feel like a dunce. I completely forgot.

"No worries, sir, I've got food at home."

"Next time, Cardis, I'll get you one."

He only shrugs. So much for any goodwill I might have earned with him at any point.

"We are going to eat this and wait for dusk," I tell Selvia. "If all the kids haven't come out by then, you and I will go to the inn for some rest."

She frowns. "What about Chance? Where are the others?"

"Chance will stay here in case they come out overnight. Hopefully, they will come out before then."

"Why is it taking so long?" She spits a little food as she asks the question. "Sorry." A little more food comes out. I offer her a drink from the canteen, and she swallows. "Mistress always yelled at me for talking with my mouth full. When she allowed me to talk, that is." She looks down again.

"It's not polite, this is true, so it would be a good idea for you to learn how to wait until you swallow to speak." She looks like she's been slapped, and her overreaction reminds me of how poorly she's been treated. "But that can come with time, Selvia. No one is born perfect." She perks up a little, and I answer her earlier question. "The forest decides how it needs to test everyone. Sometimes it takes longer than others."

"Yes, but, it doesn't ever take this long around here," she points out, taking another big bite.

"I've heard that. We have to be patient." Easier said than done. I try not to let on that I'm worried.

I hear commotion at the forest's edge and turn to face it, hope flaring in my chest. A boy has come out, and I take my leave of Selvia to evaluate him, the hope petering out as quickly as it appeared. He's clearly Unchanged and I direct him to the two remaining bags. He grabs his and heads towards what must be home. Notably, no family is waiting for him. I check his name off my list.

I look over and see Saada back sitting on the stump. Cardis has moved back to the ground. She's staring after the boy, too. She looks over at me, and our eyes meet. I can sense her fear from here. One child left. Only Eloise and the sun is starting to set.

OH YES, RUNNING.

Eloise

How have I been so stupid? I've been out here, running around, looking for impossible situations to *avoid* them, and I have embraced two of them already. What. An. Idiot. Saada didn't tell me what would happen if I didn't run from all three. Would I still be able to block my magic? Will I get three more chances to block my magic? Do I only get three chances total, and it's best two out of three? How much trouble am I in already?

I feel nauseated and drop my head between my knees and breathe deeply. There's nothing I can do about the other two situations. I think back. One, for sure, was an impossible situation. The bear. No normal bear would leave helpless prey like that. I had to have used magic to tame it and get it to leave. Stupid.

The girl with the leg? Selvia, I think it was, that could be either way. I haven't heard of the Quest providing real people to assess people's magic. It seems much more likely that I happened upon Selvia, not that it was a magic situation presented to me. I feel slightly better with this thought. And I hope it's best two out of three. I examine the skin on my arms. No changes. I choose to view that as a good sign. All is not yet lost.

I stand up and groan. I'm sore from being flung against a tree stump, and my hands ache from holding onto my knives so tight…and the tree. Not to mention the cuts from the blackberry vines. This Quest isn't going the way I had hoped. I know that come tomorrow, I am going to hurt much worse. Experience with long hours of physical activity in the garden or helping Cardis with one of his projects has taught me this much.

I have to keep going, so I start walking down the path, again, daring the forest to bring about another challenge. Willing it to test me again. I won't fail this time; this time, I will run. Which will look like failing but would be me pushing down my magic. Success depends on my failure.

I continue my walk down the path, deeper into the forest. And I come to the opening with three paths again. Well, I did one and two, so maybe I need to take the left path this time. I feel defeated, but I press on.

Tall pine trees rise on either side of the game trail, their trunks, and roots obscured by the ferns and moss. For a long time, nothing happens. Absolutely nothing. Frankly, it's scarier than the bear was. How is it that silence and nothing can be scarier than a six-hundred-pound animal with three-inch claws intent on attacking me? I walk around each corner, waiting for something to jump out at me. Waiting for an attack.

It's hours later. It's getting dark. And it's getting cold. I wrap my cape tighter around me. With the sun starting to set, I know I need to set up somewhere to rest for the night. This is frustrating and disappointing. I should have been out of here a long time ago, one gold coin richer and sleeping in my own bed. While my mattress of straw is not overly comfortable, it's much more comfortable than a bed on the forest floor is about to be.

I find a fallen tree with a small, shallow gully open behind it. I decide this is as good a place as any to bed down. I set down my little pouch and free my canteen from the back of my pants. I head in search of water and wood. I find wood but strike out on water. I had finished my water a while back and hoped to find some more. I take some small, miraculously dry twigs, and some dried-out moss and make a small pile out of it.

I rub the sticks together, the way Cardis once told me about, to create fire. I would have brought matches if I had thought for a moment

I would be out here at dark, but this was supposed to be quick and easy. Run, run, Eloise. Don't let the magic catch you. Ugh.

I don't know what I was expecting, honestly, but I certainly wasn't expecting what did happen. Out of nowhere, my tinder lights all at once into a small, crackling inferno, eating up the tinder faster than I can replace it. I pray to the Celestials it will stay burning as I quickly grab some of my bigger branches and put them on the fire, building it up.

Naturally, as soon as I get my fire going and start to munch on the dried meat Cardis gave me and Saada's delicious bread, it starts to rain. Not a little rain either, a heavy torrential downpour. Because, of course.

I sigh, annoyed and now homesick. I fidget with the phoenix on my necklace as I remember Saada's rules, and I allow myself a minute to wallow. One minute. This is something she taught me after my parents died.

She told me I was allowed to be sad for a time. It was important for me to feel those feelings, but I couldn't let them take over. After their time limit was up, I needed to keep going with my life. Being sad all the time is not what my mom or dad would want. Ever since then, I have allowed my intrusive feelings like anger or sadness to exist, but I put a time limit on them. I uncap and manage to fill my canteen with a couple of swallows of rainwater. It's not the cleanest source of water, but water, nonetheless. My fire starts to show the effects of the rain, dimming as the fuel gets wet.

"You know, some of us would like to be warm and dry!" I yell at the forest. Okay, maybe I don't have full control of my emotions yet. "If you could stop the rain, that would be great. Or, you know, even better, let me out!"

The rain lightens, then stops. I hold my breath, hopeful I will get my wish to get out. I don't. No magical voice says anything about leaving. I curl up near the fire. The front half of me being kept warm while my back is cold. Eventually, I doze off there, tossing and turning continuously.

~

Tuesday, R62T22

One Day After the Start of the Quest

I wake in what I think is the wee hours of the morning. I'm facing away from the fire, and when I turn, I'm shocked to find it still burning strongly. Good fire. I notice that my necklace is quite warm despite having been away from the direct heat. I take it out of my shirt and away from my skin. I contemplate taking it off before deciding I'd probably lose it. Besides, on the outside of my shirt the heat dissipates a bit.

I debate trying to sleep some more, but the ache in my body tells me only exhaustion kept me asleep for as long as I did. I stretch and roll out my aching muscles. My back is terribly angry about yesterday's flying lesson with the sudden stop. As expected. I eat some more dried meat and bread, savoring the flavor of my favorite bread for a long moment before getting up. I kick some dirt over the fire and am surprised when it dies down quickly. I fully expected to have to find some water or a lot more dirt. I don't complain that things are going my way for once. Except the forest still won't let me out. I'm quite cross at it.

I walk in the dark, only the faint moonlight between the branches to guide my way along the path. I stumble a few times over roots I cannot see under the dead pine needles but manage to keep on my feet. I'm wondering about the wisdom of trying to move around in the dark when I hear it.

I cock my head, struggling to listen more closely. I can't be hearing what I think I hear…I hear something that sounds an awful lot like humming. I stay where I am. I even try to clean out my ears to see if I'm imagining the sound, but no, it continues. A soft, lilting sound. Not entirely on key, but not unpleasant either. It's a female voice I hear, for which I am grateful. I hope this means she's not a physical threat to me.

I come around the bend in the path cautiously, and I peer around a large tree trunk, keeping most of me hidden. Fortunately, no root systems trip me up, and I avoid brushing against the bushes. I stifle a gasp that rises when I see a woman puttering around outside of a little cottage. In the middle of the night. In the middle of the forest that has no known settlements. The cottage looks like it's been here for at least a hundred years by the moss growing on the walls and thatched roof, as well as its general decrepit appearance. It seems sturdy enough to be standing, but it also looks like it's leaning slightly to the right.

I smile. This must be impossible scenario number three. Or number one if the forest starts over. Or number two if the leg thing didn't count. My head aches trying to make sense of the math.

Either way, this is one of the times to run. I stand quietly, watching the woman work around her cottage. It appears she is planting something in some wooden, nearly rotten, window boxes. She has her hands in the dirt, her back to me. Her dress is a light blue cotton with a white scalloped trim. I marvel at how white it is given her current activities. She has what looks to be light blonde hair, straight down her back in a braid that reaches past her waist, and I look down and notice…she's barefoot. I wrack my brain trying to figure out if I must approach her or if I can run now and have that be good enough. Irritation rises within me at Saada's lack of detail about this Quest and curse.

I stand watching for a few minutes. She neither turns towards me nor seems to notice me. If it had been me, my sixth sense would have been sending off an alarm of warning that I was being watched. When nothing happens, I assume I must talk to her first before refusing the task. I begin to approach cautiously.

"Hello?" I call out to the humming woman. She turns to face me, and I get a look at her by the light of the lamp she pulls off the windowsill of the old cottage. I gasp in shock. From here, it looks like she has a whole lot of wrinkles and grey hair. I thought it was blonde, but now I can see it's actually grey. I have never seen anyone who got old.

They don't exist, they're impossible. I had seen drawings of old people in history books at school, but they're extinct now. If anyone was a picture-perfect representation of old, this woman is it. I stop in my tracks, stunned and even more uncertain of what I should do.

RUN! The voice in my head reminds me. Oh yes, running. That's what I should be doing. I am shifting my weight, preparing to run when she smiles at me and stops her humming. "Well, hello, Eloise, I've been waiting for you."

I am ready to bolt, my weight already shifted on to my back foot, but her use of my name and my curiosity stops me. A vague memory of a proverb floats across my mind, something about curiosity and a dead cat, but it's gone before I can grasp it. Instead, what I ask is, "How do you know my name? Who are you? What are you doing out here?

"She chuckles. "Come on in, my dear; we have much to discuss." She turns, walks to her door, and enters, not even glancing back at me. Clearly, she expects me to follow. I hesitate. If I'm going to run, this is the time to do it.

THAT COULD'VE GONE BETTER.

Mitac

The sky is starting to lighten on the horizon when I wake. I groan. I didn't get a lot of sleep. Turmoil over Eloise weighed heavily on my mind. I kept dreaming of her facing a bear and jumping from a tree onto its back, which is ridiculous. No one would be foolish enough to do that.

Still, better than dreaming of her being eaten, I suppose.

I know that if Eloise had made it out overnight, Chance would have come back to the inn. I never heard her return. Being a light sleeper, and with half an ear out for her, it was unlikely I missed her. Nevertheless, I quickly put on my clothes and quietly walk across the red-carpeted hall. I knock lightly. I let Selvia stay in Chance's room by herself and I didn't want to wake her if she was asleep. If Chance were in there, though, she would have heard my knock.

After no response, I walk to the bathroom to clean up. I wash my face and clean my hands and under my arms. I'm not looking to be fancy, but I need to not smell like an ogre. I quickly scribble a note to Selvia on a spare piece of parchment and slide it under the door.

I trod down the stairs of the inn, carpeted in the same rich red as the hallway, and pause as I'm about to head out the door. I spot a little bookcase in the lobby. There isn't much to choose from, but I find one that looks promising and put it outside the door of Chance and Selvia's room. Depending on when Selvia wakes, she may have a bit of a wait until someone comes to collect her. Maybe this will help keep her entertained for a little while. Even if she can't read well, there are some pictures in the book. I'll ask Chance to take it into Selvia for me when she comes back to get some rest.

I go back down the stairs and out to the cool early dawn air, my cloak flapping behind me. I hustle to the baker, who has two egg and cheese pies prepared for me. He refuses to take my money, as he promised the evening before, and I fight it, the same way I said I would. In the end, I win. I throw the coins at him and run away, chortling as I go. I can hear the baker yelling at me, in a kind way, but he doesn't give chase.

In other areas of the Realm, there are multiple pairs of Gophers and Trackers, so they don't have to contend with what to do when the sun sets. Their Quests almost always last more than a day, so there will be at least one daytime pair and one nighttime pair. Amaranth doesn't get that, I was told when I was given the assignment since their Quests are over in the first twelve hours the majority of the time. Eighteen hours if we were unlucky. Apparently, we are very unlucky because I still see Chance sitting in my seat. She must be exhausted to be sitting there rather than pacing the forest. When I get closer, I see she has fallen asleep sitting up. I gently wake her, and she startles awake with a yelp. "Mitac, you scared me!"

I smile genially. "Sorry, but it's time to change the guard." I look at the paper, still one name. I look over at Kinta's house, and the last bag is missing.

"Did Eloise come out?" I ask, hope rising. Doesn't explain why Chance didn't come back, but if Eloise managed to escape the danger prediction, I will be more than happy.

Chance shakes her head. "Not that I know of."

"There are no bags left, her bag is missing. Are you sure?" It comes out more forcefully than I mean it. I know, logically, that Chance wouldn't lie, but I can't help but ask.

She rolls her jade green eyes at me, "Yes, Mitac, I'm sure your girl didn't come out of the forest."

I ignore her "your girl" jab and ask, "When did you fall asleep?" I think I sound more accusatory than I mean to be. I'm supposed to be detached, cool, and calm. I am none of these things right now.

She yawns widely. "Not long ago. Can't have been more than ten minutes. The sun isn't much higher than it was when I last saw it. Relax."

No one in the history of ever has ever relaxed when told to relax. My irritation is increasing by the second. "Well then, where did her bag go?" I gesture widely to where the bag should have been. Where it was when I left last night.

Chance shrugs. "I'm not sure. I think it was there before I slipped into dreamland. Is one of those for me?" She reaches for one of the egg pies. I almost want to tell her she can't have it for falling asleep on the job and for looking so unconcerned about the missing bag, but I relent. She has been up all night, after all. I can't blame her. It's not exactly an exciting part of the job.

"Can you stay up for another ten minutes before you go? I need to check something."

She yawns again. "I guess if I have to. Can you be quick? I'm beat."

I promise to be quick, then jog off toward the cabin I had staked out a couple of days before. I go through the fence and knock softly on the door. I see there are candles lit, so I presume someone is awake inside.

A man with a faint blue tint in his hair and skin, and light blue eyes answers the door. He's half-dressed, missing a shirt, and looks none too happy to see me.

"It's you," he says gruffly, blinking his eyes blearily. "I thought maybe you were Saada. Though why she would knock, I have no idea."

"Saada isn't here?" I say, my voice rising an octave. Missing bag, missing aunt. I am getting increasingly concerned.

"No," he says. "She didn't come home last night. I figured she was waiting for Eloise. Wait, why are you here? Did something happen to Eloise?"

He looks around me to the outside, a challenge given my broad shoulders take up most of the space in the doorway. He stands on his tippy toes and, satisfied I'm not hiding Eloise, turns his gaze back to me.

"Eloise hasn't come out, as far as I know, sir, but her bag is no longer at the forest entrance and my Tracker doesn't recall anyone taking it."

The man turns from the door. "One sec, let me get my shirt." He disappears down a hall. I am unsure what to do. Should I follow him into the house? He didn't give me an express invitation, so I opt to wait on the porch awkwardly. He reemerges, pulling his shirt over his head, and ushers me away from the door so he can close it. It's stopped by something as he tries to tug it closed. Confused, he turns. I'm already halfway back to the stone half-wall, but I pause for him to figure out the door.

A boy's head is in the doorway, black rings under his eyes. Clearly, Cardis hasn't been sleeping well either.

"Cardis?" Gamet asks. "What are you doing up?"

"Same as you, Uncle." He nonchalantly pulls the door open wider. I can see he must have hastily dressed. His shirt is rumpled, his pants leg on one side is stuck in a sock, the other one dragging to the floor. "I overheard, and I'm worried about Eloise, too. If you're going to look for her, I'm coming as well." His eyes are steely blue, clearly determined to come with us regardless of what his uncle thinks about it.

Gamet opens the door, and Cardis slides on some leather sandals and ducks under his uncle's arm to the porch. Seems Gamet recognizes a losing situation. Or at least an argument not worth fighting.

Gamet and Cardis lead me back down the path and to the village.

Suddenly, Gamet speeds up, spying something. "Oh, thank the Celestials," Gamet breathes. "Saada."

He rushes away from me, and I see where he is looking. There, sitting on the ground, leaning against the stump, is Saada. I have no excuse for why I missed her. I must have been solely focused on Chance and overlooked her. My face flames with embarrassment. Well, now I've made a complete ass of myself.

"This is what happens when you get attached," my instructor yells at me. "You stop thinking properly. Try again!" Then he uses the cane on my back and makes me repeat the exercise.

I mentally shake the past and return to the present.

Gamet walks over to Saada and gently wakes her. In her lap, wrapped in her arms, is Eloise's bag. Mystery solved. The man glares at me as he urges his wife to get up. I walk over, against my better judgment. "Everything okay?" I ask.

He glares at me. "Fine," his eyes narrow. "She's worried about Eloise."

Me too, I think, but I keep my mouth shut.

I turn to Saada and meet her bleary eyes. "I'll keep an eye out for her and bring her home myself when she comes out."

She shakes her head. "That won't be necessary. I will wait for her."

"Oh no, you won't, dear! You're going home for some sleep. I will stay and wait." At Gamet's proclamation, Cardis steps forward.

"No, I will stay. Gamet, you need to go to work."

"Work can wait while our girl is still on her Quest. They will understand," he replies.

"I'm going to wait, either way, Uncle. How about you take Saada home and get her settled? I'll stay and wait for Eloise."

Gamet nods. Clearly dead on her feet, Saada finally reluctantly agrees. "Okay, okay. I'll go home. When she gets out, you *will* wake me to tell me." She gives Cardis and Gamet stern looks.

"Yes, dear," Gamet agrees with a sigh. Clearly, he's relieved his wife is agreeing to go to bed. "Cardis, if you get too tired, come back to the house, and I'll trade you places." Cardis nods and takes up residence on the stump.

"I'm sorry, sir." And I am genuinely apologetic. "I didn't mean to frighten you. I was worried that Eloise had taken off or maybe even hopeful she had gone home already."

Gamet looks nonplussed. "Yes, well. If you had used your eyes a little more, Gopher, you could have kept from giving all of us a heart attack this morning." No argument from me. It was a stupid move and exactly what I deserve for allowing Eloise to be anything more than a faceless Quester. Gamet turns and storms off with his wife.

"Wait!" I call after them. They stop and turn back to face me. "Eloise's bag. I need to keep it here. Quest rules." Saada hands over the bag, Gamet looks like he'd rather tell me to take a long walk off a short cliff. I gently take the bag, thanking them and apologizing again. They leave, and I place Eloise's bag next to the Healer's house, where it belongs.

"That could've gone better," I mutter to myself and head back to Chance, who suddenly looks perky having watched the exchange. She can't beat me at a physical or mental duel, so she loves watching me be taken down a peg or two from time to time.

"Off you go," I tell her sternly, trying to ignore her smug look. "Selvia is in your room, asleep. I left a book for her outside the door, can you take it to her? There's also a letter for her on the floor inside the door. When she wakes, tell her I will send the Healer to come bring her down around lunch."

Chance nods and gets up from the seat. She brushes crumbs from her breakfast pie off her and wanders off to find her bed. I pick up the remaining egg and cheese pie and take a big bite. While cold, it is still delicious, and I eat it within a couple of minutes. I wander the forest perimeter to see if there are any signs of Eloise. My eyes are not quite as keen as Chance's, so I know it's not particularly useful, especially given the dim light the sky holds right after dawn. I can't help but check anyway. Seeing none, I head back to my chair to sit and wait.

Danger, the voice repeats. I mentally punch it. I don't know how you punch a voice in the face, but I do it anyway.

A BEDTIME STORY.

Aerith

R62T21

After escaping the Illume Council unscathed, for now, I calculate my next moves. I sent Mancio back to his room, telling him we would practice again tomorrow. I can't deal with his questions right now. I have too many of my own to answer.

I wonder if the Council will buy it if I tell them in the end my dream isn't anything of import?

I doubt it. Maybe if I had meaningless visions before, they would, but given that I never had anything to share, having something now means it's important. My head is beginning to hurt, trying to think of what to do. In the event the Gophers come back with a magic male from Amaranth…I'm off the hook. In the clear. I will still have to answer for what is special about the kid, but I won't be in trouble. I'll only have to keep lying. It alarms me that it seems so easy to do. Probably easier than giving up any information about these people. Especially the girl whom I have grown attached to in my visions.

However, could I give up someone else in her place? I had seen the look in the Council's eyes when they were sending off messengers to the Gophers. It wasn't curiosity in their rainbow of eyes. I am pretty certain they are not going to let the focus of my first dreams be free, especially after what I had overheard. If the Black was thinking she needed to be disposed of then that's what would happen.

And if they bring her back rather than someone else? Well, if they bring the girl back, I don't know what to do. Perhaps we could escape together. The thought of living outside of the palace makes me shudder. My last experience went oh so well. Not to mention, money. I don't have any money to speak of. In the palace, there is no need for us to be paid.

We don't get a stipend or an allowance since we have no reason to buy anything. If we want something, we ask for it. If the Council approves, it appears in our rooms. Even when I left the palace on my freedom mission last time, the handler paid for everything. I don't even know the average cost of things outside the palace. I absently wonder if Naseem has any money. I make a mental note to seek her out as soon as possible and see if she can lend me anything for this trip. Plus, I want to know if she can fill me in on what she was about to say when the Illume interrupted her.

Of course, money is only half the equation. First, I have to escape before I can consider how to live in Amiket City outside of the palace.

I pull up short in my pacing...I can't live in Amiket; they would find me. I'm bright purple for Celestial's sake! Plus, there's the issue of my necklace. I don't know how to remove it without dying. Even if I figure that out, what then? The Illume would send every Stealth Warrior available to track me down. I wouldn't make it anywhere.

I sit on my bed and drop my head to my hands. It seems so... pointless. I feel helpless. I know in my heart that this girl is in serious trouble if she's found out. I also know I will be in serious trouble if I am found out.

As much as I want to write this girl off, I can't. I need more information before I make that decision.

Resolution in mind, I seek out Naseem.

Naseem answers her door looking more rumpled than usual. Evidently, I'm not the only one pacing after that meeting. She lets me in, then checks the hall before closing the door.

"Sorry, I don't know how wise it is for us to be seen together," she clarifies. "This is dangerous, Aerith."

My heart drops. I had hoped that I had the wrong feeling about it. My hope seems to be useless of late.

"Can you tell me what you know?" I ask, sitting on her yellow settee. "Whatever it is, I have to know. I don't know what to do. Do I give the girl up?"

Naseem vigorously shakes her head, whirling to face me. "No! Definitely not!"

"Okay, but if it's her or me, I'm not sure I can let it be me, either. So, I want you to tell me what you know. Convince me, Naseem. Please fill me in on what's going on."

Naseem sits next to me, straightening her skirts nervously. "There's a legend where I come from. It was told to us as a bedtime story. It's about the end of the Realm. I remember most of it."

She pauses, and I fight the urge to push her. Her face twists, and I can tell she's struggling with her past again.

She takes a shaky breath.

Once upon a time, there was Time, and Time was evil. He fed on the sorrow of the mortal people. He learned that the longer they lived, the more sadness they suffered, and the stronger he became. He would feast until he became so bloated he would fall asleep. The mortals would freeze where they were until Time awoke and restarted. The mortals would keep living, hurting, causing pain, and feeding Time until he fell asleep again.

One age, while Time slept, the Celestials sought ways to control Time's insatiable hunger. Their solution was to shorten the mortals' lives so they would create less devastation for Time. As the revolutions turned, the Celestials shortened the lives gradually until they realized that mortals would find a way to create great sadness and destruction in even short lives.

The Celestials came to recognize that the problem wasn't so much the time they had, as it was Time himself and the rulers of the lands. Time would whisper to them of great power and wealth. The powers would take the deals offered, and the Realm would become imbalanced. The Celestials decided the powers would need to be overthrown to reset the age and make the Realm a happier place, effectively starving and weakening Time where he could return to his basic function. The Celestials allowed the mortals to age as normal again, living long, happy lives. When they stopped being kind to each other, the Celestials would shorten their lives as a warning to the mortals. If that did not work, the next reset would occur.

Naseem sat back. "The moral of the story is to be kind to each other, or we will all die."

I stare at Naseem, my mouth agape. "I'm sorry…what?"

"I don't know if it's true; it's a story after all." Her yellow eyes bore into mine, "but often stories are based in legend and legend based in truth. We do slowly lose our longevity over time…so maybe it's time for a reset of the age."

"A…a reset?" I stutter, still trying to process what she has told me. "A bedtime story. I'm supposed to base my future, this girl's future, the other people's future, on a bedtime story?" Is she serious right now?

She shifts. "I'm not saying you have to; I'm telling you what I know. That's what I know; it's what I was going to tell you in the Council room."

"Well, thanks. Big help." I stand up and walk to her big window. Her rooms overlook the gardens at the back of the palace. Beyond, I can see the cliffs which lead to the harbor and the sea. It's a clear sky, and I can scarcely make out the sails of some of our ships bobbing on the water. Life used to be so simple, we would run in the gardens, play hide and seek. We used to be able to sit and chat, laugh, and just—be.

"You asked, Aerith."

I circle to face her, "Because I thought you had answers! Not some weird story about…nothing!" I throw my hands up. "We are talking about actual lives, Naseem. People who are in actual danger. One of them being me!"

"You think I don't know that?" she replies, deathly quiet. "You think I don't know what we are looking at here? How dangerous this is? Do you think I want you to get hurt? Or would you rather think that I want your dreams to lead to the end of the Realm?"

"No, of course not. I only wanted some answers."

"That's all I have, Aerith. It's the best I can give you."

As I leave Naseem's room, I realize that the only one who knows what's going on is me. I'm the only one who has seen the visions, has seen what's going on, and technically, I'm the only one who can interpret them. With the weight of the Realm on my shoulders, I trudge back to my room.

～

R62T22

I come to a few conclusions in the following hours.

First, this is beyond me. Of this, I am sure. If it comes down to her or me at the mercy of the Council, it's going to have to be me. Based on what I have seen, the girl needs to live to do whatever it is she's supposed to do. I don't relish the thought of sacrificing myself, though. Something tells me they wouldn't hang me or cut my throat. I imagine a far different fate.

Secondly, my best option seems to be to escape. With the girl if she shows up. Which means I have to wait for the Gophers from Amaranth to come back. I wish I could escape ahead of time; but I know she will need my help to get out. Either way, my time here in the palace is quickly coming to an end.

I go to bed exhausted that night and wake in the early hours of the morning to the talisman on my neck; practically burning a hole in my skin again. I sneak out of my quarters and wander to the oh-so-familiar room. On my way, I pass Naseem's quarters, and I am tempted to stop and talk to her about my plan for escape, even as ill-formed as it is. While we didn't leave on good terms last night, I still hope she will be willing to help me.

I decide I don't have the time right now. The sun isn't yet awake, but that matters not for the Celestials' call. I light a few candles in the room, smelling the familiar burning of the wick, and sit on the gold carpet. The normalcy of all of this is comforting.

I practice my breathing exercises, channeling everything into the amethyst orb hanging from my neck then begin again. I'm rushing the process, but it seems to be working.

When my vision clears, I see the girl has risen from her fire and put it out. She has started her walk into the forest and freezes suddenly. I start, as well. I can see that she is looking at a woman in the forest who is…old. I don't know how old, I have never seen anyone aged beyond thirty, so I have no idea how to guess her age, but she has grey hair and wrinkles. They exchange a few words, and it appears the old woman has beckoned her into the cottage.

I can sense the girl's, who I now know is named Eloise, indecision and I am not sure what she should do either. I am curious, as she must be, about who this woman in the Amaranth Forest is, but I also don't trust people who appear out of nowhere and also appear to be an age that cannot be. That's a different level of magic and I wonder if the woman has Stealth Warrior in her; some way to change her appearance. If so, why would she make herself look old? Is the idea to pique Eloise's curiosity?

The dream fades to black, and I return my consciousness to the octagonal room. Still, no light has entered. I still find it increasingly curious that my dreams are almost all present or past events. Other than the first clear one I had where I saw the kids together, everything has been current or recent past. My understanding of Dreaming is that it should all be taking place in the future. Otherwise, what good is it to Dream? If we cannot see to prepare for what's going to happen, what's the point? I don't recall reading about this or hearing about this for Purple Dreamers. Perhaps this is what we do, and it's different from everyone else.

I don't suppose I am going to get an answer to that, though. I have no other Purple Dreamers to ask, and my mentor had never dreamed anything at all. I guess I will have to wait and see how this plays out. I get up from the carpet and blow out the candles, the smoke wafting away from my breath. I wander back to my room and climb back into bed. Hopefully, next time I wake up, the sun will be firmly in the sky. I make another mental note to visit Naseem when I rise at a more humane hour.

WAIT. AND WAIT.

Mitac

Selvia joins me around lunch time. The Healer wheels her towards my station on her porch. I am thankful to her for providing me with shade today. I was so hopeful that Eloise would wake up this morning and have left the forest; however, it's nigh on noon, and still no Eloise. It's been a little over thirty-one hours. I have five more hours of waiting before I can go in to find her. I glance over to Saada, who, after an all-too-quick nap, returned to the Clearing to wait and tried to send Cardis home. She was unsuccessful. She is chewing her fingernails again. I can't blame her. I don't chew my fingernails, but I am about ready to begin. Cardis alternates between staring at a book, staring at the forest, glancing at Saada with worry, and dozing off.

I smile at Selvia as she approaches.

"Thank you," is the first thing out of her mouth when she gets near, "for the food and for the book."

"You're welcome," I return. "There weren't a lot of options for books, so I hope you don't mind my choice for you. It was that, a book about the alphabet or a book about a pirate."

Her eyes light up when I mention the book about the pirate. "I guess I chose wrong. Next time, I'll give you the pirate book." She opens her mouth, likely to apologize, but I raise my hand to stop her. "Don't

184

worry, I'm not mad. I thought the pirate book looked more interesting, but I also wasn't sure how well you could read. I figured choosing a book with drawings would give you something to look at if you weren't a strong reader and, if you were, wouldn't be as insulting as the alphabet."

She giggles. "Yeah, you're right. But I *can* read. My mom…she taught me to read before she was taken. She loved to read to me, and we would read together about all kinds of places."

I can guess why her mom wanted to read about being somewhere other than where she actually was. Selvia pauses and looks around. "Since you're still here, I'm guessing not everyone has come out?"

I shake my head. "No. We still have one more stubborn Quester left in the forest."

"Okay. How much longer do you think?" She looks to the forest. Her excitement to get going is nearly infectious. She almost makes me excited to get back to Amiket, too.

"I have no idea. It could be days, or she could be out in a matter of minutes."

"Days?" she asks, her eyes wide with alarm.

I smile at her reassuringly. "Unlikely. I have permission to go in a day and a half after the start of the Quest with Chance to locate her and bring her out if she's done." And I will definitely be doing exactly that.

"What if she's still doing her Quest?"

"In this area? Quests don't last this long unless something has gone wrong." Her grey eyes widen, and her jaw tightens. I kick myself and quickly add, "I'm not saying that something has gone wrong, only that it's not usually any other way. If we go in and we find that she's still on her Quest, we will return and let her stay until she is done. If she is not on her Quest, we will bring her out with us."

She looks at me, puzzled. "Why would she stay if her Quest is over?"

"Why would you go in and stay when you weren't supposed to be Questing at all?" She looks away, her cheeks coloring pink with shame, so I soften the blow. "Sometimes, people want to try to Change, so they stay even if the forest kicks them out. Sometimes, they get hurt, and they cannot get themselves out, kind of like what would have happened to you if Eloise hadn't come along to help. Luckily, she did because we had no idea you were in there and would never have known we needed to come get you."

"Eloise could be hurt?" She looks around at the forest, eyes wide, scared for her rescuer.

"Yes, it is possible, but she seems awfully capable, don't you think?" Selvia nods, looking back at me. "No, I think she's finishing up or she's taking a long nap in the woods." I hope the Celestials don't hold the white lies against me. A rock has taken permanent residence in my stomach, and it flips over every time I ponder what is happening to Eloise in the cursed forest.

Selvia looks a little happier at that thought. She pulls a book out from under her shirt and begins to look at it. I recognize it as the book I had left for her this morning.

I look over to Saada as I head back to my chair. She's as on edge as ever, and I hatch a plan to keep her busy for a few minutes. I walk over to her. "Saada," I greet her, tipping my hat to her. She and Cardis look up at me. I nod a greeting to Cardis as well. They both then resume staring down the forest. "I was wondering if you all have a library or a bookshop or something around here?"

Saada tries to ignore me, but I step into her line of sight. She looks up at me thoroughly annoyed. "What?" she snaps, exasperated.

"I asked if you have a library or a bookshop around here?" I repeat. She narrows her eyes at me.

"I think there are some books in the sewing shop, but you'd have to check with the seamstress." She attempts to wave me off and look around me, but I refuse to be so easily dissuaded, and she grows frustrated, her cheeks flaring out with her huffing and puffing.

I look over at the forest. "Well, I can't exactly leave right now. Chance is still getting some rest, and I have to stay until Eloise comes out. Surely you understand." She practically growls at me. "Do you think you can take Selvia over to pick out a book or two? The options at the Inn are sorely lacking for her."

She glares in my direction. "You can't leave because you're waiting for my niece, and you expect me to be okay with leaving?"

"I don't think you'll be happy about it, no," I say sensibly while I also put some magic tendrils out for further persuasion, "What are you going to do, otherwise? Burn the forest down with your gaze?"

Probably the wrong thing to say based on her reaction as she nearly growls at me. Cardis snickers and tries to cover it with a cough. Saada's death glare sent his way indicates he didn't succeed.

"Please?" I'm begging now, but I cannot stand to watch her struggle this hard. The fibers of magic start to reach her when they hit a wall. Wow, some serious reinforcements on this woman. I remember her niece as the same and I wonder where they got the skill to put up a barrier to Negotiator Warriors. And why. Ignoring this revelation for another day, I continue my begging the old-fashioned way. "Selvia has earned a good book, and I'll pay, of course." I pull out some silvers from my pouch. "You can keep the change."

She continues to look at me with thinly veiled anger but relents. "Fine, I'll do it for Selvia, but I am most certainly not keeping the change."

She stands from her stump and snatches the proffered silvers before going to get Selvia, waving Cardis to come with her. I can tell by the sound of her saccharine voice as she tells Selvia the plan, that she has affected a nonchalance and even excitement about the task at hand. Fake or not, I appreciate her efforts. I watch as Cardis wheels Selvia, who waves at me, toward some buildings near the Clearing. I wave back then head back to my post and sit again to wait. And wait. And wait.

A few more hours and we can go in to get Eloise. Knots form in my stomach at the thought of her being hurt, but given her insistence that she would not change in the forest, I don't have much confidence in any other scenario right now.

Please, Celestials, don't let me go in just to retrieve her body.

...DUSTY MURDER CABIN.

Eloise

The old woman insists upon me entering her cabin. I stand uncertainly on her crooked threshold and look inside the cottage. It's simply decorated. No pictures on the wall, one window in the back facing more forest, a window to my right where the woman was digging around in the dirt, a small metal bowl for washing, where the old woman is now washing her hands, and a small wooden counter, probably for food preparation.

A tiny two-seat table is near the wash basin, set with two simple wooden chairs. The cottage looks cute, but it smells musty, disused. There are cobwebs scattered around, and dust is heavy on the flat surfaces. I wonder why this woman would bother gardening when it was clear that the inside of the cabin needed serious attention. Oddly enough, the bed is made, and the bookshelf on the right wall is spotless. My breath catches when I see several knives on her wall, perfectly polished, hanging there. That's not ominous at all.

"Why don't we talk out here?" I suggest. "It seems to be shaping into a nice day."

Plus, I don't want to go into your dusty murder cabin.

The old woman laughs. "I would agree with you there, but the cabin will be more comfortable. Plus, I have some things to show you about your magic. Tea?"

I highly doubt I will be more comfortable inside. Wait, did she say something about my magic? I start to back away. The woman walks swiftly over to me, her agility contradicts her presumptive age, and captures my wrist. I attempt to wrench free, but the woman's grip is like iron.

"Ow! You're hurting me!" I cry out more loudly and emphatically than necessary, hoping to shock her into letting me go. It doesn't work. She drags me into the cabin by force and slams the rickety door behind us. I'm not sure how the cottage manages to stay standing.

She suddenly releases me, and I fall backward into the closed door from the unexpected lack of resistance.

"There, that's better," she gives me a smile. I think it's supposed to be comforting, but it's anything but.

I immediately turn and wrest the door open. Well, I attempt to. It doesn't budge. I stare at it in shock. The door is made of a light wood, even if it has a lock, I should be able to rip it off its hinges or break the lock or something. I keep pulling and rattling it, but nothing happens. It's sealed. Unwanted tears stream down my face.

I'm going to die. I'm definitely going to die. And in that thought I wonder, *why hasn't she started attacking me?*

I turn in the smallest radius I can and lean against the door, my eyes wide with terror, breath coming in short, agonizing pants. My vision is going dark, and I fight desperately to hold onto my consciousness.

I locate the woman in the cabin, and she's staring at me, evidently amused by my reaction.

"Are you quite done? Mitac wasn't wrong; you are a bunny."

I narrow my eyes at her. "Excuse me?"

"Rabbit, bunny, same thing." She waves me off and turns to begin making tea in the kitchen.

"That is not what I'm upset about!" I yell.

"Fine, Bun Bun it is," she chuckles at her own joke. I don't laugh with her, my blood pressure rising. "Won't you have a seat?"

I consider refusing, then run my fingers over my aching wrist and rethink that plan. I decide to perch on the single chair in what must pass as the living room. There is a hearth, cold and long-dead, and a thin yellow rug. It has the makings of a living room, but the things that would make it a place to gather and share love and life are missing. The walls were bare, the mantle devoid of personal effects, the coffee table covered in an inch of dust like most everything else. I shudder. Last thing I would want to do is gather here.

"It's Eloise, as you well know," I grit out, all of my muscles tense, ready to attack or defend. I'm not sure which I will need at this moment.

"Yes, dear, I know," she sounds kindly. Like what a grandmother in the kid's books was. This woman's sudden change in attitude and behavior makes my head spin. "Please, won't you sit at the table with me?"

"I don't take things from people I don't know," I stiffen, not moving an inch.

"Raemyn," she walks toward me with her hand extended. I jump up and brace myself for an attack. "I'm not going to hurt you, dear; I need to talk to you." Her smile seems genuine, but its juxtaposition with her earlier forceful behavior makes it untrustworthy.

Raemyn resumes humming and sets steaming hot tea at each place at the table. I can smell the bit of honey she's added to mine, and my mouth waters. The light herbal scent is hard to resist. Dandelion tea is one of my favorites.

"If you wanted to talk, why force me to come in here? Why lock me in?" I ask her, fighting the urge to fidget.

"Because I need you not to leave until I have finished."

"Oh sure, yes, of course," I say sarcastically, slapping my palm to my forehead. "How silly for me to have forgotten! We do that all the time. I frequently lock my guests in when I want to chat with them."

Raemyn's eyes narrow, anger flashing across her face. "What I have to share with you will not be easy to hear, and like I said before, I need you not to leave before we are done here. I have ensured that you will not. Now come. Sit. Down."

Raemyn points to the empty seat at the table. I woodenly walk to the chair and sit as she requested. I stare at her, waiting for her to talk, determined not to take part in this conversation. She doesn't reply and sips at her tea. My dry mouth reminds me I haven't had anything to drink in a while, and some tea would be nice right now.

I resist for several minutes before I find the cup in my hands, the smooth honeyed-dandelion flavor sliding down my throat. I resist moaning, but only just. Raemyn meets my gaze, unblinking until I look away, my gaze falling on the bookcase again.

Raemyn notices my roaming gaze as it comes to rest on the bookcase. "Nice, isn't it?" She leans over to run a hand along the edge of it. The books, like everything else in the cabin, appear to be well-used and tired, albeit dusty, which tells me she hasn't read them recently. What does she do with her time? It's clearly not cleaning.

I nod. "Where did you get it?"

"It's a fairly new acquisition," she says reluctantly. "But it's my favorite item here right now." That doesn't make a lot of sense given their current state. Then again, nothing about Raemyn makes much sense.

"So, what do you have to share?" I ask as I relent to having this conversation.

"It's about time." She quickly moves on. "So, Eloise, how is the Quest treating you so far?" She sits with her hands wrapped around the teacup, the steam trailing in front of her face.

"You said you wanted to talk about my magic," I point out to the old woman. I'm starting to think maybe she's forgetful.

"We will get there. First, I want to know about your Quest."

I sigh. "It's been…busy."

"Care to elaborate?"

I don't want to, but I shortly find myself telling her about Selvia's leg and the weirdness with the creek disappearing in the forest. I tell her about wrapping Selvia's leg and helping her as far as I could to get out. She laughs at my description of hitting the barrier headfirst. I pull my hair away from my face and she pronounces that my head does not appear to be misshapen.

I tell her about the bear, my heart beats quickly as I retell those events. She listens with rapt attention, a captive audience. I've never been much of a storyteller, but she's leaning forward, resting her elbows on the table with her tea in her hands, the steam curling up in front of her face.

I find myself gesturing animatedly as I tell her about the bear's odd behavior when I told it to eat me already. She looks surprised and I am not sure if it's because I told a bear to eat me or its behavior directly after. I bring her up to speed on the previous night, my luck with starting a fire, and wishing for the rain to go away and how it did. And wishing the forest to let me leave, and how it didn't.

"Then, I woke up and started on my Quest again until I stumbled onto you. Kind of a dull ending compared to the rest, I think."

Raemyn holds her hand to her chest. "I'm dull? I thought I livened things up around here quite a bit!"

An unintentional laugh escapes me. *No, no, this woman is dangerous. I can't go liking her now!*

"I didn't mean to imply you were boring, just that...I still don't know what's going on here. I guess if you fill me in—?"

Raemyn nods thoughtfully. "You are impatient, but you're right; we should probably shake a leg and get moving."

"Moving? Where are we going?" I brighten. If she lets me out, I can run. Like I'm supposed to. I'm so foolish for ending up locked in here with Raemyn.

I go to take another drink of my tea, and my face falls when I realize it has grown cool in the time I spoke. I recoil when Raemyn reaches over and takes my cup. I let it go without fighting her, and she holds it in her hand. I think she is about to put it over the fire, but she does not. She simply holds it.

Suddenly, she flashes red, and I gasp. Her hair, her skin, her eyes, they all turn a vibrant crimson. No sooner have I seen it then it goes away again. Her eyes are back to blue, and her hair is grey once again. I start to think I'm imagining things, but when she hands back my tea, it is as hot as when she first gave it to me.

I stare at the tea and back at her, my sluggish brain trying desperately to make the puzzle pieces fit.

"You...you're...what?" I stammer over my words. She must be magic, but why isn't she Red all the time? Like all the fire wielders?

Raemyn smiles. "Like I said, Eloise, we have much to discuss."

I try to gather my scrambled thoughts and put them back where they belong. I decide to start with what seems to be the simplest question first. "What are you?"

She smiles knowingly, like she knew this would be the first thing I would ask. "I wish it was an easy question to answer. I am magic, Eloise."

No kidding. That was obvious. I roll my eyes at her. "Right, but everyone I have ever seen who has magic stays their color all the time. I've never heard of anyone with magic changing colors other than when they first get their power. You had color, then it was gone." Like a trick. This has to be the Quest.

"I said I am magic, not that I have magic. There is a difference. But this is true," she replies, sipping her tea. Which reminds me to drink mine before it gets cold again. Although, part of me wants to see her trick again. "I am a special type of magic. I only turn the color of the magic I use while using it. Then I return to what you would call Unchanged."

My head already feels like it's spinning from even this little tidbit. I'm not even sure where to go next. Where did she come from? How did she get old? Can others get old like her? Raemyn waits patiently for my next question.

I finally settle on a question. "Are there others like you?"

"No, Eloise. I am exceedingly rare."

"Okay. So why do you live in the forest? Why aren't you in Amiket or something?"

"I don't live in the forest. And Amiket doesn't know I exist."

This surprises me. "But you have a cottage, a garden; what is all this, then?" I gesture around. "You were planting a garden, and yeah, this place looks like it could benefit from some housekeeping, but otherwise, if you don't live here, why do you have china and supplies for tea?"

"I am only here for a short while; then, I will be gone."

Well, that explains everything. Not.

"Because you'll die? No offense, but you look a lot older than thirty."

"And so I am, Eloise. So, I am. No, I will not die. I will simply pass on."

I am not convinced. I have heard this term before used for people who died but whose kids were too young for the reality and finality of death. I don't appreciate her condescension or her thinking I cannot manage death.

"My time here is limited, and I cannot answer all your questions to your satisfaction, this I can tell you. But I can share some things with you that you will need to know." Her blue eyes are piercing. Looking into me or through me, I can't tell. An uncomfortable prickling sensation passes across my shoulders and down my spine.

"Okay…" What is she getting at? What do I need to know, and why?

"First and foremost, the forest has finished your Quest."

My spirits rise, and a big breath whooshes out of me. "Does that mean I can leave now? Does everyone meet you to be excused from the Quest? Because Selvia didn't mention anyone like you. Or is that because she wasn't part of the Quest?" I fire all the questions off in quick succession. Raemyn looks mildly amused.

"How about one question at a time? When I am done talking with you, yes, you will be able to leave without knocking your noggin on a barrier."

My body sags as the tension I've carried for the last few days melts away. I'm free. I did it. I can return to Saada, the cabin, and everyone I know. I didn't tell Raemyn, but I had grown quite concerned about my Quest.

"Thank the Celestials for that."

Raemyn laughs a deep belly laugh. "Sure, the Celestials." I am about to ask her what she means by that when she moves on. "No, no one ever sees me. You are the first. Many hear me, like your friend Selvia, as I tell them to start the Quest and tell them to go, but no one sees me."

"Okay. So why am I seeing you then?" A little bit of dread starts to settle into my stomach. I am pretty sure nothing good ever comes from being the special chosen one to experience something no one else does. Some people would probably like being unique, but I am not among them.

She takes a drink of her tea, and I unconsciously mimic her movements. "That brings us to the next thing I may share, and based on what I know about you, you're not going to be very happy about it. Hence why I locked us in here."

I hold my breath. My immediate thought is that something happened to the kids or Saada or Gamet. "What's wrong? Did you do something to my family?" I am on the edge of my seat, fully prepared to attack this little old lady if she admits to hurting my family. I don't care if she was strong enough to break my wrist with one hand, I will go feral on her if she hurt them.

"Your family is fine, for now. But I must share with you that you are magic."

I hear my heartbeat in my ears as what she said settles into my brain. Magic. The condition I most dread. "So, it wasn't best two out of three?" I squeak, defeated.

Wait…I only had one situation…that I know of.

"No, no, that can't be! I know I mucked up the bear, and I should have run, but I didn't use magic intentionally. And I haven't had three impossible situations! Saada said—"

"Yes, Saada told you what was told to her and what has been passed through your generations. She did not lie nor misrepresent the facts. However, what she did not know is that not all situations are so easily discerned to be as magical as hers were."

A sinking feeling settles in my gut. "What are you talking about?"

"Selvia's leg? You used White healing magic," she held up a finger then a second as though ticking them off, "Blue magic when the water in the creek was gone, and Orange magic to create a brace for her leg." She holds up a third finger.

"But I was trying to be helpful! I wasn't using magic!" I can't explain the water but… "I didn't heal her! Selvia still had a serious injury when she left the forest!" Ha! Let Raemyn try to assert I healed her now.

She only smiles at me. "My dear Eloise, you should know that each magic has specific types. True, you didn't heal her all the way, but you gave her strength to be able to get up and took away a significant amount of her pain by touching her."

"But…I didn't know I was using magic!"

"Whether you knew or not makes no difference. Whether you intended to or not also makes no difference. You did the right thing; you were presented with a problem by the forest, and you solved it. Furthermore, as you acknowledged, the bear was another magic situation. You used Brown magic to create a tree you could climb, Black magic to attempt to fight it, and Green magic to calm it." Three more fingers joined her earlier three. Six fingers. Six magics?

"Wait, wait. You're saying I used six magics? Everyone gets one, you've lost your mind." Clearly, this old woman has been living out in this cottage by herself for too long. Or maybe it's different where she comes from. She claims she doesn't live here, but her sanity is definitely slipping. We have all been taught from an early age that if you're lucky, lucky being relative here, you get a magic when you embark on your Quest. One magic. One per person or none. No halvsies, no take-baksies.

Raemyn looks at me kindly. Almost with pity. Clearly, she knows I am not happy with what she has to share. Whether I believe it or not. "Not everyone gets only one. True, most get only one. But occasionally, some people get multiple."

"So, you're saying, not only did I unintentionally use six magics, but you're also saying that I'm one of these rare people? Me? From Amaranth. A place which does not produce any magic wielders?"

"No, that's not what I'm saying at all." I relax in my chair. Of course, I misunderstood her! The stress of the Quest has gotten to me, clearly.

"You used eight magics." She smiles, enthusiastic. I am not. "Last night with the fire and the rain, you used Red and Yellow magic. Congratulations, Eloise, you have used every magic you know." She has an odd look in her eye like she's holding something back.

My mouth drops open. I lift my cup with shaking hands to take a sip, then think better of it. I stare at it suspiciously. What exactly is in this cup? There must be some kind of drug in it. I put it back down. I shake my head as if that will clear it of whatever drug she laced my cup with. Evil, old woman!

Raemyn rises from the table and walks over to her bookshelf. I decide it's time to take my leave. I get up from my chair and take a few long strides to the door. I try to open it again, but it still won't budge. I look back at Raemyn to see if she's still looking at her shelf. She is not and she is also not her normal color, she's turned a deep black.

"I told you that you would want to leave before we were done. I promise to let you go as soon as we finish our talk. Come sit down, please."

I pull at the door again, fruitlessly. The black must mean she's ready for a fight. I decide I'm not ready to fight this old woman on her turf. I will hear her out, then I will leave by force if necessary. Raemyn must recognize the urge to flee has gone out of me as she changes back to her normal skin tone and resumes looking at the bookshelf. I look at the door one more time and give it another fruitless tug. Seeing no lock available to open it and it refusing to open for me, I return to my chair, resigned to my current fate.

My earlier relief is slipping through my fingers like water. She has to be wrong. If she's not—I drop my head into my hands. Oh Celestials, if she's not, then I'm doomed. The entire Realm is doomed. For what feels like too many times in recent history, I fight tears.

"There it is," she announces. She pulls a big book off the shelf and walks back to the table, setting it down with a loud thump. A bit of dust flies off it and gets caught in a sunbeam coming through the window. It's the first time I notice that it's after noon. I hope she doesn't need to read me this whole tome before letting me go. I know Saada must be getting worried.

SHE WAS BEING FOLLOWED...

Mitac

As soon as it hits the thirty-six-hour mark, I am going to march into the forest with Chance; nothing is going to stop me. She has returned from the inn with one hour to spare to wait with me. She looks well-rested and very annoyed that we are not already on the way home. I would be annoyed, but I am too busy being worried instead. I told Eloise to be careful, I warned her about possible danger.

I imagine storming in there to get her and telling her off. Then my stomach drops as I imagine a much worse possibility...storming in to rescue her and finding her shredded to bits by the bear I dreamed of. The same one that attacked the boy yesterday.

That last hour flies by, and no Eloise. Chance and I talk and decide we will go in together. Chance assures me that although the forest is not the city, she can still lead me directly to where Eloise is.

"Actually," Chance tells me, "it should be easier. There won't be a lot of contending spirit traces to sort through. She's been in there quite a while by herself, so other than sorting through animal spirits, hers will be the only human, most likely."

I know she's trying to reassure me, but the reminder that Eloise spent the night alone in the forest is not helping my mental state.

Danger, the voice whispers across my subconscious again. *I got it!* I think back, my face contorting in rage. *What is the danger?* I think. *If you could be more specific*, I try to reason with it. I don't know where it's coming from, so I don't know who or what I'm trying to negotiate with, but I'm going to try. *Danger,* it repeats uselessly. I give up, pushing it to the background until it's an annoying buzz.

Immediately, like she's been watching a ticking clock, Saada stands from her tree stump and comes marching over, Cardis in tow. I'm pretty sure the kid dozed off leaning against the stump. He has a print of the tree bark on his cheek and his arm.

I know what's coming, so I hold my hand up. "We are getting a game plan together," I tell them. "Then we are going in. I promise we will find her and bring her out if her Quest is over." Then, predicting her next argument, "You should wait here in case she comes out while we are searching for her."

"Then I'm coming with," Cardis pipes in. "I know the forest well. I can help."

I shake my head. "Sorry, Cardis, the forest isn't the forest you know right now; it's too dangerous."

Saada nods her head in rare agreement with me. "I don't want to lose you too, Cardis. They'll find her." The look she gives me tells me I had better find her, or there will be Ravaged Abyss to pay.

I direct them to sit in my place under Kinta's porch. Both Cardis and Saada are looking a little weather worn. They walk off, Saada's arm wrapped protectively around Cardis' shoulders. I walk over to Chance at the edge of the forest. She's looking at me expectantly, relieved that we are not bringing in two Unchanged and untrained individuals.

"Do you remember where she went in?" I ask Chance. I know her best chance of finding Eloise is to literally sniff her out and track her steps.

She nods and points to a spot on the edge of the forest. "Her bag is over there if it will help," I remind her like she also hasn't seen it sitting there all by itself, an odd, misshapen lump of material leaning against the Healer's house.

She walks over to it, and I follow. She picks up the bag and holds it for a few moments, Saada practically boring a hole into Chance with her glare.

I can't tell what Chance does, but whatever it is, it's enough to get us started. Her ability to follow the traces of people isn't quite like a dog, she once explained. She doesn't follow scent; she follows spirit traces. Most people are unaware that they leave behind evidence of their spirit everywhere they go. It's why you can sometimes tell when someone unpleasant has been in a place. Their spirit of negativity looms even after their departure, even if no one else is in the area to bear witness to their previous presence.

Some people, like certain Greens, can track animals or groups of people. A few Greens are especially sensitive to the traces of spirit and can track those traces to specific people and for far longer than the general Green magic-wielder. Chance once told me that my spirit traces aren't entirely offensive. A compliment of the highest order, she tells me. She told me that most people, especially in the city, have very off-putting traces. There are few good people in the city.

Chance leads us into the forest, where she saw Eloise enter, and we are off. I first notice that Eloise clearly followed an existing path, making it much easier for us to follow her steps. At least she had the smarts to follow game trails.

We come to a three-way split in the path. Chance walks down each, scenting them out in turn.

"I'm not sure which one she went down last; the scents are too similar."

We decide to head down the right path first until we come to another opening.

"She paused here for a while, did some walking around with…" Chance pauses and wrinkles her nose. "Selvia. This must be where she did the leg thing." There's some trampled needles and flattened dirt in the opening between the trees. Small traces of blood still line the dirt.

I am going to have to talk to Chance about her dislike for Selvia before we are in the wagon with her for several days to start back home. Now is not the time for that chat. "Okay, then where?"

Chance walks off the path into the forest, and I follow. "Here," she points to a dry creek bed. "She was here for a few minutes, then doubled back."

"Probably looking for water for the cut on Selvia's leg. Too bad the creek is dry." I remember, though, that Selvia's leg had looked pretty clean when she came out. Didn't she mention Eloise cleaning her wound with some water? Maybe she had brought water in with her and had gone to the creek to refill it? But why stay once she saw the creek was dry?

Chance heads back to the path. She walks around, heads off to the west, and pulls up abruptly about ten yards from the edge of the forest. "This is where she and Selvia parted ways. Selvia kept going forward; your girl doubled back."

I wonder why Eloise didn't bring Selvia the rest of the way. Seems like an odd place to leave her.

"She's not 'my girl,'" I correct her sternly. Chance looks over her shoulder with a knowing smile. I grind my teeth. "Whatever, where now?" I have never told Chance about the voice in my head, and I don't intend to tell her now. Let her think I have a thing for Eloise if she wants.

We double back to the path and walk further in. Somehow, we end up back at the split again.

"Well, that's interesting," I mutter.

"Indeed." Chance sets off down the middle path. We walk for a little while before Chance pauses, thinking. "She was being followed by a bear."

"The same one as the boy?" I ask, concerned.

She nods. "Yes, the same traces on him as are here. Guess we found the bear's real target."

My heart races, and my stomach drops. I feel like I'm going to be sick, but I hold it in. Eloise's chances of being seriously hurt suddenly went way up in my book. Chance takes us off the path to a small tree that has some gouges and a limb about six feet up that has only a fractured stump left of it. Parts of the tree are scattered around. I don't wait for Chance; I start searching around the area frantically for Eloise, blood, clothing, anything.

I realize I am holding my breath when Chance lays a hand on my arm, and I take a startled gasp of air in. "She's not here. She left."

"What about the bear?" I am relieved not to have found her body, but I am no less frantic to find her. I must assume that she was still intact when the bear left her as I see none of the signs of an injured person around.

"It left, too. It went the other way." She points back the way we came. I look as though I will see the bear there, even though if it was dropped into the Quest for Eloise, it's long gone.

"So, it didn't follow her?" I ask with relief.

Chance shakes her head. "Nope. Looks like your girl could be a Green." Chance almost sounds proud of that. Is it because she likes Eloise?

"Then why didn't she come out?"

Chance shrugs. "She didn't want to come with you, I bet." She smiles at me, and I scowl at her back.

Even if she did take off, even if she came out, spit in my face, yelled at me that she can't stand me…at least I would know she's alive and unhurt. The need to protect her tugs at me again. *Danger,* the voice whispers. It's the Realm's worst song playing repeatedly, and someone keeps turning up the volume on me.

...IT'S A FOOL'S ERRAND.

Mitac

Chance takes us further in, and, without surprise, we end up at the three-path trailhead again. We take the last one, the left one. I hope this is the last one we have to go down. Although, it's interesting to see someone else's Quest progression. I'm also pleased to see that it hasn't been as traumatizing as mine was. At least, so far.

Chance leads us on a long walk, taking us deeper and deeper into the forest. She stops and leads us back off the path to a large fallen tree. I see ashes from a fire and flattened dirt where someone has lain.

"Camp?" I suggest to Chance.

She agrees with the tilt of her chin. "She stayed here last night. The amount of spirit left here is significant."

Chance doesn't look around or move herself, so I do.

I know Chance would have done the same if she sensed Eloise had gone or stayed anywhere else, but my nerves won't let me abandon the space without looking.

Chance obliges me, waiting patiently, even though I can tell she thinks I'm wasting time. I give up after seeing no other signs of her. We walk back to the path and keep going. Chance stops a little way away from a curve. "She's gone."

"What?"

"Her traces, they just…stop."

"What do you mean they stop?"

She sighs, clearly annoyed. "Exactly that, Mitac. They disappear. Gone, poof, no more Eloise."

"That's impossible. Are there any other traces around from other persons or animals? People's spirits don't disappear unless they drop dead, and I don't see a body, Chance!"

"You think I don't know this, Mitac? This is *my* magic we are talking about here. I am excellent at this, and I am telling you, her spirit disappeared."

I pinch the bridge of my nose with my thumb and forefinger, trying to fend off a growing headache.

"Tell me more," I wave my hand, keeping my eyes pinched closed. "Theories?"

"I don't have any."

To her credit, Chance looks concerned and genuinely puzzled. I am not sure if she's concerned for Eloise or if she's concerned about her abilities. Frankly, it doesn't matter. Hopefully, she's frustrated enough to help me keep looking for her.

"No animals?" I ask to confirm again. Chance huffs at me. "So, she wasn't eaten. Plus, that would have left traces of blood or clothes or something."

"Correct. I sense no animals have come through here. At least none that could have or would have eaten her."

"Did she maybe turn around, and you can't tell the different strands?"

Chance's mouth pinches, but she obliges in walking around the area again. She walks back to the area where Eloise bedded down for the night. She walks the opposite direction, away from the path altogether. I wait for her until she comes back. I can tell by the look on her face what she's about to tell me, but I make her tell me anyway.

"No, Mitac, she did not come back here," she responds to my unasked question. "There is only one exit trace here. She went to the path and walked down it. Then she disappeared."

I feel panic rising in me. I try to remember my training. A big part of being a Warrior is detachment from feelings and panic. Since I am experiencing both of those currently, I lean hard on my instruction.

I picture my big, beefy instructor, shades lighter than me but still stronger than me at the time, rapping my knuckles with a wooden cane for getting distracted during my lessons. For letting fear overcome me during exercises.

To be fair to myself, they had the Reds in training out there throwing fireballs at us, and we were tied up. How are you not supposed to panic when kids who are only just getting control of their powers are hurling fire at you, and you can't move?

According to my instructor, you don't. The helpful "tip" he provided is as ludicrous now as it was then. Eventually, I learned to control my panic on my own by taking a few tips from the Dreamers.

I had overheard one of them in lessons with their apprentice, the voice floating down from the tower they dream in. Deep breathing exercises. I also added to my bag of tricks a few others like pretending I'm somewhere else, but I'm a Negotiator Warrior, not a Combat Warrior. I don't often have a reason to panic anymore, and I am woefully out of practice. The scariest situation I must get into is a battle of words, hidden meanings, and wills. I'm good at those. Not so good at this.

"C'mon, she was consistently following the path unless something pushed her off it. Let's keep going and see if you find her trace again."

Chance opens her mouth and closes it again. She shakes her. As if she knows it's a fool's errand. I know it, she knows it, but neither of us are willing to confirm it. We continue down the path and round a small bend in the trail. I glance hopefully at Chance. Maybe the terrain was blocking her ability to track? Chance shakes her head. We continue walking for quite a while. It's growing dark in the Forest, and I know that Chance is getting annoyed.

"Mitac," she says softly but firmly. "She's not here. I haven't picked up her trace since we lost it way back where she bedded down."

"I know!" I exclaim, rounding on her. "I know." I breathe deeply. "I just...I don't want to give up on her. What do I tell the city about a missing kid? Worse yet, what do I tell Saada about her niece?"

She winces. She hasn't considered facing down Saada. "Any way we can wait for dark and escape while she sleeps?"

I laugh loudly. "If you think Saada is going to sleep tonight or any time until Eloise comes out of here, you're sorely mistaken."

"Yeah, yeah, you're right. It's good she's got someone who cares about her so much." Chance lets down her guard a little bit as her face reveals some past hurt before it disappears again. "So, what do you want to do?"

"I guess our best option is to go back and hope Eloise passed us by somehow."

Chance sniffs. "You think so lowly of my skills."

"No, Chance, I'm hoping, this once, that your skills are shit and Eloise is safe outside the forest."

I don't say that I am terrified of any other possibility. I still don't tell her about the cacophony in my head, yelling about danger. Why won't it stop? The other times, once the subject of it died, the danger was to have considered passed, and the voice stopped. For unknown reasons, it keeps going. The smallest, finest thread of hope is there, and I grab onto it like a man sinking into sand.

How does a person disappear? No trace, no tracks, nothing.

As we walk back out, Chance asks the next logical question. "What do we do if she's not out there? We know kids sometimes get injured or even die during the Quest, but I have never heard of one disappearing entirely."

"I don't know. That's what bothers me so much. It's not like I have a body, some kind of evidence of death, anything to bring back to explain her disappearance. Given how the city is, I don't think they will be very happy if I come back and tell them, 'Well, she disappeared into thin air.'"

"No, you're probably right. You could lie and tell them she died," Chance offers helpfully.

"Fine, I'll tell that to the city," I respond, grinning at her. "You tell Saada."

"No way. You are not making me responsible for telling that woman. You are the one who promised we would bring her back."

"Yeah, when I thought we could. More specifically, when I thought you could."

"Ouch, Mitac, you wound me. I'm still not telling her."

I roll my eyes at her. "I didn't have a lot of choices. The woman is a force to be reckoned with, and if I didn't give her some reassurance, she likely would have killed us right there.

"Very funny. But you're probably right. She'll also probably kill you now that we've come back without Eloise."

We arrive at the edge of the forest. I peer around a tree, where I can see the location of the bags. One bag remains, and my stomach drops.

"So much for her doubling back on us," Chance says from behind me when she sees the bag.

I take a deep breath. "Maybe she hasn't grabbed her bag?"

Chance eyes me skeptically, and like I've lost my mind. "Yeah… maybe. And maybe Saada won't care that you lost her niece." I scowl at her.

We walk out of the forest, defeated. Saada stands up from the porch and rushes us. She is already fuming, I can tell. "Where is she!? Is her Quest still going on?"

"Saada, I…" I run my hand through my black hair. I consider telling her Eloise is still Questing after all, but what's the point of putting off the inevitable? Even if she was still on her Quest, we would have located her. I've been told the Quest will tell you to leave them behind if you find them still being tested. Having nothing…it's not right.

"I'm sorry." My head drops, not willing to look her in the eyes. "We can't find her."

"What do you mean?" she yells loudly.

"Saada, she's currently missing," I risk a glance up to her, and her eyes are alight with fire.

"Missing?" She sits back down, looking quite pale. "Missing? What does that mean?"

Cardis, too, looks pale as he attempts to comfort his aunt. He mindlessly runs his hand across her back, his eyes glazed over, staring into the distance.

Saada rounds on Chance. "You! You were supposed to track her! I should have known you wouldn't be good at your job when Selvia managed to sneak into the forest around you."

I can feel Chance's hackles rising and I lay a hand on her arm to try to calm her. She shakes me off. She does not like to be questioned or made out to be incompetent.

"I did track her, ma'am," she bites out with probably every bit of control she has, "but her spirit traces just…stop. There was no sign of any animals or anything in the area to have eaten her. We looked further down and all around where she last was, but there's no sign of her."

More people are coming out of their houses and heading our way. No doubt because of Saada's distressed shrieking.

"Saada," I plea softly. "This has never happened before that we know of. I wouldn't spread it around. It'll cause unnecessary attention."

"You want me to brush your ineptitude under the rug?!" She laughs heartily. "You're crazy! Incompetent and crazy!"

"Shhh, no. It's not incompetence, Saada. This truly has never happened, and Chance is one of the best Trackers. If anyone can find her, I know she can." Chance is standing square, her arms folded across her chest in defiance. She doesn't acknowledge my compliments toward her.

Saada abruptly drops her head into her hands, anguished sobs wracking her body. I put a hand on her back and try to comfort her, matching Cardis' earlier motions, but she shrugs me off and jumps up, her sobs ceasing abruptly.

"I demand another Tracker. All the Trackers," she yells this last bit to everyone who has gathered around. She looks at them frantically. "I'm going in after her! Anyone who wants to join me can!"

"Saada…"

Cardis glares at both Chance and me then chases after her. The crowd gathered around looks both concerned and angry. I quickly explain to them that we have not yet located Eloise, and she may be in the middle of her Quest. I don't share with them that we feel she disappeared altogether, so as not to incite a mob. I encourage everyone to go home and promise that we will continue to watch and wait. They seem uncertain, whispering amongst themselves in groups. I don't want them running off into the forest at night. Luckily, slowly, they trickle away.

"What do we do?" Chance asks me, watching the crowd disperse. "We can't let her be in there alone."

"I know. I'll go in with her."

I would send Chance in after them, she is the Tracker after all, but

Chance is garbage at trying to negotiate with people. She will never convince Saada to leave the forest if given the opportunity. Remembering the look Cardis gave me, and the threats Saada has given me before I add, "I'll stay at a distance to keep watch on them."

I look over at Selvia, who is watching us closely. It's getting dark and late. "Can you take Selvia back to the inn? And get some pies from Mr. Braswell?"

"Who is Mr. Braswell?" Chance looks genuinely confused.

"He's the baker. I met him at the market and have been getting those delicious hand pies from him. If you go to his bakery, maybe he will still be there with something for us. It's right down the way, on the way to the inn."

Chance looks where I have pointed and nods. "Okay."

She looks over to the forest and I can tell what she's thinking. I have to get going, Cardis and Saada are going to get harder to track the longer I wait. "Be careful, Mitac. You're the best pain in the ass partner I've ever had."

With that she turns toward the Healer's house. Kinta is still on the porch watching us closely. I walk over to her. "Can you keep an eye out for Eloise? In case she comes out while I'm in the forest? Chance needs to go back to the Inn with Selvia."

The Healer nods her consent. I make sure Chance can manage Selvia's wheeled contraption then turn for the forest. I break into a jog, hoping that Saada and Cardis haven't gotten too far, or at least make enough noise for me to follow them. I hate that it's nearly dark. This was not in the plans. So much for the "easy" Quest assignment.

...YOU ARE BUT A CHILD.

Aerith

I rouse from my sleep, confused. I am still exhausted, but sunlight is streaming through the open window. I groan and wish I could go back to sleep, but my absence would be noted by Mancio if we didn't Dream at least once together today. We practiced every single day, even when we weren't having dreams. Now that I have something to Dream, I can imagine that he is anxious to try some more. I would be, too, if I wasn't so tired.

I crawl out of bed and head for the bathroom to clean up. Within a few minutes, I am braiding my purple hair and throwing it over my shoulder as I walk out the door.

I go to Mancio's door and knock. I wait for a few minutes and a few more knocks, but he doesn't answer. I wander away to see if I can find him. My guess would be the kitchens. Mancio can't pass up a meal or a snack. I pass a few people on my way, housekeepers tending the rooms or guards keeping an eye on things. I nod politely to them as I pass. I ask one of the housekeepers I know fairly well, Esher, if she has seen Mancio. She predictably directs me to the kitchen.

Upon entry, I find him sitting on a stool at the counter, spinning while licking pudding off a spoon. I think he has more of it on his face than in his mouth. It's easy to forget when we are training all the time that our apprentices are kids who never get to be kids. It was the same for me. Same as all the Dreamers.

Once we start school and especially once we start our training, we don't get to have fun. What we get is lessons on focus, sitting still, directing our thoughts, and the propriety of being in front of the Illume Council. What a sad existence if I stop to think about it. I usually don't.

I wonder if I gave my guide similar feelings of sorrow when she had to chase me down the halls to join her for sessions or the many times I would play hide and seek…without her permission or her knowing we were playing. Enough discipline resulted in my playful nature being buried.

"Mancio," I warn him lightly but firmly. "It's time to go. Thank the chef."

He frowns and reluctantly hands back the licked spoon and nearly empty bowl of pudding. I remind him to wipe his face which he does hastily before he thanks the chef and follows me out of the kitchen. Back in the hall, we hang a left and climb the two flights of wide marble stairs to the Dreamer room. I don't feel my talisman warming which is disappointing. After all the excitement of the last couple of days, I thought for sure there would be more to show. I am anxious to know what the rest of Eloise's interaction is with the old woman. I also want to know who the old lady is. My talisman is eerily lukewarm.

We both discard our shoes at the door and walk to our places on the carpet. No need to light candles today with it being after noon. I walk Mancio through our breathing exercises, correct his position again, and stuff my thoughts and emotions into my orb while Mancio does the same with his owl.

I sit, feeling foolish, for several minutes. It feels like old times. Nothing for nothing. I am getting ready to give up when my vision changes to the cottage. I look around, or try to, to see if I can see Eloise, but she's not visible from here.

I wait and wait and wait. As I am starting to think this is an exercise in futility, the vision changes. I am inside the cottage now. Eloise is sitting at a table with the old woman. So, she decided to go in after all. Eloise has a cup of tea in front of her, and a large book rests on the table between the old lady and the young woman.

"Look, I appreciate you trying to help me, or whatever this is," Eloise tells the old woman, "but I want to go home."

The old woman smiles. "Yes, I am sure you do."

"So…"

"So?"

"So, how do I make that happen?"

"You have two choices when you leave here. One is to go on about your life like none of this happened. You will always have magic, but you can pretend you do not."

"I like that option," Eloise pounces on that suggestion. She jumps up, prepared to leave the cabin. "Let's do that."

The old woman grasps Eloise's hand and pulls her back down to sit. Eloise winces. "Before you decide, I must tell you the consequences of that choice. Should you choose not to embrace your magic, everyone in your family will die before they are thirty."

Eloise laughs loudly. I nearly laugh with her.

"So, I can return to my life, and it'll be as it has been. I hate to tell you this, Raemyn, but that has been the fate of all of us for a long time. On the plus side, I don't have to be the end of the Realm!"

The old woman, Raemyn, Eloise calls her, frowns. "I am aware of this. If you'd let me finish?" Raemyn has a bit of a bite to her tone, and I flinch for her.

Eloise waves her on. "By all means."

Raemyn points to a place in the book. "The Celestials created the universe with a time clock. Not only for each and every one of you but for humanity itself. Revolutions come and go, and the time clock on humanity gets shorter and shorter. I am sure you have noticed that it won't be long before you can longer birth the next generation before dying?"

Eloise reluctantly nods. I am perplexed by why Raemyn is sharing this information. Evidently, Eloise is, too, as she asks, "What does this have to do with me?"

"Patience. Let me finish!" Raemyn's tone has taken on a scolding quality. Eloise looks slightly abashed.

"Time is running out. Humanity is coming to its end. If you look here," she points to a spot in the book. "Every age has a Variance that resets humanity's clock. Time is put back proper, and humanity gets to live on *again. Slowly, the clock will wind down and time will run out again until another Variance appears."*

"Okay," I feel like Eloise is reaching the same conclusion I am but is reluctant to say it.

"You, dear girl," Raemyn says. "Are the Variance."

She makes the statement grandly but with a hushed reverence.

"The Variance." Eloise stares at Raemyn, not understanding. "The—the Variance. I'm going to need more than that. Explain it like I'm a child."

"To me, you are *but a child." Eloise's eyes narrow. "At any rate, if you look..." Raemyn flips through the pages with the book tilted up like she's trying to hide what she's looking at. "One second. Hold on." A few more pages. "No, not that one." She flips another couple of pages. "Okay, here!"*

She drops the book on the table, the table creaking dangerously under the sudden weight. Raemyn points to a drawing in the book. A man stands in front of several people of various magics, based on their portrayed colors.

"See here? They're talking. That could be you negotiating to reset the revolutions. Everyone would live nice, long lives; you and your family don't have to die by the time they're thirty!"

Eloise reaches out to take the book, but Raemyn holds tight to it. Something is fishy about this.

Eloise raises an eyebrow. "Okay...Let's assume this Variance thingy exists. What makes you think I am the Variance?"

"Aside from your use of all the magics?" she asks, raising an eyebrow at Eloise. Clearly, she's amused. "That necklace you're wearing tells me it's true." Eloise picks up the phoenix around her neck and examines it. "The stone, Eloise, did you notice it?"

"Sure, it's pretty." She admires the stone, and I notice the way it changes colors in the light.

"It is pretty, true, but what it really is, is a talisman. It turns all the colors of magic you can use, As you will."

Raemyn reaches under her shirt to reveal a necklace of her own. It's a lion with eyes of similar stone as the phoenix on Eloise's necklace. I consider, briefly, my own talisman. Also, she said that Eloise used all of the magics. Now, this is news. Faintly, a whiff of surprise crosses my mind.

"Anyone like us gets a talisman," Raemyn states.

"But I haven't turned any colors," Eloise protests.

"You will the more you use your magic. Plus, your hair will change over time."

Eloise's eyes widen. "Is that how you got the grey hair?"

Raemyn laughs. "No, that's because I've gotten old."

"Were you a Variance, then?" Eloise asks. I'm glad because I am starting to wonder the same thing. None of the dreamers talked about how hard it is to be a passive observer to these visions.

Raemyn shakes her head. "No, I was not and am not. I am..." she taps her lip as though thinking, "I am something else entirely. Something even more difficult to explain."

"Oh." I can't tell from Eloise's response if she's disappointed or not that Raemyn can't or won't give her more information about herself. I am, though, which causes my vision to blur before I remember to keep my emotions out of this.

Raemyn sighs and turns the book toward herself. She turns a few pages and turns it back to Eloise. She shows her a drawing of a man with iridescent hair. In several images, it shows him using various magics and changing colors. At rest, though, his hair stays iridescent, while his skin stays what must have been his normal skin tone.

"So, you think I am like this man?" Eloise points to the drawing on the page.

"No, I know *you are like this man. You are the next Variance. No doubt."*

Eloise shakes her head. Her eyes glance at the door. "No, impossible." She stands up and backs away from the table, her eyes wide.

"Eloise, the Realm needs you." Raemyn breathes it reverently. Pleading.

"No, no. Saada said that if I take my magic, then I will be the one to destroy the Realm. Destroy. Not help!"

"What's needed is for the Illume to step down. And for the rulers to start over. Along with a healthy dose of the vilest of humanity being removed." Raemyn turns the pages back, no longer hiding the pages she passes over. The images show various iridescent magic-wielders, male and female, surrounded by destruction on a large scale. I gasp. They are like my vision, and Eloise was at the forefront.

Eloise stares at her in awe, then looks at the book again. Her finger lightly traces the edges of the face of a child, standing between the bodies of a man and a woman. "Why does it have to be this way?"

"As long as time has its way, this is the way it will continue to be." Raemyn looks sad, almost apologetic, toward the poor girl seated at her table, who is essentially being handed the weight of the Realm to carry. "You are the next Variance. You are the one who has the chance to turn back the clock on humanity's end. It has never been this short before."

"Why now, then? Why didn't a Variance come along sooner?"

"The Celestials," she threw an angry look to the roof, "they thought it would be funny to tell the family who creates the Variances how to avoid their magic and what happens if they accept it. Ha. Ha. Funny, right? Those same gods thought it would be funny to also…well, that's for another time."

"That's the curse on my family?" Eloise asks nervously.

"It's not a curse, girl, it's destiny."

"I don't want destiny!" Eloise slams the book closed, nearly closing Raemyn's fingers inside. She gets up from the table again, turning her back on Raemyn. "I want to live a normal life. I don't want to end the Revolutions or the Realm or whatever!"

"Okay," Raemyn says, deathly quiet. "Then everyone dies before thirty. Your aunt, your uncle, your brother, your sister, your cousins…everyone you know and love. And one day, not long from now, the Illume will destroy the Realm, or humanity will simply die off."

"Okay, so why doesn't someone else do it? Someone further down the line? Someone who might actually want *to be chosen?"*

"No other Variance can be born until you die."

"Is humanity going to fail because we wait thirteen years?"

"You're not understanding!" Raemyn slams her hand down on the table. "Everyone else in your family will have been through the Quest. How long before the next generation is ready? And what if they keep putting it off? Or, what if it's your child in here facing this choice, and they choose to take it? Would you prefer that?"

Eloise stares at Raemyn. "It has to be my family? Can't a Variance closer to proper age come from another family instead?" She's pleading with Raemyn like the woman has the ability to do something about it. Maybe she does. After all, there's no telling who this woman truly is, and she's been less than forthcoming in her answers about herself.

"Yes, don't you listen? The destiny, or curse as you put it, is on your family."

Eloise sighs. Clearly frustrated. "Are you telling me, this was offered to my mom, my aunt, even Julieth?"

Raemyn shakes her head. "Yes and no, they mostly ran from their magic so were unable to make it to this point. Those who did, eventually refused the task."

"You're saying I can someday change my mind and not go through with it? If it gets to be too much?"

"You know the consequences," Raemyn's shoulders droop, "So yes, you could change your mind. But Eloise, who else would you have do this?"

"Someone besides me..." Eloise mutters under her breath.

"Eloise, I chose to make your Quest different, to get you to accept your magic."

"Why did it have to be me? Why did you choose me?"

"So Cardis could be in your position?"

Eloise turns from the window and frowns. "No, of course not. I don't want anyone to do it!"

"Someone has to, don't you get that?"

"Then you do it!" Eloise shouts, lashing out. "You have all the same magic, you do it. What's it matter who it is? You have the answers, you have the magic, you're already close to dead so does it matter if you die? I want to live my life with my family and maybe make my own family one day."

"If I could, Eloise, I would. I would die for you if I could. I would stop this cycle and all the others if I could." Raemyn looks sorrowful. "I have the magic, I have the power, but I don't have the freedom. You do."

Eloise is about to ask a question when Raemyn interrupts her. "You can do this, and maybe you can do it less...grotesquely. There's more this time than I've seen before, and I hope that bodes well for us all."

Eloise seems to ponder this. I don't envy her position one bit. What a rotten choice to have to make. Do you sacrifice yourself to reset the Realm, or do you risk humanity's end? I don't know what I would choose. I know nothing of the Variance, but I know that in the oldest annals of history, violent wars and disasters have been recorded. I wonder if these had anything to do with previous Variances. I would love to get my hands on the book Raemyn and Eloise have at their fingertips. *Eloise's face releases the anger she's been holding there.*

"I can see you've decided," Raemyn's voice is soft, soothing. "Now, let me help you."

"Haven't you done enough?" Eloise spits.

"No. Hate me all you want for tricking you, but it will be much easier for you if you listen to me and the advice I have for you."

Eloise scoffs. "What about this is easy?"

"I didn't say easy, did I? I said easier. Now listen, first and foremost, do not go to Amiket City. There is no training for a Variance. Once the Council catches wind of your existence, you will be hunted. The Council will want to use you for their own purposes, seek to control you, or end your very existence."

"Do they know that a Variance is necessary to reset the age?"

"They do," Raemyn nods. "But it doesn't mean they want it to be during their lifetime. They would rather postpone it as long as possible. Your family has been hidden from their knowledge, keeping everyone in it safe. Once they locate you, they will remove everyone in your family to ensure no other Variance can arise until they themselves are ready. Rather short-sighted, especially given they are never ready."

"Got it. Lesson one, no Amiket City. Then what?"

"Lesson two, you will need help."

Eloise looks at Raemyn impatiently. "Isn't that what you're for?"

"I can't stay, girl. You're going to need people around you to teach you, guide you, and help you in all aspects of the Realm. There are many who can and will come alongside you with skills you will require. Unfortunately, there are others who will come alongside you for less noble reasons. Beware the betrayers. They will look familiar, and they won't hesitate to drive a dagger through your heart."

"Who are they? How do I keep away from them?"

"You think I have all the answers?"

"What do you mean? You're the one who said you were going to give me advice. The only advice you have is to avoid being caught by the Council, I'll get help from some other mysterious people whom you can't name, and to avoid being betrayed?"

"Yes, exactly."

Eloise groans. "Gee, thanks." The sarcasm is unmistakable. I don't think I can blame her.

Raemyn shrugs and looks off into the distance, then looks alarmed. "Shit, I lost track of time! It's getting dark and it's time for you to leave. Outside of here, leave the forest immediately, but do not go to your family or your friends. Avoid your village. You will be hunted. The Purple Dreamer has already seen you." Raemyn looks up directly at me, and I am startled straight out of the vision.

I fall over in surprise. Who is Raemyn, and how did she know I was watching? As far as anyone knows, Dreamers leave no trace of their presence. Of course, as far as anyone knows, all Dreaming was of the future, not the present. I sit myself back up. Mancio's questioning look reminds me to school my shock and to come up with something fast to tell him.

"I must be tired," I chuckle. "I was having a lovely vision where the gir—I mean, boy, was taking a nap at home." A plan formulated in my mind for how to keep Eloise and myself safe from the Council. At least now I knew why she needed to be kept safe.

"A nap? So, he finished his Quest?"

I nod. "Looks like it." I cringe at the false cheeriness in my voice. I try to affect a more normal tone.

"Was he Changed?" Mancio asks eagerly.

"Since he was at home, it doesn't appear he did."

"Then why did you have visions of him? Sounds like a boring Quest to me."

I shrug, trying to be convincing. "Sometimes we do not know why we dream what we dream. When the Council next meets, I can share this with them. I bet you they'll be relieved!"

Mancio nods. He doesn't quite look like he's bought into the lie. "Come on, Let's see if the chef has any ice cream."

Mancio smiles large, his misgivings already forgotten as he dashes to his shoes and waits impatiently for me to walk to mine. This will work, I tell myself, it has to.

TAKE ME INSTEAD.

Saada

Must find Eloise. Must find Eloise.

It's the theme that is running through my mind. The single driving force for my reckless dash into the forest. I'm not sure how far I am into the forest when I realize I have no idea where I am. My arms and legs are cut up by the bushes and branches I've blindly barreled through. I reach up, and I can feel leaves and twigs in my hair.

But I must find Eloise. The Tracker, what an imbecile. To tell me that my niece has disappeared. Like she was no more than chaff on the wind. What kind of statement is that to make? Eloise might as well be my child, for Celestials' sake! You don't walk out and drop a bomb like that! "Well, sorry, we don't know where she went." What kind of heartless wench does that?

I stomp onward, my hatred, anger, and fear bubbling over into attacking this forest.

"Saada," a small voice comes from behind me, causing me to jump.

"Cardis! You scared me half to Abyss! What are you doing here?"

He cocks his head. "What do you mean? Why wouldn't I be here?"

"This is not one of your normal jaunts in the forest, Cardis. This could be dangerous. They said Eloise disappeared. Someone could have taken her. I don't want you out here. Go home." What I don't tell him is that I can't lose him, too. I need him to be at home, safe.

He stands before me, nearly as tall as me already, his hands on his hips, looking every bit Leigha's son in that moment. All fierce stubbornness, protector, and compassion.

"All the more reason to not leave you here alone," he reiterates. "It's dangerous, and you shouldn't be out here by yourself. Plus, it's getting dark."

As if on cue, it starts to drizzle, a cold rain from the stormy grey skies above us. I shiver involuntarily in my dress. I look at Cardis and back to the forest.

"Saada, please," Cardis pleads. "We need to stop."

The word "stop" triggers something deep in me. A feeling of failure.

"No! I won't stop until I find her!" I yell at Cardis, and he cowers. I realize with horror what I've done. I have never yelled, never raised my voice. Not at the kids, not at Gamet, never. I start sobbing and reach out, gathering Cardis in my arms. "I'm so sorry, I didn't mean to yell at you."

"I know," he responds quietly. "I don't want to leave her out here, either, but if we don't come up with a plan, we are only going to end up cold, hungry, possibly hurt. And probably lost."

I look around. He's right, I know he's right. Rain drips off my hair into my face. I love the smell of the rain in the forest, and normally, I would dance in it. Not today. Nothing about today is normal. My heart aches.

"We can go back," Cardis urges me softly, "gather some supplies, then continue to look for her tomorrow when we have daylight on our side. I've been marking our trail so we can find our way back out."

I am taken aback by Cardis' clear-headed thoughtfulness in a moment of crisis. While I ran into the forest blindly, no plan, no water, no cloak, Cardis followed me and managed to make sure we had a way back out. What did I do to deserve such a great kid? *Leigha, Steen, he's a good one.*

My shoulders sag, ready to give in and go home for the night. I have to believe Eloise survived one night, and she will survive another. I refuse to believe any other option.

"That won't be necessary," a voice floats from the forest. We both jump and turn toward the voice. Cardis gets in front of me, on the defensive, to protect me from whoever is there even though he has no weapons available. I feel him relax when Mitac walks out. I don't.

"I agree with Cardis that you should both go home," he confirms, "but I do have some supplies that would allow us to stay out here for the night and resume searching in the morning."

I shift from foot to foot. The urge to stay overwhelming, but the logic in my brain says it would be better to go. Cardis is glaring at Mitac. I think he knows I was about to agree to leave with him.

"I dunno, Saada, I still think we should regroup," Cardis continues, "Tell Gamet what's going on, organize a real search party that can cover more of the forest than the three of us can."

Mitac is nodding in approval of his suggestions which makes me want to reject them on principle alone. I can tell the Gopher offered the supplies as an olive branch but also to keep an eye on us. Maybe to keep us safe, or maybe to be able to take Eloise if we find her and she has magic. Most likely, the latter. Screw that, there's no way he can have her now after he bungled this thing so badly.

"Fine." I turn and stomp in the general direction I came, chin elevated, refusing to admit I need help getting out.

"There's a game trail Eloise followed, through here," Mitac suggests. "It will be easier if we take that out."

I stop and glare at him before letting him lead the way. I don't know how I missed the game trail, and I feel my face turn red with embarrassment. If I had a knife right now... His broad back would be an easy target. I'm not a violent person, usually, but if you threaten my kids, I *will* take care of you.

In much less time than it took us to get in, we come back out of the forest. Eloise's bag still sits dejectedly by Kint's. I snatch it up on our way back to the cabin. *Screw the rules.* Playing by the rules put us in this predicament in the first place.

I don't say a word to Mitac and he, wisely, keeps his mouth shut.

I hear Cardis murmur gratitude to the Gopher for his help getting me from the forest. I growl. I would have come out, sense would have reigned eventually, without either of them.

Would it, Saada? Would you have eventually come back, or would you have stayed out there waterlogged and starved to death eventually?

I go home and slam the door behind us. My husband stares at me wide-eyed but I offer no explanation. I leave Cardis to explain what's going on while squelching to the girls' room. Thankfully, Hilda and Gilda are in the living room. I crumble onto Eloise's unmade bed, her bag clutched in my arms. I smell her lavender-scented soap on her linens.

"I promise, I'll never get mad about the messes she leaves," I pray, "I'll happily pick up her clothes, make her bed every day, I'll make her favorite bread, I'll do anything, Celestials. Bring her home. Take me, instead, if you must have someone." Sobs wrack my body, stealing my breath.

For the first time in my adult life, I wish I had made a different decision in my Quest. Perhaps if I had, Eloise would be here. I was too much of a coward, too scared. Eloise isn't. What if she learned what we really are? What if she decided to do it? Guilt pierces me through and through.

I pound on the wall with the side of my fist repeatedly, wanting to hurt as much as my heart hurts. Wanting to hurt myself as much as Eloise could be hurting right now.

I don't know how long I hit the wall before a gentle, but callused hand envelopes mine, protecting me from further harm.

"Shhh." The bed shifts under Gamet's weight, and he pulls me close to him. I curl into him, making myself as small and insignificant as I feel right now. He says nothing, wrapping his strong arms around me and shushing me like I'm a small child. Like he did years ago when my sister and brother-in-law died. He rocks me until my breathing slows, my tears stop, and I drift into a fitful sleep. A familiar face haunts my dreams. One I haven't dreamed of, thought about, or cursed at in years.

PART III

The Journey

...SOME WEIRD HALLUCINATION?

Eloise

I stand from the table, less than pleased with the outcome of this odd encounter. I don't feel any different, for supposedly having control of eight different magics. I would have expected some tingling, maybe some light, something besides feeling exactly like myself.

Well, sort of. In truth, I'm lost. Utterly lost. Adrift with no life raft. There's only one thing I want to know now. I face the window and ask the question that has been burning inside of me since things started to click into place.

"How long do we have?"

No response.

I turn to repeat my question, but she's disappeared.

What in the Realm? I search the cottage fruitlessly. Where could an old woman hide in a single-room cottage? Worse yet, where could she have possibly gone? So much for all the help she was supposed to be providing. I don't feel helped. I feel like I was warned and made to be scared. But helped? No.

I check under the bed and pull open the cupboards, feeling as ridiculous as I know this search is. I notice with alarm that her bookshelf is empty and the book we were reading is also gone. Shoot, I would have loved to have read a bit more of that.

The menacing knives on the wall are gone, the sink empty, our dishes from the tea are nowhere to be found. It's like the cottage never had anyone living in it, at least not within the last decade or two. I sneeze when I stir up some dust bunnies from under the bed.

I snort, *Bun Bun*. I wanted to strangle her for that one. Rabbit was bad enough, but Bun Bun? And what was she trying to hint? That I'm flighty? Easily frightened? Prey to be eaten? *Mmmm, rabbit stew.*

I shake my head. There aren't any qualities of a rabbit that I would want attributed to myself. Quick on my feet is probably the only one I would be okay with.

I give up my search; the woman and everything she had in here are gone. I look out the windows, which are caked with dust and grime. I can barely see the planter boxes at the window. There's nothing in them. Maybe I dreamed all of this. Maybe Raemyn was some weird hallucination?

I would like to wake up now. I want to go home.

I walk to the door and turn the handle, holding my breath to see if it opens. It does. Guess the old woman was true to her word.

I step over the threshold, and a slight shimmering around me catches my eye. I turn to try to catch sight of it, but it disappears, remaining ever on the edge of my vision. I step away from the cottage and turn back to look at it one more time…to find it has disappeared. Well, that tracks with every other part of this unusual day. I step forward and fall over a tree root.

I JOLT AWAKE. My body is screaming at me in pain. I turn over, and my fire is still burning away. The sun is starting to peek through the trees in the east. Well, that was a weird dream. I smile, relief overwhelming me. I'm safe, it was a dream, nothing to be worried about. Where does one's brain even come up with such weird things to dream about? And so detailed, too!

I take the necklace out from under my shirt. Unlike in my dream, it's not hot to the touch. I look at it, examining the gem and its many colors.

I think over everything that happened. It has to have been a dream. Nothing on me or around me indicates I ever left the position I was in last night.

I sit up, rolling my shoulders and stretching. I'm pleasantly surprised to find that my back doesn't hurt like I expected. I am ravenous, though. I grab some jerky from my bag and eat the whole thing. I'm determined to leave today. No matter what, this Quest has to be over today.

I lift my canteen to wash down the dried meat when I realize it's still empty. No matter, I'm leaving.

I stare into the crackling flames beside me, lost in thought for a little while. I'm not sure if I'm disappointed or not that it was all a dream. It would be cool to have an answer for how to reset the clock on humanity, but do I want to be the one to do it? If I think about it, I don't think so.

Someone should, though, if there is a way. Not me. No, no, thank you.

Finally, I stand and put out my fire with some sand and I prepare to continue my Quest, since I still haven't been told to leave. I climb over the tree trunk I slept next to last night and head back to the path.

"LEAVE!" A big voice booms. I jump and nearly wet myself.

"No need to be so dramatic," I mumble to the forest. "I've been trying to get you to let me leave for a couple days now!"

I turn on the path, back the way I had come previously, and I see that an exit has opened at the edge of the forest. "Does this mean I'm Unchanged?" I ask the air around me.

"LEAVE!" the voice repeats itself. I wonder if it's Raemyn, but the voice sounds different from hers. Further confirmation that it was a dream.

"Alright, I get the point," I grumble. With no definitive answer, but seeing no change to my skin or, I pull my hair down and bring it in front of my face, my hair, I assume I'm Unchanged. I tie my hair back into a tight bun and begin walking out.

I step out of the forest as the sun peaks over the mountains, its rays caressing my face. The warmth is welcome, and so is the hope I feel seeing it.

Weird. All is quiet. I expect to see my bag and the table, or at least Saada waiting for me. The Clearing is empty. It is early, but I am surprised and a little hurt that Saada wasn't waiting for me to come out. I walk the most direct route to the cabin. It sits dark in the early morning. A little odd. Usually, Saada, at least, is up early making breakfast for Gamet before he leaves for work.

I walk up to the cabin and turn the doorknob to open and walk through it. I grunt when I run into the door with my shoulder. It's locked. That's the second time I've run into something solid in the last couple of days. I'm not appreciating this new trend.

I try the doorknob again in case I twisted it wrong. Still locked. The door is never locked. I am truly perplexed.

First, no one waited for me to leave my Quest, and now they have locked me out of my house. What is happening around here?

Where would we have stashed a key? I can't think of anything. We never even had a key that I knew of, but I had heard from other friends who were less trusting where they put their keys. I look under the mat at the foot of the door, no key. I check under the empty flower pot. No key. Coming up with no answer, I resort to knocking. On my own door. Annoyance flashes through me.

I wait for a minute before knocking again. Finally, the door swings open. I nearly stagger in shock when Julieth answers looking bleary-eyed. She rubs her eyes. Then rubs them again. Then blinks at me rapidly.

"Eloise?" She sounds stunned. Probably as stunned as I feel seeing her at the cabin.

"Julieth? What are you doing here?" I ask her at the same time she asks me, "You're alive?"

"Of course I am," I reply, more than a little annoyed by this whole ordeal already. "I've only been gone for a couple of days."

Julieth shakes her head. "What are you talking about? You've been gone for *months*."

"Julieth, are you still asleep? I went on the Quest a couple of days ago. It's what? Tuesday? I went in on Monday, had an Abyss of a time, thanks for asking, and came back out, finally. Also, thanks for not telling me about the family curse. Could have used that information sooner."

Julieth stares at me. "Eloise, it was Tiulla 22nd when you went in; it's now Atar 15th. It's been *two months* since the Quest started. Everyone came out except for you."

I laugh. "Don't be ridiculous. Where is Saada?" I look around her, "Or even Gamet? Why are you staying here?"

"I've been here since—"

I don't wait for her to explain. I push myself in since she doesn't invite me in. The cabin looks the same, albeit awfully unkempt. The first feeling of disquiet settles in. I look around for Saada and don't see her.

"Look, Els," I cringe at her use of my nickname. She hasn't been around me enough to be that familiar anymore. "Gamet is out back where he has been for the last couple of months, and Saada..." she trails off again in that annoying way.

I decide to head out back to get answers from someone else. Maybe she and her girlfriend broke up in the last couple of days. Can I be so hopeful? Maybe that's why she's at the cabin, and she's too embarrassed to say so. Doesn't explain why she thought I was dead, though. Or why she wants to insist it's now Atar. My sister has never been one for jokes. What a weird thing to joke about, anyway. Maybe Cardis put her up to it.

I go through the back door and out through the garden. I look around for Gamet and, not seeing him, head further out to the small meadow that lines our property. Under the tree is a crude wood plaque at the top of somewhat recently turned dirt. My stomach turns. *No...*

I walk with leaden legs to the wood plaque. "Here lies Gamet. Shilium 18 1734 – Udar 07 1762"

I don't read the rest. I drop to my knees.

Udara? Udara is *next* month. How can there be a plaque for someone who hasn't died yet? And why would someone put that up or wish ill will on my uncle? I rip the post out of the ground, trying to rip the plaque off of it. *No no no. None of this is right.*

"He died a couple of months ago." Julieth has joined me outside. I glare at her over my shoulder.

"No! He was alive a couple of days ago."

"No, Eloise, he died a couple of weeks after you disappeared on your Quest. Your Gopher did it."

I scream. "NO! Stop lying! You're lying! Why are you doing this, Julieth?" I look at her hand and notice the ring from a couple of days ago is missing. "Is this some kind of weird payback for saying that I thought it was a terrible idea to marry Elaxi?"

Julieth's left hand covers her right. Her nostrils flare. "No, Eloise. I'm telling you the truth."

"No, you're lying. You're—you—jealousy. That's what it is. You're jealous. Or mad. Or something. Where is Gamet really? Where is Saada?"

I stand from my kneeling and hurl the plaque and post as far from here as possible. I don't step on the fake grave. Even fake, I can't desecrate it like that. *What if it's real?* I dash that thought away. No, I won't accept it.

I hear footsteps behind me. I turn, expecting to see Saada. It's Cardis. He approaches slowly as though he can't believe what he is seeing. Like Julieth, he blinks at me repeatedly.

I look back to the grave, still not believing what *I* am seeing. He tentatively touches me and pulls his hand back like he has been burned. "Eloise? So, you're actually alive?"

Why does everyone insist on thinking I'm supposed to be dead?

"Cardis, tell me the truth. Is this a joke?" I plead with him.

Cardis looks like I struck him. "No, Eloise. It's not a joke. You've been gone for months. Look at the garden."

I turn to look at the garden I had walked through earlier yet completely ignored. Everything is overgrown and being choked out by the melons and squash. There is no way for this much growth to happen in a couple of days. I turn and vomit as my stomach revolts, careful to avoid the freshly turned dirt.

Gamet and I weren't overly close, but I still cared for him. Cardis' words don't penetrate. They don't make sense. I have just seen him. Tears roll down my cheeks. Julieth walks back to the house. I hear the back door close behind her.

Dizzy, I hold onto Cardis for strength. He flinches when I touch him. "Tell me, Cardis, where is Saada?" I ask, afraid of his answer.

"The Gopher...he and a friend of his took her."

"Took her where?" When Cardis doesn't answer, I ask again my eyes burrowing into his, "Where, Cardis? Where did they take her?"

"I can't be sure, but I think they took her to Amiket City." I hold my hands over my ears, squeezing. As though I can get the roaring in my ears to stop if I squeeze hard enough.

I stagger. "Why would they take her? This doesn't make any sense. How have I been gone for two months?"

"I don't know. Come on, let's go sit down before you fall down."

We go back into the cabin. Julieth is sitting at the table. Cardis and I join her. She's prepared tea for us all. I take a sip, hoping it doesn't come back up. I hold the cup with both hands to hide their shaking.

"Someone, please help me fill in the blanks," I start, looking at both of them.

"I wasn't there for most of it," Julieth begins. I snort. Of course she wasn't. She glares at me then continues, "You went into the Quest on a Monday. You were gone for thirty-six hours, so the Tracker and Gopher went in to get you. They came back out and told Saada you had disappeared. This is what Saada told me, anyway, when she came to get me to be part of the search party. It took me only minutes to be ready to go in after you. You—" her voice breaks, "—you worried us so much."

This surprises me. Julieth *wanted* to come get me. She wasn't forced?

"They organized a search party by Wednesday to look for you. Nearly all of Ashadier hunted for you, took about two weeks, but we couldn't find you. Another Warrior showed up while they were gone, looking for someone. They said a Dreamer in the palace had a dream about some boy who was supposed to have Changed. No boys had any change in all of Amaranth.

"He had already stopped in Winfair, Bruderdon, and Rothesard. No one had any magic at all. Since you were the only one with anything abnormal, the Warrior became intensely interested in you." Julieth pauses and looks at Cardis. "Cardis will need to fill in the rest as I was still walking out of the forest when it happened."

"Saada got us kids outside," Cardis picked up the story hesitantly, "She had us stay in the goat pen, and she hid in the garden. They started by interrogating Gamet, best I can guess. He must not have given them answers they wanted." Cardis looked down at the table as tears threatened to spill over. "They—" He takes a deep breath. "They cut his throat."

I gasp but Cardis keeps going. "After they finished with him, they came out to grab her. They must have heard her cry out when she peeked into the window. Anyway, they asked where the rest of us were, and she said she didn't have any kids. Only her, Gamet, and you."

That sounded like Saada. Sacrifice herself to protect everyone else. "They said that either she produced you or she would go in replacement. She didn't know where you were, not that she would have told them anyway, so they hauled her off.

"She started struggling and they hit her over the head and carried her away. We haven't seen or heard from her since."

I stare back and forth in horror at Julieth and Cardis. "The kids ran to find me," Julieth continues. "We stayed in the tiny apartment for about two weeks before deciding that wasn't workable and the Warriors were likely not coming back. I brought the kids back to the cabin and here we are. We never thought we'd see either of you again."

My mind is running like a train off the rails. I swallow back the bile in my throat. I can't feel anything. My body has gone numb. Shock, I must be in shock. I start shaking. Gamet is gone. No, Saada is gone. Gamet is dead. Oh, Celestials. And I threw his plaque into the meadow.

"I have to find it," I stand suddenly, my knees banging on the table, but I barely take notice. "I've gotta get it back before it's ruined further." I start walking for the back door then I turn, my knife off my belt in my hand suddenly. "No, I'll make him a new one, a better one." I start to head for the front door. "Why is it raining in here?" I look up at the ceiling. Wetness splashes on my face.

Two hands wrap around my upper arms, force me back to the table, and push me into the chair I had vacated.

"No, can't sit. Gotta make a new marker for Gamet." More water. "Why is the whole roof leaking?" I demand, looking at my siblings but not seeing them. "Why hasn't someone fixed the roof? I'll fix it. Hold on."

I stand up again, heading for the front door to get to the roofing supplies. I can fix it.

The hands are on me again. I swing wildly, blinded, and connect with something soft. A cry follows it.

From far away, "Eloise!"

I hear the name. *Whose name is that?*

"Eloise!" Again, that name. *Who's yelling? Why doesn't Eloise answer so the yelling stops?*

A hand connects with my face, and I blink.

"Eloise!" I blink again. Eloise…that's *my* name. Why is it raining inside?

I look at the person yelling. Julieth. She's got blood running from her lip. How did that happen?

"Eloise, hi," she has a blood-tinged grin. "Welcome back."

"Why is it raining inside?" I ask out loud this time.

"It's not," her voice is consoling. "You're crying."

"Crying?" I ask, confused. Why am I crying? What happened?

"Yes, crying." She tentatively places her hands on my arms and guides me back to the table again. I sit down but jump up again. She pushes me down and keeps her hands on my shoulders.

"It'll be okay," Julieth reassures me. "You're just upset."

"Upset," I repeat. Why? I wrack my brain.

"Breathe with me," Julieth gets in my face. I look in her green eyes. Emerald. She places her palms on either side of my face. "Breathe, Eloise. In your nose, out your mouth. Nice and slow."

I try it out. Feeling silly for breathing with someone else like I don't know how to breathe. But it helps. The roaring in my head decreases. The black rings at the edge of my vision I hadn't even realized were there, recede. Julieth instructs me to breathe a few more times.

When I do, the cause comes rushing back to the forefront of my mind, and I wish it hadn't. The blackness returns, but this time, it veils my entire being.

...SMIDGEN OF HOPE.

Saada

Revolution 1762 Udara 05 (R62U05)
Fourteen Days After the Start of the Quest

AFTER CARDIS and I left the forest with Mitac, we organized a town-wide search party. Everyone took part. In groups of threes and fours, we set out in lines, close enough to run between and send messages to each other but not close enough to see other parties. We zig-zagged, making sure to cover every possible nook and cranny.

It appeared to have returned to normal, according to Mitac. He had said the creek was dry when he and Chance had searched before. The creek was flowing normally when we went through on our search for Eloise.

We did not find her. We spent a week walking the depths of the forest. We nearly made it all the way to Winfair in the east, and as far as Bruderdon in the south. Eloise did not appear. There was no sign of her or her things. Each day, my desperation grew. My prayers to the Celestials grew more and more frantic. My bargains with them grew more and more outlandish. I would have given my life to see a sign of her anywhere.

Mitac and Chance came with me and Cardis, but I still wasn't convinced it wasn't for any reason other than to take Eloise to Amiket when we found her. And that's how I thought of it the whole time. When, not if, we found her. Because we would.

Gamet stayed behind to look after the younger kids and keep an eye on Selvia, who Mitac firmly had to tell could not come with us. There was no way to get her wheeled chair through the forest.

Every one of us carried packs of supplies, and my feet and back ached fiercely. Outside of laundry, I didn't do much physical activity, and it was showing.

Cardis was a trooper, trailing along with us, and showing us his knowledge of the forest flora and fauna. I am certain part of his showing off had less to do with trying to impress us and more with trying to take my mind off my missing niece, who I was supposed to be a guardian for, watching out for, keeping safe.

If the Celestials didn't take my life in exchange for Eloise's, I'm pretty sure Leigha would find a way to come back and kill me for losing her daughter.

On the last day, near the opposite edge of the forest, I finally relented.

"She's not here, is she?" I asked no one in particular. I didn't expect an answer.

Mitac looked at me with pity. Chance looked…well, she looked like she always has. Slightly annoyed and bored. Cardis' face contorted to a deep scowl, his eyes brimming with tears.

Chance took the opportunity to share with the next closest group of people we were heading back, and they should, too. Presumably, each group sent one person to the next group until we all were heading home.

OUR QUARTET MAKES the long trek back to Ashadier, mostly in silence. We sleep fitfully at night, or at least Cardis and I do, but the Gopher and Tracker seem to sleep fine. Back in the village, everything looks the same despite our absence. People straggle out of the forest in small groups. They all apologize to me and ask me to let them know how else they can help. I have never been so proud of my Ashadier family and so heartbroken all at once.

"I'm sorry, I really am." I look over and realize Mitac is apologizing to me.

I shake my head. "It's not your fault. Turns out you weren't completely wrong. She disappeared."

I fight back tears. I still cannot fathom where she went or what happened. A rock forms in my gut as an option I had not considered comes to light. What if she accepted our magic? What if she somehow escaped the forest? What if she didn't want to come home? I give in to this last smidgen of hope. I don't care if she hated us and wanted to leave all along and this is how she did it. At least she's still alive. I know it's not true; I know it's denial at its finest, but I'll enjoy it for as long as I can.

I start to walk away, Cardis behind me, when I see another Black Warrior heading toward us. I pull up. This Warrior looks nothing like a Gopher. He's the same dark black color but has a leather vest, and I can see two black sword handles sticking up from behind him. I had seen Mitac's weapons on our trip, but by then, I knew he wasn't a threat. At least, not an obvious one.

"Cardis," I whisper urgently, "Hide."

I don't know for sure that this Warrior is trouble, but the hard look in his face does not give off friendly feelings. I am hopeful that the Warrior is far enough out not to see Cardis, who is positioned a little behind me. Cardis only hesitates for a moment, then disappears around the nearest building. I walk a little closer to Mitac. Better the evil you know than the evil you don't, right?

"Mitac, what is going on?" I whisper.

"The city might have sent someone to look for us when we didn't come back in a timely fashion," he whispers.

"Why would they send someone armed?" I'm still eyeing the swords on his back.

"I'm not sure. Maybe because there hasn't been any communique to Amiket about why we are delayed? Perhaps they think we have been taken hostage." Mitac laughs, and I would join him, but I'm too scared.

"Friend or foe?" I ask.

"Friend." But I hear him mutter under his breath as he walks away, clearly not for my ears, "I hope."

Mitac puts on a smile and approaches the other Warrior. They shake hands. They have friendly looks on their faces, but I can tell they're sizing each other up. They talk together and I decide to take my leave. I look to be surplus to requirements for this conversation.

I head back to the cabin, trying to look as nonchalant as possible, so as not to draw attention to myself. When out of the eyeline of this new Warrior, I speed up to a fast jog. Despite my tiredness and aching feet, I run, limping, as fast as I can manage. I know this is important. The unease I felt around Mitac originally is back in spades.

I crash through the door and find Gamet and Cardis waiting for me. I am grateful Cardis knew to return to the cabin.

"What was that all about?" Cardis asks after I burst in.

"Another Warrior," I pant out, and I turn to lock the cabin door, something I haven't ever done. The door lock sticks before finally sliding into place. I turn to face Gamet and Cardis who are both looking at me with wide eyes. "One that Mitac doesn't know. He thinks they were sent to check on him and Chance because they haven't yet returned to Amiket after the Quest. I'm not so sure."

"So why did you come in like your hair was on fire?" Gamet asks, getting up from the table.

"Call it a feeling coupled with the swords strapped to his back. I think it's better we get out of here."

Gamet looks out the cabin window. "I think you may be right. But I think it's too late. Kids!"

I look outside the window and see Mitac and the other Black Warrior striding toward our cabin with purpose. He's more menacing than I thought. The kids appear around in the hall, all except for Selvia who, Gamet explains, has been going to Miss Halsey's shop to read during the day. I pray to the Celestials she stays there while we deal with whatever this is.

I take all my kids out the back of the house, and I tell them to stay quiet and stay low. I ask Cardis to watch over them. He ushers the kids to the goat's shed, and I plant myself in the garden where I might be able to hear what's going on.

"Hello, sirs," Gamet addresses the men. I smile. You can take the man out of the noble, but you can't take the noble out of the man. His training is clear. He must have invited them into the house, or they shoved their way in because all the voices grow muffled.

I wait and wait. I am tempted to peek into the window, but I fear they will see me if I do. I look back at the shed and see the kids growing anxious and bored at the same time. Cardis is doing a wonderful job of keeping them quiet, but they only have so much patience.

I hear a commotion coming from inside, and I can no longer resist looking. I slowly rise from my crouched position. Only enough to see into the window. I gasp. Gamet is tied to a chair and slumped over, and I see blood running down his chest. I stuff a fist into my mouth, but a sob still escapes me. Mitac looks over at me. I barely have time to think about where the other Warrior is when hands grasp my arms and pull them behind my back. I struggle against the restraint, but a tie is placed around my wrists. Tightly. I resist crying out; I don't want the kids trying to rush out to my aid.

"Stop fighting," he snaps at me, jerking my arms upward, pulling painfully on my shoulders. An unbidden yelp escapes my lips. I see Cardis poke his head around and I try to tell him with my eyes to go back.

"Stop giving me a reason to," I resist stubbornly. My wrists are already burning from the tightly wrapped ropes, and I can feel my fingers going numb. Fear races through me.

"I'm not. Your missing niece is." Eloise. They are after Eloise. Why?

"What do you want with her?" I demand as though I'm in a position to demand anything. As though I'm not practically hog-tied.

He ignores my question and asks his own, "Where are the other kids?"

Thinking fast on my feet, I ask, "What other kids?" It's a no brainer on my part that I will take whatever punishment this man has for me in place of the kids. I might be terrified of what they're planning to do with me, but my instincts to protect my kids overrule all of that.

"The other members of your family, you dolt."

"I don't have anyone but Gamet and my niece." I raise my voice, trying to get the message across to Cardis. I hope against hope that they won't search the cabin. It will be too easy to see that we aren't the only ones living in the cabin as soon as they do a cursory search.

He grunts and looks at Mitac. I silently beg Mitac not to reveal the others. I don't risk looking at them, but I trust Cardis has heard me well enough to deduce what he needs to do. I pray to the Celestials they stay hidden. Mitac nods, confirming my lie and I sag in relief.

"Well, lucky you, then, you get to come back with us." I stiffen again.

"I can't go with you!" I start fighting the ties again. The burn on my wrists worsens, but I ignore the pain. I try to fight the restraints, try to free my arms. I fling myself backward, trying to catch the Warrior off his feet. He only chuckles and lifts my arms again; I hear a pop on one side, and I scream as pain radiates through my left shoulder.

"Actually," he sneers as he leans closer to my ear. His breath smells of tobacco and alcohol. "You can. Your niece isn't here, and your… husband…is indisposed." Gamet. Oh, Celestials, what did they do to Gamet? I choke on another sob.

"Why would you need to stay here? Unless you can tell us where your niece is, you're her replacement." I thrust my head back and hear a satisfying crunch of his nose and smell the tang of blood in the air.

He pushes me away from him roughly and I land on my face in the dirt. "Dumb bitch. Wait until you see what's coming to you. Once more, where is your niece?"

His voice is garbled, probably from the blood dripping down his face. He hauls me back up onto my knees. I spit the dirt out of my mouth. My dislocated shoulder twists even more. Luckily, my other one remains in its socket. For now.

"I don't know where she is. She never came out of the forest." I'm being honest. I try to meet Mitac's eyes, to plead with him. Hopeful for some humanity. He doesn't look my way. "Please, is my husband okay?"

The man shrugs and spits blood off to the side of us. At least he doesn't spit in my face.

"Don't know, don't care." I look at Mitac again. He meets my gaze. I try to get him to tell me or to at least check on my husband, but he's staring at me with a cold look. So much for him being a human with a soul. At least he doesn't spill about the kids. Maybe that's the full extent of his kindness.

"Let's go." The other Warrior roughly gets me to my feet. "We have a train to catch."

I struggle again, fruitlessly. I know I'm not going to get free, but panic doesn't care about that. I push, I pull, I twist…then my world goes black.

...SIREN FOR DEATH...

Aerith

Revolution 1762, Atar 09 (R62A09)
About 1 1/2 months after the Quest

I'M RELIEVED. It has been several weeks since the Council heard about my first round of dreams, and nothing has happened since. We've had several meetings, and I continue to tell them I have nothing new to report. I reported that the boy I had seen in my dream ended up being of no import. They seemed to accept the lie readily, clearly feeling the burden lift. It seems their desire for it all to be nothing is so great that they'll accept my weakly concocted story.

I sit and dream with Mancio each day, but we see nothing, and I am grateful for this, too. Turns out, I'd rather have nothing to do than be the siren for death and change. Leave that to the other colors, thank you very much.

The Council calls our regular meeting and me and Mancio approach as we always do. I feel light as a bird, relaxed. I smile at Naseem, who gives me a pinched smile in return. She's less convinced that I've gotten away with my lies.

I told her what I had seen with Raemyn and Eloise after it happened, and she insisted I needed to be careful and needed to leave. The longer nothing happens, the more I disagree with her assessment of the situation. I still wake up in my comfortable bed, we eat delicious lunches and dinners together, and life returns to normal. What more could I hope for?

When the Council enters this time, they look less than amused. Instead of calling everyone forward in order like they normally do, they call only me in front of them, telling Mancio to stay where he is. I break out in a cold sweat.

The Council grills me for over an hour, the other Dreamers standing nearby. They don't dare look bored or ask to leave. I answer their questions while trying to maintain an even tone of voice and not betray how fast my heart is beating. Finally, it looks like they're going to let me go. Unhappy, but they seem ready to accept what I have been selling them.

"She is lying," the Black magic-wielder states with deadly calm. My breath catches in my throat.

"Excuse me?" I try to sound offended rather than surprised and terrified.

"You're lying. I can sense it. Your heart rate is high, your breathing is shallow, and you smell from sweating." My suspicions about the Black Council member renew. He must be a Truth Finder. I do what I know best in this situation: deny, deny, deny.

"I have been standing here for an hour," I growl.

He waves my statement off. "You're still lying. The sweat is stress, not heat."

I start to chew the bottom of my lip before I remember that will make me look guilty and stop. "Believe what you will, but I am not lying to you. It was a simple error like I told you previously."

The Black Council member is glaring at me with unadulterated hatred. Until recently, that look would have had me on my knees begging for him to forgive my lapse in judgment and have me spilling my secrets unabashedly.

Now, however, I feel a supernatural internal strength. I continue to look him directly in the eyes. Almost daring him to come after me. Refusing to back down.

"We know differently," he sighs after a long pause. "Mancio?"

I raise my eyebrows. *What fresh Ravaged Abyss is this nonsense?*

Mancio steps forward and bows and kneels like he's been taught to, but he does not stand again. "Yes, sir?" his voice is quiet and shaking.

"Stand, then tell everyone what you told me," the Black man orders then holds up his hand. "Wait, one second. Bring in the scribe!"

Mancio rises from his knee. Murmuring breaks out around the table, and a small, hunched, Unchanged man shuffles in holding a quill, ink pot, and several pieces of parchment. He sits at a small desk in the corner I've never noticed before. I feel sick. What does Mancio know? I didn't tell him anything other than what I've shared with the Council.

After the scribe is seated and prepared, the Black Illume waves Mancio on. He looks nervous, as he should be. He's never had to address the Council, but could his nerves be for whatever he is about to reveal to contradict me? Or does he not care?

Mancio spares me a glance, but the look is not one of fear but of smugness. Whatever this is, it's not good.

"Aerith has not told you the truth of what she has seen," he starts. I begin to protest, but the Unchanged Council member raises a hand to stop me.

Mancio continues, "What she has truly seen has been of several kids, but most often of a girl who is going to bring destruction before peace. She has also seen she has access to all the magics and is something called the Valence."

My mouth drops open. What the ever-loving Abyss is happening here? My head spins as blood drains from my face. I struggle to control my reactions.

"Valence? Do you mean Variance?" The Orange Council asks.

"Yes, Variance," he corrects, nodding confidently.

"How do you know this?" The Green Council member asks slowly, clearly skeptical.

"Because I have seen it, while Dreaming alongside her."

"Impossible!" I protest, "He is only twelve. He does not have access to Dream yet! He is still five years from the Quest. How can you take a boy's imagination as truth when I, who have access to my powers, have actually Dreamed things?"

"The thing is," the Black Council member growls, "you are lying to us. What he speaks is truth. And no one outside of the Council knows of the Variance. It is a tightly held secret. As a result, the only way for him to know would be to have been told by you or to have Dreamed it." Cold seeps through my bones as fear takes root. "It doesn't matter if you told him or the Celestials gave him dreams, it's the truth and you—" he points directly at me, "—are lying."

"I—" I start to argue but don't get any further.

"Additionally, the aunt of the accursed Variance is here. You'll get to know her soon enough." The Black Council sneers at me, his perfectly straight teeth at odds with the venom he spits out.

"Guards!" The Black Warriors step forward. "Take her to the dungeons."

I am about to fight before I recognize the futility. I have been found out. Resistance at this point will only result in a more severe punishment. Two of the guards each seize one of my arms roughly. Their black skin is quite the contrast to my vibrant purple.

I catch Naseem's eyes as they start to drag me out. She stares at me with worry written all over her face. At least she doesn't give me the "I told you so" look I've been giving her when we had perfectly normal Council meetings. I don't hold her gaze long; I don't want her to get into trouble for knowing me. I wonder if this is the last time I will see my one and only friend.

"What should we do with her once she's there?" the guards ask.

The Illume deliberates. "Torture her until she tells the rest of the truth."

My stomach drops. Of the three options I considered as an outcome for this, torture is the worst. Falling behind locked up forever and death. I only hope I can hold out long enough to let Eloise get a head start.

"It doesn't matter much, does it?" The Yellow Council member asks. "After all, we know it's likely to be that girl from Ashadier since she was the only one in Amaranth to have anything go weird with her Quest."

"We know it's likely," the Red Council member continues, "but we don't know for sure. We also don't know the rest of it. Like what will she do? How important is she? Why does she matter at all? I, for one, would very much appreciate answers to these questions. Paired with Batair's visions of the other two Vales, I think it's prudent to see what other information we can get from her."

The other Council members nod along in agreement. The last tendril of hope for a quick death disappears. I grew complacent. I shouldn't have. I should have left when Naseem told me to. I want to tell her she was right, but I don't get the chance.

The guards stalk me out through the double doors. I have never been to the dungeons, I have never needed to go there, thankfully. This might be to my detriment now. I am wishing I had scoped it out so I could have devised a contingency plan for escaping. Arrogance. Stupidity. Complacency. I never knew these would be my downfall.

I walk between the guards, wishing they would ease their grip on my arms. My pinky fingers are going numb. "You know I'm not resisting, right?" I ask them, looking back and forth as we descend yet another flight of stairs. Notably, these stairs are stone rather than marble, and the hallways are getting smaller and darker. That might work to my advantage when I try to escape. It'll be easy to see anyone coming or going. Of course, it also means I'll be easier to see coming or going, too.

The guards chuckle. "Nice try, princess, but we're not letting you go."

"I didn't say let me go, but you don't have to hold on so tight. It's starting to hurt."

"Whine, whine, whine. Get used to it. This is barely the start," the guard on my left sneers at me.

I hang my head and plod on.

There are torches in sconces on the walls. The dim, flickering light shows only more stone, more walkways. I can see up ahead there is a slightly brighter patch of light and beyond that what looks to be the first of the cells. As we approach, I take careful note of the exits. Or lack thereof. There are no doorways, no offshoot paths, no hiding places. Clearly this was designed as a one way in, one way out kind of dungeon.

Great, that'll make it easier. Oh, who am I kidding? I can't escape. I couldn't even survive a couple of days in the damned city.

The cells are about eight feet square with low ceilings. Merely tall enough for the average person to stand. The back walls are made of stone. Each cell is connected to the next, round bars made of a rough iron between them. The space between the bars less than twelve inches. Although I'm quite slender, I'm not slender enough to get through that.

A small cut out in the stone raises my spirits considerably. Could it be another exit? If so, there might be a chance after all. We draw closer. I see two Black guards sitting in the nook playing a game with black and white stones on a little wooden round table between them. They have light black skin and black hair. Warriors, but not strong ones. Behind them, I see more stone. No doorway. My shoulders slump.

The guards jump up from their game, nearly knocking it off the table. I presume they are not supposed to be playing games while on duty. They bring their left hands to their chests and bow to the guards holding me.

"This one is here for torture until she reveals her secrets," the one on my left tells them. They straighten and take a look at me. Their eyes widen when they realize who I am.

"The Purple Dreamer?" one of them asks, stunned.

"Yes," the one on my right confirms. "She's had a vision, and the Illume wants to know about it. Do what you must to get her to spill her secrets, short of killing her."

The weaker Warriors do their weird chest bow thing again to their superiors and take me roughly by the arms and walk me down the hall.

The smell down here is overpowering of ammonia, sweat, and waste. The further we walk, the worse it gets until it's nearly choking me. I try to hold my breath but realize this is foolish as I will be living down here for the near future and can't very well hold my breath forever. I let my breath out and take a deeper breath in. I cough as I choke on the odors. The guards chuckle.

"You'll get used to it," the one on my right says, smirking.

"That's right. Me and Ivon have been down here for years. Of course, we get to go up and get fresh air when our shift is over. Can't say the same for you all." He sneers at me, and I shudder.

I get a better look around and notice there's not a single window or opening in the stone. I shouldn't be surprised. The dungeons are underground, after all.

The first cell is occupied by a dirty young man in a sackcloth. Unfortunately, the grunge look is universal. Each cell seems to only have a single occupant, so rushing the guards is out of the question. A large, heavy lock hangs from each cell's door. Not likely to be able to snap it off. I am walked past six cells before I see a much less dirty figure in the dungeon attire. I recognize her from my dreams. Saada. Eloise's guardian.

I refrain from speaking. If I let on that I know one of the prisoners, I will surely be moved to a cell where we cannot communicate so easily. The guards unceremoniously open the metal door with a key they produce from their waist. I make note of its location. A loud screech follows the opening of the door. Sneaking out is going to be impossible if the door alone makes that much noise. My options are shrinking with every observation I make.

The guards shoo me into the too-small cell. There's a wooden bench that I suppose is meant to be both my sitting area and my bed. The lack of a mattress is not lost on me, but no one has any form of a mattress. Shouldn't there be rules against this kind of treatment? Even for prisoners?

The guards do a rough pat down of me, presumably feeling for weapons. I wonder where in my silks they think I could hide something. I begin to protest but one of them slaps me across the face with promises for more if I won't do what I'm told when I'm told to do it. My cheek cuts on my teeth; I swallow a faint hint of blood. I contemplate spitting in the guards' faces.

I stand quietly for the rest of the humiliation. They toss me my own sackcloth and ask me to change. I ask if they'll turn around and give me privacy. They slap me on the other side of the face, making me even. They do turn around, though. I quickly peel off my purple silks and purple shoes and pull on the bag as fast as possible in case they decide to turn around. They turn moments after I settle it on me, and I hand over the purple silk.

They look through it, then ask for my brassiere.

"Can be used as a weapon," the guard identified as Ivon explains when I narrow my eyes at him.

I manage to get it free without removing the sack and hand it over.

Satisfied, they leave the cell, securely locking it with a heavy clink before storing the key and walking off.

The burlap is rough and scratches uncomfortably on my delicate skin. I am missing my silks already. I sit on my bed, or whatever you might call it, and let myself cry. Fear settles on me like a heavy blanket, suffocating me.

COMPLETELY NORMAL.

Eloise

R62A16

When I come to, I'm lying on the couch. I groan. My head is killing me. I look around; there's no one in the living room with me. The sky outside is dark.

Cardis comes out of the hallway in his pajamas, his hair mussed. His face is drawn and tight by the candle in his hand. He startles when he notices me looking at him.

He doesn't stop and continues to the kitchen.

"I don't know what to say," I tell his back.

"You could start by telling us where you've been for the last couple of months," Cardis snaps without turning around.

I shake my head. "I don't know. I went into the forest, and, as far as I know, I came out in a couple of days."

He brings me a cup of tea and sits in the chair across from me with his own tea. I relay to him all the experiences I'd had in the two days I had been in there. I don't tell him about my strange dream. It's not relevant, and it *was* a dream.

"So, you went to sleep and woke up, and the forest told you to get out?" Cardis looks perplexed and annoyed.

"Yes, Cardis."

"I don't believe you. Why are you lying to us?"

I blink. "I've never lied to you, Cardis. Have I? Can you not trust me now?"

He shakes his head. "No, I can't. Gamet died when they questioned him. I was the one who discovered him in the cabin. I buried him. And you were gallivanting in the forest!" He pushes off the chair and storms off.

This has to be the worst homecoming ever. I drink the rest of my tea in silence.

~

LATER THAT MORNING, I make my way back out to the garden. I can at least get it under control while I try to sort out everything that has happened and try to get my brain around it all.

The sun moves slowly higher as I work steadily. I let my tears flow freely as I pull weeds, use one of my knives to trim back overgrowth, and pull off vegetables that have matured. Cardis is right; there is no way the garden would have gotten this out of control nor grown this many vegetables if it hadn't been at least a couple of months. Thinking about it makes my head hurt.

Every time I think about Gamet, more tears slide down my face. I don't bother to try to stop them. More water for the garden. Crying can be cathartic, and right now, my soul needs some catharsis. I am feeling incredibly guilty for not being here to take Saada's place. Even though I didn't consciously do anything to keep myself in the forest.

Maybe Gamet would still be alive if I had been here. Saada would still be alive. Julieth would probably still be getting married. Well, not everything in the alternate universe can be perfect.

I continue to work on the garden mindlessly, with a large pile of vegetables on my right and a pail of water on my left. How did everything go so wrong? How did I lose so much time? I couldn't have slept by the fire for two months. I would have died of hunger and dehydration long before then. Not to mention, the fire would have burned out for lack of fuel. Nothing adds up.

I ponder the dream I had, wondering if it was real after all. I look at my hands, covered in dirt, of course, and wipe them off. They look to be the same color as always. My hair, now fallen out of its bun and perpetually stuck to my sweaty face and neck looks the same chestnut brown. If I had powers, especially eight of them, I would surely look different, right?

Although, Raemyn didn't look different until she was using her powers, and she said I was like her.

I look around for something to practice on. My water pail is nearly empty from watering the parts of the garden I had finished weeding. I concentrate on it, similar to how I saw Raemyn concentrate on the tea.

I'm not sure if I want the water to get hot or the pail to fill, either would be fine, but nothing happens. The water is the same tepid warm, and the level stays low. I half-chuckle to myself. Of course, nothing happened; it was a stupid dream. That somehow lasted for two months. Completely normal.

I finish in the garden as the sun begins to set. Neither Cardis nor Julieth come out to talk to me again, so I give them their space. Hilda, Gilda, and Leck are also mysteriously missing.

They're probably scared of me. I would be if I thought someone was dead and then they walked back in the door.

After I finish the garden, I search out Gamet's grave marker in the meadow. It takes me a while, but I manage to find it. I break down all over again when I see it. I hold it to my chest.

"I'm so sorry, Gamet, I'm sorry I wasn't here for them to take me," I cry. It should be Gamet here, alive and well. Saada by his side. Sitting on the couch, cuddled together like always.

The image shatters almost as quickly as it forms. That's not how it would be. Saada and Gamet would turn the Realm upside down to find me, to rescue me, if I had been taken. They wouldn't be sitting on the couch relaxed and happy anyway. It's an illusion. A wish. Unrealistic.

If I could convince Amiket I don't have magic, they would let Saada go, right? They took her under the belief that something was weird with my Quest, if I can show them there's nothing weird about me, other than a missing couple of months of time, they have to let her go.

I take the marker back to Gamet's grave and pound it back into place. It's time to plan a trip to Amiket. Somewhere in the back of my mind, a whisper of warning comes across. Raemyn said not to go to Amiket, but I can't leave Saada there. She wouldn't give up on me; I won't give up on her.

39

MAYBE I DO HAVE A CONTAGIOUS DISEASE.

Eloise

R62A23

No one wants to talk to me after my return. I spend the first week wandering the village. It's much quieter than usual. People seem to avoid me, like I have an illness they might catch because I was an anomaly in the Quest. Who knows? Maybe I do have a contagious disease.

I can't tell if the village is quieter because I'm the one wandering the paths and everyone is hiding, or if it's actually less lively. I have spent the last week getting the garden back under control and teaching Hilda and Gilda how to take care of it. I have a plan to get Saada, which means I will need to leave. Julieth is still working for Mr. Braswell, and her income, plus the garden and Cardis' hunting, can help keep the family fed and afloat.

I walk to the path near the Clearing and stop at Miss Halsey's store, hoping she will give me some kind of answers as to what is going on with Ashadier. The dress form I used to spend so much time standing in front of is missing from the big window. I wonder why she hasn't put another lovely dress on it for display.

"Knock, knock," I call as I enter the store. A little bell above the door chimes, announcing my arrival. Miss Halsey comes around the corner, her flaming orange hair standing on end. It looks like she cut it into a pixie cut, much more manageable for her.

She stops in her tracks when she sees me and frowns.

"Not you, too." I throw my hands in the air. "Please, will someone tell me what is going on around here?"

She seems to weigh her options before answering. "I'm not sure I should be telling you—"

"Please," I beg again. "I need to know."

She sighs, resigned. "Fine. In the time you were gone, we organized a search. I'm sure you heard about that."

I nod. I am still amazed that the whole town came looking for me yet did not find me. I am also amazed that they all wanted to come looking for me. Not Saada and the family, of course, and I would expect Mitac and Chance to do it out of duty, but the whole town, other than a few who were too young and those who stayed to watch them, came after me.

"After we came back, things were different," Miss Halsey's hands shake. "Our water sources started to dry up, one by one, and without Gamet, we have been searching by pure luck to find more, and with little success. As you can imagine, without water, our gardens and trees are failing, and food is getting harder to come by. We also had a big forest fire in the area we were harvesting for our orders. Took out most of our carts and many acres of trees."

She gathers some supplies and puts them into a bag. "Unfortunately, it also took out the carriage horses. No one has the money to replace them, so we haven't been able to get orders out to Rothesard. Mrs. Braswell has been in Rothesard for more than a couple of weeks trying to get someone to loan us horses and let us make payments so we can get some money flowing back to the town. Many families have already left, I will be leaving soon. I can't stay in a place that can't afford to buy what I'm selling, or I will also starve. I love Ashadier," she swipes a tear off her cheek, "but this isn't the Ashadier we once knew."

I take a look around the shop for the first time and notice the bare walls and empty shelves. "Miss Halsey, I'm so sorry. What can I do?"

She shrugs at me. "Nothing, dear. I don't blame you." She pats me on the shoulder. "Others might, but I don't."

"Wait," I stop her as she turns to walk off. "Are you saying Ashadier blames me for all the bad things that have happened? I wasn't even here!"

"You don't need to convince me, but bad luck like that leads to a lot of superstitious and strange thinking among folks. You disappeared and no one could find you, but then you reappear like you never left after two months? That's weird and raises a lot of questions and fears."

"I don't know what happened!" I exclaim. "I swear. I went in and came right back out the next day. I have no idea how two months disappeared." I snap my fingers. "Like that."

"I know, Eloise, I know. Now, if you'll excuse me. It's a long trip to Rothesard." She picks up her bag, settles it on her shoulders, and grabs a trunk to which she has added some wheels. I step out of her way, and she pulls it over the threshold, closing the door firmly behind her. "I hope we meet again, Eloise. My dress looked wonderful on you, and I wouldn't mind making another someday. Under other circumstances, of course."

I nod, and she trundles away. I trudge back to the cabin. Ashadier thinks I'm the cause of all the bad luck. My gut churns. I have found reason after reason to stay in Ashadier in spite of knowing what needs to be done. I need to go to Amiket. I need to find Saada and prove to the Council I am no one to be afraid of. I swear the phoenix on my necklace warms once I make my decision. I give it a squeeze. Hoping if it has any magic at all, it has the power to give me courage.

When I enter the cabin, Julieth is sitting at the table with Cardis. The kids are at school, although I don't know why Cardis isn't there. He takes a look at me and turns to leave. "Wait!" I call out to him. "Now wait one minute." I stomp my foot. "This is ridiculous, Cardis! You can't run away from me forever."

"You don't think so?" he asks.

"No, but I also know that we have been through too much as a family for you to hate me so much for something I had no control over."

"Or so you say," he grumbles.

"What? You think I wanted to disappear? You think I wanted Gamet to die? For Saada to be taken? For all of us to lose the closest people we had to parents? Do you believe that?!" I am yelling now, but I'm past caring. All I want is my family back. For everything to go back to normal.

Cardis shakes his head. He has tears in his eyes, and he sniffles.

"Cardis, I came back, Like I promised. And I came as soon as I could. I didn't know I had been gone so long. I found out everything that's been happening here, and I know everyone blames me for it. I would have thought you, my very own brother, would understand. If anyone was going to be on my side, I thought you would be."

Cardis looks away. "I thought I would, too." He walks off, and I'm rooted to the ground, stunned by his response. What happened to my brother? I look at Julieth, hoping for some support or something. She only shakes her head and gets up to pour herself a fresh cup of tea.

I sit at the table. "Well, that went wonderfully."

"What do you expect?" Julieth asks. She sits down with her tea and puts one in front of me as well. I stir in some sugar and cream and sip at it mindlessly.

"I expected my family to trust and believe the things I say and not think I'm lying to them." I pause. "Where did Elaxi go?" I finally ask the question that's been weighing on my mind. I've been home for a week, and I haven't seen her once.

"She didn't want a family," Julieth's shoulders droop.

"Neither do you," I point out.

"Yes, but I have one now."

"You don't have to stay," I tell her. I loathe the idea of her getting back together with Elaxi, but I won't be the cause of more strife around here.

"It's fine. I should have probably broken up with her a long time ago."

"So, you had to come here and she just…broke up with you?" I'm trying to fill in the blanks. I thought they would be together forever, even though that's not what I wanted for Julieth. Julieth nods. "I don't know what to say. I'm sorry."

Julieth shrugs. "I doubt you are."

"You're right," I sigh and finish off my tea. "I didn't like her from the first time she got you in trouble for stealing at the market. I don't know why you wanted to be with someone so toxic."

Julieth closes her eyes. "I thought she was my best chance to have what Gamet and Saada had, what our parents had. She treated me nicely most of the time."

"Most of the time?" I ask.

"Yes, most of the time. I don't want to get into it. Suffice it to say that after I started taking care of the kids, I went back to the apartment to get some of my things, and it was empty. Not even a note. She just left."

"Julieth, we have had our issues, but I hope you know you deserve much better than that."

Julieth shakes her head. "I don't. Who wants an eighteen-year-old with a list of crimes attached to her and a tendency to drink too much?"

I don't know what to do with that. I didn't even know about her drinking.

We sit in uncomfortable silence for a little while longer. I fidget with my teacup, and she stares at the wall.

"Julieth, I think it's time for me to go get Saada."

She sighs, her eyes snapping back to the present. "I wondered when you were going to do that."

"You knew I would go?"

"I had a feeling." Julieth smiles at me weakly. "You feel responsible for her being gone, and you've never been one to let those kinds of things go if you can fix it. You can't fix the forest burning or the lack of water, but you can try to get Saada. I think it's a foolish mission, so you know."

"I can't leave her there. If need be, I'll take her place, so they'll release her. Ideally, I can get her out without having to do that."

Julieth sighs. "What do you need?"

"Not even going to try to talk me out of it?"

"Would it change your mind?"

"No, but I would have expected something. Are you eager to be rid of me?"

"Not at all. You're a big help, even though you've been moping around here for days on end since you came back."

"Hey!"

She shoves my shoulder playfully and stands up. I stand up with her, ready to get packing now that the decision has been made. Before I can walk away, she pulls me into a hug.

"I've missed you, Els." I stiffen at the unfamiliar display of love. "I hate that we lost so much time because I couldn't get out of my own grief. And out of the bottle."

I nod, unable to speak.

"So, again, what do you need? How can I help you?"

"If you've got any spare bread or dried meat, I wouldn't turn it down. It's a long trip." I grab my leather bag from beside the door and walk to my room.

"I'll get some things for you," I hear her call to my back as she heads to the kitchen.

I empty out my bag, still partly packed from the Quest. I push aside the clothes I'd packed in anger that morning, and something gold catches my eye. A gold coin? Where did that come from?

I sit on the bed, truly recognizing what I'm about to do.

"Two minutes," I mutter. I will allow myself two minutes to feel sad. To feel scared. To feel disappointed in my brother.

At the thought of Cardis, I sock my pillow, already a flat piece of nothing, but it feels good. Angry tears escape my eyes as my fist connects over and over. Why can't Cardis understand? He and I had always been so close, and now he was driving a wedge between us.

Julieth stops at the threshold as I finish my punching parade.

She holds up a small box and something wrapped in parchment. "I came to give you some supplies." She comes over and sits beside me on the bed, away from the pillow I was pummeling. "How long?" she asks.

"How long, what?" I take the box and the parchment and shove them unnecessarily roughly into my bag.

"How long did you give yourself?"

"What are you talking about?"

"Ever since you were little, when you were told about the trick of letting yourself feel your feelings for so long, that's all you've ever done. So, how long did you give yourself? A minute? Two?"

"Two," I mumble, surprised that Julieth remembers these little details from our time together. Before she left us.

"Two minutes. For a lifetime of loss? That's not very long."

"What are you talking about?"

"Two minutes might be enough time for a small frustration like kicking your pinky toe on the coffee table. Or for not doing well on a minor test.

"But two minutes to grieve the loss of your aunt and uncle? That's not enough. Not to mention the loss of two months of your life. The loss of your relationship with Cardis. Grief needs time and space to be felt proportionate to the loss." I stare at her. "Gamet deserves more than two minutes," she continues. "Saada deserves more than two minutes."

I am rendered speechless. Where did this wisdom come from?

"Eloise," she uses my whole name affectionately like she used to. "Saada was trying to get you to feel your feelings even a little bit, so she figured she would set the bar low and hope that you would learn to manage it yourself one day. One day is here."

I shift uncomfortably on the bed.

"We spend so much time focused on survival, on doing our best, on trying to make the most of our limited years here, that we don't let ourselves live or feel. Life isn't about merely surviving or forcing yourself to get over things quickly because time is limited. Life is about living."

"But we *don't* have time," I argue. "We have thirty years, at the most."

"Yes, this is true. No man escapes this fate. But is it better to have lived those thirty years trying to avoid anything negative? Or is it better to let our hearts feel and lead the way? I'm not saying we need to spend years in mourning, even if we had a thousand years to live, that wouldn't be appropriate. But we don't have to feel bad for, well, feeling bad."

I nod. "But right now, I need to rescue Saada."

Julieth gives me a hug. "Okay, but it's a long trip so you have some time to feel and process everything you've been through in the last… well, for you, couple of weeks, before you get to Amiket. Do you have a plan?"

"Well, I figure I'll go to Amiket and…rescue Saada?" I realize at this moment how weak my plan is. Or how little it resembles a plan.

"Let's start with the first part. How are you going to get there? How are you going to get to the train?"

"If the Illume is after me, I can't take the train. They could be looking for me, and I would rather they didn't take me in on their terms."

"How are you going to get to the city?"

I ponder this. "Walk, I guess."

"That's going to take weeks. Have you considered that?"

"I don't know what else to do. The horses and carts were destroyed in the fire. Plus, they can only travel by the road which leaves me exposed."

"Let's assume you're walking. Fastest way to get there is as the crow flies, through the woods and straight across through the Cantuè Plains and the Kahli Desert. That's going to take a lot of planning. What are you going to do about food? Water in the desert? New shoes?" She looks pointedly at my boots which are holding together but won't last hundreds of miles.

"I don't know," I admit, frustrated. "I know I have to go."

"I'm not trying to stop you; I'm trying to help you get your supplies together."

"I know." I'm grateful for Julieth's questions. Even though it's maddening to have all these holes shot into my plan, I realize she's not the one making them. They were already there, I didn't fill them in, I was blind to them. Plus, her concern is comforting. My concern about her ability to care for the kids when I go abates. She has been managing for a couple of months without me. While the house wasn't kept spotless, everyone looked decently cared for.

"Listen, I have some money stashed. You take some of it with you, so you have back up in case you can't get small animals or need to buy food. And I was going to give you new boots for your birthday, but the cobbler hadn't finished them yet. He should be done with them by now."

I throw my arms around her and hug her. "Thank you," I mumble into her neck. "I don't want to take your money, though."

I reach back behind me on the bed to the coin and hold it out to her. Julieth's eyes grow wide in shock. "Where did you get that?" Her tone is hushed, like she's afraid if she talks too loudly it'll disappear.

I chuckle at her before pushing it on her to take. "You can't fool me. You're not any better at hiding money than Saada was. What I want to know is where you got a gold coin."

"Eloise, I didn't give that to you. Honest. I've never even seen a gold coin before." She turns it over, examining it, feeling the weight in her hand. She tries to bend it between her teeth, but it remains stolidly flat. She hands it back to me.

I take it and study it, too. It's about an inch wide, with smooth edges. On one side is a pressed image of what must be the palace in Amiket. On the other, an image of Isynt Vale. I run my fingers over it, feeling each groove. Suddenly, I recall the Gopher and his bet with me. It's the only way a gold coin could have made it to my pack. My brow furrows, I can't figure out why he gave it to me when I definitely lost the bet. By two months, no less.

"You could use this more than me," I try to give the coin back to Julieth.

She shakes her head. "No, it's yours. We will be okay. The twins had been working on the garden while you were gone, and the time you've spent with them seems to have made them semi-proficient. If you can give them another lesson or two, we'll be in good shape.

We are also one of the few houses left in the town with water access still. And Greta has a kid on the way, we're okay, Els. You, however, are about to embark on a cross-country trip that is going to take a long time and a lot of resources." I'm relieved to hear our goat is pregnant. If it's a girl, she'll go to the neighbors. If it's a boy, he will stay with us, and we will raise him until it's his time to feed both families.

I reluctantly put the coin in my bag. I remember the jar of coins Saada had been keeping in the living room closet. I decide not to tell Julieth about it until I'm leaving. Then she can't try to give it to me.

I bury the gold coin under some folded underclothes, an extra couple of shirts, one good pair of socks, and an extra pair of trousers.

"Here, don't forget this." Julieth hands me a familiar parchment-wrapped package. "You never know when you might need it. And these." She gives me the flats I wore for the festival.

I stare at both in my hands. They feel so different now than they did that night. I got to be the woman I imagined in a fancy dress for one night. For one dance. Something niggles in my memory looking at them, but I can't place it.

When would I have need for an elegant dress? The shoes could be a good replacement if the new ones fail, but a dress? I start to get up to put them away when Julieth takes them from my hands and puts them in my bag. "Take them. Trust me."

The dress, thanks to its silky material, doesn't take much space so I allow it to stay in the end. A small cook pot with a spoon, an extra roll of twine, and matches inside of it joins the other items. I leave the room and locate a tightly wrapped bedroll and a large piece of canvas. I tie the bedroll to the bottom of my leather bag. The canvas gets rolled as small as possible, which isn't as small as I would like, and tied closed. It joins the bedroll on the bottom as well.

"One more thing, Els." Julieth hands over a rolled piece of parchment. "This might come in handy."

I unroll it and see a map of Isynt on it, marked with the various towns and cities from here to Amiket, as well as the rivers, gorges, and the places the train stops. It's heavily worn.

"I uh…I spent a long time studying it over the years. When I, you know, wanted to leave."

I scrutinize her face. "Don't you still want to leave?"

She looks around. "I don't know. Maybe someday. Right now, being here with the kids, it feels okay. I'm probably going to screw them up, though." She gives me a half-smile and I return it.

"It's what parents do, isn't it? Screw up their kids? But, for the record, I don't think you'll do it on purpose. The same as our parents and guardians never meant to mess us up."

I lift the leather bag and grunt under the weight. And I haven't even added water yet. I wish that our goat was a horse or at least a donkey to carry this thing with me. This is going to hurt. I put the bag back down in the corner.

"I'll harvest some fresh vegetables before I go and see if I can get Cardis to help me pickle them or dry them. Think I can get him to come around before I leave?"

"I'm not sure; he's pretty upset. Maybe he'll cool down in a couple of days. I'll try talking to him again, see if he will at least listen to you. Rationally."

"Thank you, Julieth, I don't know what to say."

"Say you'll bring Saada home. And that you'll come home with her."

"I promise." I hope I can keep this promise. Although, I suspect, it'll be much longer than two months before I can make good on that promise.

SO NOT DYE, DEFINITELY MAGIC.

Saada

R62A16

Time has lost all meaning. I have no idea how long I have been here. I'm not even sure exactly where "here" is.

When I finally came to, the first time, I was in the back of a carriage, bound and gagged. The gag seemed a bit unnecessary given that, based on the view of the passing scenery, we were somewhere on the pass to Rothesard, which is largely deserted most of the time unless supply runs are being made.

The rhythmic clip-clop of the horse's hooves on the hard-packed dirt lulled me back to sleep before I even had time to register the pain I was in.

When I awoke the second time, the Gopher and the other Warrior were in the carriage with me. No sign of Chance or Selvia if they had decided to bring her after all. Based on the Gopher's sudden change in attitude and behavior in Ashadier, my guess would be that they left her behind. Cruel bastard.

The travel from Ashadier to Rothesard passed painfully. No one ever puts my shoulder right, so every movement causes pain.

The trip normally takes a week but since I was unconscious for part of it, I only had to endure two days and nights. I slept in the carriage, bound, while my guards slept outside in tents. They gave me bathroom stops but no privacy, so I found it hard to do my business. Especially since they would only release one hand and the other was tied either to a tree or to one of themselves.

Each time they did, I laughed. Where did they expect me to go? I have one good shoulder, one that is still out of socket and terribly swollen, and nothing is around us except for trees, more trees, and, for a change from the trees…Celestials-damned *trees*.

Even if I was in good shape and my body was in perfect condition, I still couldn't outrun two Warriors. Nor their weapons. I bet that the weapons on their backs are not the only ones they have. Nonetheless, I took deep breaths of the pine forest when I was let out of the carriage, which had begun to smell with my unbathed odor. That might have been the last time I saw Amaranth, my home.

On the morning of my third day of consciousness, we pulled into Rothesard. They kept me in the carriage until the train arrived then surreptitiously hustled me into a private car. This week-long journey was no more comfortable than the carriage ride. The only difference was that I had never traveled by train before. I would have loved to enjoy it, but all I could focus on was my impending and likely doom.

The Gopher put a hood over my head when we got to Amiket City, and I was unable to see where exactly we were going. I bounced around the carriage uncomfortably with my hands tied behind me. Unable to anticipate the bumps or curves coming my way, I hit the Warriors. One of these would grunt in disgust and shove me off of him. The other would help me right myself without complaint.

I was sure I would have gained a few new bruises on my shoulders and head after that trip. Luckily, the train stop at the end of the line is near Amiket City, so we didn't have far to travel to wherever they wanted to take me. I am left with my head in a sack even after being pulled from the carriage.

I couldn't tell much about the city with my eyes covered but a few things struck me. It was dark when we arrived. There wasn't light penetrating the bag over my head. Although it was dark, my ears were attuned to the many noises of the city around me. How can such a place be so busy at night? I heard people hawking their items on the street, some begged for bronzes from the Warriors before they were harshly rebuked. A few people laughed, but more often, I heard the anguish of hunger, sorrow, and need. My heart broke for them.

I had always thought that the people who lived in the city would be well-dressed, well-fed, and happy. What I heard painted a different picture in my mind's eye.

The smells around me were far different from home. Above all, the salt in the air and the wetness of everything struck me. I remembered Amiket was near the sea, but having never been to the sea, I did not know how it smelled. Now I knew and I couldn't decide if it was pleasant or not. When a breeze blew through and stirred up the scents of long-dead fish, I decided I didn't like it. If that's the smell of the sea, no thank you.

One person took one side, another took the other. No words were exchanged, but I recognized the hands to be different from the ones that pulled me out of the carriage the first time. They must have handed me off to other guards. Blinded like I was, I didn't bother to fight. What was the point?

I hoped the kids were okay. I hoped Gamet was okay. I hoped Eloise was okay. I kept back my tears until the long walk ended and I was thrown into a cell. I fell inelegantly to the floor and my chin scraped painfully on what I found out was a stone floor. Added to my shoulder and other bruises, I was sure I looked like something dragged behind the horses rather than pulled in the carriage.

The guards finally ripped off the hood and I got to see I was with yet two more Black magic-wielders, although their skin was lighter than that of the Gopher and the Warrior who came to fetch Eloise.

They patted me down, none too gently, and demanded all my clothes but my underwear. They were so kind as to provide the burlap I was now clothed in. I was left with no brassiere, no shoes, and, most importantly, no hope. With a shriek of pain, I forced my shoulder back into place and I spent the first couple of nights crying and supporting my arm, trying to keep it from popping out of place again. The other prisoners would occasionally yell at me to shut up, but I ignored them. They couldn't do anything to me anyway.

The guards, however…they could do things to me. A fact I

discovered after my first night. If I continued to cry into the day, they made sure to give me something to cry about as they put it. I learned the only safe time to cry was at night. It didn't stop the abuse during the day, but it seemed to lessen it.

I also learned there were two rotations of guards for both day and night. The first rotation of guards, the day guards, were the harsh ones. They meted out punishments for anything. Ate the gruel too slow? Hand rap. Ate too fast? Hand rap. Didn't hand over your waste bucket fast enough, skipped for the next two days. This did not help the smell in the cells much.

The second set of guards were the nice guards. They worked the night hours, but they lured you into a sense of safety and comfort, into feeling like you were going to be okay. They were the reason it was okay to cry at night. The gruel was still bland and disgusting, the beds were still solid wood, and the cells still smelled, but they had more allowances for us.

None of the prisoners were willing to get to know me. I tried to talk to the man in the cell next to me, but he walked away and ignored me, preferring to stand in the corner than talk.

Clearly socializing was not on the docket but the question remained of why none of the prisoners talked to each other. Preference or forced?

I answered that question the second time I tried to talk to my neighbor. I got another rap across the knuckles with the cane for trying. I tried at night the first time, and they allowed me to learn my mistake before I got punished for it by the day guards. My knuckles were still swollen from the punishment, and I was afraid to attempt it again at night to see if the night guards would let us talk or not.

On my third day—at least I think it was my third day, there are no windows and no access to light to tell—the guards bring another person down. I watch eagerly and am shocked when I see she is a rich purple color. I didn't even know Purple magic existed! Maybe she fell into a vat of dye? Her eyes turn toward me, and I see her irises are also purple. So not dye, definitely magic.

I see a flash of recognition in her gaze, and I wonder what it means. I would surely remember if I had ever seen a Purple woman before.

Knowing what is coming next for my new cell neighbor, I turn away to provide her with the limited privacy I can. I may not be able to see her, but I can still hear everything, and I cringe with each resounding slap. She, like the rest of us, will hopefully find out quickly what is and isn't allowed. Talking back to a guard or asking them questions is definitely on the not allowed list. Being unfailingly obedient and toeing the lines, even the lines you didn't know were there, is expected.

My heart goes out to this poor woman next to me. After the guards lock her in and walk off laughing, I turn back to look at her. She is sitting on her bed/bench, head in her hands, crying softly. Her purple hair is a curtain in front of her, blocking me from seeing anything more. I don't invade her privacy. I let her have her space. She needs this time. Wherever she came from, whatever she was doing, was likely better than this.

I DIDN'T NEED RESCUING!

Mitac

R62A15

When I got home, I stretched out in my bed, grateful to be back. The four walls, familiar yet foreign since I spent so little time here, stared back at me nearly blankly. The only decoration on the white walls is the rack for my long sword and my leiomano. What a disaster this Quest was.

I know I will be called to the palace. I know I will have to answer questions about what happened. For the first day, I just wanted to sleep.

My bed, still and unmoving, was supposed to be a welcome change from the train and carriages, but I missed the sound of the engine, the wheels on the rails, even the squealing of the brakes. It could also be that in the silence of my apartment I could hear that voice in my head again. It had been quiet. In the quiet, it resumed its melody. What am I supposed to take that to mean?

I should have gone to find Chance as soon as I made it to Amiket, but it was late by the time we passed Saada off to the dungeon guards. I didn't think she would appreciate me showing up so late. Besides, one more night with Selvia couldn't be so bad for Chance.

When I saw Elgin showed up to find out what was going on for the Council, I immediately gave Chance a new plan for Selvia, refusing to

268

leave her behind. Chance protested only minimally, thankfully, and the two took off together that day. I didn't need Selvia to be made a part of this. I explained to Elgin that Chance needed to get home so she could let the Council know what was going on. Elgin explained he had already dispatched his own courier as soon as he arrived and heard about Eloise's Quest and her status of missing at the time.

I had to work hard not to show disappointment over that turn of events. I hadn't wanted the Council notified yet. Although, I wasn't sure what waiting another week would possibly do. We had searched as thoroughly as searching could be done, and she was still nowhere to be found. Another week wouldn't change that.

The second day after coming home, I checked in on Selvia and Chance, who seem to be surviving for now. Chance tells me when they got back to the city, they went to see a Healer who helped Selvia's leg immensely. She's allowed to walk now, which has helped Selvia and Chance establish a somewhat comfortable living relationship. I tell Chance I'll come back the next day to discuss our plans.

I hit the market to shop for some food since my cupboards were bare. I picked up some bread, cheese, and bacon. On a whim I snag half a dozen eggs. They cost a small fortune, but they'll be worth it. I haven't had eggs at home in a long time. Plus, I'm still thinking about Mr. Braswell's egg and cheese pie. I wonder what he did to make it taste so good and I wish I had asked. Of course, now I'll never know. I'll never be allowed in Ashadier again.

THE SUN IS STARTING to peek through the window of my small apartment. One of these days I may remember to put a curtain up. Today is not that day. Today, I need to get Selvia and figure out my next moves. With her and with Saada.

I quickly climb out of bed and I'm out the door in a few minutes. I'll bathe properly after I come up with a plan. I hope that Chance has some ideas.

The roads are wide, made of packed gravel. In the brisk early morning, the streets aren't too crowded, yet. Later, there will be carriages being pulled by horses, people riding horses, people in carts being pulled by other people, and people on foot. That many people crowded in such small spaces makes my skin crawl.

I glance to my right. High up on a hill, much higher than everything else, is the palace. At least what I can see of it. Most of it is hidden behind stone walls and tall trees. The four towers loom above the trees, red roofs gleam in the sun. The marble below is spotless in spite of its light color.

A road winds down the hill from the palace, disappearing into the city.

The houses are worn down, made mostly of cheap wood, a poor choice for being so near to the salt and the sea. I think back to the houses I saw in Ashadier. Were these any better than those? For all the cracks people make about the far country folks, I think their living conditions might be better.

An occasional brick or stone house comes up here and there, but a lot of them look like they were put together hastily and with the cheapest materials they could find. Here and there wash lines are hung with drying clothes, stretched from one corner of a house clear across to the neighbor's house. In some cases, the line is short because a lot of the houses are packed tightly together.

There are no trees within the city. In fact, there is truly little greenery at all. A few rose bushes around some houses, some creeping vines around others, little patches of weeds and grass. Other than the citizens, with all their magic, there is so very little color.

How had I not realized how depressing this place is?

Chance lives in a run-down little shack on the outskirts of the city. I've offered to help her fix it up, but she always shrugs me off, insisting what she has is good enough for the little time she spends there. I hate it. It's unsafe, but no amount of badgering has gotten her to let me make it safer for her. She doesn't know, but I will often walk past the house in the morning and again before bed. To make sure she's safe.

When I walk up, I notice aghast, that her door is tilted off its hinges and immediately think someone has broken in and done something to her or Selvia. I don't remember seeing it like that the last time I came by and dread settles in my stomach. I didn't walk by last night, too tired to do so.

I shove into the single room place and find Chance and Selvia both asleep. I feel immediate relief. Chance jumps off her place on the couch in a hurry, a knife appearing in her hand out of nowhere. She's dressed in a night shift that hangs crookedly off of her shoulder. Selvia, for her part, stirs and wakes confused. At least she doesn't pull a knife on me.

"Celestials, Mitac! You scared me half to death!" She lowers the knife and adjusts her shift. "What are you doing barging in like that?"

"Your door is hanging off its hinges! I thought someone had broken in!"

Chance looks around me and I look too. I see her door is now completely off its hinges. I'll fix it later. Chance glares at me. "Someone did break in, you!"

I shrug. "Are you going to be mad because I was trying to rescue you?"

"Yes! I didn't need rescuing!"

I grunt. I look over to Selvia, who is watching our exchange with some amusement. She is sitting up on the edge of the bed. The bandage on her leg looks a lot smaller than when I last saw it. Selvia looks more well-nourished, and I am instantly grateful to Chance for taking care of her.

"Are you going to stare at us?" Chance asks in a huff. "Or are you going to explain why you're here?"

I refit the door into the crooked frame, wedging it in so it will stay, then I take a seat in one of her rickety wooden chairs, which groans threateningly under my frame. "I was coming to get Selvia and to make a plan."

Chance puts on a robe, seeming to remember she's barely dressed, and busies herself making tea. While the water heats over the fire she starts, she places cups in front of each place setting and a third on the counter then takes a seat.

"A plan for Selvia?" It almost sounds like she's disappointed by that.

"Yes, that, and a plan for the package I came back with."

Chance nods in agreement. "That plan."

"I'm not sure what exactly we do with Selvia," I start. "I could take her to the orphanage, I suppose…" I trail off waiting for Chance to share her ideas.

Selvia is watching us closely. I feel bad for having this conversation with her in the room, but there is no other place for her to go. Chance ponders my statement stoically, getting up to check the water. Unnecessarily. I know that water isn't hot yet, but Chance doesn't want to be under my gaze while she thinks. I may not know everything about my partner, but we have spent enough time together for me to know this.

"I don't think that's the best thing for her," she turns back to face me. "Maybe she could stay here a little while longer? Maybe until we get our next mission?"

My stomach twists. I am not sure what the palace is going to do with me after the botched Quest. Although it seems that everyone agrees there's nothing more I could have done, that doesn't mean the Illume will agree, especially since there's a dream from the Purple magic-wielder involved.

"I'm sure it will be fine," Chance soothes in an uncharacteristic show of empathy. She pats my hand, also a rare action for her, as she retakes her seat. I know she is referring to me and not Selvia staying with her.

"Staying with you would be fine, but we can't leave her to fend for herself when we have a mission."

"Maybe we could drop her off at the orphanage and pick her up after?"

"It's not a daycare, Chance! You can't drop her off and pick her up. That's not how orphanages work!" I scrub my hand down my face.

Selvia clears her throat loudly. We turn to look at her. "I could stay here when you all go. And I'll cook and clean and keep the house tidy until you return."

I laugh at the preposterous idea, but Chance doesn't. "Oh, come on," I scoff, "You can't be considering this!"

"Well, why not?" I try to imagine Selvia left here by herself. In this place with the door falling off, no security, and barely enough space for a gnat to fit.

"For starters, up until recently, you didn't want anything to do with

Selvia! Secondly, what will you tell people when you suddenly have a kid hanging out?"

Chance agrees. "But the kid has kind of grown on me. She's quiet most of the time, and she can make some decent food. I dunno, I don't think the orphanage would be right for her. I can tell people she's my cousin. I told that to the guards at the entry gate. Parents drop dead all the time; why not hers?"

Leave it to Chance not to mince her words. Selvia doesn't seem to mind. She continues rolling with the train.

"Plus," Selvia pipes in, "I can keep the place safe while you're gone! Didn't you say someone broke in while you were gone this time?"

I round on Chance, shocked and annoyed by this information. "Not helping," Chance groans.

"Why didn't you say anything? How many times have I told you to let me help you put this place into a more suitable state?"

"I don't want you to! Besides, there's nothing here to steal."

"Well, Selvia can't stay here while we're gone if you have thieves raiding the place!"

Chance tries to brush me off. "I'm sure they wouldn't if they knew someone was here. They'd probably think I was here if they saw her coming and going. Because who in their right mind would leave a thirteen-year-old alone?"

"Yeah, my point exactly. Listen, if you want to keep her, that's fine, but I have a condition."

Chance lifts her chin, a sign for me to go ahead.

"I get to fix the place up. Reinforce the walls, put the door back on, put locks in place…things like that. Maybe fix your leaking roof while I'm at it." I jerk my chin to the part of her roof that has a pan perma-stationed underneath it.

Chance scowls at me. "That's my water reclamation pot."

Selvia giggles. "It's not supposed to be *in* the house!" I tell her sternly.

Chance gets up and pours hot water over the tea leaves. She brings the cup on the counter to Selvia after adding a little sugar. I can tell she doesn't want to give in to my help, but she also knows I won't budge on this.

"Fine," she relents with a sigh. "Fine. You can do a few things. Only a few, Mitac! And I insist on paying you for your time."

"Nope. No payment, and I will do as I see fit. Or I turn Selvia over to the orphanage where she can be reasonably safe."

Selvia snorts into her tea. "Unless it's vastly different than the one in Ashadier, it's not safe. Also, I don't appreciate being used as a pawn in whatever game this is."

"It's not a game," Chance corrects her quickly. "And I'm trying to keep you here so hush."

"Agree to his terms, then. I get to stay, the house gets to look more like an actual house and not something an amateur threw together in a weekend, and Mitac gets whatever it is he wants out of this weird arrangement."

"I resent that. I worked hard to build this."

My mouth drops open so wide that I think my jaw hits the floor. "You built this yourself?"

Chance grits her teeth, her jaw pulsing.

"Chance, you did well for not knowing what you were doing, but please, let me help."

Chance sighs loudly, sipping her tea. "Okay. You win. You both win."

I give her a grin, trying to keep it from being smug. "Now that we've settled that, how about the package?"

"Selvia, why don't you get dressed and go to the market. See what you can find for supper," Chance suggests.

"I know you're trying to get me out of here so I don't overhear your plans." She grumbles but does as she's asked. Chance gives her a coin pouch, reminding her to tuck it into her waistband to keep it safe.

I open the door for her and wedge it back into place, instructing Selvia to knock when she returns.

"Okay, the package?" I ask impatiently.

"What about her?"

"What are we going to do?" I press.

"What do you mean, 'what are we going to do?' Why do *we* have to do anything?" Chance stands and clears the teacups and places them in the sink, frustratingly unconcerned about Saada's fate.

"It's not Saada's fault her niece didn't come home. She's not going to be treated well, and I bet if Eloise does turn up, they both end up dead." Chance stills at the wash basin, her back toward me. "We need to get her out of there."

Chance turns to face me. "Why are you so set on rescuing everyone all of a sudden? First Selvia which, fine, she was being treated like a piece of shit. You should hear the things she had to say.

"But then you went on this weird thing about Eloise which I tried to stay out of. She's not that much younger than you and if you have a thing for her, like, cool, but don't drag me into it."

"Woah, wait, I don't have a thing for Eloise. There's something you should know."

"Do I have to know? We've done fine without knowing everything about each other," she persists.

"Yes, I think you should know. It might help explain some things."

Chance sits across from me, one leg crossed over the other. "Go ahead." She already sounds bored.

"I have a thing, a voice in my head. And it only speaks sometimes."

Chance raises an eyebrow. I knew I was going to sound like I'd lost it. I rush on. "The thing is, it only ever says one word. 'Danger' and it's only done it three times in my life. Once before my dad went to work, once when my brother went to Amiket City for training, and a third time around Eloise."

"I'm failing to see the significance of an imaginary voice."

"It's not imaginary. It's damned annoying, though. But the day it said it about my dad, he was crushed under a tree and died. With my brother, he came here to train, and I never saw him again, no record exists of him after he finished school. I presume he's dead. So, when it said the same thing about Eloise, I panicked. I tried to warn her, but the voice didn't stop. Part of me wonders if she's still out there somewhere."

"Because of a voice in your head?"

"Yes." I pinch my lips. "Because of the voice in my head."

"So, you want to rescue Saada because?"

"Because…I don't know. I feel like it's the right thing to do."

"Mitac, are we worried about keeping our jobs, or not? Because a little bit ago I could tell you were upset about the possibility of not having any more work from the city, now you want to break into the palace to rescue a village woman from the most-fortified dungeon to exist?"

"Yeah, yeah, that's right," I confirm.

"Which part?"

"All of it. I want to keep our jobs and rescue the woman."

Chance laughs heartily. "Those are mutually exclusive statements."

"There has to be a way."

"I've been down there, there isn't."

This comes as a surprise to me. "What do you mean? You were down there?"

Chance shakes her head. "Not the point. It's underground; two guards on duty all the time and heavy locks on the cells. Not to mention that if you should get her out of the cell by some miracle, her clothes will give her away. Plus, she will have no shoes. Plus, you still have to get her out of the palace itself. Silly me, I thought this would be difficult."

"Chance, please?" I'm not used to begging, and I prefer not to use my magic on my friends, but special circumstances call for special measures.

"What do you want me to do, Mitac? Get you a job in the dungeon?"

"Yes! That's perfect!" Suddenly, the formation of a plan comes to mind.

"Mitac, I can't do that. I don't have that ability."

"No, you don't, but I do!" I stand up hurriedly, knocking over the table. I bend down to set it right. "Listen, when we get called in front of the Council, back up whatever I say."

"Um, how about no? You're going to get into some hair-brained scheme that's going to wind up getting you hurt or killed. Then what?"

"Don't worry about it. I got this."

"I always worry!" I hear her call out to me as I dash out of the shack, wedging the broken door in place again. I move that stupid door up to the top of my fix-it list.

IT WASN'T POWER...

Aerith

R62A30

The last two weeks have been torture, literally. The guards are determined to get me to talk about my dreams, and I have come close to telling them everything I know several times. Then I remember what's at stake, and I remember how they have been treating me. Anger boils over in my veins, igniting me from the inside out, and my spirit becomes unyielding, unbreakable. I have never felt such strong emotion before, and I am not sure if I like it or not. I feel powerful with it. I never thought that I was powerless in the palace, but the power I thought I had was an illusion. Created only by keeping me satisfied and comfortable. Apathy. That's what it was. It wasn't power, it was apathy.

No one ever realizes how strong they are until they're forced to be.

I have never been so physically uncomfortable in all my life. I am utterly humiliated every time I have to use the bucket in the corner to take care of personal business. As desperately as I try to keep myself covered, there is nothing that can stop the shame of having someone watch you. And they do.

I made the mistake of asking the guards on my first day if they could not watch while I went to the bathroom. Now it's a game. If they hear the bucket shuffle, they immediately come over and stare at me until I finish. Then they laugh until they get back to their seats.

"They exploit your discomfort," Saada had told me in hushed tones that night. "Don't show your weaknesses or what makes you uncomfortable. They'll use it to break you."

Despite the humiliations I had faced and the pains, I refused to let them in on it. I ate the food with a smile. When they watched me use the bathroom, I stared them in the eyes, fire in mine. When we got a new sack to change into, I brazenly did it in front of them. I refused to hide.

They hadn't grown bored with me yet, but I held out hope that they would eventually.

The only time I get to leave my cell is the times I wish I didn't have to. A short walk to a ten-by-ten windowless room with a heavy, solid, iron door. A cold iron bench, waist height, greets me every day. The iron is rusted, and I have received more than one cut from being bent over it. Inside, I have recently become accustomed to whips, canes, and implements with barbs on the ends.

Endlessly, they ask me, "What are your real dreams?" "Where is the girl?" "What is her name?" "What is she going to do?"

When I refuse to answer, they bring out the toys, as they call them. They spare no skin. I heard their directive. Get answers; Don't kill her. They're not succeeding on either account.

I have several cuts on my back that are open and, I fear, festering with infection. If my skin weren't purple already, it would be in various shades of purple from bruises in multiple stages of healing. I am also pretty sure I have a broken rib because breathing is an exercise in pain.

The worst, aside from being unable to sit or lie comfortably, are the cuts on the bottom of my feet. I do my best not to hobble when I walk with the guards or in my cell, but it's hard. My lips are chapped from dehydration and from the endless bites they're receiving while I try not to cry out. I will not break. It's a tune I repeat over and over.

Saada and I didn't have much time to talk. In broken sentences, stolen pieces of conversation, we were able to share our lived experiences to this point. Silent tears streaked down her cheeks as she relayed the loss of her husband and the presumptive loss of Eloise.

I could do nothing about Gamet to comfort her. I couldn't hug her or even touch her. What I could do was tell her about Eloise. Minimally. Giving her too much information would be a cross to bear that would make it hard for her to keep secret.

"She's alive," I whispered to her hoarsely one night. The guards had started their rounds at the end of the cells. We had seconds to talk before they got close enough to hear us.

"What?" she said loudly.

I flinched and listened closely for the guards to come hurrying over. I heard the measured, even steps of the guards; it didn't sound like they had sped up. "She's alive. I can't tell you more. But she's alive."

The guards had gotten too near for us to continue our conversation, and we fell silent again. A new light took place in Saada's eyes after that conversation, though. She returned each day less broken. It appeared she was rallying.

I had presumed that my dreams would stop when I could no longer sit in the Dreamer room or could no longer focus, and focus was hard to come by in this place. I was wrong.

I still had my talisman, the only personal item I was allowed to keep, and it occasionally still heated up, signaling a vision. I would do my best to rest casually on my hard bench, making it look like I was catching some sleep rather than Dreaming.

The first series of dreams filled me in on the two months Eloise had lost.

I watched in my visions as her village came under curse after curse. I watched her village struggle with water. I watched the fires burn down their major source of income. I watched as people went hungry; I watched people leave in droves. Ashadier, already the smallest village in Amaranth, was quickly becoming nearly non-existent.

My heart ached for them. And when Eloise returned, she believed her time with Raemyn had been a dream. Nothing about her appeared different, but I, too, had been there. I had seen what happened in that cabin. I knew it wasn't a dream for her, but I couldn't explain it, nor could I alert her to it.

I would Dream of the others, too, though less frequently. They were on their own journeys and were safe for the time being. Eloise, however, was in imminent danger, and it appears the Celestials want me to help her. If they want me to do so, though, they need to get me out of this dungeon. So far, no sign of help was coming.

I watched Eloise prepare for her trip here. To rescue her aunt. And I admired her for it, but I also didn't want her to come.

I have overheard the guards talk. In some of their exchanges, they discuss Eloise. They discuss the Illume's plans for her. The exact scheme seems to be up in the air, but it appears to reside between killing her on capture or finding a way to harness her powers. Neither possibility is good. It would be better for Eloise to stay where she is.

When I rise from my visions, Saada always looks over. Fear in her eyes. In whispered snatches of conversation when the guards are switching over or when they doze off at night, I have filled her in on what I have seen of Eloise, as much as I dare to keep her going.

R62A31

I come back from another dream of Eloise. She's preparing to leave. She's gotten her sister on board, helped teach her smaller cousins how to grow food in the garden, and she's attempted to mend things with her brother. None of which have succeeded. He remains stubbornly unreachable to her. The Celestials insist on giving me these visions, but they won't get me out of here where I can help her, and they won't show me what's next. Not for the first time, I wonder why they bother to show me any of this at all.

I look over to Saada, who gives me a querying look. I shake my head, my signal that I will tell her later. It's not safe right now. The guards are awake and paying attention to us. I think they hope that I will tell Saada what I know and that they will overhear us. I have learned that this guard duty is a very low station. Being in the dark twelve hours a day, every day is not desirable. If any of them hear what I have been Dreaming up and relay it to the Council, I could bet, and so could they, that they would buy themselves a better post.

I sit carefully, my backside sore, on my bed and face Saada. She lays on hers, facing my cell. She mouths a word to me. I look at her quizzically, and she mouths it again.

Eloise?

She must be asking if I was Dreaming of Eloise. I give her an almost imperceptible nod. She closes her eyes and breathes deeply. I can't tell if my Dreaming of Eloise brings her comfort or greater pain. She rolls away from me, and I attempt to lie on my bed as well.

In this spare time we have, I consider how I will get us out of this situation. Our best chance, as I can see it, is to escape when they're transferring us to the other room for another lovely day of pain. Unfortunately, they only transfer us one at a time. The guards never unlock more than one cell at once. They also keep their keys attached to a chain on themselves. Like us, they're chained to their circumstances.

I have watched their routine, trying to find anyone I can sweet talk. I have attempted several times. Tried to get to know the guards and learn about their lives. So far, I've only made inroads with one of the night guards, Tanlar.

He's barely got any magic. His eyes are black, as is his hair, but his skin is barely a fog grey. I have ascertained that the others make fun of him frequently for his low level of magic. When he is with one of the dark Warriors, we don't speak, but other, lighter Warriors, are willing to let us talk. Sometimes, they'll even bring their card game over for Saada and me to join in.

I find out Tanlar has two kids, but his wife died in childbirth with the second. At night, the kids stay with his sister while he works, and the only reason he does this job is because it pays well enough to make sure they can stay in the city with moderate accommodation.

He tells us he grew up here, and he has no idea what he would do if he lived anywhere else. Something I can relate to. Saada gives him a little information about her village, upon my prompting, and he sits wide-eyed at her description of her people and how they are towards each other. Having never left the city, he has never seen people behave like she depicts.

In time, Saada opens up more on her own. She always stops shy of talking about her kids. I remember her telling me she had told the city there were no other kids, so she speaks fondly of her husband instead. She also avoids talking about Eloise, as do I. Tanlar never asks.

While we share about ourselves in the evenings with Tanlar, I see this as a way out. He might be convinced to let us go. I wait for the change of the guard, determined to try to talk to Tanlar some more, but I am disappointed. Tanlar isn't on duty tonight.

I lay as comfortably as possible on my bed, facing away from Saada, who has also given up for the night, and wait for sleep to overcome me.

That night, I Dream while I sleep. I have never had a vision while sleeping before. I watch Eloise talk to her sister and finalize her pack. I am yelling at her to stay put, but of course, she can't hear me. Eloise tries talking to her brother again, who continues to push her away.

I know she must be getting ready to leave soon when she harvests fresh vegetables and packs them. Eloise approaches Cardis and asks for help with pickling or drying them. He refuses, so she wraps them instead and ties them to her bag with everything else. Her last task is to fill her canteens. She straps her knives to either side of her hips and hugs each family member.

Cardis reluctantly takes the hug but doesn't hug her back. He's going to hold this grudge despite her leaving. I continue to yell from my position, my consciousness floating above the scene. I try to get her to hear me. To stay put. She doesn't hear me, and with a last look at her cabin in the dawn morning air, she hoists her pack to her back and heads through the garden to the woods beyond.

I wake from my dream and hear myself shouting, to my horror, "Don't come here, Eloise!" Furthermore, the guards are staring directly at me. The whites of their eyes give away their position in the alcove. There is no way they didn't hear that.

WHAT AREN'T THEY HIDING?

Mitac

R62A31

I pull out my ace in the hole when it comes time to face the Illume for what happened with the Quest. I had expected them to call me and Chance in sooner, but we have been home for a couple of weeks before they do. It was like they wanted us to relax, think we were off the hook, before they brought down judgment on us. I don't mind. I knew it was coming, and my training had helped rid me of pre-emptive anxiety over things like this.

We use our time off wisely, or I did, at least. I got a new roof, thicker walls, and a proper door on Chance's house. I also put locks on the windows and got her a couple of rugs for the floors. It's starting to look like a house. Selvia did a lot of the work alongside me. She was a good apprentice, holding things and anticipating what I would need next. The further we got into the project, the more she was able to help.

I noticed that our time together taught her a lot about construction in general because I came over one day toward the end of our project, and she had put together a small bed for herself from the scraps of wood we had left over from the walls and roof. It was rough, but she showed me proudly how she fit on it and told me how Chance was able to take her bed back. I wanted to offer a couple of suggestions, make a couple of tweaks to make it look better—the overall structure seemed sound—but thought better of it when Chance glared at me.

Chance and I leave Selvia at their newly remodeled place and begin our long journey up to the palace. We stay fairly silent on our walk on the hard-packed gravel roads. Or at least, I do. Chance is clearly anxious about what I have planned and keeps peppering me with questions.

"Relax," I smile as a carriage passes us by. "I got this."

"Sometimes, Mitac, your ego drives me crazy."

"What ego?" I snark at her.

She huffs at me. "You know what I'm talking about. Couldn't you share something of what you have planned with me?"

"Chance, you know as well as I do that you don't lie well. I need you to be as surprised as the Council, so it doesn't look like we are in cahoots on this. I have a plan, trust me."

She huffs again. An annoying sound. Also, an indication she's annoyed at me, too. We make our way off the side roads to the main road leading up to the palace. It's not an easy climb. We get stopped at the guard gates at the base of the hill and explain our business. They check their list of approved visitors and open the wide iron gates to let us through.

The winding path is lined by stones and lush green grass beyond. Tall trees block our view of the palace the majority of the way up. And if it's not the trees, then it's the tall walls around the palace. Few get an unobstructed view of the palace. It's the first time I've been in since I was summoned for this job. My jobs get handed to me by a courier who, once the job is complete, pays me as well. I bring Chance in on the jobs as a matter of course. I don't know when the last time she was in the palace, either.

"You've been inside, right?" I ask. She said she had seen the dungeons, and I am still very curious about what brought her to the dungeons.

She nods stiffly, her face ashen. I've never seen Chance scared. She's usually calm and collected. I can tell she's truly out of her element right now. I want to ask her why she was in the palace previously but think better of it. This isn't the time, but I am going to give her Ravaged Abyss about this later. Who knew some finery and big buildings was all it took to still her tongue?

At the top of the hill, we are let directly into the palace. No introduction needed. We must be on time. An Unchanged man dressed in gold silks with humorously puffed out sleeves and wide-legged silk trousers leads us to the Council room. Two very Black Warriors stand guard. I don't recognize either of them.

They open the double doors and admit us access. This is the same room I was in when I got my job in the first place. The table is in the same spot, with the same chairs, the carpet and rugs exactly as they were. Nothing is out of place. I'm not surprised, not really.

People such as the Illume don't tolerate change well. Another guard is guarding the back exit, as dark as her friends who allowed us in. I nod to her, not recognizing her either, but she returns the nod out of professional respect.

I had half-hoped I would recognize a guard or two in the palace, but if I got down to it, I knew I likely wouldn't.

During my two years in school for training I didn't socialize a whole lot. Especially not with the Warrior class. If I did talk to anyone, they were usually in the Negotiator class. The other Negotiators helped hone my skills and my sense of lies and trickery. We always tried to outdo each other, seeing who could convince the others of the most outlandish stories. It was a good way to learn how to channel a lot of magic in the smallest of threads.

Negotiators learn how to put up walls to keep others out. By the time we finish training, those walls are impenetrable to nearly all invasions. The best Negotiators send out a lot of tiny threads of magic to get past complex and tight defenses. I am among the best. My threads can barely be felt, which is why it was so weird that I couldn't find a way through Saada's or Eloise's walls. I haven't thought about it for a while, but I need to one of these days. If we can get Saada out, maybe she can teach me something.

I look over at Chance, who looks as uncomfortable as she did on our walk in, but she doesn't look surprised. I assume that means she has been in this room before as well. I am about to give up and ask her when the door in the back opens to admit the Council.

They all file in, taking their respective seats and largely ignoring us until they don't. Haughty and arrogant as ever. I can see the Blue Council member is different than the one who was in power last time I was here. I assume his predecessor must have died while we were gone. I don't recall a vote being held last time I was in town, so in the months we were gone, one was called in an emergency session and "democracy" was upheld. The biggest problem with emergency sessions is that they're only announced a week in advance. None but the closest can make it to that vote.

The Green magic-wielder seems particularly interested in Chance. She sits tall in her chair, staring her down. Chance is stiff, but I can tell she's trying not to fidget. The Green smiles.

"Well, well, hello again, Giselone, it's been a while."

My head whips around to look at Chance and I force myself not to laugh. Giselone? What kind of name is that? No wonder she goes by Chance. Chance's mouth curls into a snarl before she schools it back to boredom with an underlayment of nervous energy.

"Sister," she nods at the Green.

I swear, if it weren't for years of training, my mouth would have dropped open. Chance's sister is a Council member—which means Chance must be nobility. Or have come from nobility. I nearly choke. I want to know why she didn't tell me. Or why she decided to become a Tracker rather than rest on her piles of gold.

"Mitac," Chance's sister calls on me, pulling me from my thoughts and forcing my gaze back to the Council. "Giselone. You—"

"Chance," I interrupt.

"Excuse me?" She's mad, but I don't care.

"She goes by Chance now, not Giselone. I sure would appreciate you using that name for her. It would keep me from getting confused as well." I smile, but I know I'm walking on thin ice. I'm pulling on my magic, and I shouldn't be. Not for this. But I feel waves of disrespect coming from Chance's sister, and I am not here for it. This woman doesn't deserve respect any more than Chance deserves her disrespect.

Chance nudges me, a sign to leave it alone. I shrug her off and wait for the Council.

The Green waves me off. "You were assigned to Ashadier for the Quest; is that correct?"

"Yes, Chance and I were," I emphasize Chance's name, pointedly staring at the Green Illume.

She narrows her green eyes at me. The two women could be twins. I suddenly wonder if they are. "Can you tell the Council what happened there?"

Chance opens her mouth to speak, but I speak over her. "We arrived in Ashadier two days before the Quest. We got set up in the inn and familiarized ourselves with the Questers the day before. I processed their names and signatures, which I see you have in front of you." I gesture to the stack of parchment on the table. "Chance took them to their places around the forest until it was time for dawn."

The scribe in the corner scratches out notes onto a separate stack of parchment. They only bring out the scribe for proceedings that might end in discipline, I've heard. I'm not surprised we're in trouble. Even though I can't fathom what more we could have done.

"Then?" The Black Council member urges.

"The Quest began. It was a little odd, though," I scratch my chin.

"How so?" the Yellow Council member asks, leaning forward, resting her elbows on the table. She tents her fingers in under her chin.

"Everything began normally," I state, "but one boy came out injured by a bear. He said it swiped at him, then lost interest before running off again." I avoid bringing up Selvia. That's a piece of information no one needs to know about. It was weird, but it wasn't going to do any good other than put Chance and Selvia in danger.

The Council looks at each other, unimpressed. "It's a forest, of course there are bears. He's lucky he didn't get killed."

"Yes, sir," I muster every ounce of respect I can forge, "but Ashadier has no known bears in the area, and given that many of them hunt, they would know. And the Quest is touted to be safe, but this bear was not."

I try to put a lid on my anger, but it's complicated by the fact that I am still angry about my own Quest.

The Council shrugs. "So, the country bumpkins were wrong. What's weird about that?"

Anger rises again, but I hold it back. "Perhaps. But I'm sure you're all more interested in the missing kid?" They're all staring me down. "She went in and didn't come out." I know it'll frustrate them, my lack of detail, but they've earned it. I almost laugh.

The Orange Council rolls his eyes. "We know that idiot. The reason you're here is to figure out how you let her get away."

"We didn't. We mounted a search with the town," I explain, "we tried to find her, we found traces of her, but then her traces disappeared. We searched and searched, hoping to find her. None of us ever did. When we came back out, the guard you sent to find us was there and I am sure he filled you in on the rest."

The Council nods, clearly dissatisfied with my explanation. "Do you think someone in the town helped her to escape?" The Blue Council asks. "Her aunt or uncle, maybe?"

I shake my head. "No, all of her family were with me who came on the search." I don't mention Julieth was in another group. They don't need to know.

"But someone else in the village could have," she presses.

"No," Chance pipes in. "I don't think so. Her traces of life disappeared completely. It's not like she ran off. If I didn't know better, I would think she was eaten whole."

The Council deliberates amongst themselves.

"Truly, she's not out there," I reinforce. "Or the Celestials have shielded her." The Illume seem perturbed by this thought, and I'm getting the sensation…do the Celestials shield people?

What is the Illume hiding? Better question is probably, what *aren't* they hiding?

"Is that the way of it, Giselone?" Chance's sister asks.

I grit my teeth. Chance nods. So far, so good. Of course, I haven't lied either, or said anything she should object to. Yet.

"We have her aunt," the Red Council reminds me as if I've forgotten. I don't let on that I haven't. It's better if they think I am detached. "Down in the dungeon. You are aware of her…fate?"

I don't respond. "If she doesn't turn over her niece, this," he picks up the parchment on top, "Eloise. If she doesn't tell us where she is, she faces torture until death."

I shrug, pretending it has no effect on me. I build a careful shield around what I am about to tell them next. This is my ace, a special strand of magic I have learned and practiced in secret. The ability to hide lies and pass them on as truth.

"I'm a Negotiator. I didn't get a lot of time to talk to her on the way back here due to her condition and being unconscious for a big part of the trip, but I am sure if you put me down there with her, I could negotiate my way to some information."

Chance looks over at me, surprised. That's what I needed. The Council looks unimpressed.

I pull on my magic again, adding conviction and sweetness to my words. "I am sure she knows where Eloise is; she doesn't have the right incentive. She probably believes you're going to hurt Eloise if you find her."

The Orange Council member goes to speak, but the Red stops him. "So, you're friendly with this woman?"

A few more threads wrap around my next statement. I am grateful I have practiced and strengthened this skill so much. It takes a lot of my energy to do it, but it will be worth it if it works.

"The thing with the far country folks is they're trusting if you're nice. If you ask Chance, she'll tell you I was very nice to them, and they grew fond of me. This will work in my favor. If you make me a guard down there, day or night, I am sure I can get her to talk."

"It's true," Chance backs me up. Thank the Celestials she's caught on. "He made many so-called friends there. People who started to trust him, even though it was unwise."

"You helped bring her in," the Red Council points out, his eyes narrowed. "Why do you think she'll forget that you killed her husband and suddenly be willing to trust you?"

"I'll convince her I wanted no part of it, and that I was trying to protect her from something worse. In time, she will grow to trust me again, and I'll sneak her treats and give her respect. She'll be ready to spill her guts thinking I will protect Eloise when, in actuality, I want to bring her in."

I can feel my magic extending on my words. Like a whisper of wind as it floats toward the people seated behind the table. I am both protecting my words and trying to get through their shields.

The Council ponders this, and I steal a glance at Chance who is rubbing the back of her neck anxiously. The Illume seems prepared to accept my idea when the door bursts open. A guard comes rushing in. "She's coming," she pants out. "The Dreamer, Aerith, was screaming at her not to come, the girl, but she's coming. That's what she must have Dreamed."

I feel the tendrils of my magic snap. Shit.

I am relieved to find out Eloise is alive, but it's replaced by dread that she's coming here. Where the Council wants her, and it's rarely a good idea to be where the Council wants you when you're an enemy of the Vale. A new plan forms, and I gather my magic again. Quickly creating strands and preparing them to shield my next set of lies. I'm going to need a nap after this.

"Please, sirs and madams," I gently call attention back to myself. They slowly stop talking and look at me. "I would very much like to go searching for her."

I hear Chance shuffle uncomfortably. Eyes at the table widen in surprise. "I doubt she will come directly here; she will likely try to find a way in and could harm someone. I bet I could apprehend her while she's still on her way and bring her back here more quickly and safely."

"What is your interest, here?" the Yellow Council member asks with suspicion. "Why do you care?"

"Penance," I spit out quickly. "I would like to atone for the mistakes in Ashadier. It won't be easy to find this girl, traveling will be uncomfortable, and I have certainly earned this punishment. Keep her aunt in the dungeon, I'll lure the girl back with promises that you will free the woman in exchange for her."

"We aren't going to, you know that, of course," the Yellow clarifies. I'm not sure if she's trying to dissuade me or encourage me.

I nod. "Of course, she betrayed the city and, especially, you." I give a slight bow. Wondering if I am going overboard but instinct drives me forward.

"I should go with him," Chance pipes in from my left. I glare at her.

That was not part of the plan. She was supposed to follow along but stay behind. There's no need for her to get herself into trouble and this will definitely end with all involved in serious trouble.

"I, too, made mistakes in Ashadier," Chance clarifies. I can't imagine how much it is costing her to swallow her pride for this. "I would like to prove that I am as excellent a Tracker as the Illume once believed of me."

Chance's sister guffaws. "Oh, please! You chose Tracking to piss off our family. You're not actually good at it."

Chance's green face turns a darker shade of green as blood rushes into it. Anger or embarrassment? I can't tell from this angle.

"Chance is a great Tracker," I rush to defend her. This sibling of Chance's is making me irrationally enraged. "I have worked with her many times before. If you don't trust us to find Eloise, then send someone to babysit us. See that we are on the up and up."

"Excuse us," the Black Council stands, and the others follow suit. Together, they walk out of the room, the doors closing behind them.

"What. The. Abyss." Chance is whisper-shouting as she marches over to me. "What do you think you are doing?"

"Playing for time," I murmur back. "We need time."

Chance fumes, her eyes narrowed, brows furrowed. "Next time, you tell me the plan first!"

The Council returns a few seconds later. The Black Council speaks directly to us, a stern look on his face.

"Both of you are one mistake from being jobless, homeless, and possibly headless."

They don't make empty threats, so I know they're being serious. "We will send you with another Warrior, the same one who came to get you from Ashadier, I think. He has proven he's willing to go the extra mile when necessary."

He sneers and I would like nothing more than to take the dagger I bought from Eloise and thrust it into this man's throat. I know he's referring to Gamet's murder.

"You will have three weeks to locate her and bring her back."

Three weeks isn't very long, a trip to Amaranth alone takes several days. But I bought us a few more weeks to figure out what we are going to do next. I pray to the Celestials that Saada can hold on for a few weeks while I try to locate her niece and come up with a better plan to get her out. One that hopefully doesn't get my head removed in the process. Or hers. Or Eloise's.

At the thought of Eloise, the stupid voice in my head is back.

Yes, I know! I yell back at it. *I'm doing what I can!*

IT'S THE BEST WAY.

Mitac

"I still think you're being foolish!"

Chance has taken it upon herself to yell at me the whole way back from the palace.

"You didn't have to invite yourself!" I yell back. I'm not actually mad; it's kind of funny to see her so riled up.

"And let you run off to get all the glory?"

I snort. "Glory? What glory? There's no way this ends with me still alive. And now you've assigned yourself to the same fate!"

We storm into the house, flinging the door open. "Look at that," I place my hand over my heart, "The door didn't come off."

Chance growls at me. Actually growls. I laugh.

Selvia is standing at the stove, stirring something over the fire, which smells so good it causes my stomach to grumble.

"It's the best way," I tell Chance.

"Getting yourself killed is the best way?" Chance shrieks. "Going on a fool's errand to find some village girl! That's not foolish?"

"Okay, maybe it's a little foolish, but I bought us, and her, some time."

"Three weeks to locate a girl who isn't going to want to be found? Then what? We bring her back like it's no big deal?"

I catch Selvia stealing a glance at us. Chance is standing as tall as she can, her hands on her hips. Her short stature makes it almost laughable.

"I haven't quite gotten that far, Chance. My plan hinged on getting close to Saada so I could hopefully get her out. Now it's changed and we are going for Eloise. I think she's in trouble, and I think it's best if we find her, not the Illume. After we get her safely stashed, I can figure out how to get Saada out."

Chance scrubs her hand down her face. "Do you even hear yourself? Let's say Eloise is willing to come with us. In spite of the fact that you killed her uncle, we aren't going by ourselves, or did you forget that fact? Elgin isn't going to let us take the girl."

"I didn't kill Gamet!" I protest. I was there, but I didn't actually do it. The knife slicing across his throat, the blood coating the floor, the spray reaching even me…it haunts my nights. I scrubbed and scrubbed my hands as soon as I could after that, but nothing could scrub my soul for being there. For not stopping it.

"It doesn't matter who did, you were there, weren't you? Did you stop it from happening? Make any efforts?" Chance puts voice to all the errors I made that day, and it cuts deep.

"No, but how could I? It was over so fast, I couldn't do anything," I defend weakly.

"And you think that Eloise is going to accept that as an answer? You don't think that maybe she'll put up a fight?" Chance has a good point, but I'm not changing my mind.

"Well, we did have that bet…" I trail off.

"What bet?" Chance narrows her eyes at me.

"I bet her a gold coin that if she came out Changed, she would come quietly." I know it's not worth anything, but I wonder if I could appeal to Eloise's honor or something.

Chance doubles over in laughter, startling me. Selvia continues to watch us silently, stirring the stew.

"You—" Chance wheezes, "—you idiot! Do you honestly believe that will make any difference to this girl, whatsoever?"

"I don't know." I shrug, a small smile is on my face. "I don't have a lot of options. I'll appeal to her honor."

Chance laughs more, her hand on the table to hold herself up. "Stop it, stop it, I can't breathe!"

"Listen, either way, we're in this," I grumble at her, starting to feel a little annoyed. "There's no backing out now. We have three weeks to figure out what to do, but we need to leave immediately. I'm going to go talk to Elgin and get a plan together to leave tomorrow bright and early. I'm talking first train out."

"Ugh, this is utter lunacy!" Chance throws her hands up.

"Excuse me," Selvia's voice suddenly chimes in. Chance jumps, I think she forgot Selvia was in the room.

"I might be able to help a bit," Selvia offers. "Eloise helped me in the forest. She trusts me. She might be more willing to come if I am with you."

I ponder her suggestion, but Chance immediately shoots her down.

"No way, no how. You are not coming with us. This is going to be incredibly dangerous as it is, and while I admire your tenacity and desire to help, I won't let you get into harm's way."

"Now, hold on a second Chance," I chime in, "That may not be a bad idea. Selvia can come with us all the way until we locate Eloise then we can send her back here on her own."

Chance is shaking her head vigorously. "You want this girl, this child who is barely old enough to feed herself with utensils, to come with us then travel back across the country. Alone!"

"Hey! I take offense to that!" Selvia butts in. "I have been far more resourceful than you know. I could do it! I promise to stay out of the way as much as possible and only do as I am told."

"No way," Chance persists, "You're a Negotiator, Mitac, you'll have to find a way to convince Eloise to come with us."

"It may not be so easy, Chance. Saada had a wall. I couldn't get through. As did Eloise." Chance's eyes widen. She knows a bit about my magic and how skilled I am.

"She's not going to listen. Selvia could be the difference between Eloise cooperating with us or hiding from us. Again."

"I don't care, Mitac, find another way." Chance turns away. "I'll get ready to leave first thing in the morning. I'll meet you at the train station," she calls over her shoulder.

I shrug at Selvia and give her an "I tried" look and she shrugs right back.

I step out of the house and lean against the wall. I'm spent. My magic took everything out of me.

As soon as the door closes, I hear Chance's raised voice. "You, girl, are going to get yourself killed! You're reckless with your life like it doesn't matter!"

When did Chance get so protective of Selvia? It's heartwarming.

"It *doesn't* matter," Selvia sounds defeated. I can't have heard her right.

I hear Chance's feet moving quickly. "It doesn't!?" she yells, "What the Abyss do you mean it doesn't? Do you think we brought you back here because you don't matter? Do you think Mitac paid to get you out of the orphanage because you mean nothing? Do you think I keep you here because you don't matter?"

The next words come out more softly. I know I shouldn't be listening to this private moment, but I can't help it.

"You matter, dear girl," Chance is saying, "Your life matters, your being matters. You belong here, with me, with Mitac. I know that the orphanage didn't give you a good understanding of that, but every person matters to someone. You matter to me, to Mitac; I would even bet you matter to many of the people in Ashadier."

She pauses. I hear someone crying. I should have soundproofed these walls better.

"I want to hear you say it. I want to hear you tell me that you matter."

Selvia sobs harder. "I—matter." Selvia doesn't sound like she believes it. Not yet, but if Chance keeps at her like this, one day she might.

I never thought putting Selvia with Chance would be such a good match. I don't know Chance's past, even less than I thought after today's revelations, but I wonder if they aren't healing each other in these moments.

"No one gets to ever tell you that you don't matter. Not in any way that makes it true. I will tell you every day until you believe it. I will do it until you know it. Until you treat yourself like someone who has a right to exist." Chance's voice has dropped, gone soft and caring. A voice I've never heard her use before.

Rested enough, I move on. It's time to find Elgin and get this mission underway.

YOU'RE NOT THRIVING.

Eloise

Revolution 1762 Onas 04 (R62O04)

MY PACK IS STARTING to feel heavier the longer I walk. I yearn for the luggage Miss Halsey had, the one with the wheels. Right about now that would be very nice. Of course, I think as I traipse over fallen trees and dead brush in the depths of the forest, it probably wouldn't work very well here.

I have been on the road, road being an operative word since I'm decidedly ignoring the roads, for several days already. My new boots gave me blisters the first couple of days, even with my good socks. Those days were slow going and shorter. My socks had to be washed out in the creeks due to the blood that had built up. Luckily, calluses were slowly starting to form, and I was pushing through the pain a little better these days.

I ate various berries and known mushrooms along the game trails. I wish I had Cardis and his wealth of knowledge with me as he could identify some things that I wasn't sure were edible. At night, while not nearly as effective, I would set up snares on the game trails. Once I had gotten lucky and caught a rabbit. I skinned and gutted it, leaving all the pieces behind for the forest or carrion animals.

I cooked it over some fire and stored the meat that I didn't want to finish that day in one of the jars which had held some dried vegetables. It seemed to be okay, and I was able to heat it and eat it the next day. So far, I haven't gotten sick from it.

While I trekked through the forest, I tried to catch sight of the carriage pathway occasionally to make sure I continued to head the correct way. One of the days, I had heard a small team of horses and a wagon coming, heading toward Ashadier. I took it as a good sign that help was on the way for the beleaguered town. I barely had time to duck out of the way before they came running past. I couldn't be sure, but I thought I saw Mrs. Braswell driving the team. I waited in the brush for several minutes until the sound of the horses' feet disappeared.

On the morning of the fourth day, I rise from my bedroll in the early hours of dawn. I yawn and stretch my sore muscles. It appears no matter how long I sleep on the ground, my body is going to be upset about it. Of course, my back has not been quite the same since the Quest, and that may have something to do with it. That and my bag of supplies.

I pack up my site, making sure to cover my tracks so it doesn't appear anyone was there, and head back out, chewing mindlessly on some licorice I had found growing along the way. It wasn't very tasty, not my favorite snack, but it was better than nothing and my food stores were getting low. Plus, it helped with the bad breath. Mint would be better, though, if I could find some.

I approach my snare with prepared disappointment. Nothing has been in them for a few days, and I am getting frustrated—and hungry. Today, my snare is moved from its spot and is no longer set. I figure I must have failed to set it properly. I gather my equipment and put it back in my bag to try again tonight. I do find it odd how disturbed the area around my snare is like it had caught something. It must have gotten free somehow.

"Looking for this?" a voice behind me asks. I whirl around, my heart nearly stopping. In Cardis' aloft arm is a fat squirrel, clearly starting to prepare for winter.

"Cardis, you scared me to death!" I clutch my chest in mock pain.

"No, Sister, you're still alive," Cardis' face is flat, lacking enthusiasm, and his voice holds no inflection. He must still be mad at me. "Though you're not thriving."

I narrow my eyes at him and sigh, holding out my hand. "Nice to see you too. Can I have my squirrel now?"

He pauses to consider it, then tosses the deceased animal to me. I catch it and take one of my knives out of its sheath to start processing it on a nearby log.

"So, Cardis, how did you catch up to me?" I ask without looking up from my work. Cardis taught me everything I know about skinning animals and my hand shakes a little as he studies my work. I always get nervous when someone watches me.

"You're moving slow," he mocks me. "And you leave tracks that could be followed by anyone."

"I do not!" I protest. I pull the hide off the squirrel in one pull, quite proud of myself. I hold it up for Cardis to look at, and he appears mildly impressed.

"Nice work, who taught you that?" There's a glint in his eye. I smile at him. "And you do, too!"

I frown and toss the inedible entrails off to the side, leaving us with a nice bit of meat.

"Why are you here anyway? You didn't even hug me when I left." Cardis gathers some nearby wood and starts a fire for our breakfast.

"I waited a day then figured you would probably die out here if I didn't come to help you."

"So, you still haven't forgiven me," I cut the squirrel into manageable pieces and put them on a stick I found, making a skewer.

He shrugs and takes the skewer. He holds it over the fire, rotating it slowly as the meat starts to sizzle. He pulls some salt and dried garlic out of his bag and hands it to me. I sprinkle it over the meat. The salt pops when it hits the fire. My stomach rumbles with the smell. I wish I had thought about herbs when I left.

"Is that teenage boy for 'I'm sorry'?" I wonder if Julieth has something to do with his presence here now.

He shrugs again.

"Fine. You can go home, Cardis. This isn't going to be easy or safe. It's not like in your books. There are real consequences here."

Cardis scowls. "You think I don't know that? Why do you think I came after you? You can't hunt big animals, you can't identify plants like I can, you probably didn't even bring anything to defend yourself at a distance."

He's got me there.

"I was doing fine. I could throw a dagger if needed."

"So, a rabbit or squirrel every few days is 'fine'? Or leaving tracks behind so anyone can stumble on them and find you to capture you is 'fine'?"

"It was enough."

We sit in silence for several minutes. I take over turning the meat over the fire, giving Cardis a break.

"Figuring you're walking about twenty-five miles a day on a good day, you're going to need a lot more than that, or you're going to die of hunger. Your body will start eating your muscles, then your organs when you run out of fat stores."

I grunt. "I would have made it to a town long before that happened, Cardis."

"Then what? You go into town, pull out your fancy gold coin, get recognized, and taken? I'm sure the Council feeds their prisoners well. But, hey, at least you'll be in the same place Saada is, right? Isn't that the plan? Why bother going out of your way to avoid detection if you want to be where she is, anyway? "

I ponder this.

"You're burning the meat," he points out. I rip the skewer off the fire and blow out the fire that had started on one of the chunks. We divide the meat, Cardis insisting I take the bigger pieces, and eat. I hum with approval. I didn't realize how much difference some salt and garlic could make.

"I just…I don't want to be in their hands for too long," I chew and swallow. "I thought, maybe once I got to Amiket, I would find a way to, you know, rescue her?"

Cardis nods skeptically. We finish our breakfast and put out the fire.

"Sounds like a solid plan," Cardis states flatly. "It should only take us a couple of months to walk there."

"Not if we keep standing here!" I match his sarcastic tone. Even though it's a long distance and we have to go over the more difficult terrain, I estimated about four weeks. At most.

"Then let's go," he waves me onward.

"Seriously, Cardis, go home. You can't come with me." He laughs at me, and I scowl back at him.

"We have long since passed the stage where you can order me around. Julieth is taking care of the kids; she even helped me pack, because she thinks you need help, too."

That's what I thought. He didn't come because he wants to be here, he's here out of obligation. I decide to push his obligation. I'm not going to make this any more pleasant for him than he's making it for me.

I throw my hands up in the air. "Fine! Whatever. Let's get going."

Cardis picks up his stuff and I notice his bow and arrows attached to his bag. He did come prepared.

We walk in silence for a long while. Both of us, I think, waiting to see who will break first. Finally, I've had enough. "How many books did you pack?"

"Three," he answers without hesitation. If he's surprised I knew about his books, he doesn't show it. "One about the other towns we might come across, one about the plants and fungi, and one about magic and curses."

I side-eye him. "Magic and curses?"

"Sure, it's a new one Julieth got for me. I haven't had a chance to read it, and it might contain something useful about our family curse. Maybe we can find a way to break it?"

I get a sinking feeling in my gut. I continue to operate along the lines that my time with Raemyn was a hallucinogenic dream. Something caused by being thrown into a tree, but every time I think about it, it feels more and more real.

It's dusk when Cardis and I start looking for good places to sleep. I had glanced at the road a couple of times today, so I knew we were headed east still, a good sign since we need to cross the Vale to get to Amiket. I am glad we haven't been walking in circles.

We find a semi-comfortable place and unroll our bedrolls. Given the warmth and cloudless sky, we don't bother with a cover over our heads. We each set a snare trap a little way away and meet back at camp where I set about boiling some water for tea. We eat some dried fruits, quietly, just the sound of the fire in front of us, each of us lost in our own thoughts. Or I am, at least. I think about Saada, I wonder how she's doing. I think about Julieth with the three gremlins, hoping what I taught Hilda and Gilda is enough to keep them going while we are gone. After we eat, I smother the fire, but not before Cardis interrupts my efforts.

"One second." He removes a small tin from his pack; inside is an odd-looking mushroom. To my surprise, he thrusts it quickly into the fire, where it ignites and then turns into a burning coal. He instructs me to finish smothering the fire. I do so, and he uses the tin to scoop up the strange coal mushroom and puts it in his pack. "This will hold an ember for a long time, and we can use it in the future to start more fires."

I'm once again impressed with Cardis' knowledge and am begrudgingly grateful for his presence.

BROKEN NOSE?

Eloise

We must have only been asleep for a short while before I was awoken. It is still pitch black around us, the stars dotting the sky brightly. There is no moon tonight, a fact that may be working in our favor. I can hear voices not far off chattering. Odd for the middle of the night. I quietly extract myself from my bed and nudge Cardis, placing a hand over his mouth so he won't make a noise.

He fights me briefly before he recognizes me, a finger to my lips telling him to be quiet. I can tell he now hears the voices. I take my hand from his mouth, and he too rises into a crouch. I pull a knife from under my pillow. Cardis produces his bow and knocks an arrow.

Cardis motions for me to stay, and he starts to head toward the voices. I grab him and pull him back. No way am I letting him go after the voices alone. I point to myself. He shakes his head violently, insisting he go. We have a silent but heavily gestured argument before he gets his point across. He's the one with experience in the woods, tracking animals, and being quiet. I don't.

He walks off and I wait, knives at the ready, still crouched.

"Put down the knives," a voice behind me demands once Cardis is out of earshot.

I jump up and prepare to fight. I've never had to fight someone, and the act of hurting a human gives me pause. Long enough of an opening for her to bring the tip of her blade to my throat.

"Drop them, or I'll slit your throat, then your brother's."

I get a good look at my attacker. As good as I can in the dark, anyway. She's tall, taller than me and broad of back. I have a hard time telling her actual build. Her clothes are loose and flowing, but she holds her sword steady, not even a wobble in the long blade. Here is someone who has clearly faced an actual opponent or two in her time.

I reluctantly drop the daggers, hoping Cardis might return and put us in better numbers. She instructs me to turn around and quickly ties my wrists with a rough cordage. The point of her blade keeps steady pressure in my lower back as she orders me forward. As we pass my daggers, I see her bend down to grab them. I mourn the loss of my good knives and my only source of protection.

"Are you from the city?" I ask, my voice shaking. She has to be. Who else would be interested in kidnapping me? I start to run through possibilities for escape; they all seem bleak.

"No questions," she increases the pressure on my back. I speed up to get away from it. In the dark, I can't see the roots and branches. I trip on several, one sticking up far enough that I fall on my face. Without my hands to catch me, I land face-first in the dirt. A sharp pain cuts across my face, and I feel something warm running down.

Blood, I think, when the metallic liquid makes it to my lips. My face feels swollen immediately. *Broken nose?*

The woman reluctantly helps me up to my feet and keeps her hand wrapped around the knot between my wrists. This keeps me on my feet when I trip but also pulls on my shoulders each time she catches my fall.

We make it to the edge of a grove, and I can see the flickering of a large fire. Around the fire are several people sitting, talking, eating, and a few dancing to music which must be playing in their heads. Their ages range from infant to adult, and they're all dressed in brightly colored clothes of lightweight materials. I've never seen so many clashing colors altogether. It's like they took patchwork quilting to a whole new meaning.

"Where do you suppose she is?" one of the older males asks a younger female.

He looks vaguely familiar, but I can't place him. He sounds jovial and calm. I assume the "she" he is referring to is me.

"Not sure," the woman replies in a soft, airy tone. "She will return when it is time."

The man throws his hands up in defeat. "Never ask a Dreamer for a straight answer."

A Dreamer? I examine the woman more closely. She has long, wavy black hair, but not black skin. I can't see her eyes to see if maybe she's a weak seer. Then again, my understanding of Dreamers is they all have access to one kind of Dreaming. Plus, aren't they all identified by the other Dreamers in Amiket and taken there at birth or shortly thereafter?

"She is coming," the woman turns her gaze in my direction. I try to straighten my posture under scrutiny. I can sense Cardis is watching me, but I don't look at him. He wisely stays hidden as we pass. If I didn't know he was there, I wouldn't have seen him.

"Eloise," the supposed Dreamer welcomes me, "Welcome to the Wayfarers."

I tilt my head. What are the Wayfarers? Maybe she said Winfairers? I didn't think we were that close to Winfair, but maybe we were? I hope not, because we don't need to be traveling that direction, we should be heading directly toward Rothesard, not north.

"Excuse me?" I ask. "Who did you say you are?"

"The Wayfarers, girl," the woman repeats impatiently, her voice not as light and airy as it had been. "We've been waiting for you."

"What do you mean? I think you have the wrong person. I've never heard of a Wayfarer."

"No, girl, we don't. I have been Dreaming of you for months now. You are Eloise of Ashadier, daughter of Steen and Leigha, sister to Julieth and Cardis, who is hiding behind that tree over there."

She points directly towards Cardis' hiding place. From the corner of my eye, I see movement and involuntarily look to see him walking out on wooden legs, like a statue forced to move. His bow is at his side, his knocked arrow in place, and his arm is tense as though he's prepared to draw it any moment. I pray he doesn't.

"Thank you for joining us, Cardis." He doesn't nod or acknowledge her statement. He stares at me then glares at the woman holding me at sword point. "I had hopes that you would know of us, at least a little, it would make this so much easier." My gaze returns to the Dreamer.

"Have a seat." She points us to a log. I inexplicably find myself seated on it with Cardis next to me. I don't even remember walking here. The woman gives me my knives back and walks away. Apparently, she thinks we are subdued? I am very confused by everything that is going on here.

"I want you to know, first and foremost, that your aunt is safe. Sort of."

Cardis and I look around frantically.

"Where is she?" I ask. "If she's safe, I demand to see her!"

"She's not here," the Dreamer grunts. "She is at the palace in Amiket, and right now, she's not in pleasant circumstances, but she's alive. We have someone keeping an eye on her. For now, your path follows ours."

I don't have any idea of what's going on here. A glance at Cardis tells me he's as lost as I am. "I don't know how you know so much about me, but someone better explain and quickly." It's a threat, but I know it's an empty one. Even with two knives and a bow, we are hardly a threat to this many people.

"We are the Wayfarers." She repeats herself like it's going to make it make more sense. "I am Nyana, the Dreamer for this band of hooligans."

I look around at the nearly silent group. The only ones making noise are a few kids off to the side chasing each other through the forest. "The Wayfarers are nomadic people. We move in groups, as you can see, and belong to no one land. Few know of us, but I thought maybe your mom would have told you stories of us."

"Our parents are dead," I say blandly.

"I am aware that none of us are immune to time's cruelty, but your mother, Leigha, knew of us and lived with us for a time."

Cardis shakes his head. "There's no way."

"She did. Shortly after her Quest. It seems she had a little panic about her choices in the forest and ran away. She had met one of us during her Quest and found us afterward. I was only a young girl at the time, of course, but I remember her staying with us for about six months before she felt she should go home."

My mouth is hanging open and I snap it shut quickly. How did we not know about this piece of history? Saada would have said something, I'm sure, about our mother running off to live with nomads.

"She mentioned the curse on her family and asked us to keep an eye out for her kids, if she had them. We have done so, coming in from time to time to check in on you and make sure you're doing okay."

I turn to the man who had been speaking to Nyana earlier. "You! You're the traveling salesman!"

He takes a bow, taking his tall hat off his head. "Grady, at your service."

"But," I struggle to find words, "If you knew about us. I'm so confused. What are you doing here? How is a Dreamer not in Amiket? Why make yourself known now? I presume it wasn't an accident you found us, based on what you were saying before."

"So many questions," Nyana smiles at me kindly. "I will do my best to answer all of them. We Wayfarers do like to keep our ways a secret. I am not known to the city, nor is anyone here." She waves around. "We have existed for generations with the city not knowing of us. We are very careful to present ourselves to cities only when we must, and we never go to Amiket as they force you to register your visit. Any Wayfarer who leaves is spelled to silence about our activities."

"Then how could you expect us to know anything if my mother couldn't tell us?" Eloise asks.

Nyana is undeterred. "Your mother was quite powerful in her magic, she was able to resist the spell but swore she would never tell, only to her kids if she felt she should."

"She accepted her magic?!" I shout at the same time Cardis protests, "Our mother had no magic! She looked like us!"

"Not all people in your family resisted their magic, Eloise. Your mother accepted it."

"But she didn't bring the end of the Realm. And she wasn't a color. How is that possible?"

"Somewhere in your lineage must be some old, old Wayfarer blood. We do not change colors. We do not have one type of magic. We can use many types. True, some of us are stronger in some things than others, but we have access to all."

To prove her point, she brings flame forth in her hand, turning red, and extinguishes it with some water from her other hand, turning blue. I gape. My head is starting to hurt.

I sit straight as a lightning rod, a faint buzzing running through my mind. Nyana goes on. "While your mother accepted her magic, she chose not to accept her role as the Variance, a decision we believe she may have made once she discovered she was pregnant with Julieth and no longer felt she could risk it."

"Julieth," I croak. "Julieth would have been the next in line."

Nyana nods. "Yes, she would have been. I do not know what Julieth chose to do. We did not have anyone of our lineage in the Quest she was in. She may have successfully hidden her magic from even herself."

"So, it was real?" I ask quietly, my stomach dropping. "It wasn't a dream?"

"No, it wasn't. It's all very real. Like this is."

Oh, Celestials. The tunnel vision is back. Panic crawling up my spine. Dread. The world around me disappears momentarily, and a vision of me surrounded by the dead with peeling skin snaps in place. I gasp and groan. Reality returns as quickly. *What was that?*

"Why can't one of you be the Variance? You all have all the magic you said. Why hasn't one of you done it rather than my family? Why me?"

The Dreamer sits on my other side, wrapping an arm around me. "We know it's scary, but what makes you different, your family line, is that you have access to and equal strength in all of the magic. Your power will surpass all others in a way that none of us can do."

"I don't know what to do," I grasp at straws. "I don't have any magic. I…I tried. Nothing happened. And I can't go to a school to learn, that's what she said."

"No, there's no school that will help you, and those schools aren't helpful anyway. The way they use their magic is brutish. Forceful. There are better ways to use it. We can teach you the Wayfarer way. How to work with your magic, not force it."

"What wasn't a dream?" Cardis asks angrily. I forgot he was sitting there listening, probably with little idea of what's going on. "Who told you that you couldn't go to school? What do you need to do? Will someone tell me what's going on!"

...OH, GREAT NEGOTIATOR.

Mitac

R62O03

The next morning, Chance, Elgin, and I boarded the steam train, and we spent the last couple of days trying to come up with a game plan to find Eloise. This is incredibly difficult since Elgin has no desire to be with us and would rather go in, tie her like a farm animal, and drag her back. Both Chance and I would rather opt for non-violent methods. This isn't a surprise since Elgin's magic is sourced from fighting and mine negotiation. Unfortunately, with all of us sharing one sleeper car, Chance and I have little time to talk without Elgin to try to come up with a better plan.

"I don't know why you're so worried about trying to get this girl to come willingly," Elgin complains for the hundredth time.

"Because it would be a heck of a lot easier to bring someone cooperative back than someone who is fighting us each step of the way," I reply back for the hundredth time.

He huffs. "It worked on her aunt fine. It doesn't matter if she wants to be there, the Council says bring her back, we bring her back. However we have to."

"Without hurting her," I remind him.

"No, without killing her. They didn't say we couldn't hurt her. They only said we couldn't kill her. What a pointless undertaking, anyway. Why is this girl so special?"

"That's not for us to know," I tell him.

I try to keep my responses to him around duty and honor rather than emotion as he won't respond well to emotional pleadings, something I learned during our first round of travel back from Ashadier with Saada in tow. I also learned that trip that my magic is ineffective against him. That has also made this more difficult. I need to find a way to separate us from him.

"Whatever. We find the girl, bring her back, I get paid. Then hopefully move on to something more exciting." He rubs his thumb lovingly over the sword he has in his lap. I don't know why he has it out of its sheath, but there it sits, scaring off everyone who dares glance our way.

"Why don't you head back, and we will take care of this?" I suggest.

"Yeah, you don't have to be bored hunting some girl," Chance chimes in quickly. "You could stop off at an inn somewhere in the Kahli desert and chill. We should be there today. We'll pick you up on the way back. Some liquor and women? Free downtime?"

I flinch. This is not appealing to his honor. He does appear to be considering it, though.

"It would be nice..." I glance at Chance. Does she have some magic I don't know about? "You promise you'd come get me on the way back?"

"Of course!" I chip in. "I don't think we need all three of us for this silly girl."

"I'll think about it." He gets up and puts his sword back in its sheath before leaving the carriage without a word.

I look over at Chance, bewildered. She sits back, arms crossed over her chest, a smirk on her face. "Okay, spill. How did you do that?"

"Easy. Every time he left, he went gone to get something from the bar. He downs it in one go, eats some mint, and returns. He's sneaky, but he's got a soft spot for liquor. I was guessing on the women, honestly. But most of the men I've seen in the bars tend to drink and take women to bed with them." Her face twists with disgust.

I think about it, and I'm not sure I've ever seen Chance drink anything other than water or juice.

"Well, while he's gone, let's talk about what we are going to do."

"Lead the way, oh, great Negotiator."

I roll my eyes at her. "I figure we start in Rothesard. Ask some questions, find out if anyone has seen her or heard from her."

"I disagree." Chance leans forward, elbows on her knees. "Presuming she left when the Purple Dreamer saw it and not before, she would still be in the forest. I think it would be smarter to start in Ashadier and work our way east. Most likely, she will want to avoid the roads, which means she will be a lot slower than we will be."

"Why ask me to lead if you're going to shoot my idea down?" I grumble at her. "Okay, we go to Ashadier…they're going to chase us right back out with pitchforks and torches. I am sure I am public enemy number one around there. And you won't be liked much more than I will be."

"Maybe not number one, but pretty close to it. But I think I can get information."

"How so?"

"We don't have you enter Ashadier to start. I will go in alone. You can hang out in Rothesard or nearby in the forest while I ask around. I will hopefully be able to convince them that I am there on a goodwill mission and that I'm not a threat to Eloise. I can even frame it that you're an evil person, and they have every right to hate you. Align myself with their side."

I nod. "That could work. I don't like you going in alone, though. They might hurt you."

"Unlikely," she pans. "You're not the only one who can negotiate things, you know."

I have to admit her plan has merit. I may not like it, but I know Chance can take care of herself. She can't beat me in a sparring match, but she's no slouch when it comes to defending herself or fighting. At least for a Tracker.

I look outside and see we have switched the mountainous gorge for the Cantuè Plains and are chugging hard and fast for the Kahli desert. There's another day of travel in front of us. I kick my feet up onto the bench and rest my head on my hat against the window. Chance leaves the carriage, perhaps to spy on Elgin some more. I reluctantly admit that she did some good reconnaissance. Perhaps I'm less necessary than I thought.

I'M in a carriage bouncing uncomfortably on the hard-packed road. Across from me is Selvia, staring at me blankly.

"Are you sure about this?" Selvia asks me. "You have to be sure. Otherwise, you're going to get us killed."

"I'm sure," I find myself saying.

"Okay, Eloise, tell us what you need us to do."

Eloise? I'm Mitac.

I look down. I'm in a delicate, feminine body. Definitely not my own. I look at my hands, soft and tanned, not rough and black. What is going on here?

"When I tell you what I need you to do," my voice is Eloise's voice and my Mitac brain has no knowledge whatsoever of what I'm going to say, "I need you to do it without question."

The voice is certain, confident. I am not. I need to get out of Eloise's body and into my own. I hear the voice again, screaming. *Danger.* I try to claw my way out of Eloise's mind. Nothing happens. I pull on the invisible ties keeping me rooted in place.

R62O04

I jerk awake, my leg falling off the bench across from me. Chance is watching me in mild amusement.

I rub my eyes, confusion veiling my mind.

"Good morning, sleepyhead," Chance grins cheekily at me.

"Where are we?" I look outside and see the desert passing by. Cacti, sagebrush, old fire pits, and animals dot the landscape. Here and there, steps lead down under the dirt-laden ground. Underground housing, for the people to keep cool. Nearly every resident in Kahli is ill-suited to live in Kahli. They're fair-skinned, red-haired, and don't tolerate sunshine.

The desert sun is unforgiving. It is unsurprising that the majority of people who would be out of the house have already found shelter for the afternoon.

"Passing out of Kahli, almost to Amiket."

I look around for Elgin. "He got off in Kahli like we suggested," Chance mentions, correctly interpreting my searching gaze.

My shoulders relax. Until I remember my weird dream. I chalk it up to exhaustion and try to scrub it from my mind.

"Thanks," I tell her. "I had no idea I would sleep for so long."

She only shrugs. "No big deal. You must have needed it. If you don't mind, I'm going to catch a quick nap before we get to Rothesard. This will be the last comfortable bed we have for a while."

I drop my other leg off the bench and Chance stretches out. I leave her to her nap and go to get a meal.

I can't help but size up the other passengers while I'm in there. No one makes eye contact with me, but that's okay. I don't need them to. There are a few magic-wielders, but most of them are Unchanged. I don't see any obvious threats, and I tuck in.

"Are you a Warrior, sir?" A young kid, probably no more than seventeen, stands in front of me. He's a tall, stocky boy with long brown hair and a short brown beard. And shockingly green eyes.

I debate denying it, but my look belies my magic anyway. What's the point? For that matter, why did he ask?

"Of sorts," I hedge.

"Did you oversee one of the Quests this year?" he asks. He boldly sits across from me at the table. I'm taken aback by his brazenness.

This is an interesting line of questioning. I try to sense deception or ulterior motive from him, but I can't feel anything. I wish I were a Truth Finder.

"I did," I finally answer.

"Was it a good one?"

I scratch my chin. "A good one?"

"Yeah, did you have a lot of Changed kids?" He looks me directly in the eye, unblinking. It's unsettling and causes me to fidget. I clear my throat and take a bite of my food, chewing slowly while I contemplate if I can answer his question.

"It was alright, I guess," I try hard not to fidget some more or look away.

He nods. "I had my Quest this year, too." He leans forward like he's going to tell me a secret. I find myself matching his body language. "I came out Unchanged, can you tell?"

Then he laughs heartily and stands up. He claps me on the shoulder.

"Have a good ride," he walks off confidently.

What on Zarvan was that?

...NOT FORCE IT.

Eloise

R62O07

I had fallen into a fitful sleep the night the Wayfarers found us and brought us into their little circle. It's been a few days since then, and I have learned a lot about them.

For one, they live strictly off the land. They hunt and forage, rarely ever buying. I asked about their clothes, and they said they would forage for those too, though it was said with a twinkle in their eye. I later learned from Nyana that they forage through discarded clothing for pieces they need and put their clothes together. This made sense as to why they looked like dancing rainbows.

They have horses and a wagon where they keep some of their larger items like cook pots and winter weather gear, but they have no permanent housing. And they like it that way. They move according to the patterns in the weather. In the summer, they mostly spend their time in Amaranth, where they have a ready supply of water and shade.

I asked them why they weren't in the forest when I was being searched for, and they laughed at me. They told me they were and that they simply spelled the groups who saw them to not see them after all. Those with the ability to cast those spells, gifted in mind alteration, were pointed out to me. I stayed far away from them, preferring to keep my mind exactly as it is.

The Wayfarers are also capable of starting small gardens for vegetables they can preserve through winter. Cardis spends most of his time talking to those in charge of that process. He shares what he has learned, and they share what they have done and has worked. Both sides seem equally fascinated by the other's knowledge. Each night, Cardis returns with a huge smile on his face, excited to share what he's learning. I keep half an ear on what he has to say, but I'm not fully paying attention.

My mind is currently trying to light a fire. And failing. I growl in frustration.

"You haven't heard a word I've said, have you?" Cardis asks me, his shoulders drooped, and face fallen.

I drop my hand. "I have, I'm sorry, I'm trying to do this on my own. So far, I haven't been able to produce any magic unless one of the Wayfarers is guiding me. What if it's them doing it and not me anyway?"

"You're trying too hard, Phoenix," a voice comes from behind me. I turn to face my least favorite Wayfarer, Gorduin.

"It's Eloise, stop calling me that," I snap. Every time he calls me Phoenix, I'm reminded of the necklace around my neck and what it means.

Gorduin is a boy around my age; he's not exactly sure because the Wayfarers don't keep meticulous records, but he was able to enter the Quest this year. He is frustratingly talented with his magic.

The Wayfarers sneak into the Quests when they're about the right age to gain access to their magic. Unlike everyone else, they don't go through the proper channels to do so, and, unlike everyone else, they don't go to school to learn their magic. They learn it from each other, each person passing it down in perpetuity.

Of course, what comes naturally to them doesn't come naturally to me. Gorduin shoves his stocky frame between me and Cardis on our log. Cardis grunts and walks off.

"That was rude," I point out. Gorduin scratches his light brown beard. "Was it? I didn't notice." He smiles at me, and I scowl at him in return.

"You have to work with your magic, not force it." I roll my eyes.

He's told me this over and over. Gorduin is assigned as my teacher of sorts, for my magic. He's new to it, but because he's my age, the Wayfarers feel I would be more inclined to learn from him.

I tried to get Nyana to teach me, but she laughed at me and told me that she had too much to do to be able to train me and that Gorduin would be happy to help. Of course, he was happy to help and rub it in how great he is. *Gah!*

"You turn bright red when you're trying to make your magic work for you, and not a flash like you're about to produce fire. I can always tell. You also look constipated. Are you having problems going to the bathroom?"

I feel myself flush and not from trying to use magic. "Inappropriate!"

"So…yes?"

"Agh! Go away!"

He shrugs. "As you desire. But you're never going to get to your magic if you keep trying to force it." He gets up from the log, unaffected by our exchange, and walks off.

I notice Cardis staring after him as well. Boring holes into his back. Cardis comes back and sits with me again. "Brute," he mumbles.

I murmur agreement and return to trying to access my magic. I keep hitting a wall. At least, that's what it feels like.

Although, one time, I literally did hit a wall of rocks when I was supposed to be breaking it down. To say my fist did a better job than my supposed magic would be an understatement. I was seriously beginning to doubt I had any magic at all. I had watched the Wayfarers around me using magic for various tasks. At random moments during the day or evening, people would turn a pop of color, and something would happen. I had watched them, trying to see what they were doing that I was not. I couldn't perceive any difference which made it all the worse.

I remember the first session I had with Gorduin. He told me to breathe and feel my magic flowing through me. He stood behind me and held my hands, palm up, in front of me. I had watched as a small spark had revealed itself there and jumped in shock and surprise. He smiled with me, then told me he had done most of the work. I tried arguing that I had done it, so he told me to try on my own. Utter failure. Every time I worked on my own, nothing happened.

"You'll get it, Eloise," Cardis hugs me reassuringly. "I have faith in you."

"Thanks, Card. I guess I'll keep trying to have faith in myself." I feel deflated.

We sit there quietly, me trying to get to my magic, him pouring over a book. I glance over once and see he's reading the magic book. I hope he finds something of use.

～

R62O08

The next morning finds me where every morning has. Standing with the messengers. They are the ones to receive the ravens, if there are any.

The first time I had seen the half-dozen pitch-black birds fly into camp, I had darted into a tent in fear. Then I saw the messengers standing there with their arms up in front of them to receive them. Each bird went to one specific messenger. When the birds were visible, the messengers turned a deep Green and didn't return to their normal color until the birds had their next task and flew off into the distance.

"What are they doing?" I had asked Gorduin.

"They're getting information from around the Realm and sending some back," he said easily.

"Why doesn't everyone use them? It would probably be faster than taking the trains back and forth to send and receive information."

"It would, but the ravens are notoriously picky. They're smart birds. Only trust certain people. They're a good judge of character. It's hard to find someone they'll work for, and they don't transfer their allegiances."

I stared at the birds, waiting patiently for their person to read and write. They hold out their legs and accept some food, and then the bird and human will connect head-on. Only then will the bird take off.

"What happens when their person dies?"

Gorduin looked at me, his eyes dark, losing their natural humor. "They die."

I gasped.

319

"Not right away, but they become listless and stop caring for themselves. They will keep coming back here, looking for their person. When they are unable to find them, they will pace around here, refusing to leave or eat. Despite all our best efforts, they can't be consoled."

This morning, we stand quietly, watching a few birds come in.

One particularly flighty one lands with a scroll on its leg. "That's the one from Amiket," Gorduin whispers in my ear, his beard tickling me.

My heart rises into my throat. *Please let there be word of Saada.* The only reason I am still here and not on my way to Amiket is the reassurance I have received that Saada is reasonably safe. My feet itch to get going, to get her out of there, but cooler heads and better judgment continue to hold me here for now. I need control of my magic before I go anywhere, and this is the best place I can learn it.

The messenger reads the note, writes a reply, and sends the bird off after a snack. I know better than to wait to find out what it contains. They always take everything directly to Nyana, and if it's fit to share, she will.

I DON'T APPROVE...

Mitac

R62O05

I stretch out my tired limbs and disembark the train. I look around. Rothesard. It doesn't look much different than the last time I saw it. It's getting cold, though, and the trees around me are tinged with gold. Not the pines, of course, which will remain their green throughout unless they're topped with snow, but the other trees in the area obey the seasons. I'm bumped from behind by someone else trying to get off the train.

I hitch my bag onto my shoulder and mumble an apology as I step onto the platform. It's busy, people everywhere.

I walk toward the carriage stands. Time to purchase the next leg of our trip.

Chance slows and turns on the walkway. I look at her, my eyebrow raised.

"Tell me, I am not seeing what I think I am seeing," Chance grinds out next to me but clearly loud enough to be directed to the person coming after us, bag on her back. "Tell me, I am not seeing Selvia coming to us."

I chuckle. "Oh yes, that's Selvia, alright." The petite girl, her bag almost as big as she is, jogging toward us, her black hair pulled back into a low ponytail. Her grey eyes are wide and eager.

Chance stands with her hands on her hips. Her green eyes staring down Selvia.

Oh boy, this girl is in for it.

"What on Zarvan are you doing here?" Chance asks, tight-lipped.

"I came to help," she crosses her arms over herself, tipping her chin up. "There is no way you are going to get anyone in Ashadier to talk to any of you about Eloise. You essentially came in, lost one of the town's favorites, killed the water finder, and dragged off a beloved wife and mother."

The speech comes across as rehearsed. Like she'd been thinking about how to present her plan. I grin at her; she wisely does not return it.

"I got Ixis to watch the house for us," Selvia drops her bag on the ground. It lands with a loud thump. *What did this girl pack?*

"Ixis? Who in the Abyss is Ixis?" Chance asks, her voice rising.

"The Healer who saw me when we got to town, remember?"

"NO! I don't flipping remember! That still doesn't answer why you're here when I specifically told you to stay home!"

Selvia spreads her arms open, palms up in offering. "I'm here to help! I am a sorrowful orphan who was taken in by a Gopher. Then she was abandoned by said Gopher, and I came back, all by myself." Her eyes widen like a cat begging for a treat. She clasps her hands in front of her and twists side to side.

I burst out laughing. This girl is good.

"You weren't abandoned!" Chance yells at Selvia.

Selvia doesn't even flinch. So far from the girl I rescued five months ago who was terrified to make a single mistake. Now she's here demanding she be allowed to help.

"No, but they don't know that. What were you all going to do? Storm in and force them to give you answers?" Chance stiffens. Selvia gets a gleam in her eye. She knows she's right.

"However, I can go in and say that I know what the city wants with Eloise, and I want to warn her. Who is likely to get more answers? Me? Or him?" She points at me.

"Hey! What did I do?" I protest. *Innocent bystander attacked on the sidelines.*

"We weren't going to send him in." Chance looks over at me for backup. I don't think Selvia is wrong, so I'm not going to enter this argument. "I was going to go in. Pretend I'd had a falling out with Mitac and get them to tell me what they knew."

Selvia snorts. "You must think we're stupid to think that would work."

Chance shakes her head. "It was a long shot, but the best plan we had."

"Well," Selvia flourishes her arms out to the side again and takes a bow, "now you have a better one."

Chance's eyes narrow. She's not happy, but I can tell she's not going to argue.

"Well, come on." She grumbles all the way over to the carriages.

I put my space between the furious Green woman, certain this conversation is not over.

I quickly negotiate our fare to Ashadier, paying double to leave tonight with haste. I load the bags, including the one that weighs as much as Selvia.

Selvia reaches in after she settles in and pulls out a book for the trip. I sneak her a smile. I'm damned proud of this girl. She sits with a measure of confidence. She still fidgets, and I can tell she is anxious that she bested Chance, but she's taking what she wants. I know Chance is worried for her safety, but this girl across from me is far removed from the girl in the orphanage. I see a glimmer of hope for her yet.

Selvia glances at Chance, biting her lip. Chance finally looks over at her and pats her on the knee.

"I don't approve," she rubs her eyes, "but you're already here, so for now, you can come along."

Selvia beams.

I settle in across from the girls on the maroon bench seat. The carriage driver closes the door, and I feel it sway as he climbs up into the driver's seat. The carriage begins rumbling down the dirt road, bouncing and shaking back and forth.

I finally break the long silence. "Okay, so we get there, and you run into the village and ask questions?" I ask Selvia pointedly. If she's going to come up with a plan, she had better have a fleshed out one.

She thinks for a moment. "No, I think it would be better if you didn't come into the village at all. The whole thing will fall apart if they see me arrive with you. It would be better if you waited somewhere outside of town. Maybe in the forest. Then I can report back when I have an idea of where she went."

She looks at us, twisting her hands in her lap. Chance puts her hand over hers to still them. Neither of us disagrees with Selvia's plan so far.

She continues, "We should all be dropped off somewhere outside of town. I'll walk in like I couldn't afford a ride. If we're a day or more outside of town, it'll look convincing because I'll have had some time to build up some filth. I can even walk behind the carriage for a while before we stop each night."

Chance nods. "That's a fitting punishment for not listening to me."

"C'mon, can you deny that this is a good thing?" Selvia cajoles.

"Yes, I can," Chance shifts to face Selvia. Concern written all over her face. "What we are doing is potentially dangerous, Selvia. Did you never stop to think what would happen if the other Warrior was still with us? Or what Eloise might do when she sees us?"

"Of course," Selvia flips her hair casually, but her voice trembles slightly, "but the other Warrior is gone, so problem solved. Also, Eloise won't see you. When we find her, I will go talk to her, same as in Ashadier. I will convince her that we are here to help her. That should prevent her from getting violent."

I shake my head, my black locks swinging side to side with the motion. "That's not how people work. Not always. And we can't assume that Eloise will be easily persuaded. Nor that she won't change her mind the moment she lays eyes on us."

"Fine," Selvia snaps. "What do you think we should do?"

I hold up my hands and smile. "I was helping Chance point out why it's dangerous for you to be here. I wasn't trying to suggest I had a better idea."

We settle into an uneasy silence for several hours, none of us having a better idea. I doze in and out of sleep.

"Have you ever fought?" Chance asks suddenly. I jump at the break in the steady drum of the hoofbeats and the creaking of the carriage. I look at her and realize she's talking to Selvia. I return to dozing, or pretending to, keeping my eyes only half-closed. A mastered trick from the Academy. People will reveal so much more about themselves if they think you aren't paying attention. A wise person never truly stops paying attention. To everyone. To everything.

"Sure," Selvia replies. "The kids in the orphanage were mean. I didn't fight back, usually. It got me into more trouble. But sure, I've fought."

"I mean, physically fought," Chance clarifies.

Selvia frowns, brow furrowed. "Oh—well, no. Not really."

Chance nods. "That's what we will fix while we travel. Every night before we bed down, I will teach you some maneuvers to protect yourself. As well as some to fight back with. It won't be much, but six nights of practice should give you at least some basics. Hopefully enough to help keep you safer." She looks Selvia dead in the eye, as serious as I've ever seen her. "I want to emphasize how stupid this stunt is."

Selvia looks away, starting to look like the girl from the orphanage again. "I wanted to be useful. I wanted to help and show you that I can do things."

Chance lifts her chin, so Selvia's eyes are forced back to hers. "There's nothing you need to prove to me. There's nothing you need to prove to anyone. If you spend your life trying to prove yourself to others, you'll never know what you're truly capable of. Live your life for you. Not for anyone else."

"Is that what you do, Chance?"

"I try. It took me a long time to learn it." She turns in her seat to more fully face Selvia. "I grew up in nobility. I was taught every day of my life that I had something to prove. I'm the oldest of three, barely. It was—is—my job to take over the family, the money, the social standing. Everything.

From the time I could sit up on my own, I have been educated in the propriety of being a lady in society. How to sit, when to curtsy, how to eat, how to drink, what to say, and more importantly, when to keep my mouth shut."

I feel sorry for Chance, listening to her. It sounds like a terrible way to live. I continue to pretend I'm dozing, but I'm eagerly listening. Eating up her confessions.

"I wasn't good at learning the last part. I questioned everything. It seemed frivolous, dumb. I voiced it, and I was beaten for it. I was told I wasn't meeting expectations. That I needed to do better, be better. So, I tried.

That year, one of my best friends—she nearly starved that winter." Chance's voice cracks. "I was so worried that I was failing my family and not meeting their expectations that I nearly let her starve." She falls silent for a moment. I can almost see tears welling up in her eyes. "My family firmly believed you had to work for what you got. No handouts. Ironic, given that their riches and power were generational. No one has worked for anything they have in centuries. But I let them poison my mind. I told my friend she had to work for what she wanted, and I would not hinder her by providing her with further help. It would only make her reliant on me.

She was one of the hardest-working people I ever knew. She worked every day, all day, and many times into the night. Still, I told her she wasn't working hard enough." Chance shakes her head. "It's not worth it," she croaks, her voice thick with emotion, "Be you. Be uniquely you. The world has Mitac and me; Celestials know the world has enough nobles acting like each other. What the world needs…is one of you."

With that, she turns back and faces the window. Closing the opportunity for any response Selvia might have had.

I close my eyes the rest of the way. So maybe being noble wasn't all it was cracked up to be after all. My chest aches for Chance, my poor heart cracking. I wish she had wanted to tell me. Maybe one day she actually will. Until then, I tuck the information away with a much better understanding of who my partner is.

...THE VOID OF SILENCE.

Mitac

R62O10

Each day we get closer to Ashadier, Chance and I take Selvia aside and teach her basic knife skills. I have to admit she isn't that bad. She has a natural defense. I suspect it's from her time in the orphanage. Although she may not have done it consciously, it did make her very aware of her place in space and naturally alert to her surroundings. I feel bad she had to go through that, but I am grateful now that she has.

Most of our time is spent teaching her how to handle one of the smaller daggers. The holds, the ways to use it for defense, and how to do serious damage if needed.

"You can't hesitate," I remind her a few days later when she pulls back from using all of her strength. "If you do that in a real situation, you could get seriously hurt. Now try again; give me what you have."

"But I don't want to hurt you," she objects, her gray eyes going wide.

"You won't. I pat the leather armor on my chest under my shirt and the bracers on my arms. Now, again!"

She groans in frustration, doubled over, panting. I know she's tired and she's sore, but she needs this. "I can't! I'm too tired!"

"Do you think anyone who might attack you cares if you're tired?" I urge her, calling forth every last bit of resilience she has. I remember my training in the Academy, and I wonder if I'm pushing her too hard.

I mentally shake my head. No. She needs this. The only way to get stronger is to push yourself beyond the point of exhaustion. I will *not* let her go in there defenseless. I will *not* let her make it easy for them. She can fight. She can win. Most importantly? She will.

When faced with an enemy, when faced with a blade, when faced with a choice to live or die, she will choose to live. She will gather all of her strength, like I'm urging her to do now, dig deep within herself, and fight tooth and nail to live.

The words I overheard from Selvia in Chance's house come back to me. She may believe she's not worth anything, but she will find her sense of value one day. Until then, I will help her find the tools she needs to survive.

"C'mon, think of every kid in that orphanage who put you down. Who stole from you. Who mocked you. Who told you that you weren't wanted."

Anger flashes in her eyes. Oh yeah, I found the sore spot. "The girl with no mom, whose dad told her she was worthless. The girl who couldn't do anything right, whose mom is a murderer and left her."

I notice her grip tightening on the dagger, and I prepare for the lunge. She surprises me by lunging and twisting slightly, coming in under my left arm. I can feel the point of the dagger hit my leathers. I spin away from her and gently grasp her arm. I push on the pressure point in her wrist and she drops the dagger with a yelp. She looks disappointed.

"That was much better," I encourage her. Pride courses through me. I pick her up and swing her around. She yelps in surprise.

"You managed to get to my leathers!"

She perks up a little.

"I don't expect you will be able to stop a trained Warrior, but I want you to do enough to keep yourself safe or scare off lesser attackers." She nods.

"Go get some rest," I tell her. I stow my stick I had been using as an impromptu training blade. Selvia bounces back to the carriage, her step light. What kind of father could have ever looked at her and thought she was worthless?

The sun is starting to dip below the horizon. The horses are hooked to a line tied between two trees off the path. They're grazing lazily, happy to be free from duty for the night. Chance has started a small fire and is roasting something over the flames. It looks suspiciously like a couple of rats, but protein is good, so I am not going to ask or complain. We haven't come across big game of late.

The carriage rocks slightly as Selvia climbs into it. I head over to my bedroll and undo everything, preparing for the night. I see my canteen is full, and I thank Chance, tipping the canteen in the air toward her before I take a big gulp.

The shade and the sunset are feeling good right about now. The summer heat is unrelenting on the unshaded path. Even in the carriage, it's like an oven. I have joined our driver from time to time on the bench, our hats helping to keep us cooler. The breeze on the bench helps, but not by much.

Chance and I have decided today is our last travel day with the carriage. We will pay the driver in the morning and send him on his way. The rest of the way will be up to us on foot. Selvia will finish the last few miles by herself, Chance and I are staying off path in the forest to wait. This is the part that gets my stomach in a twist.

Selvia re-emerges a few minutes later, her hair let down and brushed out. She sits on a stump near Chance.

"What is that?" Selvia asks her, pointing to the mystery meat over the fire.

"Do you want to know?" Chance asks, one eyebrow raised.

Selvia shakes her head. "If you have to ask, probably not. At least it smells good. I think I saw some herbs growing around here when we were walking. Do you want me to get some to spice it up? It looks a little bland." She stands. "No offense," she adds quickly.

Chance waves her off. "None taken. By all means, if you can find something to make it taste better, please do."

"I'll be right back!"

Selvia dashes off back down the path. I chuckle at her enthusiasm and move to sit where Selvia had been posted a moment before.

"Nothing like youth, eh? Ten seconds ago, she was exhausted, could barely stand, and now she's running into the forest for herbs."

Chance nods, turning the spit but remaining silent. Her gaze far off.

"Okay, spill." Chance looks over at me in surprise. "You're being even more quiet than usual. What happened? Ever since we got out of the carriage, you have been off. I can't quite put my finger on it, but something's up, and I think it would be good if I knew what."

Chance shrugs. "Just thinking."

I've learned over the years that sometimes staying quiet is more beneficial than talking to get someone else to talk. People feel the need to fill the void of silence. Chance knows me well, so she continues to pay attention to the spit, content to let the silence continue. It's frustrating when you've worked with someone for a while, and they know your tricks.

"Is it Selvia? Sending her in by herself?" I probe.

She shakes her head. Her green hair falling into her face before she pushes it behind her ears on both sides. "No, she can do it. I saw the blow she landed on you." Chance smirks at me.

"Hardly a blow," I mutter, pretending to be put out.

"No, I told Selvia about something I haven't thought about in a long while, and it stirred up some old feelings. Things I don't typically talk about." She pins me with a pointed glare.

I know she's referring to the conversation I heard in the carriage, the one I wasn't supposed to hear.

I raise my hands in defense, signaling I'm not trying to push. She returns to spinning the meat on the spit, and I pull out a map I have stashed in my bag. Based on what I can see, we are about five miles from Ashadier.

"I'm going to talk to the driver about the plan for tomorrow."

I don't bother to wait for Chance to acknowledge me and walk off to find him. He's set up behind the carriage, having a drink. He doesn't join us for our meals. I'm not even sure I have seen him eat. He's an average man, average height, average hair…everything about him is forgettable. I wish we could be as forgettable as he is. I envy him. Unfortunately, no one will forget a Tracker and a Warrior traveling together with a young girl.

"Hey," I approach. He jumps, slightly startled. With the dimming light, I know I sort of disappear into the surroundings. "Tomorrow, we are going to go the rest of the way on foot. You will be free to go. I'll give you your money in the morning. Any chance I can convince you to come back in about a week to get us?"

He grunts. "No way. It takes nearly a week just to get back to Rothesard. No offense, sir, but you ain't pay me enough to work the horses like that. I know nobody runs this-a-way no more, no work and all. Not sure how you 'spect to get back."

I shrug. "My hope was someone would come across us. We'll figure it out."

"I bet the Tracker and ya could walk tha' far, no sure about the little one."

"She's tougher than she looks, but you're right, it wouldn't be fun. Thanks anyway."

I wander away. Though that reminds me…

I expected her to be back by now. It shouldn't have taken but a few minutes for her to find the herbs and bring them back. I walk back to the fire, half expecting her to be there sitting with Chance. I don't spot her. Chance is still absent-mindedly spinning the meat.

"Has Selvia come back?" I ask when I'm in earshot.

Chance turns to look at me, blinking. "No, how long has she been gone?"

"My guess? Better part of half an hour."

Chance frowns. "I don't like it." She gets up and pulls the meat off the fire. "Tell the driver what we're doing and to watch the fire if he doesn't want to burn down the forest."

I do as I'm told and begin scouting the area for signs of where Selvia has gone. "Hold on, I'll go grab a shirt of hers or something." She heads back to the carriage. I continue to look.

"Mitac!" Chance calls, her voice high-pitched, strained. I sprint back to her, worried for what she's found. I'm surprised to find her still standing at the carriage door.

"Look," she points inside. I look in and see nothing.

"What am I looking for?" I ask perplexed.

"Her bag!" Chance has turned and started walking away.

"What bag?" What am I missing here?

"Exactly!" Chance calls over her shoulder.

Oh shit. Her bag is gone. I jog after Chance, who's heading in the direction Selvia had started off in.

"When would she have grabbed it? And where is she going?" I ask.

"Not sure, but I wasn't exactly paying attention after she headed off. Maybe she snuck back and grabbed it? But why?"

BUT NO SNARKY REMARKS.

Eloise

R62O19

I'm glaring at Gorduin, who is grinning in the afternoon sun. He's amused watching me fail over and over to grasp the concepts he's trying to teach me. His amusement fuels my defiance. I stand straight and ignore the flushing heat up my back and neck. I shiver in the cold air. As hot as summer has been, fall is getting cold fast.

Nyana explained they were only still in the forest because it's where I needed to be for now. Normally, she said, they would have moved to the warmer desert climes until Naheia in the spring.

Since the second day of training, I have refused to let Gorduin physically touch me to guide me to my supposed magic. If I'm going to do this, I am going to do it. Not him.

The problem is that it's been *months,* and I'm still no closer to accessing my magic. I *am* plenty close to wanting to pummel him, however.

"Breathe!" he yells at me.

"Not helping," I grind out as I try again to produce water. "Why are we trying for water when it's freezing out here! Why not fire?"

"Because water isn't destructive, so if you go off the rails with your power, you're not likely to hurt anything. Now…"

I try again. I feel my eyes bulging out with effort.

"You're not breathing; you're going to pass out!"

I drop my hands and inhale deeply. "This was so easy during my Quest. Why is it so difficult now?"

"The Quest amplifies your power. After leaving the Quest, you must learn to amplify it yourself. If you'd let me guide you, you would have an easier time sensing your way through the blocks."

He approaches me, and I take a couple of steps back. He narrows his eyes and deliberately penetrates my personal bubble. He takes my hand in his, standing behind me. He clasps my hand, curling my fingers inward, leaving my index finger out.

"It's like a maze," he draws my index finger through the air, creating an imaginary maze. His voice is soft, caring, and it rankles me further. One could think it mattered to him if I managed to control my magic. His aloof attitude the rest of the time negates that.

"It might stay the same from use to use, but until you learn the maze, it takes a while. You keep running into the walls instead of around them. You're trying to force it, like those in the schools learn. Eventually, they learn to break the walls, which makes it continuously hard to access their magic on an ongoing basis. For us, with the maze, we learn to navigate quickly and can conjure what we need second nature, without thinking about it."

"What's it matter if I break through the wall or run around them?"

"Which is easier, Phoenix, to run around a wall or climb over the rubble?"

"Depends on the size of the wall. Won't the rubble get smaller over time?" I grumble at him stubbornly.

"How long does it take for stone to break down?"

I sigh in frustration. In theory, it makes sense. In reality, I can't see the damned maze so I can't push through one way or another. Everyone here can seem to grasp their magic so easily.

I have watched people pop blue and water comes out of nowhere for the night's dinner. Pop orange when thinking of a new way to fix something. Pops of red each night when starting the bonfire, yellow when determining when to move or change the set up for the night for impending weather changes. But still, nothing for me. I throw myself a pity party. I gather myself again.

"Please," he pleads, "let me help you. I'm begging now. It's painful to watch you struggle to destroy something that should be beautiful." He brings forth a shower of rainbow. "Beautiful."

I have to agree, even though I can't stand him. "Fine. But no snarky remarks."

"I make no promises," Gorduin says, his voice a deep rumble.

I turn to face him, and he forces me forward again. "Hold out your hands like you were."

I do as he asks. He rests his hands underneath mine, lightly, barely touching. The hair on my neck stands on end and I wonder if it's from his magic.

"Good, now breathe. In and out. Slow. Find the threads of magic, the ropes." His voice is deep and steady, calm. "The more you do it, the thicker the strands will get. It's probably very small right now." We breathe together. "Picture the water coming into your hands, feel the flow between your fingers, feel the magic coming in with your breath, and leaving on exhale."

I roll my eyes but breathe in, trying to find the strands of magic. I think I feel one, a small one. It's the thinnest strand of silk, like a spider's web in my mind's eye. It can only be seen under the right conditions, or you walk right into it.

I mentally reach for it, and it ripples with the movement of my breath. I take a deep breath and hold it, the strand stilling again. I reach, not daring to breathe out. I grasp it, lightly, trying not to break my tenuous hold.

I breathe out, the strand still in my hand. I try not to get too distracted with excitement. Even getting to this point has been a serious challenge. I feel sweat bead on my brow from the effort.

"Let it go, Phoenix," Gorduin encourages me, "You have to let the strand go, or it won't work."

I breathe in and out once more, trying to release the strand I fought so hard to get hold of. How can I drop it when I barely got a hold of it? I breathe in again and let go of the strand. It's like releasing a rubber band pulled too tightly. It snaps away from me, and I nearly weep when the nearly invisible strand disappears altogether.

Come back! I mentally shout at it. But it's hopeless. It's gone.

"Open your eyes," Gorduin encourages me.

He should move away from me. If he's smirking at me, I will hurt him.

Instead, I see a trickle of water across my palms and off the side to the ground. I jump, and the trickle stops.

"I did it!" I yell, raising my fist triumphantly. "Or wait, was that you?" I turn.

Gorduin holds his hands up in defense. "No, Phoenix, that was all you."

I marvel at the wetness still covering my hands, staring at it. I shiver; I *do* have magic. My excitement fades as a second, more pervasive thought penetrates. *I am the bringer of the end of the Realm.* My balloon of happiness pops with the thought. If that's the case, then I need to practice so much more.

"I want to do it again." Doubts about whether I can do it again come unbidden to my mind. I'm tired, but I want to try again.

"With or without my help?" Gorduin asks genuinely, a smile on his face.

"Without. I need to see it's mine. My magic." What a strange thought. Butterflies have taken flight as I consider having access to this new skill. I'm eager to see how much I can do.

"Do it, Phoenix; show me what you've got."

Gorduin holds out his palm, a small flame dancing above his now red skin.

I hold out my palm, face down this time above his flame. I breathe in, reaching for the strand. It is a little easier to find this time, but not without effort. The spider's thread, there, scarcely in reach. *Is it brighter this time?*

I grasp it. I think it is. It feels more substantial.

Gorduin reminds me once to relax, and I make the effort to loosen the tension in my shoulders, then let the rubber band go. A small trickle falls and puts out his small flame.

I dance excitedly and hug him. He holds me for a second then I pull away, feeling awkward. I still don't like him, I remind myself firmly.

"Is it like that for all the magics?" I ask. "Like, can we access it as easily as that? All the time?"

I am amazed at what I am able to accomplish. A small thing, no doubt, compared to others, but a battle hard fought and won. At least, for me. Victory tastes sweet. I wipe the sweat from my forehead.

He nods. "Yes. Some will be easier to reach for than others, but they all follow the same principle. When you find the one that's easiest, that will be the magic you are most aligned to. Plus, as you get stronger, you will change colors when you use a lot of it. For example…"

He looks over at the yet unlit bonfire for tonight. I see him take a breath in. I swear I can feel his magic, like electricity crackling around us, as he reaches for it, stretches the strands, and then lets it go. The bonfire lights up in a blaze and I see Gorduin briefly turn a bright red. Then he returns quickly to his normal tanned self.

He turns to face me, a smug grin on his face. "Now put it out."

"What?" I ask, startled.

"It's too early for the bonfire. So, put it out. Quickly, before we ruin the wood."

"I can't do that! I had barely a trickle!" I'm flabbergasted. Why does he think I can suddenly produce a deluge?

"You can, and you will. Unless you want everyone mad at you for starting the bonfire?"

"But I didn't, you did!" *Dirty, rotten…*

He shrugs. "Put it out, and you won't have to find out if they'll take my word over yours."

I narrow my eyes at him. He twirls his finger in the air, instructing me to face the blaze. I do so reluctantly.

"Psst," he hisses in my ear, causing me to pull away, "If you're angry, it gets harder to find the strands. At least until you're an expert." I want to stab him in his smug face.

I spare him one more glare, then try to calm my mind and relax.

"Breathe," I tell myself softly. "In…out." I feel the threads coming at me, this time more of them. I take another breath and find I can gather more with a second breath. Then I release them. A bucket's worth of water falls on the fire. It does exactly nothing to the fire. It crackles on as if I asked it kindly to please consider stopping.

Gorduin chuckles before he reaches out and sends his own torrent of water to the bonfire.

I storm off, but he follows me. "Phoenix, stop."

He grabs my arm, and I jerk out of his grasp. I spin to face him, furious. "My. Name. Is. ELOISE!" My shout draws stares from around the camp. I feel heat rising in my cheeks.

"Listen, El-o-eeese," he emphasizes my name, making it clear he prefers the nickname he gave me, "I wasn't laughing at you, I promise."

"It sure as Abyss feels like it!"

"I was chuckling because your face looked like mine the first time I managed to pull multiple threads. And you turned a bright blue which I found to be quite flattering on you."

"Not helping! I didn't get anywhere near enough to put out that fire!"

"No, you didn't. And you weren't going to."

"Then why have me do it at all! Why are you setting me up to fail?" *Of all the dirty tricks. What a rotten, horrible person. Liar!*

"I wasn't setting you up to fail. I was showing you that you can draw more magic to yourself. And you figured out how to do that all by yourself. You figured out how to use more breathing to bring more. The next time you take a breath to pull that strand, there will be the same amount as there was for two breaths. Then when you take two breaths, you'll double it. And so on and so on until you have the most you can personally hold. I thought you would find more value in learning it yourself, figuring it out on your own, rather than me telling you."

Oh…well, that makes sense. I'm still pissed, though. Definitely *not* forgiven. Definitely still don't like him. Hate him. Loathe him and all the other synonyms for hate there are.

Reluctantly, I ask, "So, the more breaths I take, the more I can have. What happens when I get that rope, and I only want a single strand worth?"

"Well, that's the next step after. Learning to separate the threads before releasing them. But, for now, let's see what other magic you can call to."

YOU PLAY YOUR PART...

Saada

I heard Aerith's yelling when she Dreamed about Eloise coming. My heart broke in two, and ever since, I have been worried sick. Literally.

The guards cut down significantly on the torture they put me through, but increased Aerith's considerably. I could hear her screams through the walls, and I saw the blood on her clothing, or what passed as clothing. The guards gave her less and less food, and I tried to sneak her some of mine, but it only ended with both of us losing everything for a week. My stomach had never been so empty.

As hard as we had struggled over the years to bring in enough to feed the family, we had never actually gone hungry.

I feared that if I did have something to spill, I would have, and I was grateful Aerith had limited how much information she shared with me. At the time, of course, I had been outraged, insisting in our whispered conversations I would *never* jeopardize Eloise. Here I was, facing the hardest trial of my life, and I was ready to tell them anything they wanted to hear.

Meanwhile, Aerith, who had no reason to protect Eloise, was holding out. Or she was too broken to share anything.

In the first several days after she had inadvertently shared about

Eloise's plan to come, she had whimpered, groaned, moaned. Even in her sleep. Then, she abruptly went eerily silent.

She didn't say anything; she didn't even look at me. She stood in her cell, staring blankly, until exhaustion forced her to collapse. Sometimes into bed, sometimes on the floor. Calling for the guards to help resulted in only more punishment for both of us. They remained stolidly unconcerned with her mental and physical state.

I whispered words of encouragement to her, trying to get her to come around, to at least recognize I was there, but I also thought maybe she wasn't so wrong to think that disassociating was the way to go.

I hoped that wherever her mind was, she was free from the pain and hunger. When we did get food back, she merely picked at it, clearly driven only by a basic need to survive. She was becoming skin and bones before my very eyes, and I was at a total loss for how to help her.

On this day, I roll over and Aerith is not in her cell. I have no way to tell time, so I have no idea if it's a normal time for her to be gone or not, but I have not seen breakfast. Usually, the guards do not take either one of us until breakfast comes at least. I think they like to watch us lose our breakfast as a result of their punishments.

I notice her door is open, not unusual in itself, but paired with the early hour gives me an ominous feeling in my stomach. I look around at the other cells, prisoners still sleeping soundly, suggesting even more so a very early or very late hour. One of the guards comes by, pacing, checking our doors. He closes Aerith's door and reapplies the lock.

"Where is she?" I dare to ask.

I hope this is one of the nice guards, I can't remember for certain. It's worth asking, even if he isn't. Maybe I will get an answer. If not, at least I will have tried.

The guard looks at me as if debating what to tell me. He doesn't immediately call me forward to rap my knuckles, so I take that as a good sign.

"She was taken for special treatment." He sneers at me and heads back to his station in the alcove.

I dare not ask what "special treatment" means, but I can bet it's not a vacation. I also find it quite disturbing that her cell has been relocked without her in it. It suggests she isn't returning, and I like that even less.

Aerith was one of my few friends or at least a person I could sort of trust in here. In a way, we had developed a bond even though we couldn't talk. We found our own way to communicate, and that was enough.

I watch her cell all day, as if by staring, I can make her reappear, much like I had done with the forest when it had kept Eloise. But she doesn't appear. And for the next week, the cell remains empty. I mourn the loss, weeping in the night. I refuse to eat and barely drink. I become much like she was, catatonic. Staring off into the void of nothing.

My brain shuts down. I still feel the pain, physical and emotional, but I completely disconnect from it.

I remember in Ashadier, we had a pair of horses that were closely bonded. One of them died, and the other went into a similar state. I feel this is what I have become. A horse who has lost its closest confidant and friend.

The next day, the guards open my cell, and I vaguely register them bringing me up off of my bed by the arms. Instead of taking me left, deeper into the dungeons, and toward the small chamber in which they beat and humiliate me, they take me to the right. We pass the other cells, my feet dragging on the floor as I am unwilling to walk. For all I know, I may also be unable to walk. I haven't tested my legs in several days.

We head up the stairs, and the bright light coming through the windows we pass makes me blink. It's painful. I want to tell the guards to turn it off but remain unable to speak.

They drag me along the marble halls, less painful than the stone floor of the dungeon. They avoid the carpet runners, and I guess, after a good while, this is because my feet are bleeding. I remember one of them saying something about it and not wanting to get in trouble for staining the carpets. They take me up another staircase and another; I have lost track of where we are going altogether. Plus, the bright light keeps making me close my eyes. Finally, they stop dragging me, and the sharp pain in my feet dulls to a throbbing ache.

When I wake, I'm lying in a bed on my stomach. My legs are hanging awkwardly off the side, my head turned to one side.

How did I get here? Where is here? How long was I out for?

"Healer!" one of the guards yells quite loudly, and I flinch, but I don't think he notices.

A woman in white, with white hair, and white eyes, comes over. She reminds me of someone…I can't remember her name, but someone from my village. I try to search my brain but come up empty. I'm tired. I close my eyes again.

"Another one?" she asks.

"Yep, been about two weeks like this."

Two weeks? It's been two weeks. I didn't think it had been that long.

"How long has she been down there with your treatment?" The Healer sounds less than impressed with their duties in the dungeon or how they care for us…or don't.

"Oh, almost three months or so, I think," one of them snaps. "I don't know. We don't keep close track."

"Clearly," the White woman says sarcastically. "Well, get out then. Let me see what I can do."

"How's the other one?"

I hear the curtains pull while the Healer works on getting me into bed.

"About the same," she responds, grunting with effort. "I have gotten her to eat a little bit, though. But what you see is what you get."

"Well, when she comes around, her cell is waiting for her." The guard sounds cheery. I want to throw up. The Healer ushers them out of the room and finishes getting me into bed.

"You can relax now, Aerith," I hear the Healer tell someone.

"Thank the Celestials. It's hard to fake this stuff, you know?"

Aerith. The name and the voice are familiar. Where do I know her from? I want to ask them, but I can't seem to find my voice.

"Luckily, those guards are idiots and can't recognize the real thing from acting." She gets my feet into bed and gently turns me over. "This one, though, she's not acting."

I hear the rustle of the bed and movement. I see a blurred purple shape standing near me. "Neither was I when I got to you. Do you think you can bring her around, too?"

That voice…I know that voice.

"I think so. It's going to take some time, though."

"Thank you, Helia; I will never be able to repay you."

"Hush, girl, this is my job. You play your part if anyone comes. In the meantime, help me get her cleaned up."

Together, the two women undress me, wash my many wounds, and dress them with salve. Then they carefully put me the rest of the way into bed and close the curtains. "Sleep, Saada." I can't tell if I'm awake or dreaming, but I think I hear Aerith's voice saying, "When you wake and are well, we will get out of here. This I promise to you."

WELL...SHIT.

Mitac

R62O17

Seven days. Seven long days. Selvia disappeared into the forest seven days ago without a word. Chance and I have been on her trail since but have not seen her. Other than traces of her spirit, we have had no luck whatsoever catching up to her.

"This is ridiculous!" Chance screams, and not for the first time. "She's thirteen, how can she be outpacing us?"

"I don't know," I murmur. "It doesn't make sense."

I circle the area where we have paused to drink some water and eat our catch of the day, a fish from the brook. I see nothing. If not for Chance's ability to trace Selvia's spirit, we would have long since lost her completely.

"Maybe we need to think about this differently," I suggest, pulling out my map. I trace my finger along the approximate path we have taken through the forest. We have zigged and zagged, gone forward, gone backward, gone in circles, but all the while...

Chance quirks an eyebrow at me. "How do you mean?"

"Well, she has us running all over this damned forest; what if we look at where she's heading and try to cut her off rather than follow her directly?"

Chance shakes her head. "No, it's too risky. I could lose her trace altogether. As it is, it's faint, and if we abandon it, I may not find it again."

"But she's primarily heading toward Ashadier," I suggest, showing Chance what I'm looking at. Chance looks on with a sigh. "What if we went to Ashadier?"

"No," she says sternly. "She might not be going there. She might not make it there even if she is. She could also be making it look like she's heading that way, and she doubles back and doesn't go there at all."

"Chance—" She's not thinking rationally. If I didn't know better— "Chance, are you afraid she's going to get hurt before she gets there?"

She looks away, telling me I'm right. "Chance, she's not completely defenseless, and there's not much in this forest to get her. Remember what Healer Kinta said? They don't have predators out here."

"It's not only predators that I'm worried about; she could dehydrate. Starve. Trip and hurt her leg again."

I nod. "Yes, there are a lot of things that *could* happen, but there are also a lot of things that could *not* happen. We can't keep chasing her because you think she *could* get hurt. Our better option to get her, to catch up to her, is to head to Ashadier. She's more capable than she was and spent time out here by herself before."

I leave my statement hanging in the air and walk away to fill our canteens. If Chance won't budge, I might have to split off from her. She can keep Tracking her spirit, and I can head to Ashadier.

I run a hand over my face. Celestials, if those people see me again, they will surely kill me first and ask questions of my corpse after.

I put the lids back on the canteens, waiting for Chance to come to me. Expecting her doesn't stop her from sneaking up on me. I suspect she stepped on the branch intentionally to alert me to her presence. I still jump.

"I can't do it," Chance hangs her head. "I can't leave her to her own devices and hope she makes it to Ashadier. You might be okay with that, but I'm not." She sits beside me, and I look at her. "I think—I think we should split up." She worries her lip.

I grin wryly. "I had the same thought." Chance's eyes widen. I don't think she expected me to acquiesce so easily. "Don't get me wrong, I don't like it. I like to be able to keep you safe and know where you are. We've been partners for a while now and the idea of not bringing you with me or keeping you nearby…" I don't finish the statement.

Chance rubs the back of her neck. Emotions. They make her anxious.

"I've gotten kind of used to having you around, too, you big lug." She shoves me with her shoulder.

I swallow thickly. Choking on my own emotions. As much as she worries about Selvia, I worry about Chance. I stand and dust myself off, Chance doing the same. I open my arms to her. She scrunches her face up at me, and I try to keep the hurt I feel at that from crossing my face.

I am about to drop my arms when she steps forward slowly into them. I give her a hug, this tiny woman practically disappears into my huge frame. I am grateful that for this moment, the voice in my head doesn't scream at me. I hope that means she will be minimally safe.

I release her, and she steps back. Neither of us says anything as we pack up and part ways. She takes a moment, her eyes closed, before she sets off east. I turn west to Ashadier.

We never say goodbye.

∼

R62019

I pack up my campsite and take a moment to stretch out my limbs before picking up the pack. It's been two days since Chance and I parted and…well, I miss her. I didn't realize how much I would miss her snarky comments, her casual put downs, and backhanded compliments. All those things she does to keep her walls up were apparently working on bringing my own walls down.

I hope she's okay. I hope she's found Selvia. I hope she's already on her way toward me with the girl who is probably receiving the lecture of a lifetime. Probably one to rival the horse woman from the orphanage. I chuckle.

Ashadier is a few miles from where I stopped for the night. Last night, I bedded down figuring it was better to approach in daylight, but now I feel exposed. Maybe I should have snuck in. I don't exactly know what to expect, and I feel off-kilter. I'm not used to not being in charge. Ever since I finished the Academy and started working, I have been in charge.

True, Chance and I work as a partnership, but in the end, I often end up making the decisions. I don't usually end up in a situation where I don't already have a good idea of what to expect. My stomach twists painfully.

I ran through the various possibilities last night.

On the possibly good side would be that Selvia made it to Ashadier, Chance beat me there, and they've already talked to the town and have a good idea of where to go next. Or even better, that Eloise is there waiting for me. Chance would jab me, call me slow, and we could walk off into the sunset.

The more likely possibility is that I'm about to walk into a viper's nest. I remember thinking at their village market that you wouldn't want to make an enemy of these people. I had unfortunately done that, even if I hadn't meant to.

I approach the village slowly, coming out of the forest the same way Chance and I had entered to search for Eloise so long ago. The Healer's house sits as it had that day. No bags against it. The sun shines, like it did that day, only cooler.

It's Sunday, but it looks like the Clearing is empty. No market which strikes me as odd. This would be the prime season to have it, and it seemed it was something that they did rain or shine anyway. On the one hand, I'm grateful because there are fewer eyes to see me as I come into the village. Exactly zero, as it turns out.

Unease creeps up my spine. The village is quiet, too quiet. I keep my guard up. I wish I had stashed my weapons. I don't want them to see me as a villain. Well, more of a villain.

I make my way slowly to Eloise's house, my head on a swivel. Keeping an eye out for anyone I might recognize. Eloise, Cardis, Selvia, Chance, but I don't even see Mr. Braswell.

I knock. No response, but I think I hear shuffling on the other side.

"I don't want to do this through the door, but I will if I have to," I plead, hoping whoever it is can hear me. Silence.

I knock again.

"Listen, there's a lot you don't know, and I need your help." Lay my cards on the table from the outset. I try to float my words on magic to reach them. It reaches a wall and stops. What is it with this family? Why are they so impenetrable?

"We know enough!" Julieth calls from inside. "Back to kill someone else or cart them off for not having answers?!"

"Julieth, I didn't kill him. And I do need answers, but I won't force them. None of that was my choice."

"And I bet you're here because you want to be, right?" she snaps at me. I flinch, my own words to Eloise coming back to me. I wonder who told her.

"Yes and no," I admit. "The Council sent me, but they don't know why I wanted to come."

I think I hear someone laugh from inside.

"Ditch the weapons. All of them. Even the hidden ones. Then, we will talk."

I take off the leiomano and the sword, setting them on the bench on the porch. I pull the knife I bought from Eloise from a holster on my belt and put it down.

"Pull up your shirt and pant legs," Julieth directs from the window where she's staring out at me.

I do as she asks, impressed with her thoroughness but also knowing I could still hide a multitude of weapons where she wouldn't see them on this kind of cursory search. I turn around for her without being asked.

The curtains drop in front of the window again. I hear hushed conversation behind the door. The lock slides free and the door opens. An arrow is pointed directly at my heart.

"One wrong move," Julieth spits at me. "I'll make you as dead as Gamet."

I nod, understanding. She steps out of the doorway, the arrow unmoving as she does. I step into the dark cabin, and she points to a chair at the kitchen table. The house is about as well-kept as when I was here last. A few more small items clutter the living room and kids' toys. I wonder where they are and where Cardis is. Who was Julieth talking to before opening the door?

"Sit." I do so, carefully, so as not to break the chair. "Speak."

"Thank you for being willing to hear me out. I noticed there's no market out there today?"

Her eyes narrow, probably trying to see what my angle is. "This isn't a social visit."

I hold up my hands. "Sorry, I was only curious why that was."

"Most of the town has left," she quips. "Speak."

"Thank you for hearing me out."

"It's going to take a lot for me to be convinced you're not the scum of the Realm that doesn't deserve to die. So don't thank me yet. I have no problem being judge, jury, and executioner. You left my uncle here dead, the body sitting in the chair you're in now, blood everywhere. Did you know Cardis is the one who found him?"

I flinch. I hadn't known that. It was possibly the best scenario. Other than Julieth finding him. I had wanted to dispose of his body, bury him for all of them, but I could see no way to do that and not expose the children. I had been looking for them and had seen them hiding in the goat pen. Luckily, Elgin was focused only on getting answers and didn't notice them.

I nod. "I am so incredibly sorry for all of this." I wave around. "I don't even know where to begin. Everything went seriously sideways the moment I met your sister."

Julieth blinks in surprise. She hadn't expected that. I debated if I should tell her about the voice. In the end, I decide full honesty is the best I can do. I tell her about the voice that has eerily accurate premonition, that I still hear it every day, that I take it to mean Eloise is still alive.

Julieth remains silent, her face stoic. She stares at me stonily, holding the arrow still at my heart. She doesn't confirm she came out of the forest or where she is.

"I had no idea her Quest would go so wrong. You have to know, I worried about her as much as you all did. I wanted that voice to be wrong. I don't know Eloise that well, but I feel this deep pull to protect her. I can't explain what it's like. It feels like an invisible tether that has a metal hook attached to my spine. It pulls constantly, causing a deep ache.

"I know Gamet died, and I was in the room, but you have to know I had nothing to do with him dying. I had no idea Elgin would do that, and I had to keep it together so I wouldn't be sick in front of him. He's the kind of Warrior who sees force as the best way to get answers and when Gamet wouldn't give him any…" I trail off and turn my gaze down. I can't look into her eyes and talk about their uncle's death. I simply can't. My breath starts coming in short gasps, and I try to slow it down.

"It happened so fast," my voice cracks. "If I had known, I would have— I would have—"

I can't breathe. I wrap my arms around myself. *What is happening to me?* I close my eyes, but I can't get rid of the memories.

Memories of that day come speeding back again. The knife sliding through his neck, his blood spurting forth from his neck, coating Elgin, splashing onto me. The blood pooling on the floor. His blue eyes going vacant, pupils widening. His empty gaze accusing me. *You did this.*

Hands clutch my arms. A voice from far away penetrates the memories. "Mitac," the voice penetrates my panic, Barely, "Deep breaths."

The memories back off with each breath I manage into my struggling lungs.

"I didn't think you cared so much," Julieth says when I finally settle. She returns to her seat, finally dropping the bow.

I take a few more deep breaths, waiting for the memories to fade, the rushing in my ears to stop.

"I haven't been able to stop thinking about the what-ifs of that day since. What if I had detained Elgin somehow and given all of you time to run? What if I had tackled him in that room when he took his blade out? What if I had killed him? What if I had let him kill me instead?" The last comes out as a whisper. Tears flow down my cheeks. I wipe at them quickly. I haven't cried since…maybe since I was a little kid.

"The truth is, I could have done something. Anything. And I did nothing. You should want to kill me." It comes out in a rush. The truth. What I think about that day. Maybe returning here wasn't to get answers. Maybe the truth of it is to get absolution. Or maybe…maybe I wanted to walk into death's arms, and I was too much of a coward to do it myself. I hang my head in shame.

What kind of person does it make me? That I would put my death on someone else's head? To leave someone else with images that will never leave their brain so I can get rid of the ones in mine? A monster. Yes, that's what I am. I look up at Julieth, finally.

She shakes her head. "No, Mitac, I don't want you dead. I wish I did. It would be so much easier. To see you as a heartless person. To hate you. But I can't. Because you aren't."

"I might as well be," I take a deep breath. "I still took Saada in, knowing what was waiting for her. I think I was shocked by what happened. I couldn't think of anything to do other than to stay with her as long as possible. To try to keep her safe. But that's no excuse. It's not good enough.

And then, when the Council called me, my plan was to try to get assigned to the dungeons so I could find a way to get her freed from the cells." I scoffed. "That plan fell apart when they ran in saying Eloise was seen leaving here."

Julieth blinks in surprise, but I don't acknowledge it.

"So, I changed my plans and begged to be allowed to come after Eloise. Promising to earn her trust and bring her back." She frowns. "I had no plans of doing that at all, of course, but I had to be convincing."

Julieth arches an eyebrow. "And you're not trying to win me over now? What if you're trying to get information for that exact purpose after all. Why should I trust you?"

I shrug. "I don't know. Really, you shouldn't. Logically, I've given you no reason to trust me or my motives. I come from Amiket; I'm hired by the Council who probably wants Eloise's head. I can only tell you in earnest that my only aim is to protect her. With my life, with every breath left in my being. It's as though the Celestials have given me this higher purpose and—" I lay my hands on the table, palm up, "—that's all I have. If that's not enough, then I will clear out and continue my search blindly. No matter what happens, I won't stop looking."

Julieth rests her chin in her hand. She bites her cheek, mulling over what I've said.

Suddenly, she stands and walks into the kitchen. She doesn't take the bow. I take that as a good sign that she trusts me enough not to kill her while her back is turned.

"You're here for information on where Eloise is?" Julieth asks from the kitchen.

"At least an idea, if you have one," I call back. I contemplate getting closer to her but decide against it. She never said I could move.

"Not much."

She returns with a pot and cups, then goes back into the kitchen. I pour some water into the cups and drop a tea steeper into each.

She comes back with a plate of cookies, and my stomach growls loudly. Living off of rabbit and squirrel has left me with a deep, permanent kind of hunger. Sometimes, I need something sweet to take the edge off. I resist immediately scarfing them down, uncertain if she's poisoned them.

She sits across from me and adds some honey and cream to her tea. She takes a sip and sighs. I follow suit and inhale the aroma of chamomile, lavender, and honey.

"Trying to get me to sleep?" I ask wryly.

She smiles at me over her cup. "If I were, I would also be going to sleep. But no, whenever someone has a panic attack, Kinta recommends this blend. It's calming. It *can* make you sleepy, but my aim was to help soothe your soul."

Thoughtful. Julieth takes a bite of a cookie, and confident she hasn't poisoned them, I eat half of one in one go. The sugar dances on my tongue. "Celestials, that's good," I tell her. The chocolate is smooth, smoother than any chocolate I've had before.

Julieth blushes and smiles. "The sugar in the chocolate and the little bit of oomph it provides should counteract the sleep-inducing effects of the tea. If not, you can sleep on the couch."

Both the tea and cookies are amazing, and the lack of sleep on the go makes me think I might need that couch after all.

"As for where Eloise is," Julieth breaks in. "I don't know. She left here almost three weeks ago. I had half-hoped she would give up and come home by now. Or be in Amiket."

My shoulders droop. "No, we haven't seen her. Chance and I have been scouring the forest looking for Selvia, and we haven't seen either of them. Selvia hasn't come back here, has she?"

She looks at me confused, so I briefly explain what happened with Selvia and why Chance and I split up.

"I haven't seen either of them that I know of."

"Well…shit."

We sit quietly, drinking our tea and eating the delicious cookies.

"Where are the kids? And Cardis?" I ask.

"The kids are in the back. I wasn't sure what you wanted so I sent them to the meadow for a while. I sent Cardis after Eloise, so hopefully, he's wherever she is. I wanted her to have someone who knew what to do to survive."

"I can understand that."

Julieth quickly catches me up on what's happened in Ashadier, explaining that there's no market because there aren't many people left in the town and that the town is struggling to recover after fires and the loss of water.

"It's like the whole town is drying up," Julieth's eyes fall to the table, her hands folded in front of her.

"What are you going to do?" I ask earnestly.

She shrugs. "We are doing okay. The girls are running the garden fairly well, and we still have water. We share what we can, and I can't see leaving here. Not when this is where Eloise knows as home. And not with three kids."

"Well, I don't have much," I tell her, "But you're welcome in Amiket at my house. If you ever need to get out of here."

Julieth snorts. Nothing I didn't expect.

...ALL-POWERFUL.

Eloise

R62O21

Gorduin and I are a little way off into the forest, practicing. Again. And I'm struggling. Again. I thought after I got a feel for the water magic, the rest would be easier to do. Turns out that isn't quite the case.

I have managed a little flame, but not a lot. I still have no control over the weather, and my tracking is abysmal. On the plus side, I have gotten better with water. I still need a water source of some kind nearby or air that's humid to make it work, but I am able to control more of it, and I can actually direct it to where I want it.

A jar shatters, and I jump.

"Damn," I mutter.

"You lost your concentration," Gorduin deadpans. He's sitting on a log nearby, his chin resting on his hands, elbows propped on his knees.

"I'm aware," I grunt back.

"Want some help?" I'm convinced he asks this knowing it will irk me. He asks all the time, and it always rankles. He has all the control over *his* magic. He can conjure a little of everything, but his favorite is lightning, the one I'm trying to control now.

He lazily waves his hand to my broken jar, and it puts itself back together again.

"You know I don't," I snap at him.

He shrugs and points to the jar. I clench my jaw and try again.

I can feel the threads, the little static inside me, I can grasp them. The problem is that instead of conjuring a little lightning in a jar, I end up creating a bolt that destroys the jar. Maybe the jar is faulty. It shatters again, a little blue bolt of electricity hitting it.

"There's nothing wrong with the jar," Gorduin states, putting the jar back together again, his skin flashing a light orange to do so. I sneer at him. I hate that he can do that. He can't read my mind, exactly, but he can read my emotions, and, unfortunately, he can usually guess what I'm thinking on top of it.

I try again. Threads of static. I stare carefully at them. I learn that's how you have to do it. You pick which ones you want. And, as I've seen with the water threads, different threads have different powers. Gorduin told me that the better I get, the more threads I will see and the more obvious their differences will be.

With the lightning, I still can't see what the different threads are so I'm blindly grabbing one and trying. I'm getting lightning, but it's too strong for the jar. I grab a different one, the smallest one I can see, and release it to the ether.

The white-hot light appears in the jar and stays. The jar stays intact.

Gorduin jumps off the log. In surprise or celebration, I'm not sure. I jump up and down and walk over to the jar.

"Yes!" I exclaim, holding the jar aloft. "I have light!"

Gorduin smirks. "Yes, good job, Phoenix. It's getting dark. We should head back in."

"Eloise!"

I whirl around, nearly dropping my hard-earned jar of light.

"Selvia?" I squint at the bedraggled girl approaching us. Her black hair is in tangles, full of brush. Her pants are torn, her shirt ripped.

"Oh, thank the Celestials I found you!" She rushes over and gives me a hug. I grunt from the force of it.

"I've been searching for you for days!" She drops her heavy bag on the ground. "I can't believe I found you."

"Well, here I am," I respond weakly, "I don't know—what are you doing here? What happened to you? Were you attacked?" I look around behind her, looking for whatever or whoever did this to her.

"Mitac and Chance…"

I narrow my eyes. Mitac, the Gopher who murdered my uncle.

"They're not with me," she reassures me. "I left them when we got near Ashadier."

"Come on," I tell her. "Let's go to the clearing so we can talk." I glance to Gorduin, making sure it's okay. He gives me a slight nod and picks up Selvia's bag. We walk back to camp together.

"Ah, there she is," Nyana welcomes us warmly when we walk into the clearing. I think she's talking to me, which is strange because I almost never see her, but then she approaches Selvia and embraces her.

Selvia looks as shocked as I am.

"Here I am?" she questions the woman.

"Selvia, Selvia, I have had some dreams about you young lady." Nyana wraps her arm around Selvia's shoulders and takes her to her wagon. Selvia looks back at me with alarm, but I nod and encourage her forward. Gorduin and I look at each other before I shrug and follow. Nyana has always been a weird one, I've been told.

Inside the wagon, Nyana has set Selvia on the bench and motions Gorduin and me to join her. Nyana sits across from us.

She folds her hands on the table between us. "Now, share with your friends here what's been going on."

"I don't know who the guy is," she hooks her thumb at Gorduin.

"Gorduin," I fill in for her. "He's one of the Wayfarers."

She raises an eyebrow at me. I fill her in with as much as I know about the Wayfarers, and she listens without interrupting.

"So they're safe," Selvia concludes when I finish.

"Yes, safe for us," I confirm.

She nods. "Okay then. Well, Chance and Mitac are on a mission from the Council to come get you. They were sent with the same Warrior who killed your uncle, but they managed to ditch him along the way. I decided to come along, figuring I could help and maybe find you before they did."

"Why would you want to find me first?"

"I don't know. Chance didn't want me on this trip." She looks away.

"I thought if I found you first, I could show her that I am good enough to be part of their team."

I shake my head. "Selvia—" I start. She interrupts me.

"I took off into the forest when they weren't watching and got a head start. I slept little and kept moving whenever I was awake to stay ahead of them. I went every which way in the forest, looking for you. I got lucky to finally find you."

"Is that why you look like…this?" I gesture to her shredded clothing.

"Yes." She nods, and I visibly relax.

"You almost found us several times," Nyana tells her. "But I kept the wards up around us so you couldn't see us, and we didn't see you."

I face her. "Why did you do that?"

"Someone was following her, a person with evil intent," Nyana speaks slowly. Picking and choosing her words carefully. I wonder what she's not telling us. "I couldn't risk letting them in with her."

"So, you left a little girl to fend for herself in the forest? With someone who means her harm?"

Nyana shakes her head. "You don't get it, do you? You are worth far more than one girl, no matter how much she may mean to you."

"No." I refuse to believe that. I am no more and no less than anyone else. "Everyone is someone's someone. Everyone matters, not me alone."

Nyana flashes black and slams her hands on the table. She rises from her bench and towers over me. "Without you, there is *no one else!* Without you, everyone dies. Don't you get that? You heard Raemyn, she told you, right? You are required to reset the age, reset the power balance. Everything requires balance and time is running out."

"The Celestials," I try to offer.

"The Celestials, the master watchmakers? You think they can do this? They started this mess, but they are powerless to stop it."

My eyes widen. I hear the sharp intake of breath from my companions on either side of me.

"What do you mean?" Gorduin asks. "The Celestials are all-powerful."

"Not against this. This is beyond what they can do. You are the mechanism, the sand in the watch, the wrench in the gears. Only you can stop time."

I sit in stunned silence. This isn't what Raemyn told me.

"What if that's not true? How am I supposed to believe you?"

Nayana turns and digs under her bench. She pulls up a book. I gasp. The same one Raemyn had.

"Here," she pushes the book toward us, "If you don't believe me. It's all here. The creation of the Variance, the start of the world, everything." She sets the heavy tome on the table in front of me. I rest a hand on it, afraid she will take it back.

"Who wrote this?" I ask. "Why are they experts? Do they know what they were talking about? Plus, how can we be sure I'm even the Variance? My powers are shit, in case you haven't noticed. If the difference between the Wayfarers and myself is that I have all the powers and all the strength, why can I barely use any of it?"

"Practice," Nyana hisses. "You must practice more."

Now I'm getting angry. "I practice every single day! Almost all day long! How dare you say I don't practice?"

She waves my objections off. "It's not enough. You stop too much. You give up too easily. You are too easily dissuaded."

"I am trying my hardest," my voice warbles. "I don't know what else to do."

Gorduin wraps his arm around my shoulders pulling me close, but I stand, my knees painfully hitting the table in front of me. Gorduin stands to let me by. I leave the table, the book, the woman accusing me of not trying hard enough and flee the wagon.

...NOT THE ONE YOU NEED TO BE WORRIED ABOUT.

Mitac

R62O25

I don't overstay my welcome with Julieth and the kids. Julieth introduces me to the three youngest, Hilda and Gilda, twins who have been caring for the garden. And Leck, who has been taking care of the goat who is turning more oblong by the day, he tells me proudly, as she grows her kid inside of her.

I leave the next day, thanking them for the insight they were able to provide and the couch to sleep on. I don't tell them I didn't actually sleep on it. They seemed proud to offer it, but the springs dug painfully into every sore spot on my back. The floor worked better.

"I hope you find her," Julieth tells me as she shakes my hand.

"I'll do my best," I reply as I walk out the door. I give her a singular wave and head back into the forest. Julieth told me Eloise would not be taking the road, but I need to move faster than she was, so I stick to the roads to start. As I walk, the voice in my head gets louder, and the tug around my spine gets more insistent, pulling me into the forest. I decide to follow it, what's the worst that can happen?

I vaguely wonder if this is what Chance feels when she's tracking someone. I shouldn't be able to track people, but I also shouldn't have a voice in my head giving me warnings. Time to roll with it.

I walk a ways away from the road when I sense it. Someone behind me. My hand automatically closes around the knife in its holster, releasing it from its hold. The motion can be done with almost no perceptible movement. I keep walking, my steps deliberate and careful. Without letting on I know someone is there, I start picking through a wider path. It will give my attacker more opportunity but also give me some room to move, and I need it.

When I reach an opening, I dive behind a small boulder as a knife whizzes into a tree I had been in front of seconds before. I misjudged what was behind the impromptu shield, my shoulder slamming into a sharp rock hidden under some moss and pine needles.

I push away thoughts of the pain and quickly roll back to my feet, staying crouched. I turn to look at my attacker and see a familiar face looking back. A pissed off face twisted with rage.

"Get out here, Gopher, and face your death with the dignity you didn't offer Gamet," Eloise threatens.

I've never been so happy to see a face before. The drumbeats of "danger, danger, danger" bounce off the walls of my mind, but she's here. She's safe. And the pull around my spine eases. I sigh in relief and let my guard down long enough for her to send another dagger sailing past my head. I duck again, my shoulder screaming.

I notice my shirt is covered in blood, a sharp relief to the white linen.

"Eloise, please, hold on."

"No way." Her eyes flick briefly behind me. I was so focused on Eloise that I miss the person behind me until it's too late.

"Stand," a deep voice demands, something sharp at my back. The person behind me sees fit to relieve me of my sword and leiomano. I cringe when he tosses them to the side. They're good weapons, but they don't like to be thrown around. I don't dare look to see where they landed.

I stand slowly, assessing my situation. Eloise at my front, an unknown male at my back. A glance around me doesn't immediately show another person.

"Walk," the voice is paired with a jab in the back. I reluctantly follow Eloise, who has marched off into the forest. A short distance in, we come to an opening in the trees. I shiver when I walk through something that feels like a cold shower across my skin, but I emerge dry on the other side. And on the other side, a large clearing has appeared. I blink, then blink again. That was not there seconds before. I look behind me and see the same forest we walked through to get here.

"What is this?" I ask tentatively. I don't know if she'll tell me. "What are we doing here?"

Eloise purses her lips but doesn't share. She marches onward toward the middle of the clearing, where several downed trees have been turned into a sitting area.

"Sit," the man behind me puts a hand on my shoulder and forces me down. He didn't overpower me; I have more questions than answers at this point, and obedience will hopefully give me some of those. He finally comes around in front of me, and I gasp in surprise.

"You—"

He smiles. "So, you do remember me?"

"You were on the train," I remember our unsettling conversation just before we got to Rothesard. "What is this? Who are you?"

"Answers will come in time."

Eloise has walked away. She returns with a woman I don't know and—

"Selvia!" I exclaim. I look around to see if Chance is next to appear.

Selvia gives me a shy smile and stays partially behind Eloise. She probably thinks she's in trouble, which, to be honest, if I wasn't so relieved to see her unhurt, I would definitely be giving her a lecture.

The woman I don't know has long black hair that falls in waves down her back. She is tall, taller than even Eloise, and walks with an easy grace. She looks as though she barely touches the ground. Her face is hard, unlike her nimble walk. I do not take her for an easy woman to cross.

"Mitac," she says, her voice light, "I'm glad you could join us. As you can see, we have a couple of your people here."

I nod. A thousand questions race through my mind. Who is this woman? How does she know my name? How did Selvia get here? How did Eloise? Why is Eloise still here? By now, she should be nearly in Amiket. We only started with Ashadier to try to get some information on how she might be traveling.

Looking at Selvia, I'm reminded she ran away from me and Chance and a little part of me aches to find out why. Did we treat her so poorly? Did she hate us?

"Drop your weapon, Gorduin; Mitac is not the one you need to be worried about."

"Definitely not," I agree with haste. I wonder who we *are* supposed to be worried about.

"I am Nyana," the woman explains. "I am one of the leaders of the Wayfarers. You have been brought into our encampment because you've been deemed not a threat." A huff from behind me. I would guess it's Eloise. Nyana looks sharply. "He's *not* a threat, Eloise."

"Tell that to Gamet," Eloise mutters behind me.

Either Nyana doesn't hear, or she chooses to ignore it.

"So, Mitac, where is Chance?"

"We split up, looking for Selvia," I look at Selvia, who looks ashamed. "Looks like I found her first. What is the threat? Eloise, why are you still here? Selvia, why did you run?" I look at each person in turn as I ask my questions.

Nyana answers all of them. "The threat is someone moving through the forest, looking for Eloise. Eloise is still here because we have reason to believe her aunt is reasonably safe in the palace at this time, and she needs to learn. Selvia ran to prove something. Satisfied?"

"Not by half, but it'll do for now."

UNBIDDEN TEARS...

Mitac

R62O30

I'm starting to go stir-crazy. It's been five days, and while I have learned a lot about the Wayfarers and their magic, I am anxious to get moving. I need Chance. Each time I try to leave, though, something stops me. That damned tugging on my spine yanks me right back. Nyana doesn't even stop me. She watches with amusement.

Cardis and I settle into a tenuous alliance. He doesn't forgive me for Gamet, but neither do I, so I could never expect him to, but he agrees not to stab me in my sleep. He makes no such promises for when I'm awake.

"There you go, Phoenix," Gorduin coaches Eloise, who is creating a small snow flurry. She gets several flakes before sagging in exhaustion. Gorduin catches her, and my hackles rise when he gets too close to her. He helps her sit down, and my inner guard settles when he backs off of her. "Much better. You're getting better!"

"Not fast enough," Eloise grits out. "I'm still useless!"

"Not useless, Phoenix, never useless. Inexperienced, ill-practiced, but not useless. You can find the threads of your magic for all of them now, can't you? Didn't you successfully Track Selvia in the forest earlier this week?"

"Yeah, but she left plenty of other clues of where she was going," Eloise whines.

"Stop it, Phoenix, you Tracked her. You said you could tell the difference between her and the animals. That's huge."

Eloise shakes her head, then carefully gets to her feet. "Again," she stands upright, squaring her shoulders.

Cardis smiles at her with pride, Selvia with respect. I watch her with caution, trying to look at all the potential threats around us. Nyana has assured us we are safe. The encampment is invisible to the outside unless Nyana lets them in, or she dies.

I step away from the group, craving some isolation. I stand in the shade of the trees, willing Chance to appear. To find us.

The breaking of branches in the forest puts me on high alert. I jump to my feet, reaching for my sword, which isn't there. Nyana took them, letting me know I wouldn't need it while I was with them. I didn't argue, I was so happy they were safe after being thrown around in the forest.

Now I wish I had them.

Out steps Elgin, and in front of him, with a dagger to her throat, Chance. I stop breathing. We shouldn't be visible, but Elgin is looking directly at me. Not through me, *at me.*

"Run!" I yell through the trees. I can't look to see if they have done so, but there's a flurry of activity behind me. I need Eloise to get out. Before Elgin sees her and knows she's here.

Elgin is sneering at me, tightening his grip on the blade. I see a small trickle of blood down Chance's throat. I growl. How dare he?

Elgin chuckles. "I knew you were weak," he jeers. "If it weren't this girl, I would have gotten the other one. Either way, I knew how to break you."

I watch and wait to see what he means. I struggle to come up with options. What can I do? If Chance wasn't here, no problem. I would take him out without a second thought, but Chance is in my way.

She stands awkwardly, pulled back against Elgin's front. I look her in the eyes. *I'll get you out of this,* I try to send her telepathically. She doesn't look scared, though; she looks *mad.*

I start to move toward the pair, and Elgin presses harder on the blade. I immediately stop. Blood trickles down her neck faster. The bright red against her deep green is startling.

"See? Weak. Caring for others makes you an inferior opponent, Mitac."

My heart drums against my ribs, and my pulse pounds in my head. "What do you want?" I finally ask. I don't know what to do other than try to buy some time. For what or whom, I don't know. Time for the others to get away. Leave me to die as long as Eloise gets away. And Chance, Celestials, I need Chance to get out of here.

"What I always wanted. The girl. She's the key to everything."

"She's not here," I try to send my magic with my words, but it doesn't make it. I'm too anxious and scared to even make a real attempt at it. I know my magic doesn't work on him, but I wasn't above trying again. And again.

"You're a terrible liar. Bring the girl to me, and you can have this one."

I glance at Chance. She darts her eyes back and forth in a non-verbal "no" to me.

"She's not here," I repeat.

"Fine," Elgin says, and I breathe a sigh of relief when he drops the knife.

My relief comes too soon. He takes the knife and drags it across her throat. In the same way that he did across Gamet's. The result is the same. Blood everywhere. Someone screams.

～

Eloise

Mitac told me to run; why didn't I run? Why am I still here?

Gorduin took Selvia back to the camp, promising to get others, and Cardis and I went wide. I froze when I saw the blade drag across the Green woman's neck, Mitac's Tracker. I watched Mitac scream and crumple to the ground. Then I darted out of the trees, not even thinking twice.

I rush toward the three, completely ignoring Mitac and Elgin, and kneel by the Tracker, pulling her into my lap. I don't care if she bleeds all over me, I don't care what kind of person she is, I don't know her name, but I know she's dying because of me, and no one should die because of me.

Her green eyes are fading, the pupils getting wider. She looks me in the eye, and I reach out for magic. Any Healing magic I can find. I don't know why I think I can Heal her. I haven't been able to Heal anything more than a simple cut, but I'm going to try. Distantly, I hear the crash of metal and the soft thumps of body on body.

I tune it out, trying to keep my attention on the task at hand.

"Hang on for me, Tracker," I tell her. I wish I knew her name. "I can't Heal you if you die all the way. So, hang on. If you work with Mitac, you must know how to be stubborn."

I think I see a faint smile.

I close my eyes and search for the threads. I despair when darkness is all I can see. I breathe deeply. Focus, I have to focus. Try harder.

I search and search. Darkness—then…there. A white thread, but it's so small. More deep breaths. More threads. I start gathering them. I don't even care what they're for. They could be for making potions, but it doesn't matter. There's a woman dying in my arms, and I'll take anything resembling Healing magic at this point.

I gather everything I can find and release it with a long exhale. I stare at the Green woman in my arms.

The open space on her neck looks minimally smaller. The blood has slowed, and I repeat the process multiple times. The slice on her neck completely closes, the blood completely stops.

I look back at the Tracker in triumph. Then dismay.

Her eyes are wide, vacant. Staring into the distance. The blood stopped because her heart stopped. I didn't save her after all.

Unbidden, tears come to my eyes and fall down my lashes. I shake the woman in my arms. "No, no, no," I repeatedly shake her. "Wake up! I did it…I closed it. I did everything!"

The woman doesn't respond, continuing to stare blankly. I let out a hoarse cry, holding the woman close to me. Gripping her tightly, trembling.

I did everything, everything I could. And it wasn't enough.

A clang of metal-on-metal breaks through, and suddenly, the noise of the world around me rushes in all at once in a loud cacophony. I look up and Mitac is in a blind rage, fighting off two Black Warriors. He's using nothing but his fists, but they're moving so fast I can barely keep track of them. Cardis is fighting with the first one, managing to work a blade in a way I've never seen him do. Gorduin and Selvia have reappeared. Gorduin has turned Black, and he, too, is fighting against yet another Warrior.

"Get back, Selvia," Gorduin pants between parries. "You'll be safe in the clearing. Go!"

Selvia laughs. "No way, miss all the fun?" She spins, a small blade in her hands.

While Gorduin has the Warrior distracted, she stabs him in the flank. The man howls and turns to face her. Gorduin takes the opportunity to drive his knife into the middle of his back. The man collapses, alive, but appears unable to move.

Selvia and Gorduin, having given up trying to make her return to the Wayfarers, run off to help Cardis. Between the three of them, they make quick work of the Warrior. Putting him on his knees, dagger to his throat the same way it was to the woman in my arms.

I continue to hold her close, as though if I hold her, I can bring her back. But I know better. No one can bring back the dead.

Selvia takes guard over the Warrior while Cardis and Gorduin help Mitac take care of the other two. Mitac looks around, chest heaving. His eyes meet mine. Hope shining bright.

I pull the woman closer to me and shake my head. I couldn't save her. I couldn't save her. I'm supposed to be the strongest magic-wielder in the Vale, probably in the Realm, and I couldn't do anything.

Mitac rushes over, dropping to his knees, and rips the woman from my arms.

"Chance," he sobs into her hair. "Celestials, Chance. I told you not to come with me. Why did you come with me!"

I stay where I am, unable to move. His grief overflows to me. A weight so heavy I can't move or breathe.

He cries. No, he sobs. Deep, heart-wrenching sobs that shake his body. His body caves in on itself, folding over Chance's body. He rocks back and forth with the woman. He doesn't even look at me. He roars to the canopy above us. Wordless sounds of anguish. I swallow back my own emotions. Gorduin, Selvia, and Cardis stand by, looking lost for what to do.

Selvia approaches slowly. She kneels next to Mitac, her eyes wet with unshed tears. Her chin trembles uncontrollably. She reaches out, her hand shaking, and she touches Chance's hair lightly. The green strands fall from her fingers like a waterfall. Selvia leans heavily against Mitac.

Mitac looks at Selvia and wraps an arm around her. He pulls her close to his side. Together, they cry. Chance, Mitac, Selvia. Looking at them, they could be mistaken for a family and, in a way, perhaps they were. The best kind of family. The family that chose each other.

I swipe tears away from my own cheeks.

"Mitac," Gorduin approaches slowly, gently placing a hand on Mitac's shoulder, "we should get back. These two might know something." He gestures to the paralyzed Warrior and the first Warrior.

Mitac takes a deep breath, seeming to try to collect himself.

"Oh, they know something, alright. At least that one," he tilts his head to the first Warrior. Mitac finally rises from his position, placing Chance in Selvia's lap. Selvia continues to stroke the woman's hair. She's murmuring something, but I can't quite catch it.

He walks stiffly to the first Warrior and knees him in the face. The man looks unfazed. He gives Mitac a coppery smile, saliva and blood dripping from his mouth. Mitac rains blows on his face with his fists. Again, and again. Each time I flinch, but internally, I cheer him on.

Gorduin finally restrains Mitac.

"I'm not saying he doesn't deserve it," Gorduin struggles to hold Mitac back, "but we need answers first."

"He needs to pay!" Mitac shouts, defeated. "He killed her. He killed her. He just…he killed her." His voice trails off as grief seems to overcome him again.

"He will pay. But first, let's get answers."

"I'll never tell you anything," the man says through his swollen face and missing teeth.

"We'll find out, won't we?" Mitac snaps and drags him back toward the clearing by the wrists. The man doesn't even fight.

Gorduin lifts the paralyzed Warrior and walks off with him. I get up as carefully as I can, and Cardis and I remove Chance from Selvia's lap and carry her. After a few steps, I notice Selvia isn't with us.

Selvia, where did Selvia go?

I look back, and Selvia is kneeling where I left her, blood splattered all over her tan skin, her grey eyes stormy. She's clenching her hands over and over. She's staring at Chance.

"Hold up, Cardis," I say, setting Chance's feet down gently. I walk back to Selvia.

"Selvia," I say softly. She doesn't move. "Selvia?"

"She's the only one who believed in me," she says, absently, seemingly unaware of my presence.

"Selvia," I repeat. She blinks and focuses on me. "Let's go."

57

...VERY DOOMY.

Aerith

R62F03

Saada's slow progress concerns me greatly. I had hoped we would be long gone by this point, but it's been a week, and she still hasn't come out of her near-comatose state. The Healer, Helia, kept telling me not to worry, but I could see the worry in her eyes, too. She might be less worried about Saada and more worried for me. With each passing day, the guards from the dungeon get more and more persistent with checking on me. I can tell they are starting to think I am faking it. I play comatose well, but we are risking a lot. Helia, especially. She didn't ask to be dragged into this.

When I went into my catatonia, I was brought to her. I had severe infections from my countless wounds and was severely nutritionally deficient. When I came out of it after a few days of intensive healing and care, I found her to be a friend and ally.

It made sense, a Healer to be on our side since the work the dungeon does directly contradicts her work and ethos, but I had thought everyone inside the castle was loyal to the Illume.

She and I had begun to make plans to get Saada out when she dropped into our laps unexpectedly. Now, we are making a new set of plans, how to leave, but all of the plans we come up with require Saada to be awake and able to move under her own power. As of yet, that is not possible.

Day after day, she lay in her bed staring at the ceiling, unmoving, unblinking. From time to time, Helia came by and put drops in her eyes to keep them from drying out as her lids refused to stay closed. She worked out a way to give her food and drink directly into her stomach, too. Saada was putting on some weight, not looking nearly as gaunt, and the wounds on her back are healing slowly over time, but her mind seems irreparable. This is what scares me the most. What if she doesn't come back at all?

Helia had tried to encourage me to leave on my own, insisting she would send Saada when she roused, but I pointed out that as soon as I disappeared, Helia would not have a job anymore. Letting me escape will cause her to suffer punishment as well. No, we will all need to leave together. Helia isn't convinced yet she needs to leave, but I will make sure she comes. One way or another. She can't stay and suffer because of us.

"We still need to deal with your talisman," Helia points out.

I feel the orb around my neck. It's been neither hot nor cold since I've been in the dungeon. It's like the Celestials have stopped talking through it at all. I nod.

"I don't know what to do with it. The Council says if we remove it, we will die. They said it's tied to our heart, which is how they keep track of our health."

"Okay, so maybe that's true," Helia thinks aloud. "Why do you think they haven't come to check on you since you woke up from your catatonic state? Don't you think they would have noticed?"

"I have considered that, but I think maybe they turned it off? Or paused monitoring for now? I'm not getting calls for the Council meetings either. I think we all get called at the same time, and mine hasn't been cold since they sent me to the dungeons. So maybe they have a way of turning it off?"

Helia nods. "That's a possibility. Should we try to remove it, then?"

My heart begins to race. "What if we do, and it kills me? What then?" I don't know what to think about my own death. I never contemplated it before, even though I probably should have given the treatment I was getting before being in Helia's care.

"We could snap it back in place if you feel any ill effects as soon as it comes off." Helia comes over to examine the metal around my neck, looking for the clasp. "It looks simple enough to remove."

"Do you think that'll alert whoever is monitoring me that it's been taken off?"

She comes around to face me, examining me. "Yes, it's a possibility. Maybe you should climb into bed. That way, if they do come up here, I can tell them I was removing it to clean around your neck." I walk stiffly to my bed and climb in under the sheets. "Okay, I'm going to watch you carefully, and you tell me the moment you feel anything strange. Then I'll put it back."

I nod my understanding. My heart still racing. Helia turns the necklace around and gently releases the clasp. So far, so good; I'm still breathing, and my heart is still beating.

"I feel okay," I tell her.

I lift my head off the pillow, and she removes the necklace and places it on the bedside table. I still feel fine. Anxious, but otherwise fine. Helia watches me carefully which isn't helping my anxiety. After a few minutes, my breathing evens out, and I think I'm going to be alright. I smile at her.

"I think I'm free," I tell her. *Oh, happy day!*

Suddenly, the doors bang open, and two Warriors burst into the room. I quickly close my eyes and feign sleep. "What's happened?!" They yell.

"What are you going on about? What is the meaning of this?" Helia sounds indignant.

"Her talisman," one of them utters. "It's not on her!"

"I took it off to clean her," she defends. "Unless you'd like for her to never recover?"

"Well, no, but that can't ever stay off her or she will die," the other iterates.

"It's only for a moment. How long can it be off her without causing ill effect?" I silently applaud Helia for her deviousness and forethought in gaining valuable information.

"Not long," the first conjectures, "A couple of minutes at most."

"Well, it's been almost that long now, so if you'll excuse me—" I hear the necklace rustle on the bedside table, and I feel her placing it back around my neck. My leash is back in place, and I'm disappointed. It doesn't appear I will die without it, though, because it had definitely been several minutes since we removed the necklace. However, it looks like it still keeps track of me.

I hear the Warriors leave back out the door now that the necklace is back on.

I AM SITTING at Saada's bedside in my insufferable patient gown. If I wear normal clothing, it will be too hard to sell that I am an invalid. I need to be ready to jump into bed at a moment's notice. For now, though, the guards left moments ago, so I will be safe for a little while. I open the book on my lap and read aloud to Saada. It's not an exciting book, but it's better than sitting in complete silence. Who knows? Maybe she can hear, and it will get her brain working. The book is a manual on Healing, and I have been reading it to her day after day. We have been covering medical ailments in alphabetical order from "abdominal pain" to "fever" where we are now. Fever is a super long chapter. It seems like anything can cause a fever at any time.

"How do you keep all this straight, Helia?" I ask her as I read the fifteenth condition that can cause a fever.

"Easy," she replies. "I don't! Why do you think I have the book?" I notice it does look rather well-used. "Some things we see a lot of, and I don't need the book to help me treat those things anymore. Other things are less common, or don't behave the way I expect, so I do more reading on them at the time."

"Like Saada's catatonic state?"

"Exactly. I treated her, at first, like I treated you and others from the dungeon. When she didn't respond, I started reading. Unfortunately, for us, I didn't find anything in there I don't know or haven't tried. So, it's a waiting game."

My feet fidget of their own accord, anxiety, I am sure. I read that one last week to Saada, and I show many of the classic symptoms. Feeling a heaviness on my chest, fidgeting, a sense of impending doom, inability to sleep, loss of appetite… The cure section for anxiety in this book is sorely lacking.

Deep breathing exercises, talking with someone, and thinking pleasant thoughts. All useless drivel. I am very well versed in deep breathing, given my profession. I have been talking to Helia every chance I get, and thinking pleasant thoughts is hard to do when you have a sense of impending doom. It's not like it's unreasonable to be anxious in the situation we are currently in. I would love to be able to see an end to this. All the endings I see right now are very doomy.

I close the book, unable to pay attention to the words I am trying to read and get up from my seat. I walk over to Saada and pick up the brush on her nightstand. I pull her long hair off to the side and brush it gently. I hum an old song to her, a lullaby I think, though I don't know where I might have heard it.

As I am about to repeat the song for the third time while braiding Saada's soft hair, I hear another voice join me. I think it's Helia but when I look over, she is absorbed in her herbs and her mouth is unmoving. I look at Saada and can see her mouth is open, eyes on me. While I have been in her line of sight before, this is the first time she seems to be looking at me. I continue humming, listening carefully to see if she is humming with me. I can hear the echo of her voice, and I tie off her braid. I put it down and step a little further to the side. Saada's eyes follow me.

"Helia! She's looking at me!" I yell.

Helia jumps and drops the bottle she's holding. "What?"

"Saada," I clarify, "her eyes are following me. She's looking at me, not through me!"

Helia jumps up from her seat and rushes over, her white skirts billowing. She stands on the other side of the bed.

"See? When I moved away from her head, she followed me."

"Are you sure?" Saada's eyes roll slowly to Helia. "I'll be damned…" Her hands fly to her mouth.

Saada still doesn't blink, but she follows. "This is good, right? It means she's coming around?"

"Yes," Helia nods cautiously. "I think so."

"How long…?" I start to ask. I want to know when we can look at getting out of here. I am hopeful we can get out of here soon. Before the guards catch on. Before Eloise gets here. Before the whole palace crumbles around us.

Helia shakes her head. "No way to know, Aerith, same as it was before we saw progress. Her brain appears to be healing from the trauma, but no one but the Celestials can tell us when she will rouse. Time will tell."

I hope it's soon. We need to be gone a long time ago. I tell Saada that, like she has control, then feel bad. She has no more control over this situation than I do.

"When your brain is ready, Saada, we will leave. We will get out of here and—well, I don't know yet. But we will get out of the city and go somewhere. And we will find your Eloise too."

Saada continues to stare at me, unblinking. I hold her hand in mine, patting it. Helia comes over and pulls a table next to the bedside. On it, she lays two maps, the top one I've never seen before. One glance and I can tell the top one is a map of the place I have always called home.

"I thought this might help," she waves to the maps. "It shows the passageways in the palace. Some of them are not known but by a few."

I look closely, and I do indeed start to see small paths which I have never noticed before. It looks like some are behind large pictures or statues. Little notes in an unfamiliar hand indicate the specifics of each. How to open false walls and enter these places.

"How did you get this?" I whisper in awe. I am certain the possession of this map would not be allowed by the Council. "Did you find all these?"

Helia shakes her head. "No, no. I have several useful friends here who found these and shared them with me over time. I keep the map and notes, so if it's found, I am the only one in trouble, but I have used this to get others out before. I think we can come up with a reasonable plan to help you escape."

"Us," I reaffirm sternly. "You're coming with us."

"No, Aerith. I won't leave the people here. Others, like you, need me. When the time comes, I know how to let you out without any suspicion falling on me. It has worked before; it will work again. Just—when it comes to it? If this girl of yours is as important as you think, can you find a way to get word back here? Let me know so I can save the good people still left in here?"

I look at her in surprise. Never have I mentioned the specifics of my dungeon stay or why I was being punished. "I may not know specifics, but I can read the signs. It's time, isn't it? For a new person to rise and reset the Revolutions?"

I nod.

She slumps where she sits. "Thank the Celestials. I am tired of watching us bury people in their prime. Although, of course, this means that this place will fall. It always does."

"Maybe it won't this time." I try to sound brave, convincing. I'm not sure I am succeeding. Helia smiles at me and pats my hand similar to how I pat Saada's from time to time. "Maybe it can be different."

"Aerith, you are sweet and kind but spoiled rotten and naive."

"Hey!" I protest.

"Oh shush, you know it's true. Do you think the Council will bow down to someone else? This is what happens, in the end. The Council must be dismantled or give up their power. Balance reset. They hold too much power; they will never give in."

"What do you mean, balance reset?"

"Do you know how the age starts over?" she asks me. She probably knows my answer is no, but she asks anyway. I appreciate her not assuming I'm uneducated, even if I am. I shake my head in embarrassment. This wasn't exactly a part of our curriculum. If it's as Helia says, it would make sense why the Council wouldn't educate us on it.

"Well, as the story goes. The reason we all start dying sooner is that the powers of the world are out of balance."

"You mean the colors?" I picture the mass of people, one color more heavily represented than the others. Maybe we have too many Blacks and not enough Yellows? Or something?

"No, the other powers. The power over people's lives. The Council determines everything, good or bad. Mostly bad. Have you never noticed that they mostly serve themselves? Wouldn't it make more sense for them to be located a little more centrally so people in other areas could have a chance to choose their rulers? Or the rules imposed upon them?"

"I started thinking about that recently, but I was always told they were here because it was easily defensible."

"Sure, but wouldn't it be even easier if they were inland, away from sea attacks? A place where they can see things coming for miles? Maybe even underground? I mean, if the real concern is safety." She pauses, and I consider what she's implying. "Also, have you never wondered why there aren't more Dreamers?"

"The Celestials only give us one at a time. And then a replacement when it's time."

The words Naseem told me before come back to my mind. She had her doubts about the goodness of the Council. Suddenly I wonder, why hasn't Naseem visited me in the time since I was pulled from the Council room? It's probably pretty well-known we were—are—friends. I wonder if they've done something to her. Trying to see what she knows. My stomach twists.

"If you want to believe that," Helia challenges, "but I have it on fairly good authority that other Dreamers are born. And they're identified and killed if it's not time for a replacement. I have even heard there are Dreamers who are not attached to one type of Dreaming or magic. In fact, there are people who have access to multiple magics. What are the odds that every person in existence only gets one magic? Those are the ones they tell you about. The others are silenced, permanently."

"So, if that's true, how do we know about them?"

"Because," she smiles conspiratorially, "not all of them get caught."

She stands up and steps away from me. I watch her closely. She moves her hands, and a gust of wind blows through my hair. I gasp. I look around and see the doors and windows are closed. Next, a flower appears in her palm then turns into ash as it bursts into flames, which is then put out by a burst of water. In all of this, Helia remains White, no change in her color. I try to find the source of the tricks she is playing but see none.

"You're one of them," I hear from the bed. I whip my head around and stare at Saada.

"What?" I turn. "Saada, was that you? Say something else!"

"Stop yelling," she croaks. "You're a Wayfarer."

She's looking directly at Helia who has come to the other side of her and is smiling at her.

"Yes, ma'am. I would recognize you anywhere, Saada," Helia pumps her fist. "You're finally awake!"

"What?" I repeat.

"You were there?" Saada asks, her voice still raspy. She tries to reach for her water, but her arms are so weak from disuse they fall back against the bed. I wrap an arm around her shoulders and sit her up to stabilize her while Helia gives her a little water, reminding her to go slow.

"I was. I wouldn't expect you to know me, but I used to see the pictures your sister painted of you."

"You're here," Saada states, confusion written all over her face. Probably the same confusion on my own face. "The Wayfarers never come to Amiket."

"I had to come; we needed someone else in the palace after our previous spy died. Most of my magic lies in Healing, so I make myself white and present that face. I got a job here; to do the most I can do for the Wayfarers. I send messages back with the ravens when I can. I have informed them you are here."

Saada blinks, a silent cascade of tears escaping down her face. "I didn't think I would find anyone I could trust. Now I have found two."

I lean down to hug her as does Helia, and we stay like that for several moments. I have so many questions, but this isn't the time to ask them.

100 DAYS...

Mitac

R62F10 – 100 days after the Quest

WHEN WE GOT BACK to camp, I paid attention to nothing. My only goal was to make Elgin pay. The bastard killed her, and he wasn't even sorry for it. Something had broken in me then. I took great pleasure in punching his face in repeatedly. I nearly punched the kid, Gorduin, when he made me stop, but he was right. We needed answers.

The camp was in chaos, however, and Elgin would have to wait. We tied him to a tree securely; we didn't bother securing the other. He could use neither arms nor legs.

"Nyana is dead," we were told that night. Gasps broke out in the camp. That explained why Elgin could see us.

"What happened?" one colorfully dressed woman asked.

The man, who appeared to be in charge now, hesitated. "She was murdered."

A pall fell over the crowd. Dying of age would be expected, but how did someone get through the wards to her? That could only mean one thing. There's a traitor in the Wayfarers. But who?

Obviously, outsiders like me, Eloise, Cardis, and Selvia were the first questioned. We were quickly exonerated by Gorduin, who said we were fighting the other Warriors on the edge of the camp at the time. Some remain skeptical and look at us cross when we walk around.

But in all the questioning, no one came up as an obvious suspect.

Worse yet, we weren't allowed near the prisoners we had taken until the questioning was done. Someone saw to it they ate and drank, but we were confined.

When we were released, we were told that they, too, had been murdered.

I had unleashed my fury on the messenger who told me. Elgin was supposed to pay. And I was the one carrying the invoice!

We buried Chance and Nyana in the forest. I made sure Chance was in a grove of trees that closely matched her skin. I kneeled beside her grave long after dark. Then the Wayfarers mourned. For several days they didn't speak, they wore their brightest colors, offered prayers to the Celestials, and all was silent in the camp. It was eerie. I had been a part of many celebrations of life, but I had never seen an extended mourning like this.

I was grateful for their silence, though. I didn't want to talk to anyone. I walked a razor's edge of grief and rage. Anything could tip me one way or the other. One moment crying, the next breaking something, once even my fist.

"Mitac," Eloise scolded me as she held my hand. I had punched a tree. Something had cracked.

I winced as she unwrapped it to look at it. Scrapes decorated my knuckles. She held my hand in both of hers, closing her eyes, and within moments, my scrapes nearly disappeared, and some of the pain eased.

I never stopped marveling at her use of magic or her turning colors when she did. While Healing my knuckles that day, she had turned a brilliant White.

"I left some of the pain," she stated. "To maybe teach you a lesson. Take it easy on your fist. Or at least the trees."

She scowled at me, and I scowled back.

I had come back to her a day later with a repeat injury. On my left hand. She only healed the scrapes and left the broken hand.

At the end of the tenth day of death, from which the Wayfarers measure their mourning period, the new leader, Grady, approaches us.

"It's time to go," Grady stands in front of where I'm seated eating some breakfast. I look up at him in surprise. It shouldn't surprise me, I guess. The Wayfarers are nomadic, so I've been told, and I've been told they've been here longer than usual, for Eloise.

"Okay, we will start packing up. Where are we heading?"

"No," Grady shakes his head. "We aren't going, you are. All of you outsiders."

"We didn't do anything wrong," I protest. "You cleared us of any wrongdoing."

Grady shrugs. "You could have found a way. No one can trust you. We can't have someone here we can't trust. So, you all need to go."

"What about my magic?" Eloise asks. "What are we supposed to do about that?"

Grady lifts his shoulders again. "Not my problem."

"It'll be everyone's problem if we don't get this figured out! Weren't you listening to Nyana?" Eloise's skin flushes.

"Frankly, girl," Grady says harshly. "I think she had the wrong person. You're not powerful at all."

Eloise stands and gets directly in his face. "Excuse me?"

"Even if you are the right person, you're being hunted. It won't do for them to find us again and worse to find you with us. We work hard to keep ourselves secret, and we want to keep it that way. We can't be involved in all of this."

"So, Nyana thought it was too important for me to leave, that it was too dangerous, but the moment she drops dead, it's suddenly fine? You can't be involved?"

Grady slaps her. I stand and tackle him.

I get one good punch in before Cardis and Selvia pull me off the man.

"We are a peaceful people," he dabs at his split lip. "We are not here to hurt people, and you clearly are. And if you are the Variance, you need to go. It never comes without strife and conflict."

"And you don't think that maybe keeping me alive might be

important? Helping me learn my magic? What if I can do things another way?"

"It is always that way. If you thought they could be reasoned with, don't you think we would know by now? Don't you think it's been tried? You aren't the only one who has someone in Amiket City, you know. Unlike yours, though, mine shares information. Also, you will learn more as you practice. You've been given all the tools you need. You will be fine. We trust you."

Is he trying to imply that Saada should be sending messages? I wish she would, but I assume she has no way to. That fact that his spy can do so is great and is the only reason we have stayed and why Eloise is arguing to stay. If we didn't know Saada was doing okay, we would have moved on long ago.

"Trust me—" Eloise sputters half-laughing, "you trust me. Excuse me, but it doesn't sound like you trust me so much as you want to hide." Grady shrugs but doesn't deny the accusation. "Cowards. The lot of you." She turns to walk away. "Fine, we will be gone by midday."

"That should be sufficient." He turns then looks over his shoulder. "Also, you should know, we got a note from our person in Amiket. Your aunt is on the mend, and they have a plan to get out."

Eloise's eyes widen in a similar fashion as mine.

"Get out?" she asks. Grady could have led with that information.

He nods. "I don't know the specifics. We code everything in case the ravens are intercepted. But they have a plan of some kind."

"Did they say where she will meet me? Who is 'they'?"

"No specifics, remember? We know nothing more. Have a safe journey." He turns and starts to walk off.

"Wait!" Eloise calls after his retreating back. He looks over his shoulder. "Where should we go, now?"

He shrugs. "Wherever they won't expect you to go." Then he walks off, leaving us to chew on that.

After breakfast, we pack up our gear in silence.

Finally, Eloise asks the question we've all been avoiding. "Where are we going to go?"

I've been mulling that very question since we were told to leave. Somewhere they don't expect Eloise to go doesn't help. The only places they would expect her to go would be Ashadier or Amiket to rescue Saada. Short of that, Zarvan is open to us. Which helps us none. I prefer a more set path. Not that I want to be cornered, but I don't know enough about the Vales to figure out what to do now.

We shoulder our packs and say goodbye to a few more people. None of them seem confused or upset that we are leaving. I guess Grady must have had a meeting to fill them in on the plan. Doesn't make me feel better about this whole thing. We leave the circle we've sat around every day for the last month and leave the camp behind we knew as home.

"Thought you were leaving without me?"

We turn to see Gorduin jogging over to us, his pack square on his back, a quill of arrows on his waist, his bow resting lazily in his hand.

"What do you think you are doing, Gorduin?" Grady pops out from the camp, staring him down. "You can't leave."

"Why not? I swore the oath, I won't tell anyone about the Wayfarers. But I feel I need to go with them. You may not want everyone to go, but I can definitely go. You can't hold me here."

Grady looks shocked by the statement. I wonder if anyone has ever dared stand up to the Wayfarer leaders before. Being a peaceful people, conflict management probably isn't high on their list of skills. I can see the internal struggle he is having in trying to respond. I can almost bet he wants to lash out in anger, demand he stay, or maybe roll over and let him go. In the end, he settles on one question, "Why?"

"Because I can help her. We all could, but if you won't let everyone else help, I will help her. Maybe we will see each other again one day, cousin, but if we don't…then I wish you peace and wellness."

Grady is Gorduin's cousin? I look back and forth between them. I don't see much family resemblance. Other than being dressed similarly, but the whole of the Wayfarers is dressed that way.

Grady sputters. "Peace and wellness," he mutters finally then puts a hand up, in a gesture of dismissal, and walks away.

"I didn't say you could come with us," Eloise frowns at him. I smile at her obstinance. She doesn't like Gorduin, and I can't blame her. He's cocky.

Gorduin shrugs nonchalantly. "If I don't come with you, then I go off on my own. But I can help you and little man." I feel Cardis bristle next to me. I know he hates that nickname. "I know a bit more of the lands than you do. We can work out together where we want to go."

"*I*—where *I* want to go," Eloise emphasizes. "You are not coming with us, whatever we decide."

"You know, if you had gotten Grady convinced the Wayfarers should come with you, then I would have been part of that." He's being logical, and I can tell it's making Eloise mad. Her face gets more and more red each time he speaks, and her breathing comes in angry grunts.

"I would have insisted you stay behind." Eloise is being petty, but he laughs, and I struggle to contain my own laughter. She storms off, and I hear her calling out to him, "I know you're back there, but I also know I can't stop you unless I tie you to a tree and I'm not wasting my rope."

I hear him laugh. "How long do you think she'll be angry?" he asks me and Cardis.

"Probably forever," Cardis states flatly. Cardis jogs up to Eloise. "So...where are we going again?"

Eloise keeps walking aimlessly.

After walking about half an hour, Eloise finally stops the group. Gorduin has wisely kept his mouth shut the whole time and also stayed away from Eloise. Every once in a while, he throws out a suggestion like, "You're going to walk in circles if you go that way..." or "If you want to be caught, sure, walk along the path." Each suggestion makes Eloise more and more tense.

Eloise pulls her map out from her bag. It looks a little worse for wear after all the packing, unpacking, and moving, but it's still legible enough. I step closer to it and invite Gorduin to do the same. Selvia and Cardis join us also.

"Fine, Gorduin, where would you have us go?" If the boy wants to be smug and think he has a plan, then let him make it. I'll happily shoot him down for Eloise.

He comes up alongside Eloise cautiously, like approaching a wild animal. To be truthful, I bet she could turn into one if he says the wrong snarky thing right about now.

"Well, if I was thinking of a place you absolutely would not go?" She nods to his question he mostly did not ask. "Halberg...or Eaglyn...or

Staksu." He points to each place on the map as he lists them. He states the last two quietly, clearly knowing what he is suggesting.

She stares at him, flabbergasted, her mouth hanging open in shock. "Um…what? Are you insane?"

"Sometimes." She glares at him. "Look, what's more likely? That you stayed in this Vale? Or that you left it? Or that you went to a land whose ice bridge is famous for being there one year and not again for maybe five?"

I begrudgingly agree with him. Damn, I wanted to knock him down a notch or ten.

"Okay, fine. How in Zarvan Realm do you propose we get to any of these places? From what I know of Halberg, we can only cross during winter…and that's if the ice bridge forms. Big if. What do we do until winter? As for Eaglyn or Staksu…good Celestials, man! We aren't allowed in those places; we will surely be killed!"

"Exactly why they won't think you'll go there. For Halberg, the travel will take us some time. We won't be able to take a straight shot, and we can't hire anyone. You're a wanted woman by the Council. Everyone will be looking for you soon. Chances are, we will arrive in winter, and we can see if the ice bridge forms this year. It's been a few years, so we might have some luck…"

"And if the bridge isn't formed?" Selvia pipes in. "Then we've wasted months getting somewhere that we would have to retrace our steps to get back from."

He nods as though Selvia has given him the key to his plan. "Exactly, the other Vales are a better option."

"That's not what I'm saying!" Selvia objects. "Definitely not what I was saying."

"That is what you're saying, you can't hear it, though. Or don't want to. We make our way to the opposite shore. It's going to take a long while…but when we get there, we hop a boat or commandeer one and sail ourselves to another Vale."

"Let's say we do that…what's the point? What are we waiting for?" Eloise asks. Good point. Why leave at all? We have to do this thing, whatever the thing is, what's the point of leaving now?

"A sign, something that tells us it's time to come back, obviously," Gorduin states.

"Obviously," Eloise's voice drips with sarcasm. "Yes, so obvious. Well done."

"He's right, you know," Cardis exhales in resignation. "If I were looking for us, I would start here. Then search all the known places in Isynt. The last place I would check is the other Vales." She whips her head around to look at her brother then throws her hands up in frustration.

"You are both lunatics. Clearly!"

"Also…" Cardis pulls out a book he's been carrying in his hands. "I found this." He flips open the pages to the last pages. "I thought this book was a basic magic book, I thought it would come in handy here. It turns out it's not about that at all. It's a history book about magic. Wildly fascinating." His eyes light up. I look at everyone else, and I'm glad to see that most everyone is as confused as I am about this.

Cardis seems to notice he's losing his audience and moves on, clearing his throat. "Anyway, what's helpful is this bit here in the back. There's a mention of the ability to use multiple magics, and the author states the ability has been bred out of most of the Realm, but he posited that some out there may still be able to wield more than one magic." He glances at Gorduin, the living proof of the author's presumption.

"He also wrote this bit here." Cardis points to the very last paragraph in the book. I look over his shoulder at the weathered pages. The rest of our group jostles for position to see.

Supposedly, there are books that explain the special purpose of those who wield this special magic and that they are capable of resetting our lifespans. The problem is that these books are under lock and key in Amiket and possibly the other Vales. This author has requested access multiple times and has been denied. This author has also been threatened with bodily harm if anything about this comes out. I put it here in the hopes someone can continue the work this author has begun. I am next to seek the books in Eaglyn Vale. To perhaps find the answers I seek. To perhaps find a way to use this power I've been given.

I look up and Eloise is still reading. I think maybe she's started over from the way her eyes fly over the words again and again.

"Who wrote this?" she asks, her voice hoarse. The remainder of our party stays quiet. Cardis closes the book so we can examine the author's name.

One name across the front in gold embossment.

Faizu.

It doesn't mean anything to me and a quick look around shows similar looks of ignorance to the author.

"Where did you get this?" Gorduin asks, picking up the book and flipping through it. It looks to be in good shape I can tell from here. Cardis flinches at Gorduin's rough handling and snatches it back, holding it close.

"It was in my stack of books. I think maybe I've always had it?" Cardis scratches his head. "What's weird is I've read every book I own more than once, and I don't remember ever reading this one."

"Regardless of *that* mystery," Eloise jumps in. "I think we have our next path. Amiket is a dead end for this book, but Faizu said he was going to Eaglyn. Perhaps we follow the trail there."

Gorduin smiles broadly. "Shall we?" Gorduin asks with a bow.

Eloise nods reluctantly. "Lead the way."

Gorduin takes the lead, Eloise and Cardis behind, myself at the back with Selvia. We make a quiet, thoughtful procession through the dense forest. Each lost in their thoughts. *Who is Faizu? What did he learn? Was he a Variance? What happened to him?*

I turn to ask Chance her thoughts about leaving the Vale and my face falls when I remember the horrible truth. Too often I forget what's happened to her. In camp, I would find myself wandering around, unconsciously seeking her out. When I would find Selvia doing the same, I would hug her, and she would cry. I would do my best to avoid blubbering like an out-of-control emotional wreck. I saved that for my tent. Then I would find myself trying to seek her out once again.

I'm not sure if it's denial but I don't know what else to call it. My brain refuses to accept what seems so cruel and impossible. This is an adventure she will never get to have. I don't even know if she would have wanted to come, but what I wouldn't give for the chance to hear her call me an idiot and remind me how dumb this whole thing is.

100 DAYS...

Saada

Each day, I feel myself getting stronger. We quickly caught up after I roused from my comatose state and realized Helia was a Wayfarer. Helia had been with the Wayfarers when Leigha had been there. Helia had been much younger, but Leigha had painted images of me while she was with them, and Helia had come once to Ashadier when they did their check-up runs on the family. While she had gone to the Council Academy when she turned seventeen and faked her powers being singular, she had never forgotten me. Helia had finished her time in the Academy and came to the palace to feed information back to the Wayfarers. Seemed their Dreamer then and the one they have now had sensed the coming of the Variance who is, evidently, Eloise.

I took all this in calmly, letting Helia talk and share what she could between visits by the dungeon guards. They are getting more restless. As our physical forms look quite normal, they are convinced that mentally we should be normal. We are now, but we are definitely running out of time.

"Helia," I move closer to her. "We need to go. The guards are not going to buy our act for much longer."

She nods. "I know. I am being selfish. It has been so long since I have had friends to talk to. I wish I could keep you here with me and keep you safe, but I have no way to do this. I think tomorrow is our day. You will tie me up to the pillar over there," she nods to a marble column in the middle of the room. "You need to do it tight enough to be convincing, and one of you needs to hit me over the head, make it look like you knocked me out. Actually knock me out if that's what it takes."

I shake my head. "I can't, Helia. I can't do that."

She looks at Aerith. "Then it has to be you. Can you do it?"

I look at Aerith. She has been quiet most of the days while I and Helia talked about the Wayfarers. She has asked the occasional question, but mostly, it looks like her world has been rocked to its core. If it wasn't for Leigha sharing with me about the Wayfarers, I would be in the same position. Possibly comatose again. I give her credit for handling it with as much grace as she has.

Aerith nods. "I think so. What are we going to do about my talisman?"

Aerith had filled me in during the last couple of days about their experiment with her necklace. It wouldn't kill her if she removed it, but it could get all of us killed if she keeps it on since it does seem to act as a tracker of sorts.

Helia walks over to a small bookshelf and pulls a book down. "I've done a little reading on magical shields. I think I can shield it from sending out your location and fool it into sending out fake information. The only problem is, I'm not sure how long I can hold it, especially if I'm unconscious."

"You can still come with us," Aerith suggests again.

Helia shakes her head. "We've been through this. I serve a purpose here. I can't leave."

"I know," Aerith's smile turns to a grim line. "I had to try, didn't I?"

"You've done so much for us," I clasp her hands in mine. "I know I am grateful for anything you can do to get us some more time."

"Helia, you have been a wonderful friend," Aerith echoes. "I don't know what we would have done without you."

All three of us sit in silence for a moment, feeling the weight of what we are planning and about to do. I am eager to go find Eloise, but my nerves have me chewing on my fingernails again. *Celestials*, I pray, something I don't do often, *please keep us and Eloise safe. And help us find her. Guide our way.*

"So, after we tie you, we go through the water cisterns and out to the waterways?" Aerith interrupts my hasty prayer.

"Yes, that's the cleanest and easiest way out that isn't regularly monitored. Try not to muddy up the waters in the process. If you do, they'll come to check it and possibly find you. The waterways will drop you into the lake and then the ocean, where the two meet. You can then swim around the palace, past the walls, and end up at a small footpath that leads to the Gorge. It's not going to be easy, but it's doable."

I haven't heard the whole plan until now. We had talked about getting out of the palace but never what we would do after that. I see a major flaw in the plan.

"I can't swim," I declare, anxiety knotting in my gut. "I'll drown."

If the only plan is to swim, I'll be going nowhere fast.

Aerith and Helia, who are discussing the finer details of surviving in the wilderness on the way to the Gorge don't hear me. "I can't swim," I repeat, raising my voice. They still don't look at me. I wave my arms. "Oi! I can't swim!"

Their heads turn to me. "You can't what?" Aerith asks.

"Swim. There was never anywhere to swim in Ashadier or Amaranth Forest. I never learned."

"Well…shit," Aerith says in an uncharacteristic moment of unrefinery.

Helia looks thoughtful. "Let me think about that for a moment. You can't swim at all? Not even to paddle like a child?"

I shake my head. "No. None of my family can. I don't even know what it looks like to swim."

Helia lets loose a low whistle. "Well, there's another option. But you won't like it."

"Worse than drowning?" I ask.

Helia grins. "Maybe."

"Out with it," Aerith demands.

"The only other tunnels that lead out—are the sewers."

"Well…shit," I echo Aerith's earlier statement.

We burst into a fit of giggles. "Literally," Aerith confirms. "But it's that or swimming."

"I think drowning might be preferable," I mutter. "I don't want to pick up some kind of disease in the sewers."

Helia shakes her head. "The sea is not for a weak swimmer, let alone someone who can't swim at all. You're going to have to go out through the sewer. When you get to the end of those pipes, it'll drop you into a processing building. It's in the north end of the Gorge, near Halberg. But it's outside of the walls and barely has anyone there. They only work every other day and, from what I have heard, are quite lax because, who would escape through the sewers?"

I laugh sadly. "Exactly."

Helia looks at me and looks at the clothes we have laid out for tomorrow, then over to the packs we have planned to take with us. "We need to make some adjustments. The land near Halberg is cold all of the time. You need warmer clothes. And you need an extra set of shoes. Those ones will be ruined. I had expected you to put them in your packs for the swim, but you cannot walk the sewers barefoot."

We begin unpacking our bags, removing the lighter clothes and putting in the heavier ones. Unfortunately, they take more space so we cannot take as much with us. We also need to take food and other supplies with us to hunt. We won't have access to vegetation as we had planned either. This whole thing is much more complicated than the original plan. What a disaster. All because I didn't learn how to swim. I vow if I ever see the kids again, *when* I see the kids again, they will be learning to swim. Somehow. I don't care. This won't be the limiting factor in future escape plans. Of course, ideally, we will never need another escape plan.

Helia pulls out some of her dried vegetables and meat, a few ointments for cuts, some small bandages, and a handful of potions. She explains to Aerith they're for protection. One will start a fire, one will put someone to sleep, one is very deadly. We wrap that one in some bandages so as to keep it from breaking.

"If need be," she explains handing over the deadly one, "you could take this one yourself. If you're captured." She looks at us, tears welling in her eyes. "It might be preferable to the punishment they will have for you otherwise. There's enough in here for the two of you or two others. Use it carefully. It takes a long time to make, or I would make you more." We nod in understanding.

We stuff them into the bags. She gives us each an extra pair of wool socks and some small flat shoes. "Tie the boots you will wear to your pack before you get into the sewer and replace them with these flats. They're not great for long-term travel but should work for the sewer. Try to stay to the edges so you don't walk into the deepest areas. Wash your feet off as soon as you get out and discard the shoes somewhere where they won't be found. The workers may be lazy, but that doesn't mean they won't report something like that."

Both Aerith and I nod in agreement. Night comes quickly and we look at each other, all of our preparations carefully hidden until tomorrow, and realize this may be the last time the three of us are in a room together. We hug and share a pot of tea. A raven appears at the window, a note on its leg. Helia at once rises to get the note and feeds the raven a bite to eat before it takes off to wherever it goes at night. I wonder how it knows to come back.

Helia reads the note, and her frown deepens.

"You have to go," Aerith and I nod. We know this. "Now. Right now. I have received word that Eloise has been sent on her way from the group. She is being hunted by the city…and they're going to come get you, too."

"But we are infirm," I protest. I don't want to leave in the middle of the night. Not like this.

"They're not going to care. Several city Warriors were murdered, and they'll likely blame Eloise. You have to go. By morning they will be here. It's time."

Aerith and I gather our supplies while Helia reminds us, again, of where we need to enter the sewer and how we get out from there. She reminds us to keep the map she gave us dry, or it will be ruined. She also unnecessarily reminds us to avoid well-traveled areas. I can tell she's doing it because she's nervous and because she cares about us.

She holds Aerith's talisman and concentrates on it, looking back at the book from time to time. She had done the same earlier to test it and no guards had come running like before when she took it off of her.

Satisfied, she unclasps the necklace from Aerith's neck and attaches it around her own.

Aerith bites her lip. "How will I know when to dream?" she asks.

"You will know," Helia reassures her. "Nyana has never needed a special talisman. The Celestials will find you."

I give Helia a hug. Aerith does the same before bringing up a pot and hitting Helia in the head, catching her off guard. The hollow sound of the pan reverberates through me. Helia's head turns sharply, and she collapses to the ground.

"You knocked her out!" I exclaim. "Why did you do that?"

"It has to be convincing," Aerith replies, "If she knew the blow was coming, she would brace or potentially defend herself automatically. Now come on, help me get her to the pillar."

I continue to stare at Aerith in shock as she begins dragging Helia over. I finally come back to my senses and help. I reluctantly tie one of my newest but now closest friends up and we gather our things. Aerith glances at Helia once more.

"Maybe having her wear the talisman will fool them long enough to think I'm still wearing it."

"Maybe," I'm unconvinced but not interested in belaboring the point. There's nothing we can do about it now.

My stomach balls, threatening revolt as we walk to the doors and Aerith peers out. Signaling the all-clear, we dart out and make our way as quietly and quickly as possible to the door behind a portrait in the hall.

"Please be there," I mumble under my breath. We push the portrait to the side, and both breathe a sigh of relief when a doorway becomes visible. We push it open with some effort; it clearly doesn't open often. Good. Hopefully it's a long-forgotten passage.

Behind the doorway is darkness. Once the door closes, we are enclosed in a space too small to stand in. I push away claustrophobia and pray that this won't be our coffin. I reach out to either side of me, feeling the rough walls on either side of me. Crouched, we begin to pick our way forward slowly. We can see nothing, making our progress achingly slow. I keep one hand in front of me, Aerith doing the same. It stops me from running into her back several times, and she manages to avoid walking into a wall as the space turns several times. Luckily, there have been no branching paths to choose from.

I wonder how long our luck can hold out when I hear multiple bells toll, deep and resounding even in the tunnel. Maybe even louder in the tunnel. I clap my hand over my ears. That can't be good.

INTO THE UNKNOWN.

Aerith

The bells' tolling causes me to nearly jump out of my skin. I hit my head painfully on the stone ceiling above us. I rub the sore spot. My back aches from being bent over, and I wish we had asked Helia how long this tunnel was.

"We have to keep moving," I urge Saada in a whisper when the bells stop. "Whatever that is, it's probably got to do with us. If anyone knows about this passage, we will have company before long."

We move forward, our feet sounding too loud in the dark space. My hand trails on the wall, feeling it change from dry stone to damp stone. I pray that means we are almost out of the palace. The smell is getting stronger, too. What was a dry, dusty smell is now a musty, moldy smell. Not as bad as the dungeons, but not much better, if I'm being honest.

Several minutes pass with the scuffling of our feet and breaths the only sounds to join us.

"We got lucky," I say when the bells don't repeat, and no one appears to join us in the passageway.

A scratching noise in the passage behind us floated toward us. We paused, afraid to make any noise. The scratching continues for a moment, then stops.

"A rat?" I whisper in Saada's ear.

I feel her shrug.

We wait, holding our collective breath for another minute. When the sound doesn't repeat, we continue our crouched walk, trying to pick up the pace.

The scratching sounds again shortly after we start walking. We freeze again.

What kind of rat only moves when we move? Not a rat, that's what.

I hold my breath, listening again for the sound. Nothing. I wage a silent war in my head. Do we keep moving and hope they don't move faster than we do? Or do we wait and see if they think the tunnel is empty after all and leave?

Saada makes the decision for us, nudging me urgently forward.

I start walking again, Saada's prodding finger continuous.

"Keep going, no matter what," Saada whispers. "If they stopped when we did, they know we're in here. We have to get out."

I nod, then remember she can't see me. "Agreed."

We half-run in our crouch, making more noise than is wise. The occasional drip from the stone roof falls on my face, startling me each time with how cold it is. I hope that it's not sewage leaking down. I nearly gag at the thought. I keep my head partially tilted down to keep it from landing in my eye or worse, my mouth.

My head scrapes painfully on the roof of the tunnel, and we are forced to drop to our knees and crawl. We are breathing heavily from our partial run, and now we are making even more noise as our knees shuffle along and our backs and shoulders rub on the other surfaces. What if this narrows into nothing? What if Helia was wrong? What if Helia *lied?*

I shake my head, no, if this tunnel doesn't lead out, then Helia didn't know. I refuse to think she purposefully misled us. There are so many other ways she could have gotten rid of us, much easier ways.

Is that a flicker? Light? My heart rises in my throat. Light at the end of the tunnel is good!

I realize with dismay, the light isn't coming from in front of me but from behind me. Someone is close enough to cast our shadows in front of us.

We redouble our efforts, trying to make it to the end.

"Found them!" someone behind us shouts.

"Faster," Saada whines at me.

"I'm trying," I insist. I can feel the trousers I'm wearing tearing and my knees along with them. I don't stop. I keep going. I have to keep us going.

We scurry, the tunnel getting shorter and narrower until we are on our bellies like snakes. I hear the occasional whimper from Saada behind me.

"They're almost to the end!" the woman behind us yells.

Rather than scaring me with how close she is, she actually helps. We move faster, knowing that our slithering is almost over. If we are almost at the end, I'm not slowing down for anything.

The flame of the light is getting closer, lighting up the dark stones around us. I grunt with effort, Saada doing the same behind me. I feel her breath on my ankles as she pants to keep up.

Almost there, I can smell sewage. That has to mean we are almost there. I take shallower breaths, trying not to think about what I'm breathing in.

I slither forward, and my hands feel nothing in front of me. I teeter on an edge of some kind, my body blocking the light behind us, and before I can contemplate how to get out of this shoot safely, Saada pushes into me with a cry.

I fall out of the tunnel, landing painfully on more stone, chest and face first. And there's something wet. I gag. The drips in the tunnel were questionable. This most definitely is not water.

"Help!" Saada shouts, and I remember her cry. I push away thoughts of what's covering my front, keeping my mouth closed, and reach for her hands. She's holding tight to the opening. She grabs painfully onto my hands, and I pull. I think she's stuck in the small opening, but when she comes free, there's hands reaching out behind her.

She lands more gracefully, with a splash in the sewer but on her feet. I close my eyes just in time.

"Run," she commands, and we do. With the guards behind us, their light casting only enough for us to see the side of the sewer where it's mostly dry.

Saada has lost a shoe, and I'm covered in excrement, but we are upright. I hear shimmying behind us and a couple of splashes; the guards made it through. We run faster. My lungs burn from the effort. I pray they don't have any bows while I wait for the singing of the string and the sharp stab in my back. It doesn't come.

I try not to think about what happens when we get to the end of this. If we get to the end. The guards are likely in better shape than we are. Bed rest didn't exactly help either of us build muscle or stamina. Fear keeps us running for now.

If the guards in here don't catch us, surely the ones at the end of the tunnel will. They have probably been alerted to our current path. I push aside the panic and keep going. Fleeing the evil at my back. Leaving my home, my friends, my life behind. Into the unknown. Charting a new path, relying only on the dreams of a future where we live in peace.

MORE WILL COME.

Timekeeper

Time goes in circles. It has no beginning, no end. It has always been, it will always be. At least, that's what we have always been led to believe. I hope for something different. I plan for something different. The Variance is the start, but she's only a start. A hiccup in time's plans. More will come.

THE END
FOR NOW…

Acknowledgments

I would be nowhere if it weren't for all of the support of my amazing partner, who took on more than his fair share in taking care of the house, the kids, the cars, the animals, etc., so I could take the time to write, edit, read, re-write, re-edit, and re-read. Not to mention the countless hours driving me around the state and into other states so I could get more editing time on the go. There's no one I would rather do life with.

I am grateful beyond words for my little writing tribe: Audrey Lynn (author or Quartz Mountain and Sapphire Falls) and Meredith Kasian (author or The Wielder's Discovery). They have both been invaluable in providing encouragement, support, advice, resources, and have shared in the tears and joys of this process.

A thousand thanks to my alpha readers, Lusann, Jessica, and Edward, who saw the earliest and roughest chapters in this book and still continued to read it. I promise this book is so much better because of their feedback.

To my beta readers who saw a slightly better draft than my alphas and gave me valuable developmental feedback – many rounds of gratitude.

The thorn in every author's side, my editor, Tabitha Chandler. In spite of my endless errors (some of them quite repetitive) and my never-ending questions, she never gave up on me. She gave me thoughtful feedback and support for all of my little wins. Most importantly, she listened to me whine about all of my errors I had to fix.

I could go on for ages about all the things I am thankful for, but I think this is quite enough. So, my last gratitudes go to you, dear reader, for taking a chance, picking up this book, and giving it a read. I hope you have enjoyed the Realm as much as I have, and I look forward to seeing you in the next one!

About the Author

A.C. Marholin lives in the beautiful PNW with her fiancé, two kids, three dogs, and one cat. She used to write a lot as a teenager, but it wasn't until finding the indie author community that she believed she could do it herself. She is now the author of this book in your hands with many more planned.

Before becoming a writer, A.C. has worked in multiple jobs, but few brought her as much satisfaction as being a nurse. During the day, she can be found educating nursing students, nursing assistant students, and other healthcare professionals within the hospital. She loves to teach and watch students learn something new.

A.C. has tried many hobbies, but only a few have ever stuck with her. Photography is a long-lasting passion, and she has thousands and thousands of photos that span from the United States to Mexico to Mozambique. She enjoys traveling, especially by boat, and hopes to retire to a boat to write full-time one day in the future. As long as that boat has enough room for the books she wants to read.

Get in Touch:
www.acmarholin.com
instagram.com/book_leigh
linktr.ee/book_leigh